THE HOUSE IN THE WOODS

Zoë Miller was born in Dublin, where she now lives with her husband. She began writing stories at an early age. Her writing career has also included freelance journalism and prize-winning short fiction. She has three children.

www.zoemillerauthor.com
@zoemillerauthor
Facebook.com/zoemillerauthor

Previously by Zoë Miller
The Perfect Sister
The Visitor
A House Full of Secrets
Someone New
A Question of Betrayal
A Husband's Confession
The Compromise
A Family Scandal
Rival Passions
Sinful Deceptions
Guilty Secrets

The House
in the
Woods

ZOË MILLER

HACHETTE
BOOKS
IRELAND

First published in Ireland in 2021 by HACHETTE BOOKS IRELAND
First published in paperback in 2022

1

Cataloguing in Publication Data is available from the British Library

ISBN 9781529305159

Typeset in Sabon by Bookends Publishing Services, Dublin
Printed and bound in Great Britain by Clays Ltd, Elcograf S.p.A

Hachette Books Ireland policy is to use papers that are
natural, renewable and recyclable products and made from
wood grown in sustainable forests. The logging and
manufacturing processes are expected to conform to the
environmental regulations of the country of origin.

Hachette Books Ireland
8 Castlecourt Centre
Castleknock
Dublin 15, Ireland

A division of Hachette UK Ltd
Carmelite House, 50 Victoria Embankment, London EC4Y 0DZ

www.hachettebooksireland.ie

Dedicated with love to my wonderful siblings who were there at the start of it all and who are still cheering me along: Peter, Margaret, David and Kevin

Summer, 1964

The woods are full of secret things. They are alive with the rustle of small animals scurrying through tangled undergrowth, the buzz of insects, the call of birds fluttering through the branches, the soft coo of a wood pigeon. Outside on the lane that comes up from the beach, the sun beats down and white heat shimmers in the air, but under the brown-green shade of the trees, all is cool and secretive. The leafy canopy is dappled with patches of blue where the sky peeps through. Shimmering beams from the slanting sun turn the greenery to iridescent glitter. A gurgling brook runs over a weir onto a bed of ancient stones.

The child is sleeping in the pushchair, lulled into a doze by the heat of the incandescent day and the rhythmic movement of the wheels as she is pushed up the lane and onto the uneven track that leads through the woods and towards Heronbrook, the small house in the glade.

Through the branches of the trees, there is movement, someone coming ... two people ... flashes of colour piercing through gaps in the shimmering greenery, a pink T-shirt, a white vest, a tanned arm, the glint of blonde hair in a patch of sunlight, murmuring voices, a tinkle of silvery laughter. Unaware they are being watched, they pause, half-hidden by foliage, and they come together in a long, slow kiss.

Then, in the clearing, the curtains close on the bedroom window at the back of Heronbrook, the room with a view of the dazzling brook. Whispered exchanges of love swirl in the warm, trapped air. The couple melt into each other in the muted luminosity, limbs entwined; he lifts his hand to her flushed face, tracing the contours, smiling into her widening eyes and bending to kiss her as the dance between them heightens and intensifies.

The child stretches and flexes her small limbs. She rubs her eyes and opens them slowly. She looks around. She knows where she is. She's been here before. And she knows how to slide down the straps restraining her arms, how to wiggle clear, how to grasp the side of the pushchair and lever her little body over it so that she is free. She is hungry. She wants her mummy. She sets off, toddling through the woods, pine needles and windfall branches scratching the soft skin of her small chubby legs.

It is a while before anyone notices that she is missing.

Evie, present day

I am not dead. Yet.

I am lying on my back. My head is seized in a vice-like grip. Beneath that I am hurtling through time and space, swaying and shifting to the scream of an ambulance siren that cuts through the fog in my brain.

Something clamps my mouth and nose. On the next out-breath, I feel suspended between wavering life and soft darkness and I sink down with increasing rapidness, as though there is less of me to dispose of moment by moment.

A voice comes through a mist of pain.

'We're losing her ...'

Something pinches my skin, dragging me back from sweet oblivion, preventing me from dissolving further into the void beneath me.

'Evie, stay with us ...'

Shredded thoughts ebb and flow in my consciousness. I have done terrible things. But I have paid the price. The worst that can happen has already occurred. I feel the cold, hard loss of him in my brittle bones. The love of my life, Lucien, is gone.

Was it last week, last month, last year, or even yesterday? My muzzy head can't recall, but the dark realisation that I had something to do with it pours through my limp capillaries like black ink. I want to surrender and slip into peaceful depths.

The screeching siren jerks me back. I am being propelled along even faster.

Heronbrook. The name rushes through whatever is left of my fragmented consciousness. It never left me. Then again I couldn't let it go.

I hear a child's heart-rending sobs. The image of an empty pushchair slams into my head before cracking into smithereens.

My fault. All my fault.

The siren cuts out mid-shriek. All movement stops. There is a metallic clang and a rattle and I am being trundled out to where coolness sweeps across my face. Then the momentum shifts and I am being rushed along to the rhythmic click of wheels, the patter of hurrying footsteps keeping pace.

More voices.

'Blunt trauma to the head ...'

'Severe concussion ...'

'We almost lost her ...'

Another thought-fragment surges, slicing through thick depths as sharp as a scalpel: someone has put me here. Someone wants me dead. Who, though? The knowledge is bobbing around in my head like out-of-reach flotsam.

They have tried already. Tried to kill me. I see myself crawling along a lane, my hip hot with pain, dragging on the pitted surface. It seemed like an accident. At the time.

But I survived. I remember lying in a hospital bed and Jessica visiting me.

I went back home to Heronbrook.

Now I am being pushed around a corner. I hear doors clanging open, then flapping shut. A louder voice, closer to me, 'Evie, you're in Accident and Emergency. You've sustained a head injury ... stay with us ...'

Why hadn't I heeded the warnings? There were warnings and from the way I feel, suspended between my bittersweet existence and a thick, soft darkness, they might just have succeeded in snuffing out my life this time.

Another seed of memory – Amber. She was with me last night, wasn't she? Was it last night? Or yesterday?

What did happen? Dear God, I need to know if she is safe.

Think, Evie, think.

Don't go under just yet.

Four Weeks Earlier

The sound of high heels click-clacking purposefully up the length of the hospital corridor came to an abrupt stop outside Evie's room. In the sudden silence, a flutter of nerves caused her hand to shake as she reached for the control pad, but she managed to press the button and adjust her bed so that she was sitting upright and feeling less vulnerable by the time Jessica popped her head around the door.

'Aunt Evie?'

'Hello, Jessica,' Evie said, conscious of a wobble in her voice. As her niece walked into the ward, Evie's heart clenched. To a passer-by, it would look like a normal hospital visit. But in reality, a family silence that stretched back a lifetime of hostile years pulsed like a dark cloud between them. Then, channelling her Evie Lawrence award-winning-actress persona, she pushed that thought aside and smiled apologetically. 'Thanks for coming. You're very kind. I'm furious that I've been caught short like this. I'm sorry for putting you out and dragging you all the way over here on a Friday afternoon when you should be at work.'

This wasn't supposed to have happened. Then again, a lot of events that had shaped her life, all seventy-five years of it thus far, hadn't been in her original blueprint.

'Not at all,' Jessica replied. 'I was due a half day. It sounds like you've had a terrifying time. I'm glad you had my number to call.'

Evie breathed out. Jessica sounded as though it was perfectly normal to get an urgent phone call from an aunt who'd found herself stranded in a south Dublin hospital with nothing between her modesty and the world at large but a papery-thin hospital gown. More significantly, a long-alienated aunt, and only for a chance encounter with Jessica in a Wicklow hotel at the start of summer, Evie wouldn't even have had her contact details.

Jessica placed an M&S carrier bag of new supplies beside the locker before she pulled across a plastic chair and sat down. 'Oh dear,' she said, examining Evie's bruised face and bandaged forearm with concern. 'Tell me more about what happened.'

'The bruises and scratches look worse than they feel,' Evie said. 'A motorbike came up the lane behind me when I was walking home from the beach. It went out of control and sent me flying. Whatever way I fell, I crashed back down on my hip and fractured it.' She gave her niece the same details she had given the police earlier that day. The man and woman had looked out of place, darkly robust in their navy uniforms compared with the soft pastel colours worn by the hospital staff. As Evie had answered their questions, the woman had jotted details in a notebook that looked too small to hold anything of significance.

'The lane is full of potholes,' Evie said. 'I'm not surprised the bike went out of control.'

'You could have been killed,' Jessica said.

Evie shivered. 'I'll live. They fixed my hip as best they could in the operating theatre yesterday afternoon.'

'How are you feeling now?' Jessica asked, her oval face wreathed in concern. With a breathtaking pang, Evie caught a glimpse of her own late mother, Ruth, reflected in her niece's face – a faint impression, latent genes slip-sliding through generations.

'OK – on mega painkillers, which are a help.' Evie forced a smile. In time her bruising would fade but the neat dressing on her hip was minuscule compared with the degree of discomfort and immobility it was causing.

'Do you know who caused the accident?'

Evie grimaced. 'I don't.'

'Didn't the person give a name when they called the ambulance?' Jessica frowned.

'Whoever it was didn't hang around long enough to call one,' Evie said.

'They drove off and *left* you there? Did you see the registration plate? How did you get help?'

'It all happened so fast I didn't see much,' Evie said. 'My mobile had fallen out of my pocket and landed further up the lane. I was crawling along to reach it when Tess Talbot, a neighbour who runs the local café, came along and raised the alarm. By then the motorcyclist was long gone. The police will put out an appeal for information, but I can't see anyone admitting to running me over when they didn't stop in the first place.'

Jessica shook her head. 'That's absolutely appalling. I hope they find the culprit, shame on whoever it was, leaving you like that. Thank God you were found. I think I've got all the essentials you asked for.' She indicated the bag, where Evie spotted a cellophane package containing a packet of rolled-up briefs alongside neatly folded pyjamas, with a rose-coloured washbag tucked in beside them.

'Thank you for doing that shopping,' Evie said. 'I'll arrange to pay you as soon as I can. My closest friends are away at the moment and there's no one I could ask to go rooting around unsupervised in my house, never mind my bedroom, so it was an emergency, as you can see.' She gave a self-deprecating laugh and plucked the short sleeve of her hospital gown. A far cry from the sumptuous crimson cloak she'd once swirled around her shoulders in the role of Lady Macbeth, stalking across a London West End stage at the pinnacle of her career.

Stop. Those bittersweet days were long gone.

'And you should see the unisex knickers they provided me with,' Evie ventured.

'Beautiful bloomers, I bet,' Jessica said, a hint of a smile in her eyes.

This is what it could have been like between me and Jessica all along, Evie fretted. Warm kinship.

'So what happens next?' Jessica asked.

'I'm here until next Thursday, and then home.'

'Have you got help planned?'

'No, but I'll be well able to cope. They've already started my physio.'

'You've had major surgery,' Jessica pointed out. 'For the first month or so you mightn't be able to do much for yourself. Paul's mother had a similar operation the year before last and she had to stay with us for those early weeks. Could you get help from your friends? When will they be back?'

'Not for weeks. Lucy and Marian are vising Lucy's daughter in Texas.' They weren't even all that close – her bridge-playing friends, whom she only met once a fortnight.

'Maybe you should book into a convalescent home. I can do some checking around for you if you like?'

Evie allowed herself to relax in the glow of her niece's attention before she pulled herself together. Jessica was right, if her first and hopeless attempts at physio were anything to go by. But enlisting her help was out of the question. 'Not at all,' she said. 'I'm hoping to go home, but either way, I wouldn't dream of inflicting my problems on you. You shouldn't even *be* here. What on earth would your mother say?'

'She doesn't know I'm here and I won't be telling her,' Jessica said calmly.

Evie met her eyes but remained silent. How much did Jessica know of the cause of the bitter rift between her mother and Evie? Very little, she guessed, otherwise she wouldn't be sitting here. Married to Paul Lennox, and with two twenty-something children, Jessica was a fifty-ish, attractive woman with pale, translucent skin, her dark hair a smooth shoulder-length bob. She was wearing a smart black trouser suit and white shirt, and carried an air of crisp efficiency, as though she had a lot on her to-do list and was busy working her way through it. It only seemed like yesterday when Evie's sister Pippa had announced her pregnancy, and it had been the final straw for Evie at a time when a huge chunk of her life had crumbled in on itself, collapsing into a deep, dark crevasse. Spanning those years was the sad estrangement that lay between herself and Pippa and Pippa's family, Evie aware, always, of her sister standing silently on the edge of this glacial fracture like an avenging angel.

She blinked and marvelled at the way her niece had no idea how much this visit meant to her. 'You've been so good to look after me,' Evie said, 'but that's as far as the TLC needs to go. I know you're a busy woman. I can guess how challenging it is, trying to juggle career and home life, never mind being all things to all people.'

'I'm not a one-woman show,' Jessica said. 'There are four of us in the household and I don't run after anyone. Paul and I have raised Amber and Adam to be well able to cook and clean and empty a dishwasher.'

'I really appreciate your coming to my rescue,' Evie said when there was a lull in the conversation and she had the sense that Jessica had other places to be, 'but I'd be happier if you went home now before the car-park fees are the equivalent of a house deposit, never mind the Friday-afternoon traffic.'

'I think you have to consider your situation when you're discharged,' Jessica said.

'I'll sort out something,' Evie said, anxious to dispatch her niece with as little obligation as possible. The last thing she wanted was to be a burden on anyone, least of all Pippa's daughter.

♦

'If I hear that you've come near my family … I'll kill you with my bare hands. Got that? I'll kill you and I mean it,' Pippa had screamed at her on a snowy December day when both of their worlds had collapsed. Despite it being over thirty years ago now, they were threats Evie had never forgotten. Living in London, it had been easy to do as Pippa asked, cutting all ties with her and her family, only seeing them on the occasion of a brief visit home to Dublin when their mother had died. By the time she'd moved back to Ireland twelve years ago, it was a rift that had hardened inexorably. Then just three months ago, at the end of May, she'd met Jessica by chance in the function room of a Wicklow hotel and there had been no ignoring her.

Evie had been persuaded out of her quiet retirement to accept an invitation to speak at a fundraiser to support arts and creativity in care homes and centres across the County Wicklow region. Somehow, in the crowded gathering, Evie and Jessica had come face to face during a refreshment break, Evie momentarily blindsided by her sudden recognition – Jessica had Pippa's height and dark hair and her father's eyes. But to Evie's shocked surprise, instead of turning away, Jessica had flashed a tentative smile before introducing herself.

'I recognised you immediately,' Evie had said. Despite Pippa's old threats, Evie had found herself welcoming the opportunity to cross a bridge over the chasm that existed between herself and her niece.

'I heard about Pippa's stroke,' Evie had said. 'A cousin of ours mentioned it in a Christmas card.' She'd felt a wave of sadness at the news and the incongruous way she'd been informed.

'It's five years ago now,' Jessica had said. 'Unfortunately, Mum is living in a world of her own most of the time. She's in a nursing home in Bray – that's why I'm here to support the fundraiser.'

'Will you take my phone number and let me know if anything else happens to her?' Evie had said.

'Of course.' Jessica had smiled. 'And I'll give you mine in case you ever want to get in touch.'

Jessica had congratulated Evie on her speech and had gone on to chat about her husband and children, and her brothers Simon and Jamie and Evie's heart had filled at the way they talked quite naturally. The only awkward moment had occurred when Barry Talbot, one of Evie's neighbours, had pushed through the crowd, butted in, and introduced himself to Jessica. He'd chastised Evie for keeping such a low profile in her retirement, hoping her appearance today might mean she had decided to become more involved in community activities. She'd been annoyed at the interruption, as well as his proprietorial manner, and after a few minutes Jessica had sidled away, asking Evie to keep in touch.

Back home, over the following weeks, Evie's spirits had plummeted. Home was Heronbrook, a bungalow in a secluded woodland setting in Wicklow, close to the sea. She'd snapped it up when it came on the market four years previously and had moved there permanently after her retirement two years ago, renting out the apartment in Blackrock she'd been living in. But its usual calm failed to soothe her after the unexpected encounter with Jessica. It had shaken her, bringing home to her just how much rich family life she'd missed out on, thanks to the years of silence.

Being busy all those years had been a great distraction. There had been no time to reflect on past mistakes or wallow in heartbreak, the mask she donned in front of the cameras remaining firmly in place throughout her working years. When she first retired, exhaustion had blanketed her. But meeting Jessica had the effect of ripping a sticking plaster away from an old wound, and in the quiet of the night, her dark conscience echoed remorsefully with memories of the girl she had once been, filled with an unbridled enthusiasm for life; Pippa, with her calculating glance, hovered on the periphery of those memories, reminding her of the careless tragedy that had come between them and slammed into the rest of their lives; and the shadow of Lucien, lugging around the weight of his unfulfilled dreams like a sack of coal on his back. Lucien – it all came back to him, because everything began and ended with him.

Worse, she had begun to feel weary of life, wondering, jadedly, what was the point of it all, finding it impossible to forgive herself for her terrible mistakes. But mindful of Pippa's harsh words all those years ago, she hadn't attempted to contact Jessica until she'd found herself stranded in hospital.

♦

'Let's get you freshened up,' Chloe, one of the student nurses, said, breezing into the room after Jessica had left, picking up the bag of supplies.

'I don't want to take up too much of your time,' Evie said, embarrassed by her helplessness.

'Not at all, that's what I'm here for.'

With a stout competence surprising for her age – early twenties, Evie guessed – and a gracious regard for Evie's dignity and incapacity, Chloe helped her to shower and change.

'Wait till my mum hears I'm looking after Ma Donnelly,' Chloe said, referring to the character Evie had played in *Delphin Terrace*, an Irish inner-city-based crime drama. 'She's a great fan of yours,' Chloe went on, as she carefully towelled Evie's legs dry. 'I think she's watched every episode of the show twice or three times. How long were you in it for?'

'Ten years,' Evie said. The role of the gritty matriarch of the Donnelly gangland family was something she'd thrown herself into when she'd moved back home after spending most of her working life on the London stage and screen.

Chloe kept up a stream of chatter, finishing by helping Evie into fresh compression socks, velour leggings and a matching top. 'There you go,' Chloe said.

'Thanks so much, I feel a lot better already.' Jessica couldn't have chosen better, she realised, feeling a warm glow of appreciation for her niece. The velour outfit was cosy, and perfect for Evie's needs.

Chloe escorted her back to bed, and Evie closed her eyes and tried to relax against the pillows. But all she could see was the moment of the accident replaying in her mind: the sound of the motorbike growing louder behind her, knowing it was speeding up instead of slowing down. Reaching a bend in the lane, she'd turned to see it bearing down on her, the cyclist's face obscured by the dark visor of the helmet. Then the world whirled around, her chest tightening in panic as she was flung into the air.

Now a sudden knot of disquiet flared inside her. When she'd decided to retire two years ago, in an attempt to boost the ratings during the summer lull, the producers of *Delphin Terrace* had inflicted a series of intimidating incidents on Ma Donnelly, culminating in a hit-and-run that had resulted in the demise of her character. Evie glanced out the window to where a shaft of late-August sunshine darted its way into the narrow courtyard, alighting on the glistening leaves of a silver birch tree. Despite the accident, she was as alive as that tree, even if there were times she felt it was a life hardly worth living.

Coincidence? It had to be.

Anything else was terrifying.

Jessica swallowed back a wave of anxiety as she pulled into the driveway of her house in Laurel Lawns, a housing estate in the south Dublin suburb of Templeogue.

The minute she opened the hall door, her gaze darted around, checking for post. Nothing. Which meant nothing had arrived from the bank. Which meant a reprieve for the weekend, at least insofar as she didn't have to deal with it. She let out her breath, releasing some of the tension in her shoulders. She stepped out of her high heels and slipped off her jacket, hanging it on the newel post. Then she padded down to the kitchen, the floor tiles cold under her stockinged feet.

Her younger brother, Jamie, was sitting on a high stool at the island counter, hunched over his mobile, his leather jacket dangling off the low back of the stool. He looked up and grinned at her, the grin she knew of old: the one that Jamie had used time and time again to get away with mischief. The grin she wasn't in the humour for today. She'd had a hectic week, topped off by the visit to Evie. She'd no energy left for Jamie.

'What are you doing here?' she said.

'I bumped into Amber in town,' he said. 'I came on out on the bus with her.'

Jessica checked the wall clock as she padded across the kitchen. Four thirty. 'Amber's home already?'

'Yep. She's upstairs. She gave me a beer,' he said, lifting the bottle and tipping it to his mouth, 'and she's invited me for dinner.'

'Dinner?' Jessica dropped her handbag on the counter and tried to recalibrate her thoughts. Dinner on Fridays meant a takeout and a bargain-bin bottle of wine. Now Jamie would have to be included as well as Amber, seeing as she was home. Once upon a time it had meant a date night for her and Paul, but those evenings were long gone, as were impromptu weekends away and two foreign holidays a year.

'Don't look so startled,' Jamie said. 'I thought you'd like me popping in for a catch-up, especially when I haven't been able to do that in so long.'

'There's not much to catch up on with me,' she said.

'Isn't there?'

'What does that mean?' she asked. *You can't possibly know, can you? This fresh, new nightmare that's giving me sleepless nights?*

'You look a bit hassled.'

Jessica filled the kettle. Of course she did. Lately, being hassled was her default position. She thought of her words to her aunt Evie, delivered earlier with the capable veneer she used to face down the world, telling her aunt she wasn't a one-woman show, she didn't run after anyone, and Jessica wanted to gag.

Until six weeks ago, the daily grind had been challenging enough, her energies squeezed between her husband and her humdrum marriage, her adult children and her ailing mother, her hectic job as a receptionist in a busy GP practice, and running a home as best she could on shaky finances – the shaky finances being the unstable foundation that coloured everything. Then, suddenly, two things had happened. Her younger brother returned home unexpectedly from New York after over twenty years – or rather, she corrected herself grimly, flung himself back into the bosom of Laurel Lawns like a smouldering grenade, announcing that he'd need a place to stay until he got on his feet, but refraining from explaining why he'd suddenly decided to land home. Then, fresh from the stress of Jamie delivered into a life that was already creaking at the seams, Jessica had stupidly allowed herself to fall victim to a financial phishing scam, which had cost her the guts of five thousand euro, and which she couldn't bring herself to admit to her husband. She was still waiting to hear from the bank in writing, following their review of the case, hoping against hope that the funds might be recovered.

She took out a mug and shut the kitchen cupboard with more force than was necessary. *Calm. Breathe slowly.* 'I'm not hassled, I'm fine.'

'Hmm. I bet Evie upset you. Amber told me of your mercy mission. I hope you're not going soft in the head.'

'It was an emergency. Evie was genuinely stuck. She's getting on in years and it was nice to be able to do something for her. You'd do it for a stranger, never mind family.'

'Family? As if she'd give a shite about family. She had a cheek expecting you to come to her rescue.'

'She'd no one else to ask. I'm glad she felt able to call on family, even if it was out of the blue. What happened to her was terrifying and she could have been killed.'

'Pity the job wasn't finished off properly.'

'Jamie! I'll pretend I didn't hear that.'

'OK – sorry,' he said, raising his hands in surrender. 'I'm just …'

'Just what?' She looked at him keenly, wondering if he was finally going to reveal what had been silently bugging him since his return home – or what might have precipitated that surprise decision.

He shrugged. 'Never mind.'

'If you saw Evie, you'd feel nothing but sympathy for her. She's so petite and delicate, she looks like a child.'

'Sympathy? Evie? They don't go together for me.'

The kettle boiled and she popped a teabag in a mug, stirring it before dunking it into the brown-bin caddy. She added a dash of milk and perched on a stool at the other end of the island counter, as far as possible from Jamie and the repressed antagonism she sensed simmering beneath his surface.

Their mother's youngest and favourite child, Jamie had evolved from a truculent teenager into an angst-ridden adult who'd always been a drain on her energy and who was narcissistic enough to believe that life owed him a living. Shades of her mother; Jamie hadn't exactly licked it off a stone. Then again, a fatherless Jamie had been stuck at home during those critical teenage years to bear the brunt of their mother's alcoholism, whereas Jessica had managed to flee the nest before Pippa had become almost impossible to handle, her twin brother, Simon, also bailing out by moving to Hong Kong. No surprise that at the age of twenty-one Jamie had dropped out of college and gone to New York to seek his fortune. She'd visited him every other year when she'd been able to splash the cash, but had always felt a weight lifting off her when it was time to go home. Now in his early forties, Jamie had a huge chip on his shoulder and extra weight around his middle. His jawline had lost definition.

'You can't deny that if Evie popped her clogs it would solve a lot of problems, yours included,' he said. 'You could leave that busy job and get something part-time.'

'I don't have any problems to be solved,' Jessica said, lying through her teeth, reminding herself that he couldn't possibly know of her fresh troubles, 'and that's an awful thing to say. Anyhow, we have no idea what would happen to Evie's estate if she died.'

'Mum is her next of kin – she has to be the main beneficiary. Surely it's the least Evie could do?'

'I don't get you.'

'Evie owes her. Mum told me more than once that all her problems in life stemmed from her sister. That her life was fucked up because of her and whenever she lifted a glass, it was all Evie's fault.'

'We've had this conversation before, Jamie, you don't know if there's any truth in that.'

'Mum never elaborated, but it's clear to me Evie was the cause of her unhappiness, which led to her drinking, which then led to her stroke, and put her where she is today.'

'You're jumping to conclusions.'

'Am I?' He looked directly at Jessica.

Jessica shook her head. 'I'm so not going there again.'

'You have power of attorney over Mum's affairs,' Jamie went on, draining his beer. 'You could sort us all out. An injection of funds might stop the haemorrhage from our inheritance into that bloody nursing home. I don't know why you agreed to that expensive package in the first place.'

'What was I supposed to do? Mum needed twenty-four-hour care. I couldn't do it. Simon said he had every confidence in my abilities to sort it out, as did you. I didn't see either of you hotfooting it home to help. At least we had the proceeds of the house in Bray. Speaking of work, are you not on this evening? I thought Friday night would have been all hands on deck.'

To her relief, after three weeks living in Laurel Lawns, and thanks to putting the word out among his old mates, Jamie had got a job in a bar in Naas with a bedsit to rent over the premises. He'd also acquired a clapped-out Volkswagen Golf.

'I do get time off,' he said. 'And it's not a permanent job, just a stopgap until I get something more suitable. I could go back to college. Education is a lot more flexible nowadays.'

And who's going to fund that? Jessica bit back the words as she got up off her stool and dumped half her tea down the sink.

'I might even open my own bar,' Jamie went on. 'Although start-up investment would be critical. I wonder would Evie be interested in coming on board?' Seeing the look on his sister's face he said, 'I'm joking, Jessica.'

Jessica forced herself to remain calm, annoyed at the way he managed to needle her. Because she allowed him to, she pointed out to herself. Because she still felt guilty at the image of Jamie's twelve-year-old, unhappy face when she'd broken the news to him that she was leaving the family home in Bray and getting married to Paul. He hadn't wanted her to leave. He'd cried and begged her to stay. She'd told him she had to marry Paul because she was pregnant. She'd never admitted to anyone that she'd done it on purpose to escape the house in Bray.

Jamie's mobile shrilled. He swiped his thumb across it. 'Guess what? You're off the hook, sis. I'm needed in the pub for six pm.'

'How will you get back to Naas on time?' Jessica said, hoping she was successful in hiding her relief.

'I'll drive you,' Amber said, walking into the kitchen in a waft of Jo Malone shower gel. She was wearing skinny jeans and a loose-fitting cotton top over a white, sleeveless T-shirt. Her short dark hair, styled in a tousled pixie cut, was still damp.

As always, at the sight of her daughter, Jessica's heart felt a lift. She'd never expected to experience the depths of love she felt for her children. Her first pregnancy had sadly ended in miscarriage, so fifteen months later, when the red, wriggling body of Amber was placed on her chest on a cool April evening, her heart had expanded with a raw, primeval rapture. It had expanded again when Adam had arrived into their lives, five years later. She loved them both with a ferocity that shook her. 'You're home early, love,' Jessica said.

'I am, just one of those days,' Amber said, sounding as if it was normal for her to be home at this hour. Jessica had never seen her arrive home before seven o'clock any day she'd gone into the office. Then Jessica spotted the look in her eyes.

'Is everything OK?' Jessica said, dismay blooming inside her.

Amber shrugged. 'Yeah, 'course.'

It wasn't all OK, it couldn't be. Before her daughter turned away, Jessica glanced at her eyes again. They held a shell-shocked kind of look that said her life had imploded. Jessica's heart squeezed with anxiety. With her own life disintegrating around her, she didn't know if she had sufficient energy to shore up the pieces of Amber's, whatever had befallen her daughter. Because something certainly had.

Amber Lennox forked her chicken and chorizo penne around her plate and swallowed a wave of nausea. Her eyes felt gritty, her chest was heavy with tension, and there was a pain in her face as she gazed around the gastro pub in Naas. It was filling up with Friday-night regulars, Jamie busy pulling pints, mixing cocktails and exchanging jokes with the thirsty masses looking for their fix of alcohol to help them unwind after a stressful week. She was relieved no one paid her any attention, a twenty-eight-year-old woman sitting at a small table with her back to the wall, playing with some food and sipping water instead of the double-measure of Bombay Sapphire gin – or any gin at all – she craved. For the hundredth time she went to check her mobile before realising she no longer had it. A crashing pain resounded once again through the back of her head.

'Let me know when you're on the way home,' her mum had said, as Amber had headed for the door in Laurel Lawns with Jamie in tow. 'I can time it to order in some food – a couple of pizzas, maybe. Or Indian.'

'There's no need, I'll be fine,' she'd said more dismissively than she'd intended, remorseful when she saw the flicker of hurt in her mother's eyes.

'It's nice to have someone fussing over you,' Jamie had said, winking at her as he pulled up the zip of his jacket.

Amber had made a face at him, not quite an eye-roll. Jamie was more like an older brother to her than an uncle. She tried to sound appreciative. 'Thanks, Mum, but I can't let you know because I've left my mobile in the office, so I'll be having a tech-free weekend.'

It was the truth, but nothing like the whole truth.

'That's a nuisance.' Her mum had looked at her keenly. 'The one place a mobile is useful is in the car.'

'Thought it was against the law,' Jamie had said.

'It's in case I have an accident.' Amber forced a teasing note in her voice. 'Mum always fears the worst. I passed my test first go.'

'I trust you with my life, darling, it's the other drivers –'

'I'll feed Amber,' Jamie said. 'That'll save you trying to time something, Jessica.'

'Great idea,' Amber had said, opening the hall door, escaping at last into the evening.

♦

'Chef won't be too happy with this,' Jamie said, coming over and looking at her plate of barely touched food.

'It was perfect,' she said. 'You're far too generous with your portions.'

'It's not the food, though, is it?' he said, his eyes quizzical. 'You're quiet this evening. Not the Amber I got used to when I stayed in Laurel Lawns.'

It took Amber every ounce of willpower to wrap herself and her voice in a cloak of nonchalance. 'Hello? You mean in comparison to everyone else in here tonight? I can't help it if I'm not one of the shouty ones. I'm happy to have a bit of headspace.'

'You were, I dunno, distant or something on the drive down,' he said.

'You were too busy bullshitting about Mum going to visit Evie Lawrence. I couldn't get a word in.'

Jamie pulled out a chair and sat down. 'I'm still trying to figure out what my sister was doing pandering to that old witch. I'd never have known she visited her but for meeting you in town. I'd love to know what's been going on behind my back while I was away.'

'Nothing's going on. Mum hasn't mentioned Evie in years. I haven't seen her since I was about seven, at Great-Granny Ruth's funeral.'

'Well, Jessica must be ingratiating herself with the old crone, now that she's getting on in life.'

'Jamie! Mum's not the ingratiating kind.'

'Let me tell you something, Amber,' he said, surprising her with the intent look on his face, 'we're all capable of sucking it up when push comes to shove, especially where money is involved. And Evie's worth a few bob.'

'I'm outta here,' Amber said, picking up her bag.

'We haven't talked about you yet.'

'Nothing to discuss.'

'Oh yeah? I've just twigged what's wrong with you.' He tilted his head to one side and looked at her with shrewd eyes. 'You haven't talked about your job at all today – your favourite topic of conversation during the three weeks I stayed in Laurel Lawns. Nor have you mentioned any weekend plans with Will.' He raised an eyebrow.

'So?'

'I'd hate to think my favourite niece is upset about anything.'

She hadn't thought he'd notice. She had Jamie pegged as one of the takers in life who was so wrapped up in himself that he only saw others in relation to how they served him. Earlier that afternoon, she'd invited him home on the spur of the moment. She'd needed some company on the bus, and she'd hoped his presence in Laurel Lawns would keep her mum occupied and deflect any attention away from her. Then driving him to Naas had been a handy excuse to get away for a while from her mother's well-intentioned fussing. She'd been afraid of blurting out what had happened – Amber knew that her and her brother Adam's happiness, or otherwise, acted almost like a barometer for their mother's spirits, and had she known what had transpired that afternoon, Jessica Lennox would have been appalled. Neither did she deserve to have Amber's problems landing in her lap. In recent years her parents had been through enough struggles without Amber adding to them.

She made a huge effort to plaster a smile on

her face. 'It's the end of the week,' she said. 'I'm tired. Sorry if I didn't entertain you with good conversation. And I'd better hit the road before Mum decides a disaster of some kind has befallen me.'

'Can I get you a coffee or anything else before you head back?'

Amber automatically went to pick up her mobile and chuck it into her bag before she remembered. Her hand hovered futilely just above the table and she felt freshly stripped of something vital. 'No, thanks.'

'You know where I am if you want to talk,' Jamie said. 'I'm not just the black sheep of the family.'

She stood up. She couldn't wait to be in the privacy of her car. 'I wouldn't dream of calling you that. And I thought Aunt Evie was the black sheep.'

'Hah! Evie is the rotten apple in the barrel. I'm only in the ha'penny place, and I do have a beating heart somewhere beneath all the charming roguishness. So feel free to open up to me.'

'Jesus, Jamie,' she laughed dismissively, 'I didn't think you were into the emotional uncle business. Don't work too hard,' she said, before she slung her bag across her shoulder and headed to the exit door as jauntily as possible.

Out in the car, Amber sank her head into her hands, closed her eyes, and took a long, deep breath through her fingers. Her brain was fried and she just wanted this day to be over, to be expunged forever from her life. Then images from the office that afternoon pinged onto her darkened eyelids: her laptop being snapped shut before it was confiscated, along with her mobile; the blur of faces, some concerned, most of them blatantly curious; being flanked by two guys from the security team as she was escorted out of the CEO's office, her security pass being handed up; then stumbling out of Russell Hall into the bright afternoon, where everything looked much as normal on Baggot Street; wanting to scream at the hard slant of August sunshine reflecting off steel and glass.

Her contract had been terminated. *Effective immediately,* they'd said. *Grievous breach of protocol.* Had that really happened? *How* had it happened?

She'd found herself downtown, floating on legs the consistency of water, Jamie spotting her at the top of Grafton Street. At his greeting, she'd dredged her mind of the nightmare that had just occurred and somehow she'd managed to nail a smile on her face. Now, sitting in a Naas car park, she opened her eyes, realising that pure shock had got her through those first few hours. The sickening horror of the afternoon was lurking in the long grass like a hungry wolf, ready to tear her apart. It was scary how she could be in control of everything one minute, her expectations for the succession of weeks and the rest of the year ahead shimmering on the horizon like a promise, and the next ... it all fell into a deep, dark hole.

More than once on the way home, she found herself taking bends too sharply, overtaking dangerously, wondering what it would be like if the car flipped over and she plunged into the peace of oblivion, and in the next moment asking herself how had Amber Lennox, first-class honours graduate, recent promotee, come to this?

By Sunday afternoon, Evie knew her plan for recuperating at home unaided was nothing short of optimistic fantasy. Her attempts to heft herself out of her hospital bed and coax two crutches to bring her to the bathroom were painful and faltering, never mind the impossible feat of showering and dressing without assistance. She floundered through her dreaded physio sessions, realising that the everyday logistics of getting around Heronbrook would be impossible.

'It'll be three weeks,' Chloe said, 'before you can manoeuvre around on one crutch. Longer again before you're allowed to bend down.'

'That's great news altogether,' Evie said.

'They're the golden rules for recovery,' Chloe said. 'Ignore them at your peril. Have you arranged for convalescence?'

No.

She wanted to be home in Heronbrook. It was her spirit place, her refuge in a life that had twisted and convoluted in unexpected ways, turning bitter and sour. So when Jessica phoned her on Monday with a suggestion, Evie didn't dismiss it out of hand.

'I might have a solution for you,' Jessica said, 'when you're discharged. If you want to go straight home Amber might be able to help out. She ...' Jessica hesitated. 'She seems to have some free time on her hands and she's willing and available to help. I know the kind of support Paul's mother needed for those first few weeks. You don't want to compromise your recovery.'

Compromise your recovery – a phrase she was swiftly getting used to hearing. A cheerful way of telling her she could end up in a wheelchair for the rest of her life if she disobeyed the 'golden rules'.

Evie sighed, torn between wanting to accept Jessica's kind offer but not wanting her grand-niece becoming a sacrificial lamb, so to speak. 'There's no way I'd expect a young woman like Amber to incarcerate herself with me in the depths of Wicklow. Has she any idea what's involved?'

'Thing is, she has. She helped with Paul's mother so she knows the dos and don'ts.'

'It's very kind of Amber,' Evie said, beginning to panic a little at the thoughts of her solitude being invaded, never mind the possibility of Amber asking questions about her life, no matter how well intentioned. 'However, I don't know her and she doesn't know me. I find it hard to believe she'd be happy to pick up after her crotchety great-aunt, besides travelling up and down from your home every day.'

'She's prepared to stay over so that she'd be on hand for whatever you needed, day or night, just for that initial couple of weeks. And' – Jessica lowered her voice – 'you'd be doing both of us a favour.'

'What do you mean?'

'Confidentially, Aunt Evie, I think something has gone wrong in Amber's job, and with her boyfriend.

She's said she's on leave and that everything is fine, but I've never seen her flopping around the house like this ... kind of undone.'

There was a forlorn note in Jessica's voice that tugged at Evie's heart.

'I was telling her about you and one thing led to another,' Jessica went on. 'I told her about your lovely house—'

'How do you know my house is lovely?'

There was a pause at Jessica's end. Then, 'I saw Heronbrook featured in a magazine spread, oh, last year?'

'That was actually three years ago,' Evie said.

It could have been three weeks ago. The years seemed to whoosh by all the swifter, the more birthdays she had. The magazine had featured an 'at home with Evie Lawrence' article, and they'd taken a plethora of photographs to run alongside the interview. In her role as Ma Donnelly she'd been labelled as an actor at the 'height of her powers', which she'd considered laughable.

It was uncomfortable to think of Jessica reading about her, but the content had been light; nothing whatsoever about her personal life, which had always been kept under industrial-grade wraps. She had always shunned interviews inasmuch as she could get away with; she had never courted the tabloid press. No one in the world of the great television-watching or theatre-going public had ever caught a glimmer of the real Evie behind the roles she had played.

'I don't know, Jessica ...' Evie began, struggling put her thoughts in order. Jessica's daughter, *Pippa's granddaughter*, offering to help. 'Let me be perfectly honest,' she said. 'It was kind of you to come to my rescue with the shopping, but I'm amazed you'd suggest this, considering our years of ... alienation, for want of a better phrase. Pippa wouldn't be happy at all.'

Jessica gave a short, sharp laugh. 'Aunt Evie,' she said, 'I have far more on my mind these days besides ancient family history and fallings out. I couldn't give two fu—, pardon. Even if I did, I'm far too busy trying to keep my own life on track to bother with old quarrels. I don't think about anything at all except getting through this week and the next week after that.'

'It sounds like you don't have a spare minute.'

'It's all go,' Jessica said. 'I'm grateful Mum is being well looked after. To put it bluntly, her mind is kaput. Very little registers with her. And very little family bad blood registers with me.'

A long silence followed, Evie trying to absorb the subtle meaning behind Jessica's words – if there was any.

'I don't know what to do with Amber,' Jessica went on, her voice subdued. 'She doesn't seem to know what to do with herself.'

'Let me think about it,' Evie said.

Thoughts of Pippa's family extending a helping hand across the years of secrets and silence seemed too good to be true. But was it really wise to accept

it, considering she'd be going behind Pippa's back
in a way? Yet she couldn't afford to snub the offer.
Lately she'd been plagued by the feeling that, at
her age, time was running out. The moment the
motorbike had tossed her into the air, she'd feared
it was too late for any kind of family reconciliation.
Now she was being given another chance.

So long as Amber – whatever had gone wrong –
didn't expect her great-aunt to come up with any
heartfelt advice. She was far too withered, cynical,
and sour for that.

Amber pulled into a pick-up spot close to the hospital entrance on Thursday afternoon and switched off the engine of her twelve-year-old Clio. She stepped out of the car and zipped up her jacket against the early September breeze. She had a sudden rush of nerves, not sure what she was doing there. One foot in front of the other, she reminded herself. Breathe in, breathe out. Then she threw the strap of her bag over her shoulder and walked through the entrance to the hospital, a memory of Jamie's colourful description of her great-aunt floating into her head.

'The wicked witch of the west,' he'd said. 'That's what my mother calls her. They're sisters but they haven't spoken for years.'

It had been the day of Great-Granny Ruth's funeral, the gentle lady who had always smiled at her with soft blue eyes, and Amber had had a sad feeling in her tummy.

'Why not?' Amber had asked, intrigued by the sounds of a relative who was likened to the scary witch in the *Wizard of Oz*.

'I don't know,' Jamie had said. 'Mum doesn't want Evie home for the funeral, even though it's her mother too. Who knows' – he'd bent down towards Amber and smiled – 'she might arrive on a broomstick or turn your Granny Pippa into a toad.'

'Jamie, that's enough,' her mum had said, as she

walked past, dressed in black. 'Have some respect for the family. Amber, go to the bathroom, please, I don't want any jigging around during Mass.'

Her younger brother Adam was being minded by a neighbour, so Amber, at seven years of age, had felt quite grown-up standing in the pew alongside her mother and father, Jamie, Simon, her mum's twin, and Granny Pippa. Granny Pippa was always cross, but that day, with her eyes red from crying, she filled Amber with unease. Still, Amber knew she'd be crying if it was her mum lying dead in the wooden box.

After Mass, they had walked up the aisle behind the coffin. At the back of the church, Granny Pippa stopped suddenly and stared at a woman in the last pew, a small blonde woman wearing a dark coat with a big collar. The woman nodded her head towards Granny Pippa, but Granny Pippa made a noise that sounded like a long hiss. She lunged forward, her hands raised, her fingers curved like bony claws. Then Mum put her arm firmly around Granny, propelling her out the door.

Amber heard Jamie whisper behind her. 'Evie came after all. Let the fun begin.' She stared with curiosity at the lady as she walked past. The lady returned her gaze, looking at her with a mixture of interest and sadness and something else Amber couldn't make sense of. Her blue eyes were soft and gentle, though, like Great-Granny Ruth's, not cruel like a witch's, or hard like Granny Pippa's often were.

That had been the first time Amber saw Evie Lawrence.

Occasionally, over the years, Amber had asked her mother what had caused the rift between Granny Pippa and her sister, but Jessica had always been vague.

'I don't know what kind of row they had,' she'd told her. 'Mum never spoke of it. Evie lives in London, anyhow, so we just don't see her.'

When Evie had returned to Dublin, to an apartment in Blackrock and a role in an Irish crime drama, they still didn't see her, teenage Amber too caught up in her own life by then to give it much thought, and as time went on she was so engrossed with college and later her career that her great-aunt remained in the background of her life.

The previous evening she and her mother had visited Evie in hospital to go through some practicalities. Her great-aunt seemed delicate and fragile, a large bruise on her face turning to yellow, scabs on her forearm, her short white hair emphasising the curving cheekbones in her pale face. Back in Laurel Lawns afterwards, her mother had popped open a bottle of cheap and cheerful prosecco, wishing Amber well before she left for Heronbrook.

'It was appalling the way the culprit drove off and left Evie there,' her mother had said, as they sat in the kitchen. 'She didn't deserve that fright. We might share an offbeat family history, but I'd never hold any ill-will towards her.'

'What offbeat history?' Amber had asked. 'I know she hasn't spoken to Granny Pippa in years, but is there anything else?'

Her mother had looked uncomfortable. 'Well, obviously, that's what I meant,' she said, busying herself by refilling her glass. 'It's unusual for two sisters to fall out for so long.'

'Did you resent Evie for that?'

'No,' her mum had said, taking a gulp of prosecco, 'and please forget what I said. I don't want you going to Heronbrook with any prejudgements.'

'So there was something to judge?' Amber had said, her curiosity piqued. 'Some kind of behaviour? Bad behaviour, I presume. Good behaviour doesn't get a second glance.'

'Just leave it, Amber,' her mum had said. 'It's all water under the bridge and I've more urgent things on my mind right now.' She'd given Amber a meaningful glance.

Amber had swiftly changed the subject. She knew her parents were puzzled as to why their normally bat-shit busy daughter was suddenly on leave – the story she was sticking to like glue. Since the previous Friday she'd been going around on autopilot, feeling she was scalded all over, the surface of her skin burned away to expose a painful inner layer, her heartbeat thumping dizzyingly in her ears, all her senses teetering on the edge of collapse. Awake in bed at night, burning with anxiety, she went over that final afternoon in the office, but she still couldn't figure out why it had all gone so wrong, and she was still too shell-shocked to cry. No way could she bring herself to talk about it to anyone, least of all her parents. She knew they were still recovering financially after her father's period of unemployment, which was another reason why it would be difficult to admit she was jobless.

Escaping to Heronbrook couldn't be coming at a better time.

This afternoon, Evie Lawrence's face was creased with anxiety when Amber took her bag while an orderly wheeled her out to Amber's car, keeping up a stream of cheerful chat. He showed Evie how to manoeuvre herself into the passenger seat and stow her crutches, before putting on her seat belt.

'I don't know about this at all,' Evie said, as Amber exited the car park, 'you looking after me. I don't think it's such a good idea.'

This was a great start indeed. 'Why not?'

'If you have spare time on your hands, you should be heading off on an adventure of some sort, a break in Paris or Rome, instead of looking after a cranky old woman.'

Amber pretended she was too preoccupied looking for the correct route to the motorway to reply.

'I'm stuck between these crutches and I can't do anything at all, let alone make a cup of tea,' Evie went on. 'I'm afraid I might drive you mad and exhaust all your patience. If you want to change your mind, I'll make other arrangements. All you have to do is see me to the door, turn around, and go home.'

'It's a bit late for that now,' Amber said, finally accelerating onto the motorway. 'I have some groceries in the boot to unpack, courtesy of Mum, and a lasagne that she insisted on giving me for our evening meal. Believe me, compared with other things I could be doing in the next couple of weeks, this is better.'

'I can't believe picking up after me is a preferred alternative to whatever else you could be doing. I don't even have proper Wi-Fi – it acts up every so often and I have to get down on my hands and knees to unplug the modem, which would be one of your jobs.'

'That suits me fine. I don't know why you're doing your best to put me off,' Amber said, feeling a bit petulant.

There was a silence. Then Evie said, 'I'm sorry if I sound unappreciative when I'm actually very grateful for your help. I just find it hard to believe that a lovely young woman like you is happy to put her life on hold and come down to Heronbrook to look after me.'

Oh, feck. Amber's grip on the wheel tightened. Where was the woozy from painkillers, acquiescent patient she'd been expecting? Great-Aunt Evie seemed to be cut from a different cloth to placid Nana Beth. 'I helped out with Dad's mum,' Amber said. 'I know what to expect. And you don't know what dark thoughts were going around in my head,' she added, surprised to find herself admitting this. Having to look after her great-aunt would make her get out of bed and keep moving, give her a reason to breathe and eat and hold her dark thoughts at bay. And, she hoped, leave her too tired at the end of a busy day to lie awake sleepless half the night, agonising over everything. She was already glad of the miles she was putting between herself and Dublin, with nothing but lush greenery on either side of the motorway, the granite-faced mountains a backdrop, and, to the east, occasional glimmers of the sea.

Her great-aunt didn't reply for a few moments. 'That's true, Amber,' she said eventually. 'It sounds like life went wrong for you somewhere, so although there are decades between us, we have something in common. Life went belly-up for me and I didn't come out of it well, so there's a good chance taking care of me could make you feel worse, not better.'

'I can guarantee that looking after you will not make me feel any worse, Aunt Evie,' Amber said. 'And I'm not expecting you to cheer me up.'

'Thank goodness.' Evie gave a sigh. 'I don't have any gems of wisdom to share or sage advice. And another thing, please drop the "aunt" part,' Evie said. 'Let's be honest, I haven't exactly been an aunt to you at any stage of your life – which is another reason I'm surprised this is happening at all. You realise I'm *persona non grata* as far as your grandmother is concerned?'

'I got that impression all right,' Amber said.

'You're too polite. She hates my guts. I was

excommunicated most forcibly from the bosom of Pippa's family. Doesn't that bother you? Being marooned with me in splendid isolation?'

'I'm sorry if this offends you, but I couldn't be arsed. I've enough drama of my own to contend with. And no, I won't be sharing any of that.'

'Good, that's a relief,' Evie said. 'And let's start as we mean to go on and set some ground rules. We'll have none of this "opening up to each other" crapology. I won't badger you with nosy questions about your life, and you won't ask me about mine.'

'Agreed,' Amber said, happy to go along with Evie despite her curiosity if it meant her great-aunt wouldn't start posing awkward questions.

'It's the next exit off the motorway and left at the roundabout.'

Presently, following Evie's directions, they were driving down a winding, tree-lined laneway through beautiful woods, some of the trees so tall and ancient they met overhead, thrusting them into a cool green tunnel. At the end of the laneway they came to a large clearing in the woods where wrought-iron gates were set into an old stone wall, a plaque on one of the pillars bearing the name Heronbrook.

'I'm not sure what it'll be like inside,' Evie said, half-apologetically. 'I went out for a walk a week ago and no one has been in there since.'

'You mean you don't have an army of cleaners getting it ready for me?'

'No,' Evie said. 'And there could be a pong in the kitchen from stale food.'

'I'll hold my nose,' Amber said.

Evie gave her a long look, and Amber felt she had passed some kind of test when her great-aunt said, 'I think we'll get on OK, you and me. Just ignore me if I get frustrated.'

'Sure.'

Evie gave Amber the code to open the gates and she got out of the car, blinking in the sudden blast of sunshine. Out here in the clearing, under a silky-blue September sky, there was no other noise at all, except for a soft breeze riffling through the tall trees and the call of the birds. Heronbrook looked like it might have been a gate lodge once upon a time, and it seemed quaint and cosy enough to have come straight out of a fairy tale, but it seemed modest for someone like Evie Lawrence.

'Evie went there on holidays years ago, when she was a teenager,' her mum had told her. 'I was really surprised when I heard she'd bought it, especially when—'

'When what?' Amber had asked.

Her mother had looked vague. 'Oh, nothing,' she had said unconvincingly, before continuing, 'it's a far cry from the exciting, glamorous locations Evie could be circulating in. She could have retired to a villa in Malaga or the Amalfi coast.'

Whatever had prompted Evie to bury herself in a quiet part of Wicklow was none of her business, Amber decided, pressing the keypad and watching the gates swing open.

Evie, July 1961

As the summer holidays began, I had no idea that at fifteen years of age I was about to set the rest of my life on an irreversible path.

My sister, Pippa, and I were beyond excited to be decamping to Wicklow and the sea for two whole months. My parents had been talking about this holiday since the spring. We lived on a main road in Drumcondra, a northside city suburb where on warm summer days the heat seemed trapped in the air, oozing up tarry from the roads filled with belching buses and cars and seeping into our red-bricked house.

Four years older than Pippa, I was suspended between sheltered Catholic-schooled girlhood and the adventure of womanhood. As we drove down to Wicklow in the family Ford Anglia, my nose pressed to the windowpane looking for a sighting of the sea, I imagined my life ahead full of possibilities that sparkled like crystal held against the light. I was beginning to sense there was something in the air, like a drift of fairy dust, an anticipation of a shift in society. John F. Kennedy had been elected President of the United States of America and small seeds had been set in motion with other icons of the era. John Lennon had already met Paul McCarthy at a church festival, a teenage David Bowie was studying art, music, and design in high school. I was soon to meet Lucien Burke.

The journey down seemed to take an age, and Pippa was beginning to grumble. At last my father turned in off the main road and soon we were driving down an almost hidden lane that twisted through trees so dense on all sides that we could have been in a forest. My father jumped out of the car and opened black wrought-iron gates. He drove into a driveway, tyres crunching on gravel. He switched off the engine in front of a one-storey house, windows glimmering in the sunshine. He turned around to smile at me and Pippa. 'Now, isn't this lovely?'

Heronbrook.

The house sat in a clearing in the woods that allowed for plenty of light. The living-room-cum-kitchen was a large room to the back, with floor-to-ceiling glass doors giving on to the rear garden. From the terrace outside, steps led to a gently sloping lawn, bounded on two sides by beech hedging. At the end of the garden, a sparkling brook rippled over a bed of stones, marking the rear boundary, forming bubbling white tips over a small weir further down. The opposite bank of the brook was massed with flowering shrubs, pink and orange and lavender and yellow, a profusion of colour that dipped into the water, against a backdrop of the woods.

My mother showed us a gate in the hedge. It opened onto a pathway that led to a small wooden bridge over the brook before curving through the woods. 'The sea,' she said, to my delight, 'is less than ten minutes' walk along there.'

The moment I walked into the small bedroom tucked beside the living room, I felt it welcomed me. One window looked onto the side of the house, but the other had a view of the rear garden and the brook, and that afternoon the walls of the room were lit with reflections of flickering sunlight. When I opened that window, the sound of the water flowing over the weir was like music. It made me feel good, but in a way I couldn't yet articulate.

This was the room where Lucien and I became lovers for the first time. But that would be three years later.

♦

I loved waking up each morning to the sounds of the water. I loved crossing over the bridge, stopping to gaze down at the brook, losing myself in daydreams as I gazed at the way it kicked up white foamy rivulets. The track through the woods led back out onto the winding lane. If you turned left, it brought you up to the main road. But if you turned right, the lane curved down towards the sea, passing the entrance to a large caravan and mobile-home park. There was a small car park closer to the sea and a trail through a sand-covered incline, and when you crested the top, the first thing to catch your breath was the salty breeze and then, in front of you, the crumpled silk of the sea, rippling between the blurry horizon and a two-mile-long expanse of golden strand.

Pippa quickly fell in with a gang of children, most of them from the caravan park, where there were lots of family groups that also hailed from Dublin and others who lived in Wicklow town and spent most of their summers on the beach. I felt set apart from them by virtue of my adolescence and was happy to sit on a towel, one eye on my book and the other on the noisy children ducking and diving against a background of beach balls, multicoloured swimming rings, stripy windbreakers, fold-up stools, and sand-mottled bags with towels and raincoats.

One afternoon I lagged behind my parents and Pippa as they headed to the beach. I followed a different path through the woods, where trees met overhead, low branches dipping into the brook. *We are here*, they seemed to tell me, *we have weathered many storms. We have been here long before you and will be here long after you have gone.* I came to a small curving bridge of granite stone, covered with moss and lichen, and to me, it was full of mystery and atmosphere. Standing on it, I felt I was in a magical world of my own.

I looked further along the shady banks to see a beautiful heron in the mudflats, picking its way delicately along. I wondered how its spindly legs could hold it up so gracefully. Then I felt I was being watched. I glanced up to see him sitting high on the bank, framed by the low-hanging branches: a youth, balancing a sketchbook on his raised knees, still and silent as a statue. He seemed to belong there, in that glade with the lacy trees and dappled sunshine. Even though I felt I was intruding, I didn't want to move. He wasn't looking at me now, his eyes firmly fixed on his sketchbook, so I crossed the bridge and followed my family down to the sea.

The following two afternoons I ventured along the same path. He was there again, absorbed in his sketchbook. And finally, on the fourth afternoon, when the heron came back and I watched it flying in low before it alighted on a boulder, I heard him say, 'Are you going to say hello?'

I could have shrugged my shoulders and walked on. Instead I said, 'What are you doing here?'

We looked at each other. That moment in my life was the equivalent of throwing a small stone into a pond. A tiny plop and the stone disappeared beneath the surface. But the consequences of that small movement caused a never-ending spiral of ripples. They moved out across the surface, one rolling into the next, until they spread as far and wide as they could in ever-increasing circles, reaching out to touch off all the green banks of the pond and every single moment of my life thereafter.

'I thought that was obvious,' he said in a pleasant tone of voice. 'I'm drawing.'

'I can see that, but why here?' I asked, more out of curiosity.

'It's beautiful here.'

I found myself walking over towards him,

disturbing the heron. It flapped its wings and listed into the air, gliding downstream. I didn't make friends easily but I sat down beside him, drawing up my knees and hugging them, as though it was a perfectly natural thing to do.

'What's beautiful about it?' I was intrigued, wondering if he felt the same as I did. He seemed different to the few boys I knew who hung around my Dublin suburban neighbourhood, who were loud and brash and out to show off. This guy seemed around my age, but more grown-up, as though he had successfully navigated the messy phase of adolescence. I didn't realise then that he'd been forced by fate to grow up early.

'It makes me feel peaceful,' he said. 'I like sketching the trees, the brook, the stone bridge, the sun shining through it all.'

'I'm staying up in Heronbrook with my parents and sister,' I said. 'We're here for the summer. We live on a main road in Dublin so all this' – I threw out my hand – 'and the sea so close is like magic.' I'd never spoken of my inner thoughts to anyone like this before, least of all to 'a member of the opposite sex', as Mother Agnes would say in a snooty voice, as though such a person was far less worthy. I'd often felt like telling Mother Agnes that my lovely dad was such a human being, and that he was full of love, kindness and decency.

'In what way is it magic?' he asked.

I knew by the look in his eyes that I held his full attention and there was no need to try and be clever.

'It makes me feel happy,' I said simply, 'glad to be here. I feel I'm really me, Evie Lawrence, and I'm looking forward to all the years to come. I know I'm going to make them wonderful.'

'Evie – that suits you,' he said. 'I'm Lucien. Lucien Burke.'

'That's an unusual name.'

'I'm named after my grandfather on my mother's side.'

There was a guarded note in his voice when he said the word 'mother' and it alerted me to something wrong. 'It's a lovely name,' I said. 'It's different.' *Like you.*

'Yeah, I suppose.' He picked up a pebble and lobbed it into the brook. It hit the water with a small plopping sound.

'People ask me what my name is short for,' I said chattily, 'but it's not short for anything. My sister is called Pippa, and when people ask if it's short for Philippa, she says it isn't, because she hates that name, but actually it is. I was four when she was born and I couldn't say her name properly so Pippa kind of stuck.'

'Why does she hate her name?'

'She's called after my mother's aunt, who's tall and thin and wears mostly trousers and complains all the time. She never got married. I bet Pippa is afraid she might turn out like her because she's always grumbling about something.' I said. 'I wonder what it's like being an only child and having all your parents' attention.'

'I wouldn't know,' he said, staring into space for a moment.

He was there with his granny, he told me. She had a mobile home in the park, and his aunt and eight-year-old twin cousins were over from Croydon, London, and staying there too. He liked to escape with his sketchbook for an hour or so every afternoon.

'What are you drawing?' I asked.

He proffered his pad. 'I hope you don't mind,' he said.

It was rough, outlines of light and shade. The stone bridge, the fleck of water, the impression of trees. And me. A blurry image of me standing on the bridge, looking at the water. Even in the rough sketches, it showed my total absorption. No one had ever drawn me before. Lucien had even captured my unguarded daydreaming. I looked at him and felt something running through the space between us.

The heron returned, wheeling down to settle once more on a boulder, and Lucien picked up his sketchbook and we both sat there, his left hand flying across the page as he captured its likeness. I watched the outline of it appearing, glad that he was able to work with me beside him.

I was drawn back to him again on the following afternoons, and a week later, he told me about his parents. There was a crump in my chest as he spoke of them, his calm voice at odds with the sad story he was sharing.

A climbing accident, in Kerry, when he'd been ten. Granny Kate had broken the news to him when he came home from school that day. He still remembered the way she'd clutched at her throat as if trying to stem the flow of awful words.

His father had slipped and fallen while crossing a slope; his mother had reached towards him and lost her own footing. Climbers behind them on the trail had seen the accident and raised the alarm, but both of his parents had died soon after they'd been rescued. Granny Kate's words had slammed into his head but he'd just felt as lifeless as his old train set when the batteries had been taken out. Since then, he'd been living in Wicklow town with his granny, coming to her mobile home every summer.

I twisted my hands. How come he was sitting here, looking so normal, when this awful thing had happened? I couldn't imagine a life without my parents.

'I'm sorry,' I said. 'That's really awful. I don't know what to say.'

'You don't have to say anything. There's nothing you can say that will make it better or worse.'

It was the first time I understood that we don't have the power to change things for another person, no matter what words we might use.

'Just go on sitting here, telling me about yourself, your school, your family,' he went on, 'and how you're going to make your life so wonderful. I like hearing it.'

'If I were in your shoes, I don't think I'd like anything at all. Ever again.'

'There are lots of things I don't care about any more. But I like drawing pictures and painting and I like listening to you.'

His words glowed inside me like a shiny new jewel.

Evie, July–August 1961

'Evie has a boyfriend,' Pippa announced at breakfast almost two weeks after I had met Lucien. She lifted the milk bottle and poured milk on her cereal before looking at me to check my reaction.

'No, I don't,' I said.

'You do,' Pippa squealed. 'I've seen you with him, in the woods, on the beach.' She fixed me with a cat-who-got-the-cream look as she began to crunch her cornflakes.

I laughed. 'We just talk – that's all. It doesn't make him my *boyfriend*.'

I didn't feel any kind of embarrassment. Lucien was just a new friend. I had met him in the woods several times, and after an hour or so we'd gone down to the beach where Lucien met up with his Croydon cousins. In my hazy notions of life ahead, I wouldn't have a proper boyfriend until I was at least twenty-one. We would go out on dates, to the pictures, ice-cream parlours, on picnics and to the park. We would marry when I was the sensible old age of twenty-five.

'It does so,' ---Pippa said. 'I've seen you make big eyes at him.'

Pippa was imagining this – it was typical of her to try to get a rise out of me. She was eleven to my fifteen, and those four years had opened up a world of difference between us. Our mother had stopped dressing us in matching clothes – I now had a grown-up swimsuit, with cups, whereas Pippa still had elasticated togs and this annoyed her. She had always wanted to copy me and thought I was getting one up on her.

'For God's sake, grow up,' I said irritably.

It was, of course, the reaction that Pippa was aiming for. Anything to ruffle me. She laughed. 'Look who's talking.'

'Don't be silly.'

'Maaam …' Pippa raised her voice to catch our mother's attention. She was busy at the cooker preparing breakfast for Dad and herself. 'Evie said I was silly.'

'I said you were *being* silly,' I contradicted. 'That's different.'

'What's going on, girls?' Dad walked into the kitchen, wearing his navy suit and a tie. 'Look at that lovely sunshine out there,' he said, ignoring Pippa's raised voice. 'How lucky you both are to be here with nothing to do but enjoy the beautiful day. I wish I didn't have to go back to work but it makes me happy to think that my wife and daughters are able to enjoy this long holiday.'

It was Monday morning, and Dad was going back to Dublin to work in the General Post Office after his annual leave, returning to Heronbrook at weekends, as he would for the rest of the summer. I was annoyed he'd witnessed the childish squabble between me and Pippa. Sometimes, after hearing about Lucien's parents, I worried about my own, imagining terrible fates befalling them.

Later that week, sitting under the shade of the trees, Lucien talked about how tough things had been after his parents' deaths.

In school, he became an object of pity, kept at arm's length by his classmates as though he had a contagious illness. He knew he was a different child to the one who'd arrived home from school one afternoon, fidgeting with the marbles in his pocket, wondering why the window blinds were down. He couldn't talk about it, he couldn't concentrate; he got into trouble for doodling in the back of his exercise copies and was slapped with the edge of a ruler across his knuckles. When Granny Kate noticed the red welts across his hands, she swept up to the school to have it out with his teacher. Whereupon his exercise book was thrust in front of her, with all the evidence of his wrongdoing. The whole class held its breath, waiting to see more trouble crashing down on Lucien's head.

Even I held my breath, wondering what was coming next.

And then, he told me, Granny Kate had rounded on the teacher. Why didn't he recognise exceptional talent when it was thrust in front of him? His method of teaching left a lot to be desired.

Lucien learned to be more careful with his drawings. The following Christmas morning, he came downstairs to find a paintbox under the tree along with blank sketchpads, a set of artist's brushes, and a selection of pencils. He flipped open the lid of the rectangular paintbox and looked at the rows of assorted watercolours, the names almost as magical as the colours themselves – ochre, vermilion, emerald, cobalt, magenta, burnt sienna – each small square a smooth and perfect pebble. The sight of the colours sent a wave of something into his chest.

'I don't expect you to understand,' he said, 'but I didn't have to talk, to say anything, and all the things I had locked away inside ... they seemed to run free, down my arm and into my fingers and out, the more I painted.'

I was amazed he confided in me like this. That he trusted me with such feelings. Our eyes met and held. Something warm swelled in my chest and flew out of it, and I fancied it came to rest in his. I didn't know then that my heart had flown into his keeping. I was happy to sit there indefinitely, nothing pressing to do, just the two of us in the small hollow in the drowsy afternoon, the gentle breeze stirring the trees and the brook running by, licking the stones and kicking up bubbles like little pirouettes.

◆

The days and the weeks of the summer drifted by in a haze. Most afternoons Lucien and I met down by the brook, once it wasn't lashing rain. Sometimes I brought a book to read – I was mad into Agatha

Christie and Daphne du Maurier – while Lucien sketched. Other times I was happy to lie out on the mossy banks, listening to the water gurgling along, watching for the heron, inhaling the scents of bracken and pine trees. Lucien identified the various trees for me: silver birch, hawthorn, oak, spruce, willow, beech. Sometimes he brought his radio and we listened to music, finding out that we both liked the theme song from *Exodus*, which we'd both seen in the cinema the year before, as well as the Everly Brothers, Neil Sedaka, and Elvis Presley.

I often chatted about growing up in Drumcondra and school. 'The only subject I really like is English,' I told him, 'especially the plays. We're doing *The Merchant of Venice* next year. When I was younger,' I laughed, 'I used to put on makey-up plays at home, using the bay window as a stage.'

'Sounds fun.'

'We might be getting a television set in the next couple of years. Sometimes I go to the pictures and the theatre with my family but this way I'll get to see lots of good films and plays.'

'We have one already,' Lucien said in a jokey way. Of course he'd have one, Granny Kate making sure he was as distracted as possible from the big gap in his life that his parents had left. I had met Lucien's grandmother, a woman I guessed to be in her sixties. She was a rotund, grey-haired lady whose bright eyes assessed me shrewdly for a long moment, telling me silently not to dare mess with her precious grandson, before she said she was glad to see Lucien with a new friend.

Down on the beach, I sometimes paddled in the water but mostly sat sunbathing or reading. Lucien went swimming and played football and tennis with his young cousins and the ever-widening gang of children. Out here, with the skittish breeze, the waves frilling along the expanse of the strand, and the cacophony of excited children, something in the free and easy atmosphere seemed to give Pippa permission to be extra cheeky to me, and even Lucien, if he wasn't paying her attention. He sometimes included her when he was buying a treat for his cousins from the van in the caravan park – an ice pop, lucky lumps or a toffee bar. The first time it happened she was a bit miffed at being included in the same category as his young cousins, but she couldn't help being satisfied that he'd thought of her. She had become best friends with a girl called Rachel, who was on holiday with her family from Walkinstown in Dublin. The friendship pleased her because Rachel sometimes had her younger siblings to mind – her toddler brother, Matthew, and baby sister, Leah, who always seemed to be crying. Pippa didn't have any such annoying encumbrance, which made her feel superior.

'How come Rachel has a boyfriend yet you're still pretending you don't?' Pippa asked one morning near the end of July. I had given up explaining that

Lucien was just a summer-holiday friend. Even my parents regarded him as such; I was far too young for it to be anything else.

'Rachel's boyfriend? You don't mean that carrot-haired boy?' I said, thinking of the ringleader of the group that I'd seen Rachel and Pippa with, hanging around him like bees around a honeypot as he leaned on his bicycle and, although he was only their age, acted like he was king of the road.

'There's no need to be insulting. Rachel told me that Barry Talbot is from a respectable family in Wicklow.'

'Well good for Rachel.'

◆

In early August, Lucien's aunt and cousins went home to Croydon and I was conscious that the summer of our free and easy existence was more than halfway over. But I put that out of my mind until mid-August, when my mother started talking about going back to Dublin a few days before the end of the month to prepare for the return to school. And then Lucien told me he and Granny Kate were heading home to Wicklow town around then also, so there was no ignoring it.

'How do you feel about going back to school?' I asked Lucien one afternoon. It had rained the night before, and the brook surged along swifter and higher under the stone bridge. The woods were heavy with the scent of damp foliage but Lucien had managed to find a dry spot under willow trees.

'It's OK,' he said. 'I only have two years left now, and then I'll be free.'

'Well for you.' I grinned. 'Free to sketch and paint as much as you like,' I went on, thinking that was what he meant.

He didn't reply. He ripped out a page in his pad with a half-finished sketch of the willow tree and began to outline it again.

'I'm going back into an exam year,' I said, fidgeting with some windfall twigs.

'You'll be grand.' He turned and gave me a smile that filled me with confidence.

I began to count down each day, an ache in my chest at how quickly the hours rushed past. Inevitably, no matter how much I wanted to hold back time, the final morning came and I was awake early, reluctant to leave this magical place. We had packed up the night before and I met Lucien down on the beach to say goodbye.

'I hate leaving and I hate goodbyes,' I admitted, over-whelmed by the knowledge that the summer was shrinking into nothing but a capsule of memories, and we'd never have this time back again.

'I feel the same,' Lucien said. 'We're leaving tomorrow and I'm sorry the summer is over.'

'Are you?'

'I've really enjoyed it with you,' he said, a shy smile on his face that pulled at my heart. 'But, Evie, once you're home a couple of hours you'll be fine,' he went on. 'And you said you'd write to me so it's not really goodbye. Who knows, you might be back next summer.'

'My parents are talking about it all right.'

It was a ray of comfort, even though next summer seemed a lifetime away.

Lucien walked back up the laneway with me as far as the woods, giving me a clumsy farewell hug that felt good to me. When I turned to go, it seemed as if the sun had gone in. We left Heronbrook later that morning, Pippa chatting excitedly about going back to school and seeing her classmates again, but I felt as if I was being wrenched away from something special. I pressed my nose to the car window, watching the trees disappear, imagining they were waving farewell, feeling further and further away from Lucien as we turned out into the main road for Dublin, and I thought I was going to cry.

I was too young to feel like this, I told myself crossly, listening to Pippa chatter away. I was only fifteen. There was a whole big life waiting for me and this wasn't even the beginning.

Evie, present day

A repetitive bleep cuts through the fog in my head. My head feels encased in cement. Something pinches my neck.

Hazy images filter through my consciousness, like an old dream.

I am running through the trees, my footfall muffled by the branch-strewn forest floor, my breath coming in gasps, my heart racing. Snaking brambles and sharp-edged undergrowth sting my legs. High above me, trees meet overhead, forming a thick canopy. I'm calling Lucien's name over and over, but my words echo through the deep green chamber and he doesn't answer me.

I see the shadow of him flitting ahead of me, always just ahead, disappearing around a twist in the woods just as I come close. Where has he gone, my beautiful Lucien? I am gripped with the feeling of a terrible void. I hear a child laughing, a spontaneous, infectious laugh that abruptly turns to heart-rending sobs.

I am in a clearing, a column of sunshine pouring down, illuminating me like a spotlight. I hear shouts coming from behind me, men's voices:

'There she is.'

'We have her now.'

'She'll get what's coming to her.'

'She deserves it after what she's done.'

I turn around and around in a dizzying circle, searching for an escape route, but there is none. The voices come closer, the sound of thundering footsteps. My heart crashes around, the rest of me frozen in terror.

The woods disappear. I am sucked back to a sudden noise – a machine emitting a warning, high-pitched sound. There is the patter of hurried footsteps approaching. Someone calls my name.

If only I'd listened to Pippa …

Everything fades into a tiny black dot.

Three Weeks Earlier

Amber awoke suddenly to the taste of stale wine on her tongue. An unfamiliar scent drifted up from the bed linen. There was no hum of traffic, no everyday noises from a street outside – only the chirp of the birds and the riffle of the breeze through the trees. Eyes closed, she automatically reached for her mobile. Then pinpricks of memory surfaced, darting though her head, rushing together, exploding with fresh pain. Her heart squeezed and she struggled to take a breath.

Her eyes flew open and her chest relaxed immediately. She wasn't at home in Laurel Lawns. She was nestling in a lavender-scented bed in a small house in the middle of nowhere, going through the motions of looking after a great-aunt she hardly knew. Better again, after a week of sleepless nights, she'd actually slept right through.

♦

'This used to be Pippa's room,' Evie had said the previous evening, when she manoeuvred herself and her crutches up the hall and showed Amber into a comfortable guest room. The walls were washed in a soft white, a patchwork quilt and cushions on the bed providing pops of lilac and pale pink.

'Mum mentioned you had stayed here on holidays. When was that?' Amber asked, feeling as though she was moving around like a robot.

'Back in the early sixties,' Evie said, her tone bland.

'How come you decided to buy it?'

'It had been empty for a while.' Evie evaded her question.

'It must have meant a lot to you,' Amber said, unable for a moment to hide her curiosity about her great-aunt.

Evie turned away but not before Amber saw a shadow cross her face. Odd. Evie would scarcely have returned to Heronbrook unless it held special memories, because something had surely brought her back here.

Evie showed her a smaller guest bedroom, then a gleaming white and navy bathroom with a separate shower cubicle, and Evie's own bedroom, decorated in soft white and pale rose. 'I had everything upgraded,' Evie said, 'and the terrace outside extended. My parents used to have the bedroom across the hall from Pippa. I turned part of that room into an en suite for me.'

'It's all beautifully done,' Amber said, as they went back to the living room. It was styled in accents of eggshell and dark blue, with squashy sofas, velour throws and cushions, lamps and an occasional table. Two alcoves were shelved and held an assortment of books, ornaments, and a couple of Evie's awards. A wall-mounted television screen was set into the centre, with a stove and a basket of logs underneath. There was a white, modern kitchen at the far end of the room, a pale oak table and duck-egg-blue chairs separating the living and kitchen areas. But the most stunning feature was the view through the glass bi-fold doors, which ran across the width of the room. Outside, beyond a flag-stone terrace arranged with groupings of colourful planters and wicker furniture, the garden led down to a large stream that flickered with silvery light, everything surrounded by the woods.

Amber was glad to feel as though she'd been thrust into an alternate universe.

There was no time to think as she set things to rights, cleaning out the fridge and cupboards, restocking with the groceries her mother had given her. She plucked wilted blooms out of pottery vases, making a note to buy fresh flowers. She arranged fruit in a bowl on the table, while Evie checked out physio sheets she'd been given in the hospital, staring in dismay at the instructions.

'I suppose Nana Beth did her exercises diligently,' Evie said.

'She must have,' Amber said. 'She made a great recovery. She's in her eighties and flying around like a teenager.'

'That sounds like a challenge to me,' Evie said.

'Not particularly,' Amber said. 'Everybody is different and I'm happy to do whatever I can to help out, but I'm not able to do your lunges for you. Although I could supervise ...' she said, attempting a joke.

'No thanks. I'll keep my awkward fumbling for the privacy of my room. You could do all these contortions in your sleep. You probably have a regular gym slot and a Fitbit or whatever you call it.'

'Maybe I had,' Amber said with false nonchalance, thinking how alien that part of her life already seemed. She'd brought leggings and leisure tops with her, more for comfort than anything else, but she'd left her designer gym gear, her Fitbit, and her iPad back in her bedroom at home.

For their evening meal, she heated the lasagne her mother had given her and served it with a side salad and some crusty garlic bread.

'Thanks for this, Amber, it's the best food I've had all week,' Evie said.

'It's all down to Mum,' Amber said. 'She gave me some basics to tide us over but we'll have to get in a decent shop.'

'We'll sort all that out tomorrow,' Evie said, taking a sip of water. 'We can shop online, but we're not completely isolated,' she went on. 'The village of Glenmaragh is less than ten minutes' drive away. There's a garage with a convenience store, and the Glenmaragh View, a café and local craft shop. It's owned and run by Tess Talbot, the woman who helped me after the accident.'

'Sounds good.'

'I should be able to get out for a coffee or lunch in a few days' time,' Evie said, slicing through her lasagne. 'I don't expect you to be locked up here twenty-four-seven. You're free to pop out whenever you need to. Actually, it might be a good idea to have you insured on my car – not that there's anything wrong with yours,' Evie said hastily, 'it's grand, but I have a fairly new Kia hybrid sitting in the garage, and you might as well have the use of it. It would be handier at navigating the hill up to Glenmaragh. And for me getting in and out,' she added.

'I won't say no to that,' Amber said.

She cleared up after the meal, going out the front door to dispose of refuse in the bins at the side of the house. She listened for a moment to the call of the birds, drawing a few deep breaths of the resin-scented September air, grateful that she was miles from Dublin.

'Will I check your post?' she asked Evie, when she came back in, remembering the box she had seen attached to the front wall beside the gates.

'Sure, thanks,' Evie said, telling her where the key was kept.

Amber went back out and plucked half a dozen envelopes from the postbox, bringing them in to Evie before fetching clean linen from the cupboard and making up fresh beds. Evie's bedroom was a study in neatness, she decided. Stylishly comfortable, but tidy to the point of minimalist, it held none of the personal objects you'd expect of a seventy-plus woman, unlike her Nana Beth. For all the beautiful prints on the walls in Heronbrook, a mix of seascapes and Wicklow landscapes, there were, surprisingly enough, no photographs at all. When she came back into the living room bearing laundry for the washing machine, Evie was standing by the bookshelves, her eyes flustered, her face drained of colour.

'Evie? Are you OK? Are you in pain?'

Evie stretched her mouth in a quick smile and made her way back over to the table, sitting down slowly. 'No more than usual.'

'Were you looking for something to read? Can I get you down a book?'

'Not now,' Evie said hurriedly. 'I think it's time for my cocktail of wonder-drugs.'

'Of course, I'll organise that for you,' Amber said, going across to the kitchen and shoving some of the laundry into the machine. She fetched a glass of water for Evie and brought over the medication obtained from the hospital pharmacy, glad to see some colour returning to her great-aunt's face.

She phoned her mother to let her know everything was fine, relieved that she had escaped Laurel Lawns without burdening her mother with her problems. Afterwards they watched television, Evie lost in her thoughts and a little woozy from her meds, saying she needed an early night. Amber helped her into bed and ensured she had everything she needed within reach.

'Call me whenever you need me,' she said.

'I'll be fine,' Evie said.

'Seriously, Aunt Evie,' she said, feeling a pang at how helpless and vulnerable she looked in her bed, 'call me anytime, it's no problem at all.'

'It's Evie.'

'OK, Evie.'

Amber went down the hall to her own bedroom. Opening her wheelie case, she took out the emergency bottle of wine she'd brought. A couple of glasses would surely grant her a few hours' sleep. She sat at the table and stared at her reflection in the darkness of the glass doors. How had life brought her to this moment? A broken Amber, reliant on alcohol to help her sleep, while her career had come to a juddering stop and her wonderful life lay in tatters around her. What had she done wrong to deserve this? What had she ever done to Will? Nothing that she could think of. She sat sipping wine until the bottle was more than half empty.

Now, this morning, she could still taste the wine on her tongue as she picked up her mobile – the cheap replacement model she'd bought as a stopgap. Only her parents and Evie had this number, and it meant she could check for calls or texts without her heart rising into her throat. She hadn't downloaded any social media apps, having no wish to engage with the outside world. Showered and dressed in a jade-green zippy and black leggings, she went into the living room. She was stopped her in her tracks by the morning view through the glass doors. Evie had shown her where the keys were stored, so she fetched them, releasing the main lock and the security bolts. She slid back the doors and stepped onto the terrace.

It filled up her senses, the air like nectar, vibrant nature shimmering in front of her. Early morning dew lay like filigree veils across terracotta planters and urns overflowing with blossoms. It laced the lawn beyond. Down by the brook, a gentle mist skimmed the banks. In some of the ancient tall trees, leaves had turned golden, speckled red and bronze, and pale September sunshine sparked through slowly swaying branches. She listened to the chirp of the birds, the whispery shush of the breeze in the trees.

She thought of her grandmother and Evie being here on summer holidays along with their parents, looking out at much the same view as she was seeing now – how strange it was that she was in the same place sixty years later. She imagined she could hear the echo of their laughter, as if she could reach back across those years. She stood still, absorbing the dazzle of the sun, the splash of the brook gurgling over the weir, feeling that the crystalline calm of the moment was charged with something, as though she was being wrapped in a big, warm hug. The breeze twirled and danced, touching her cheek with a feather-like caress.

Back inside, she scanned the shelves full of Evie's books and ornaments, wondering if they would reveal anything about her great-aunt's life. Some magazines were sticking out untidily, and as Amber straightened them up, a few envelopes caught in between them scattered to the floor. It looked like some of the post Amber had brought in yesterday afternoon. She picked them up, spotting a photograph among the envelopes.

It was a Polaroid photo of a scan of a foetus, the grainy image of the small bud of life unmistakeable. The date and other details had been cut off. Had it arrived yesterday? Had it been the reason for Evie's pale face and flustered look when Amber had found her standing by the bookshelves? She must have been trying to conceal this from Amber. A secret grandchild, perhaps? It could hardly have been a child of her own – images of those scans weren't commonplace when Evie would have been of child-bearing age.

She went to replace everything just as she'd found it. Then a chill ran through her when she saw the words scrawled in block letters on the back of the photo: *You should have been killed in the womb – bitch.*

When Evie arrived in the kitchen in her dressing gown, her grand-niece had already laid the breakfast table – tea and toast, a boiled egg, yogurt, and strawberry conserve – ensuring everything was in easy reach for Evie, allowing her some degree of independence.

'Thank you, Amber,' she said, buttering a slice of toast, 'you have me spoiled.'

'You're welcome,' Amber said, her hands laced around a mug of coffee, 'and if you need help showering, it's no bother,' she continued.

'I'm determined to be as independent as possible,' Evie said.

'Of course, and we can work with that.'

The full extent of her helplessness was hitting Evie with the force of a thundering juggernaut on her first morning at home. She'd managed to get out of bed but, needing two crutches for support at all times, she couldn't so much as make a cup of tea for herself. And she had to find a way to dispose of the offensive post she'd opened the previous evening without alerting Amber to it. Her eyes darted to the bookshelves where she'd temporarily concealed it as best she could; it didn't seem to have been disturbed. A relief. The words on the back of the Polaroid image had shaken her to the core. Her first instinct had been to hide it from Amber. No need for her grand-niece to witness this nastiness.

But who the hell could have sent this? And why? Her head had felt as though it was exploding with anxious questions until thankfully her cocktail of wonder-drugs had kicked in and dulled the edges of her brain.

Conscious of Amber sitting across the table, Evie made an effort to focus on something else. 'I'll have to meet Nana Beth when all this is over,' she said. 'She sounds like an absolute paragon, not like your nightmare great-aunt.'

'I never said you were a nightmare,' Amber said politely, sipping her coffee.

'No,' Evie conceded, adding a dollop of conserve to her toast, 'but I bet your grandmother Pippa called me that. Or worse.'

'I don't remember her talking about you at all,' Amber said.

'Oh dear, indifference sucks. I'd rather incite some kind of passion, no matter how dark it is, than be ignored.' She winced. She'd spoken automatically. Woolly-minded from painkillers, she wasn't thinking straight; she didn't relish inciting the kind of fervour that resulted in offensive post. And there was no need to remind Amber of Pippa's animosity in case she questioned it.

After breakfast, she insisted on managing her morning shower herself, glad she had a walk-in cubicle, clinging to towel rails, the basin, the shower door for support, Amber having left everything she needed within her reach. Afterwards she made herself half-decent, a slow process that pushed her patience to the limits, but she needed Amber's help to dry her legs and feet, and put on her much-hated compression socks and a pair of tracksuit bottoms. And then she asked Amber to drive up to the garage in Glenmaragh for the morning paper. It would give Evie some time alone.

'Are you sure you'll be OK?' Amber said.

'I'll be fine,' Evie said. 'I can sit at the table with a glass of juice and my mobile.'

'I'll be as quick as I can.'

'No rush,' Evie said.

As soon as she heard the gates closing behind Amber, she shuffled over to the bookshelves and, balancing herself as best she could, took out the repugnant post and shoved it into a pocket of her fleece before going back to the table. She sat down carefully and, bracing herself, she stared at the fuzzy image and the repulsive words on the back.

Hate mail. She'd endured occasional bouts of it, sent mostly to the television studios, sometimes her apartment in Blackrock, par for the course, she had reckoned, by virtue of her role as the unscrupulous matriarch in *Delphin Terrace*, as well as her status and success. But this was more difficult to dismiss. It had arrived in a handwritten envelope, her name and address in block letters on the front. There was no stamp on it or postmark to indicate when it had been sent but she'd cleared her postbox the morning of her accident, so in the week after that, someone had come down the lane and personally deposited it there.

And it was someone who was familiar with Ma Donnelly's storyline in *Delphin Terrace*, because this was a replica of the menacing post that had been delivered to Ma Donnelly in the weeks before the fatal hit-and-run. Evie's heart leapt into er mouth as she wondered who could be responsible. Someone who must have known she'd been injured in the accident — much as she'd expected, it had warranted a paragraph in the national newspapers, which had included an appeal by An Garda Síochána for witnesses to come forward with any information. Had the perpetrator thought they were playing a particularly cruel joke by subjecting Evie to the same intimidation Ma Donnelly had suffered prior to her accident? If they had set out to frighten her, they had succeeded, to judge by the way she could hardly breathe. Or was it something more sinister? Maybe someone who knew the culprit? Or, she thought, her consternation spiralling, even the culprit deliberately goading her, having read about the accident and discovered her identity from the newspapers? So far, for the sake of her peace of mind, she was still clinging to the hope that her hit-and-run had been a fluke accident. So far, the police had no leads.

Christ.

She didn't want this ugliness in Heronbrook. She stuck the Polaroid back into the envelope so that she wouldn't have to look at it. She rose clumsily to her feet and made her way over to the bookshelves. The lower shelves held linen-look storage boxes, some of which contained her personal correspondence, and she managed to ease up the lid of one of them just enough to slide the envelope and its offensive contents inside.

Just in case.

On Friday evening Jessica was checking the freezer, her hands slipping and sliding across rock-hard bags of vegetables, frozen slabs of mince, pale and stiffened chicken fillets, trying to decide what needed to go on Saturday's shopping list, when Adam arrived home, bringing with him an aura of energy and lifting her heart as he marched into the kitchen.

'Well hello,' she said. 'We don't always have the pleasure of your company on a Friday evening.'

Her son took after Paul, being tall and lanky, but like Amber, he had his mother's blue eyes. Now those eyes looked at her a little sheepishly. 'Sorry I got your hopes up, Ma, but I'm not hanging around.' He went straight over to the press and, selecting a packet of chocolate biscuits, took two and wolfed them down. 'I came home to get changed,' he said. 'I'm off to a party – it'll be a late one so I'll stay over.'

'Probably safer that way,' Jessica said, mentally crossing her fingers. *And once you're careful. Once you don't knock back too many of those Jägermeisters, or whatever the current fad is.* Adam didn't always bother to come home and change on a Friday evening, sometimes arriving back in a rumpled suit on Saturday afternoon. She must be special, whoever he was out to impress. Adam had only left – freshly showered and wearing his best casual shirt and new denims, bearing a bottle of white wine from her meagre supply, having first asked her permission – when her mobile rang.

Jamie.

'Any word from the front?' Jamie asked.

'What front?'

'The front line of battle. The enemy trenches. The family warfare.'

Jessica raised her eyes to heaven, glad in a way that Jamie couldn't see her. 'I presume you're talking about Amber and Evie,' she said.

'So you agree that it's a hostile situation?' His voice sounded full of mirth. That was the thing about Jamie, Jessica decided crossly. He got away with murder largely on account of his refusal to take anything seriously.

'It's nothing of the sort,' Jessica said, knowing she sounded like a boring, by-the-rulebook older sister, annoyed that conversations with Jamie made her feel like this. She stopped that thought in its tracks and turned it around. Correction: she *allowed* herself to feel like this.

'How's Amber? Have you got a mobile number for her?' Jamie asked, changing tack. 'I was talking to her during the week, and she said she was getting a new one.'

Jessica bit her lip. Whatever catastrophe had befallen Amber, she hadn't even gone back to the office long enough to retrieve her state-of-the-art iPhone, buying a cheap model so she'd have some form of communication when she headed off to Heronbrook.

'I'll be talking to her later,' she said, 'and I'll tell her you were asking for her. She's only there since yesterday – give her a chance to settle in.'

'Throw her a lifeline to the outside world, you mean, before she realises just how stranded she is. Heronbrook isn't exactly located in a heaving metropolis and you can't get a decent pint for miles.'

'How do you know? You've never been there.'

'No harm in keeping some tabs on Mum's greatest nemesis. And no harm in making sure Evie won't turn Amber into a toad, now that she has her in her lair. Actually, sis, maybe you're cleverer than I thought, getting on the right side of Evie in the closing stages of her life. Sending in Amber to cosy up to the enemy when she's vulnerable. Maybe you have a hidden agenda, like who's going to clean up all the lolly when Evie kicks the bucket?'

'Give it a rest, Jamie. I'm not listening to this shite talk.'

'Sorry, sis, I love winding you up. Seriously, though, any word on who almost sent Evie flying into eternity? Have the police any suspects?'

'No. I'm sure I would have heard if they had. Some eejit of a joy-rider, I guess. It was disastrous for Evie.'

'It certainly was. I gotta go, I'm needed to pull a few pints. Remind Amber to give me a call.'

As Jessica put down her mobile, the sound of

the hall door closing announced the return of her husband from work.

'How was your day?' she asked when Paul appeared in the kitchen, noting that, as usual, her husband looked tired and defeated. In the last few years he'd lost weight too, his frame now thinner. His hair was almost completely silvery grey, but his hazel eyes, when they rested on her, were warm.

'Same as usual,' he said. 'One moany complaint after another.'

'At least it's Friday,' she said.

'My favourite time of the week, when I've the most hours ahead of me before I set foot in that kip again. Is Adam around?'

'He came home and went back out again. To a party.'

'Did he? Feck it. He was talking last night about watching a match with me.' He opened the fridge and took out a bottle of beer, slamming the door closed with his foot and twisting the cap off. 'How about Amber?' he asked. 'Have you found out what went wrong yet? She's not really on leave, is she?'

'I don't think so, but something's up.'

'Strange. You'd imagine she'd let us know. Unless she just took you into her confidence and you're not telling me?'

Jessica sighed. 'She didn't, Paul. I'm no wiser than you are.'

He took a slug of beer. 'How are things with you?' he asked. 'Everything OK?'

'I'm fine,' she said, as casually as she could.

'Sure?'

He was beginning to notice she wasn't her usual self. 'Sure, absolutely.' She turned away from him, checking already-checked contents of the food cupboards, hoping he'd take the hint and leave her alone. Lately she'd been turning away from him a lot, even in bed. She sensed him watching her, her back rigid with tension, then he went into the sitting room. Soon she heard the blare of the television. She could picture him easing off his shoes and propping up his feet on the pouffe.

She'd met Paul at a mutual friend's birthday party when they were both twenty years of age, soon after the untimely death of her father, and it had thrown her into his arms with a degree of passion and intensity that otherwise might have taken time to develop – or might never have developed at all. She'd decided fate had brought them together just when she'd needed him most, and when she'd discovered she was pregnant six months into the relationship, there had been no question but that they were getting married.

Paul had dropped out of college and got a job as a sales rep in an electrical company. Despite her first pregnancy ending, sadly, in a miscarriage, by degrees they'd built a life together, saving hard to put a deposit on a modest home in Templeogue, moving in just before the birth of Amber. The company Paul worked for had expanded throughout Ireland, Paul going up the ladder until he was chief sales manager. When Adam was seven years of age, Jessica had got a part-time job as a receptionist in a local beauty salon.

Six years ago, they'd remortgaged to renovate the house, including a new kitchen extension. It was light-filled with a vaulted ceiling to give the illusion of a bright and bigger space in which to entertain and relax – descriptors she'd fallen in love with when the architect had discussed the plans. In her mid-forties by then, Jessica had thought she'd finally arrived. They would have glided together into a peaceful and secure second half of life, only Paul's firm suddenly went into receivership the following year. There had been little or nothing in the kitty for redundancies, and the mortgage on their house had had to be toughly renegotiated.

Now the expensive vaulted ceiling and lighting system made her feel sick.

She'd had no choice but to give up her part-time position to take on a full-time job as receptionist for a busy GP's inner-city practice where she was run off her feet and there was rarely any good news. At least, she consoled herself, they had a roof over their heads, and even if their car was on its last legs, they both commuted by bus to their respective jobs. She knew by now that other people had it worse: classmates who sadly hadn't made it to their fiftieth birthday, families whose lives had been torn asunder by fatal illness or devastating tragedies.

But Paul's period without work had undermined his confidence and riddled his self-belief. He made no secret of the fact that he hated his present job, managing customer-assist teams in a busy call centre, where the day was spent listening to a litany of complaints from irate customers. Now they were trapped on a relentless hamster wheel of debt, which would take up to and beyond retirement age to clear, and Jessica was running the house on a budget that daren't be deviated from. Both of her children were contributing, Amber more than Adam, who was on a basic internship salary, but Jessica would far rather have seen those contributions being saved towards house deposits, something she and Paul were now unlikely to be able to help towards.

She poured a glass of wine and sat at the kitchen island while she checked her shopping list again. She itched to be free of her debt, of the weekly grind that stretched on for possibly another twenty years. She itched to do something wild and dangerous with her life, which she sensed was slipping silently through her fingers. As it was, she was caught between her mother, who even now still managed to communicate to Jessica her habitual and perpetual outrage at her life in moments of half-lucidity, her brothers, her husband, who needed her to prop up his self-esteem, and her children – Amber, who had been hell-bent on storming the heights of the corporate ladder at a dizzying speed, and smug in some kind of lust-filled blaze until last week, down to Adam, hell-bent on sleeping his way through the female complement of Morotex, the software company where he was a paid intern, to judge by the far-flung areas of the city and county in which he often found a bed for the night. Even Aunt Evie, although alienated from her sister and family, had managed to pursue a successful career.

Set against this colourful, eclectic family, was it any wonder that Jessica considered herself the bland, boring one? She longed for some space to herself in which to recalibrate her life from the inside out. She knew there was another Jessica waiting in the wings, but that's where she'd be staying for the foreseeable, especially now, considering the expensive scam she'd fallen for, the financial loss of which Paul was still mercifully unaware.

Needing to break out a little from their financial strait jacket, she'd borrowed five thousand euro from the credit union on a long-term repayment plan to upgrade the family car. In a crazy fit of optimism, she'd thought it might inject some energy into the stale, humdrum routine of their lives. Jessica had never thought she'd be stupid enough to fall for one of those scams the bank repeatedly warned about, but she had. She'd carelessly clicked on a link that had looked totally legitimate, and she'd basically transferred most of the loan fund out of her bank account across to the scammers.

She'd phoned the bank three times and got no satisfaction. Finally, she'd written to them, throwing herself on their mercy and was awaiting a reply. But she wasn't confident their decision would go in her favour and she still couldn't believe how mindless she'd been. Every time she visualised herself telling Paul what had happened, she felt nauseous. She took another gulp of wine, hearing the hum of the television coming from the sitting room, and wondered how long she could keep him in the dark.

On Sunday morning, it was raining, the soft fall veiling the trees and dripping onto the terrace. In spite of Evie's helplessness, and the bad taste the awful Polaroid had left in her mouth, she sensed Amber was moving around like someone on autopilot, albeit perfectly politely and full of willingness to help. Now and again, her defences slipped and Evie saw the dull pain in her eyes, sensing there were times when her grand-niece was barely holding it together.

This morning she noticed Amber had been staring, motionless, out the window, for almost ten minutes. 'Are you any good at crosswords?' she said.

Amber turned around, looking at her as if she didn't understand a word. 'Crosswords?'

'Yes.' Evie indicated the Sunday newspaper on the table in front of her. 'Simple clue – legendary wizard, six letters.'

Amber's face cleared. 'Ah – I get you …' She came over and sat down at the other side of the table. 'That's easy,' she said, tucking her hair behind her ears.

'I have a few here,' Evie said. 'I'll call them out. Bet you a fiver I'll solve the most.'

'You're on,' Amber said, making light of it when she beat Evie, Evie just glad that the stony look in her eyes had softened.

When the rain cleared after lunch and the sun came out, glistening through the trees and sparking off the brook, Evie made another suggestion. 'I'm going to be a crotchety old aunt,' she said.

'You mean you're not that already?' Amber said.

'I haven't even started. If you'd be kind enough to wipe down the furniture outside, we could sit on the terrace for a while. There are plenty of cushions and throws, and I have Bluetooth hooked up if we want music. It's mostly fine apart from the odd Wi-Fi hiccup. There are wall-mounted heaters if it gets a little chilly, and an overhead canopy. My crotchetiness doesn't extend to freezing you to death.' Evie could have sworn she saw a faint smile flit across Amber's face. 'We can bring out some books,' she continued. 'Feel free to help yourself.'

Her grand-niece scanned the bookshelves. 'You have two beautiful awards up there,' she said. 'I recognise the IFTA – was that for *Delphin Terrace*?'

'Yes,' Evie said.

'And the other?'

'An Olivier best actress award.'

'Wow, Evie. Mum told me you went from the West End to a role in a BBC soap opera?' She looked at Evie questioningly.

'Yes, *Spencer Row*.'

'That was some big change of direction,' Amber said, her light tone unable to cover a note of curiosity.

'It was,' Evie said shortly. 'Can you take down a book for me please? *The Last Letter from your Lover*. On the top shelf, thanks,' she said, swiftly deflecting Amber's attention.

They spent a couple of hours outside, tucked up under comfy throws, music on in the background, Evie rereading her favourite Jojo Moyes book, having suggested that Amber try Maeve Binchy when she'd said she'd never read her. She hoped Amber hadn't taken any notice of the clumsy way she'd changed the subject. No one knew the real reason she'd turned her back on her stage career overnight, returning to television work six months later. She wasn't about to divulge it to Amber.

◆

On Monday morning, Evie was sitting at the table with her laptop, Amber having reset the Wi-Fi, which had involved her crawling on her knees to reach the modem socket set above the skirting board. The radio was on, and into the calm of the morning Ed Sheeran's voice poured across the quiet of the kitchen as he started to sing a catchy love song.

Amber let a jug full of milk crash to the floor. '*Shite!*' she said, not bothering to lower her voice or hide the pain in it. She began to stamp on the splintered fragments of the jug, splattering the milk further across the tiles. Then after a few moments she stopped just as suddenly as she had started, staring at Evie, mouth open in horror.

'Oh, gosh,' Evie said.

'I'm so sorry,' Amber began, swallowing hard. 'I forgot where I was. I don't know what came over me. I'll clean up this mess immediately and replace that jug.'

'I didn't like that jug so you've done me a favour,' Evie said. 'But you'll need to clean up, otherwise I could break my neck on that milk. Still, it was an impressive display, Amber. I'm glad to see you showing the kind of passion you need to get anywhere in life.'

'*What?*' Amber put her hand up to her mouth and Evie saw the sheen of tears in her eyes.

'I was beginning to think you were a bit too meek and mild, the way you've been behaving so perfectly around me,' Evie said, smiling at her. 'Nothing wrong with looking after me so well, mind you, I've no complaints, but I'm glad to see you're normal enough. Stamping is good. Bottling it up is not. And maybe it's just as well you're wearing your trainers instead of flip-flops.'

Amber stared at her for a long moment before looking down at the shards of glass on the floor. 'Yeah, I guess,' she said, something softening in her blue eyes.

Evie felt a startling urge to sweep this young woman into her arms and tell her it would be all right – she who'd put as much emotional distance between herself and other people as was possible for about the last thirty years, scouring herself of any emotional attachment, her only connections with people coming through the act she put on for the characters she portrayed. But now her heart went out to Amber. She wanted to hug her tightly and tell her she was beautiful and kind, caring and considerate. She wanted to tell her she had years of wonderful life ahead of her, that whatever had gone wrong was surely only a temporary blip. Amber's eyes were shuttered again and Evie recognised that look; now was not the right time to say anything that might sound interfering.

Later, Evie asked her to come out to the garden and bring the keys for the back doors with her. 'I want to show you something,' she said. Following the instructions she'd been given in hospital, she manoeuvred down the couple of steps leading from the terrace to the garden. She took a pathway to the side of the house, leading to a galvanised shed with a heavy padlock securing the thick bolt on its door.

'There should be a key for the padlock on that ring,' she said.

When Amber opened the shed, there was barely room for both of them to step inside. Along with gardening paraphernalia, wellington boots, and heavy-duty storage boxes, the shed contained an old kitchen cabinet, its shelves stocked with wine.

'As we've agreed, I've no intentions of prying

into your life, but one thing I would like to share with you is my wine. I usually order in a couple of cases at a time. It's more convenient that way, instead of having them clanking around in my supermarket trolley to the delight of nosy-parker shoppers. I can't enjoy it at the moment thanks to my elephant-strength painkillers, but that doesn't mean you can't.'

Amber gave her a sceptical glance. 'I hope this is not a roundabout way of getting me so rat-arsed that I'll spill my guts.'

'I wouldn't dream of that,' Evie said smoothly. 'Besides, I've already gone through heartbreak. I assume something similar has happened to you and I don't need to experience it all over again, no matter how second hand it might be.' She paused. Amber looked beautiful and vulnerable, her cropped hair emphasising her oval face, her blue eyes soft and full of guarded depths. It peeled back a memory that punched Evie in the stomach.

'I wasn't always embittered,' Evie found herself admitting. 'I did love once, you know. It was passionate and wonderful, it consumed me, it consumed us both, it was brilliant. He was my one true, my total, love. Not everyone experiences that in their lifetime.'

'That must have been amazing.'

Evie blinked. 'That's all I'm saying, Amber – I'm not about to dump anything further on you. I appreciate everything you're doing for me and

I have a shedload of some rather nice wines I'm happy to share with you. But you're not allowed to get wasted. I don't want a rat-arsed carer on my hands.'

Amber gave her a suspicious look. Evie returned her gaze with an innocent, couldn't-care-less one, and presently Amber, seemingly satisfied her great-aunt had no hidden agenda, turned to the array of wine. 'Right. Any recommendations?'

Evie indicated her favourite Merlot and a Pinot Noir. 'Try those for starters,' she suggested. She was warmed by the quick smile Amber gave her, feeling in some small, hopeful way that she'd chalked up a reason for being alive.

During her first few days in Heronbrook, Amber was relieved to be in a place where no one had any expectations of her beyond her ability to launder and clean, prepare vegetables, stir sauces or stews in Evie's copper pots, fill pottery vases with fresh flowers, and help Evie get dried and dressed after her shower, then getting dressed herself in comfy leisure wear, wearing just a slick of lip gloss and mascara, finger-drying her dark hair even if it frizzed a little.

Time spent on the terrace was peaceful, Amber taking out the green, yellow, and purple cushions and velour throws Evie had stored away, along with glass jars and lanterns holding smooth columns of candles. The gurgle of the brook was a soothing background to the music Evie streamed. The deciduous trees released flutters of yellow-gold leaves that spiralled to the ground and skipped across the garden like big flakes of confetti. She found there was a lot to be said for escaping into a warm, comforting story between the pages of a physical book. It certainly beat a podcast or Audible when her brain was exploding with hurt. On Tuesday evening, they stayed out until the slow, dusky twilight dropped and the chattering birds quietened down, the treeline inky black against a navy sky, the evening air infused with scents of stock and lavender, Amber switching on the pretty lights that were strung around outside, enjoying a glass of Evie's Pinot Noir.

But now and then images crashed through and stabbed her in the ribs. She saw herself walking confidently through the office, enjoying discussions with colleagues, rolling her chair back from her desk and stretching her arms above her head to release stiff muscles, then Will ... having great sex in his apartment, Will pulling the drapes to shut out sounds of traffic and the view of similar apartment blocks before he turned to her ...

She still couldn't understand how everything in that life had shattered, let alone why.

◆

Amber had done everything she was supposed to do to become a success. Her school reports had been embellished with terms such as 'great potential', 'highly creative', 'intelligent'. She'd chosen the college course she'd thought would put her on the correct path, giving it her all, fitting in with college-mates Megan and Julie, forming bonds with them.

Leaving college, armed with an honours degree in Business and Finance, a postgraduate placement in the financial division of W. Healy Construction Holdings followed. Against a thrum of always-on technology, she was committed and conscientious in her approach, constantly reachable, answering emails in out-of-office hours, determined to prove herself and climb the ladder. If she sometimes felt unfulfilled and stultified, she worked harder. If she sometimes felt exhausted, she knocked back another oat-milk latte. She shopped in Zara for work clothes, she socialised in Toners and Kehoes, she knew to order a Dingle gin with elderflower Fever-Tree tonic in the Vintage Cocktail Club, she streamed Netflix must-sees through her iPad. She enjoyed the freedom that Dublin had to offer a lot more than her mother had been able to, married by the age of twenty-one.

Yet even though she'd received a good promotion three months previously, there were days when Amber had felt as though her career was one gigantic box to be ticked and she was trapped right inside it.

In late July, in the lobby of Russell Hall, an office block on Baggot Street in Dublin that housed a selection of gilt-edged firms where Amber worked, she noticed a guy sitting on a banquette as she entered the lobby in her black trouser suit, a takeout coffee in her hand. In the Russell Hall ambience of identical suits and perfectly groomed, hungry professionals, he stood out thanks to his charcoal linen suit, white linen shirt, no tie, and a head of messy blond hair that looked as though he'd just riffled his fingers through it after a shower. He rose to his feet as she came through the foyer, and somehow, on her way over to the lift, they collided, Amber squeezing her cup so that she popped the lid and some liquid spilled out.

He was all apologies. 'I'm so sorry – I wasn't looking where I was going.'

Up close, he was taller than she, his white teeth emphasised by his tan, and his eyes, so light grey they were almost like silvered water, were hypnotic as they held hers. In contrast to his blond hair, his thick eyelashes were dark. She guessed him to be in his early thirties. No sign of a wedding band. Not that that meant anything, as she knew from bitter experience. The porter, Rob, came out from his desk with a roll of paper towels and proceeded to mop up the spillage, both of them apologising until he told them good-naturedly to leave off.

'*I'm* sorry,' Amber said to the guy. 'I don't think I got your suit, did I?' She inspected his trousers, before hurriedly glancing away when she realised her scrutiny was a little too close for comfort.

'No, and I think you escaped yourself,' he said, his head-to-toe gaze sweeping over her with an intensity of interest that sent heat rushing through her. 'But your coffee has taken a hit.' He nodded to her half-empty cup.

'No worries,' she said.

'I'll get you a fresh one,' he said, looking at her as though he liked what he saw.

'There's no need.'

'Please. I've just started here this week and I feel like a right twit. Let me make amends and feel better about myself. It won't take me a minute to pop to the deli next door. Are you in a hurry back to your office?'

She hesitated.

'Come on, make me smile today,' he said, a slightly roguish look on his face.

She found herself following him out onto a bustling Baggot Street, where summer sunlight filtered through the heavy-leafed trees, and she felt like a teenager playing truant from school. He bought two lattes, putting them down on a pavement table outside the deli, and drew out two chairs, as if coffee together had been pre-agreed. Audacity, she thought, gets you what you want.

His name was Will Baker. He was thirty-three years old and had just moved into an office on the fourth floor of Russell Hall. He was setting up his own digital tech company, having returned to Dublin after five years in Rome. He gave off a warm, sexy energy she found herself responding to.

'So tell me, Amber Lennox,' he said after a while, 'where are you off to in your life?'

'How do you know my name?' she asked, disconcerted.

'Do you really want to know?' He looked delighted she'd asked.

'Yes.'

He leaned across the table, stretched out his arm and, gently, lifted the cord of her security pass where it curved around her neck, the tips of his fingers connecting momentarily with her skin, sending a sharp quiver down the length of her body. 'Easy-peasy,' he said, holding her gaze with his silvery eyes as he waved her identity badge in front of her.

She felt herself blushing. *Shit*. She was reacting like a flustered teenager. Where was the savvy Amber who'd sworn to cool it with men after the last time she'd got burned?

Later that afternoon, she was staring out the window at the patch of blue sky visible above a grey medley of office blocks when a voice spoke close to her. 'You're miles away.'

She jumped. 'Fionn! Sorry, were you talking to me?'

Fionn Heffernan. Lean, gangly, a mop of auburn hair and a kind face, he'd joined Healy's at the same time as Amber five years ago, part of the graduate intake programme. They'd become good friends as they'd continued their financial studies, attending college and lectures, swapping study notes, Fionn even coming out to Laurel Lawns for revision before their master's degrees. They socialised in a group that included Nicole, Kim, and Ryan, three other recent graduates, but Fionn was the only one in Healy's she'd confided in about her patchy love life, the men she'd dated invariably letting her down. Fionn had a long-running off-again, on-again relationship with Sadie, a nurse. At the moment it was full on.

'Ryan and Nicole are talking about the new bistro for lunch on Friday,' he said.

'Sounds good to me,' Amber said.

'How are things?'

'I'm busy with this tendering process.' She indicated a document open on her laptop. 'It's complicated and confidential. The timeline is tight. No pressure,' she grinned, shaking her head.

'Give us a shout if I can help.'

'Ta.' Then just as he was about to walk off, she asked, tilting her head, 'New suit?'

Fionn darted an uneasy glance around, making sure no one was within earshot. 'Is it obvious?'

'Well, maybe not to the others ... but I noticed something different about you,' she said, eyeing the crisp navy suit and coordinating tie. Fionn usually lived on the lower end of the scale of being terrifyingly groomed, refusing to conform to the identikit nature of it, and he just about got away with it, contrasting his sober suits with bright shirts and equally zany ties.

'This is confidential,' he said quietly, 'but I was at a job interview.' He murmured the name of a renowned consulting firm. 'I was going to tell you ... It'll be a while before I know if I'm through to the next round. What do you think?' He looked at her anxiously.

What did she think? Throughout her career in Healy's, Fionn had always had her back. If he got the job, they'd be going their separate ways and, to her surprise, Amber felt a kick of panic in the stomach. She swallowed. 'I think it's a wonderful opportunity.'

'Do you? Really?' He gave her an intent look, scanning her face as if searching for something she couldn't figure out.

'Yeah, go for it.'

He looked at her silently. Then he grinned. 'Ta, Amber. But keep it to yourself for now.' His mobile rang and he gave her a wink as he ambled off and answered the call.

The following day, when she dropped in to the deli for coffee, this time with Nicole in tow, Will was already sitting outside. And when he said, rather charmingly, that he was new to the area, Nicole insisted that he join them for lunch on Friday – it would introduce him to some of Healy's inmates. In the bistro on Friday, he made a point of sitting opposite Amber. Ed Sheeran was singing in the background and Will's gaze kept coming back to her face, his interest in her so tangible that it threw a force field of sorts around her, both Fionn and Nicole giving her knowing glances. How could she not help feeling a lift when such blatant admiration was being directed at her like a powerful beam? Even when she'd sworn not to react to any man's charms until she knew a lot more about him – like, for instance, his marital status.

Later, in the office, she put her hand to the side of her neck where he'd lifted her security pass the day they'd met, remembering how the touch of his fingers had felt, and she wondered how her skin had felt to him.

Now the memory of it cut her to the quick.

What a gobshite she'd been.

Before breakfast on Wednesday morning, Amber went to find the beach.

'I want to see you going for a walk or a run every morning,' Evie had said. 'It's part of your caring duties. You'll need it to keep up your stamina for looking after me. But nothing too punishing – make sure it's enjoyable for you.' The track to the beach had been there for years, Evie had said, becoming overgrown with thick brambles and undergrowth, but she'd had it cleared when she'd bought Heronbrook.

It had rained during the night so the ground was soft that morning, and the trees gave off a sweet, earthy kind of scent. Amber inhaled slow gulps of it as she followed the track, moving through woods where morning light flickered between the branches, and the rustle of calling birds and small animals disturbed the silence. When she arrived at the bridge over the brook, she stopped for a moment looking down at the weir, listening to the melodious rush of water.

After a short while she came to a lane that brought her down between hillocks of grass and bright green fern, the morning sky above her filled with a pearly luminosity not usually seen in suburban Dublin. She passed an old closed-up entrance to a mobile-home park, and beyond that, the lane opened out into an area that must have been a small car park but was now rather neglected. Amber jogged up a slight incline between grassy sand dunes, catching a salty, intoxicating tang before she reached the top of the incline and saw it spread in front of her – the sea.

That morning, the expanse of it all the way to the horizon was calm and full of pink-washed, silvery light. There were a few people about, further up along the beach. She jogged down to the strand, feeling the fresh breeze in her hair, the soft sand yielding beneath her, and then she was down on the hard-packed sand closer to the sea. The tide was going out, creating a wide expanse of frilly waves gently advancing and retreating across a shiny, wet surface in a pattern as old as time. Something about the ceaseless, age-old pulse under the fresh, clean sky told her that life went on; it renewed and refreshed, but it kept going. On impulse, she pulled off her runners and socks and took a few steps into the water, gasping at the cold of the foamy waves as they swirled about her ankles, feeling the solidity of the ancient seashore beneath her feet. She filled her lungs with the clear, briny air and exhaled slowly.

Heronbrook with Evie and this seascape might just save her.

On her way back from the beach, she slowed to a stroll when she came to the bend in the lane where Evie had said her accident happened.

'There shouldn't be any traffic on the lane,' Evie had said. 'It's not in regular use any more. A new slip road to the beach and entrance to the mobile-

home park opened up years ago, on the north side
of the park. I guess I was just unfortunate.'

Amber scanned the laneway. Dilapidated in
places, weeds and tufts of grass sprouted through
cracks in the old tarmacadam, the surface
subsiding into crumbling potholes in several areas.
No surprises that a motorcyclist might have lost
control or had a wobble. But what was surprising
was that they had used this old laneway in the
first place, considering the state of it. Yet, Amber
noticed, scrutinising it further, the condition of
the surface where the lane curved into the bend on
which Evie said the accident had occurred seemed
in good repair and certainly not all that decrepit.
Strange.

Amber took a slow breath and surveyed the
terrain about her. The laneway was just wide
enough for two cars to pass each other carefully.
Plenty of room for a motorbike and a pedestrian.
From the sightlines, it seemed impossible that
whoever had knocked Evie down hadn't seen her on
their approach, never mind been able to avoid her,
unless they had been driving at breakneck speed.
Even so, they must have realised what they'd done,
which meant they'd left her there on purpose.

She could have been killed, her mother had said.

She'd been unfortunate, Evie had said.

Unfortunate? Without doubt, her great-aunt
was playing down the seriousness of her accident.
Amber thought of the menacing Polaroid image.
She'd had a sneaky look for it the previous day

when Evie was resting in her bedroom, but it had disappeared. She found it disturbing to think that her great-aunt had been subjected to someone's vile abuse, perhaps a crazed fan's vitriolic hate mail. However, coming on top of someone's horrifying carelessness, it seemed to her that Evie had been a lot more than just unfortunate.

Something chilly, like a cold needle of foreboding, ran down Amber's spine.

'Come to gloat, have you?' Evie asked.

The man standing in her kitchen on Wednesday morning recoiled at her tone of voice. 'Hey,' he said, 'I thought I was coming to check in on my esteemed neighbour, not a sourpuss version of Ma Donnelly.'

'Well, rest assured, one of those individuals won't be bothering you again,' Evie retorted, 'but the other one might well be. I'm not dead yet.'

In her peripheral vision, she saw Amber sitting up straighter, her grand-niece clearly wondering why Evie had allowed this man into her home, considering the reaction he was inducing. And he was right – she'd sounded exactly like ass-kicking Ma Donnelly. It felt quite good, actually. She should have channelled the character more often in front of Barry Talbot.

She'd had a bad night, between a flare up of pain and old ghosts paying her a visit. She'd been awake long before Amber, staying quietly in bed, gratified when she'd heard the terrace door being opened, knowing that Amber was following her advice and getting out into the cool, calm peace of the morning. She'd stayed put, not attempting to heft herself out of bed until Amber was back from her run and finished her breakfast. When the intercom had shrilled soon after eleven o'clock, and Barry had announced that he was calling to check on her, she'd been half-tempted to send him away.

'I suppose I'd better see him,' she had said to Amber. 'Barry Talbot is an enormous pain in the ass but it was his wife, Tess, who found me and called for help.'

Of medium height, he had a full face that looked as if the outlines had been blurred, proclaiming his love for the indulgences of life. He was wearing a pair of trousers that strained at the waistband and a sports jacket that looked a size too small.

'Maybe calling in wasn't such a good idea,' he said. 'I can see I'm not wanted.' His glance slid across to Amber, as if he was inviting her to side with him against Evie's acerbity.

'This is Amber, my grand-niece,' Evie said, annoyed that she'd lost some of her composure in front of him. 'Amber is my niece Jessica's daughter. She's staying with me for the moment.'

'So you're the lovely Jessica's daughter. Nice to meet you, Amber,' he said. 'I'm relieved to hear Evie is not all alone and vulnerable.'

'I'm not exactly in my dotage, Barry,' Evie said.

'I never insinuated that you were, Evie – there's no shame in needing a little help at this challenging time.'

'I can think of more appropriate words than challenging. Seeing as you're here,' Evie said, 'you might as well sit down. Will you have some tea or coffee?'

'No, thanks, I've just come from coffee and scones in the Glenmaragh View.'

'How did you know I was home from hospital? It's not as if you were passing by, is it?'

He pulled out a chair and subsided heavily into it. 'Word gets around,' he said.

'It certainly finds its way to you. You know everything that's going on in this neighbourhood, don't you, Barry?' She turned to Amber. 'Barry lives outside the village,' she said. 'He has a beautiful house up on a hill on the road into Wicklow, and it affords him great views of the surrounding countryside and the local traffic between Wicklow and Glenmaragh.'

'There's no need to be so spiky, Evie. When Tess called the hospital yesterday afternoon, she found out you'd been discharged.'

'That's information about me they shouldn't have released.'

'She was going to visit you, to see how you were, a neighbourly thing, but they said you were no longer a patient there. I dropped by this morning on the off-chance you might be home.'

'Thinking I might be too fragile and frail to put up a fight against your newest endeavour? No chance, Barry. You see, Amber, Barry wants Heronbrook for himself. Not to live in, though, or to have as a holiday home. He wants to tear it down and use the site to build some kind of monstrous hotel and apartments along this stretch of the woods. Unfortunately, I've refused his offers to sell. Barry thought it might have made him enough money to allow him to sink into a comfy retirement, isn't that right?'

He stared at her.

'What a pity your accountant sold you a pup of an investment a couple of years ago,' Evie said. 'Don't look so shocked – as you said yourself, word gets around. I'm not surprised you wanted to get your hands on my home.'

Barry sighed. 'I can do without the crap, Evie, and I'm no longer interested in this neck of the woods. Too much like hard work. I'm not exactly destitute either, so there's no need to crow. Besides, we go back a long way, don't we?' He turned to Amber. 'I knew your great-aunt when she was just a teenager coming here on holidays.'

'Then you must have known my grandmother Pippa as well,' Amber said.

'I did of course,' Barry said smoothly, giving Amber a quick smile that just involved widening his lips around his teeth before turning back to Evie. 'The past is another country, isn't it, Evie? And there's quite a lot of water under that particular bridge,' he went on, giving her a dark look.

'Oceans. And that's where it stays,' Evie said snappily, conscious once again of Amber giving both of them a sharp glance. She would have to learn to hold her tongue. Amber wasn't a three-year-old child who could be easily distracted.

'Agreed,' Barry said. 'That's a piece of history we never want to revisit.'

Thanks, Barry. Now shut up about it, Barry.

'I only called in because Tess and I were concerned for you,' he went on. 'Only for Tess finding you when she did, we could have lost you.'

'*Lost* me? Since when would that have bothered you? Surely my exit would have been an occasion of celebration for you?'

'Evie, I'm not a vengeful person. And I told you I'm not interested in Heronbrook any more. I just want to enjoy a relaxing retirement. At least give Tess some credit for rescuing you?'

'I do,' Evie said, her agitation subsiding a little. Barry was right – they did indeed go back a long way, sharing a chequered history that had affected both of their lives. They were contemporaries in the same storm, travelling to the same inevitable destination, and there was no sense in being antagonistic towards him.

'Sorry for my bad mood,' she said. 'I'm finding all this frustrating.'

'I'm sure you are,' Barry said.

'I'll send Tess some flowers and thank her in person as soon as I'm more recovered.'

'There's no rush. Tess is still living off her fifteen minutes of fame in the national press. She was chuffed to see herself being credited as the saviour of the renowned actress Evie Lawrence in the article about your accident. And she managed to get in a mention of the café as well.'

'Good for Tess,' Evie said.

'Peculiar, all the same.'

'Why peculiar?'

'Not many people bar locals use that access lane, especially since the entrance to the mobile-home park was relocated. So it's strange to have a rogue motorcyclist along there. Stranger too that you were knocked down and left. You'd swear ...'

'What are you trying to say, Barry?' Evie asked.

His face was the picture of innocence. 'I'm not trying to say anything or suggest there was an ulterior motive. It's up to the police to investigate this, not me.'

'Investigate?' Evie said, hiding her fresh disquiet. 'Why should there be anything ulterior to investigate? Some eejit on a bike took a corner far too fast and I happened to be in the way. Unless you know something I don't.'

'Me? No way. I wouldn't have known anything at all about your accident only Tess arrived on the scene.'

'And pigs might fly. Nothing goes on in Glenmaragh, or indeed the whole of Wicklow, without you knowing all about it. I've no doubt if the police find out anything you and Tess will know before me.'

'If that's the case,' he said, treating her to one of his fake smiles, 'we'll make sure to keep you informed.'

Evie felt exhausted when he left, watching him walk out the door into the hall, pale sunshine slanting up from the kitchen throwing his dark shadow across the wall. Amber saw him off, opening the gate for him. When she returned to the kitchen, curiosity was radiating from every line in her body, who-the-hell-was-he and what-was-that-all-about written across her face, but Evie was far too fatigued to offer any explanations. Not only that, but there was no easy way of explaining Barry Talbot to Amber.

'If he comes calling again,' she said to Amber, 'tell him I'm resting.'

'Sure, no problem. I feel as though I've met him before somewhere,' Amber said.

'I doubt that,' Evie said, more sharply that she had intended. She reached for her crutches and rose awkwardly to her feet. 'I need a lie-down.'

'Can I bring you in anything? A glass of water?'

'A glass of water would be lovely,' Evie said, forcing a smile, thinking that a glass of wine would be far better only it was much too early in the day, apart from her medications. 'I'll read for a bit, and then fall asleep. Why don't you go off for a while? Into Wicklow? Take my car. Have a look around the shops. I find some of the small, independent boutiques carry a good range of styles you wouldn't always find in the Dublin behemoths.'

She didn't relax against the pillows until Amber had left, saying she wouldn't be long. Not that it was a proper relax.

Investigate? *Ulterior motive*? Damn Barry Talbot for upsetting her. She popped an extra painkiller, hoping it might help to reduce her stress levels.

When the police had questioned her about the hit-and-run, her instincts had been to dismiss it as an accident. She couldn't afford it to be anything else. She couldn't afford for the authorities to go delving into her past in an effort to find a motive and discover who might hold a grudge against her. Any scrutiny of her life could blow open old family secrets and scandals, and Jessica and Amber didn't deserve that. Also, an excavation of her past would soon reveal that if anyone had reason to harbour a grudge against her, it was Pippa's family.

But what if it hadn't just been an accident? What then?

Amber parked Evie's Kia by the riverbank in Wicklow and texted her mother, asking her to phone as soon as it was convenient. She sipped a coffee she'd picked up in a nearby garage while she waited. And as soon as her mum called her back and they exchanged greetings, Amber came to the point.

'You don't happen to know anyone by the name of Barry Talbot? He could be an old friend, or maybe an enemy, of Evie's?'

The word 'enemy' had slipped out of her mouth with automatic ease. It was the first time she had formulated the thought that had been hovering at the back of her mind. That Evie could have pissed off some people beyond the boundary of family? Someone prepared to harass her? Amber had taken an instant dislike to Evie's morning visitor. He'd walked into the kitchen with what could only be described as a proprietorial swagger. No wonder Evie reacted as she had. Yet something about him had sent a spike of recognition through Amber, and it was peculiar that he'd used much the same phrase as her mother had when talking about family history.

Water under the bridge ...

'Barry who?' her mother said, not reacting to Amber's choice of words, as though Evie's having enemies was something she could easily accept.

'Barry Talbot,' Amber said. 'A guy of about seventy years of age. He's a neighbour of Evie's, lives just outside Glenmaragh.' Amber realised she must have passed his house on her drive to Wicklow. It was easy to imagine him standing in his front room, training a pair of binoculars onto the road, surveying all who moved within his kingdom.

'No,' her mother said swiftly, 'why?'

'He called to Heronbrook this morning to see how Evie was. I had a strong feeling I'd met him before.'

'Like where?'

'I dunno ... it was nothing definite ... but something about him seemed familiar. And,' she had to say it, even if she felt she was catching her mother out in the act of telling a fib, 'I got the impression he knew you?'

'*Me?*'

'When Evie introduced me as your daughter, he said something about "the lovely Jessica", as though he'd met you.'

'I don't think so, Amber.' Her mother paused. 'I suppose he knew my name from Evie – she might have mentioned her family in passing.'

You sound too casual, Mum. I think you know him but you're not telling me why.

'He seems to have some kind of history with Evie,' Amber said.

'He might have,' her mother said offhandedly. 'After all, Evie's been living in his neighbourhood for two years now.'

'The history was older than that. He said they went back a long way. He told me they'd met when she was in Heronbrook as a teenager and that he knew Granny Pippa too. He also said something about a lot of water being under the bridge.' She spoke slowly, deliberately repeating her mother's own words.

A silence. Amber wished she was having this conversation face to face instead of over a phone. So much subtle, nuanced communication was lost. Then, 'I'm not acquainted with the ins and outs of Evie's life,' her mother said. It was the tone of voice she used when they had cold callers to the door and she was getting rid of them as quickly and politely as possible.

'This Barry guy seemed to think it was unusual that someone would have been driving up the laneway where Evie was knocked down,' Amber said. 'Apparently only locals know about that lane. Actually, Mum' – she hesitated before voicing something that had been bugging her since that morning on the lane – 'do you think there's any chance Evie's accident mightn't have been an accident?'

Another pause. 'What exactly do you mean?' her mother said eventually.

'I'm just ...' Amber groped for words. 'I've been there at the scene, looking around, and I can't understand how it happened.'

'Surely if the police thought it was more than an accident, they'd be on it immediately.'

'I suppose ... yeah ... You mightn't know, Mum, but did Evie ever have a child? When she was younger?'

'No, she didn't,' her mother said emphatically. Then a moment later, 'Well, not that I know of. Why are you asking?'

It was curious, Amber decided, that her mother had been so definite with her negative answer before soft-pedalling backwards as though she'd said too much. It gave Amber the distinct impression that she knew more about Evie's life than she was letting on.

'Do you think Evie has ruffled any feathers, besides in the family? Because—' She was about to tell her mother about the vitriolic post when her mother interrupted.

'Look, darling,' she said, 'I know you're not in a good place right now, but please don't read too much into all this ... this ...' Her mother's voice trailed off before rallying. 'Evie's life is her own business, whatever she may or may not have done. Just as your life is your own business. You wouldn't like me to be second-guessing why you were able to go down to Heronbrook at the drop of a hat, would you?'

A flare of pain escaped from under the virtual steel fence Amber had erected around her chest cavity, blindsiding her momentarily. 'Right. I get you.'

'Would it help if I popped down to see you over the weekend? We could have a chat then, and I'll talk to Evie?'

'Leave it for now, Mum,' Amber said, not wanting to have to deal with her mother's concerns for her just yet, no matter how kindly they were. 'Evie rests a lot during the day and I'm fine looking after her. We're keeping things quiet for the moment.'

'OK, let me know when she's up for a visit, and don't forget, I'm here for you, all the time. Call me whenever you want. I think you're doing something wonderful, caring for Evie like this. But make sure you take care of yourself as well. You're precious to me and your dad, don't ever forget that. Love you.'

This time there was a catch in her mother's voice. Amber blinked hard as the flare of pain bloomed through her body, thrusting Evie's odd problems out of her mind.

'Love you too.'

She gripped the steering wheel of the car, looked out at the choppy, steel-grey waters of the river and took slow, deep breaths. She knew she was precious to her parents; she knew she was still, in their eyes, their clever, wonderful daughter.

Which made it all the more difficult to tell them how utterly idiotic she'd been.

◆

After lunch with the gang in the bistro, Amber had been bemused at the way she and Will progressed swiftly to after-work cocktails in South William Street, Saturday brunch in The Marker, dinner in

Sophie's, the hum of expectation between them growing louder and louder. She googled him, but he wasn't active on social media with the exception of LinkedIn. Most of what she saw there fitted in with what he'd told her about himself. Educated in a south Dublin school, then UCD, then a couple of Dublin tech-finance firms, until relocating to Rome. It had suited him to live away from the bosom of the family, he told her over Asian food in Opium. His mother wasn't around and there was no love lost between him and his father. He didn't enjoy the closeness Amber seemed to have with her lovely family.

'How do you know my family is lovely?' she'd asked him teasingly, knowing full well she'd painted them in a good light when he'd asked her about them.

'Just from the way you talk about them, and it stands to reason if you're one of them.' He'd smiled at her with those silvery-grey eyes. He went on to tell her his father had always been cold and career-driven, only interested in his bank balance, and it had been tough on him and his sister, growing up in a loveless home. Amber had looked at him empathically. She'd sensed a grittiness about Will, an unyielding streak. Maybe his father had caused that.

The following morning in the office, Fionn nodded at the miniature red roses sitting in a bright yellow mug on her desk. They had been waiting for her in the foyer, Rob calling her over, handing her the tiny but perfect bouquet that had been left at reception.

Fionn cocked an eyebrow. 'Will?'

'Yeah,' Amber said nonchalantly.

'Fast worker. So long as he ...' Fionn hesitated.

'So long as he what?'

'Treats you right,' he said, looking steadily at her.

'What's that supposed to mean?' She laughed.

'I wouldn't like to see you getting hurt again, that's all.'

Their glances met and held. Then, 'I can look after myself,' Amber said flippantly, shuffling some paperwork.

'Good.'

'Any word on your interview?' she said in a softer voice.

'Through to the next round,' he said, putting his finger to his lips in a gesture of silence before heading down the floor, leaving her with a funny ache in her chest.

She was in bed with Will a week later, after going out to his apartment in Dundrum on a Friday evening, wearing a new scarlet shirt she'd bought in Zara, her dark hair slicked back smoothly. The apartment was functional and a little sterile, as though it had been stripped back to the basics and deep cleaned after the previous occupant. It didn't have any imprints of Will's life apart from a few motoring and arts magazines half-heartedly adorning the shelves.

'You're not living here long?' she'd said, curious as to his lack of possessions.

'Nah, I'm still waiting for the bulk of my stuff to be freighted from Rome,' he said. He popped the cork on a bottle of chilled champagne and filled two glasses. Amber kicked off her heels as he tipped his glass to hers and led her into the bedroom.

Compared with the rest of the apartment, the bedroom caught her by surprise. Voile panels screened the picture windows, the cream carpet underfoot was deep pile and luxurious, the high bed was supersized and adorned with luxury pillows, a silky duvet, and a matching quilt in shades of navy blue. Will drew thick cream drapes over the windows, shutting out the world, and he switched on low lighting.

'Well,' he said, grinning, 'here we are.'

Out of nowhere, she had the strangest sensation in her gut that he'd imagined this moment from the time he'd bumped into her in the foyer. Looking at the desire in his eyes, feeling her own bubbling up inside her, she thrust it aside. He kissed her in the middle of the floor, cradling her head in his hands and taking his time, allowing them both to explore the taste and feel of each other. She was as weak as a kitten by the time they came up for air.

'Take off your clothes,' he said huskily.

She opened the buttons on her shirt, peeling it off slowly, watching his eyes flicker as she made a play of removing her bra, teasing him with glimpses of curves and nipples before she finally let it drop to the floor. Then easing off her trousers, she stood in her lacy pants. Reaching for the buckle of his belt, she unzipped his powerful erection.

'Oh wow,' she said, her voice hoarse, 'look at you.'

She was going to enjoy this.

Afterwards, she woke up in the early hours of the morning, the navy sheets twisted around her hips, Will snoring lightly beside her, every cell in her body throbbing deliciously in the aftermath. She felt her mouth curving in satisfaction and her insides contracting as she recalled what Will had done, how well he had done it, what she had done.

She was in lust. Head over heels in pure, unmitigated lust.

Over the next couple of weeks, she didn't see much of him within the corporate confines of Russell Hall. There was an occasional lunch, but they mostly met in the evenings. Once she'd suggested popping up to his office, but he'd said he had back-to-back meetings in such a formal voice that she hadn't suggested disturbing him up there again. The evenings and weekends she went out to his apartment in Dundrum, she threw away all her inhibitions to an extent she never had before, and allowed herself to soak up as much pleasure and fun as possible. Occasionally she caught sight of their naked, sweat-slicked bodies in a mirror, and she didn't recognise herself.

There were even some afternoons when Will persuaded her to bring her laptop out to Dundrum and work remotely, and he did the same, both of them using the kitchen island as a desk, having spent their lunch hour in bed together, often going back to their laptops clad in bathrobes, unless Amber had a conference call – when she was unable to stop Will from putting on a silly floor show on the other side of the kitchen, doing his best to distract her. Another afternoon, he crawled under the island until he was kneeling between her legs, his face pressing into her thighs. She wondered where this wild, outrageous version of Amber Lennox had emerged from. She sensed this rampant, no-holds-barred episode in her life wouldn't last – it was far too feverish to maintain the pace and she knew instinctively that Will wasn't relationship material, sensing a detached selfishness about him underneath that unyielding streak. But that didn't stop her from enjoying it and having some fun.

She talked about him at home, letting her parents know she was seeing a new guy, Will Baker, and Jamie, who was living there in the early weeks of Will, teased her full on. She gave them the impression she'd known Will for some time, unwilling to reveal how swiftly he'd got her into bed. Afterwards, she couldn't believe how gullible she'd been, but never in her wildest dreams could she have imagined the way Will would set out to destroy her.

Now, looking back, she was beginning to think he'd been playing her all along, but she still couldn't figure out why.

Jessica drove through the entrance to Pinedale Lawns, a nursing home on the outskirts of Bray, County Wicklow. It was a large Victorian house that had been completely remodelled, and it included single occupancy en suite bedrooms. The grounds to the back of the home were beautifully landscaped, providing colour all year round. This September evening, Jessica noticed that the trees were on the turn, bursting glorious colour, leaves shot through with shades of yellow and speckled orange and burnt red. She visited every weekend without fail, occasionally Paul, Amber, or Adam coming with her, but it was unusual for her to be here now, on a Wednesday evening.

Amber's phone call earlier that day had shaken her and prompted her mid-week visit. Not that it made much difference to her mother, who didn't always register her presence. Her series of strokes had eventually brought on dementia, and she usually stared right through Jessica as though she wasn't there.

Pippa had been found in the street one day five years ago, outside her local shops in Bray, collapsed against the wall. In the following days, while the full extent of her stroke was being diagnosed, a neighbour of Pippa's told Jessica that another neighbour, Carmel, had been queueing in the post office at the time and had seen Pippa outside.

'Carmel saw her talking to someone on the pavement just moments before she collapsed.'

'Who was it?' Jessica had asked.

'Carmel couldn't see if it was a man or a woman,' the neighbour said. 'They were standing with their back to the post office, and her view was obscured by two posters hanging in the window – all she saw was a navy jacket and jeans.' Pippa had looked agitated, Carmel had told her, but it had been impossible to know if this was because of the conversation or because she'd been feeling ill.

On the one hand, Jessica wanted to weep at the waste of life, the fragile thread of acuity that had snapped in her mother one day, sending her over the edge into this grey abyss of a half-life, helped to a degree, the doctors had said, by her mother's lifelong addiction to alcohol. On the other hand, Jessica wanted to weep for herself, for her endless regret and guilt at not being the kind of loving daughter she should have been. At her frustration with these visits that she longed to escape from. Jessica liked to think that in a way it was easier on her mother, the not knowing. Better than being in her full senses, confined as she was to a nursing home, unable to walk or talk or communicate. Although there were times when Jessica sensed a tiny breakthrough, a small spark of lucidity, and she wondered how much her mother really knew of where she was and what had happened. But whenever Jessica spoke to her, making an attempt to draw her out, her mother's face blanked out again. Still, it would have been typical of her mother's behaviour to choose to blank out Jessica. They had never enjoyed a cosy and comfortable mother–daughter relationship.

The window in her mother's room looked out over the grounds to the rear. That evening, her mother was out of bed, reclining in a big high chair, staring at the wall. Amber's phone call fresh in her mind, Jessica sat down in the chair beside her mother and said, clearly and conversationally, and as though her mother was quite capable of understanding every single word, 'I hear Barry Talbot was talking to Amber.' It was there all right, she saw it – a flash of comprehension before her mother switched off again.

'Amber thought Barry Talbot seemed familiar,' Jessica went on. 'I wonder why that was.' She thought she saw a tiny clenching of her mother's jaw.

Amber's questions had shaken her. Barry Talbot calling to Heronbrook wasn't something she'd anticipated when her daughter had headed down there. No wonder she'd been caught off guard, stupidly pretending not to know him. She knew exactly who he was – she recalled only too well running into him in the Wicklow hotel where she'd met Evie, just as she was pretending not to know what had led to the last row her mother and Evie had had. But she felt satisfied that Evie wasn't going to speak of it after all these years.

'I know why he seemed familiar to her,' Jessica said. 'I bet you know too. But don't worry, I'm not going to tell her – not yet anyway. Then again, she might stumble on the truth all by herself. If she does, I'll deal with that when it happens. Not that that would bother you. You don't care about other people's opinions, do you, not even your granddaughter's? You've only ever cared about your own selfish self. Narcissism, is that the word?'

She was a truly horrible daughter, she berated herself. Then again, her mother might be pale and shrunken and devoid of her vitality, but her eyes still had the power to fling Jessica right back to a time in her life that undermined her confidence. A certain look that plunged Jessica back to the eight-, twelve-, sixteen-year-old girl who'd witnessed too many rows between her parents, instigated always by her mother's anger, her volatility, her mood swings, which ensured Jessica spent a lot of her childhood moving around her as if she were treading on eggshells. Her father had done his best to keep the show of family togetherness on the road – Jessica had witnessed his many attempts at papering over the cracks of a disjointed marriage – to no avail.

She saw him arriving home late from work one evening with a bouquet of flowers in his hand. Her mother, having started on the vodka earlier that afternoon, ready and waiting for him. Jessica and Simon upstairs on the landing, sitting in their pyjamas, while the screech of their mother's voice echoed up the stairwell.

'What's the meaning of this?'

'Sorry, I got delayed in the office. Brian is out on sick leave and I had to finish off some of his urgent paperwork.'

'Like hell you did. How dare you come home hours late, thinking a few rubbishy flowers will make up for it.'

'Pippa – please … Calm down. I called you to explain.'

'You ignorant bastard. You were just trying to cover up that you were with someone. I know you were. You don't love me. You never did.'

'Pippa – listen to me …'

'Fuck *you*!'

The sound of cellophane wrapping being ripped apart, then an eerie quiet, Jessica straining to listen, and then hearing the soft thunk of flowers hitting the wall, the sound of a stamping foot. The slam of the sitting-room door. Peeking down through the slats of the bannisters to see her father on his hands and knees picking up crushed petals. Later, after Jamie was born, her father with grooves etched into his face that should only have borne faint lifelines.

Her mother took umbrage with him over the least little thing, resulting in ornaments being flung by her, plates of food hitting the wall, a box of chocolates being stamped on and mashed into the carpet. Wondering if she had contributed to her mother's anger, she'd asked her father several times over the years if she'd done anything to displease her, or if there was something she could do to make her happy. Her father had hugged her and told her she was a wonderful daughter just as she was, and that he loved her so much, just as her mother did, but that sometimes her mother couldn't help being in a bad mood.

Jessica blinked away the images, and feeling bad about her earlier words to her mother, accusing her of caring only for herself and being narcissistic, she forced herself to make small talk about the weather and her busy day. Then suddenly needing fresh air, she said her goodbyes and left. Outside, walking across to her car, she took great big gulps of the cool, evening air, hoping it might invigorate her. But instead she felt sad and deflated. She drove away from Pinedale Lawns and turned onto the road that led to the motorway and home. A warm, scented shower at home might help.

But she knew she was clutching at straws. There was no easing her sadness and guilt at not feeling as loving as she should towards her mother. Not only that, but anything she tried to do would always fall far short of what Pippa wanted. When she'd reached eighteen years of age, the day after her mother had lost her head yet again over some trifle and had scored the kitchen table with a knife, her father began to talk to her in confidence, to gradually reveal all the events that had led to that moment.

And then Jessica had understood exactly what was wrong with their family.

From the vantage point of her custom-made chair, Pippa stared out at the patch of green fuzz, which was all she could see of the garden from here. They had wanted to wheel her down to the day room but she didn't want to go there today and she had thrown a tantrum, inasmuch as she was able to, so they had left her alone. They didn't know how much she understood, how she had sudden moments of clarity, trapped as she was in the prison of her head. They didn't understand how frustrated she got, unable to communicate or get the simplest message across. Sometimes she was glad when she became agitated and they gave her something to calm her. It was her only relief.

It was supposed to be one of the better nursing homes. So Jessica had told her. She would receive excellent care for the rest of her life. Pippa would be *so* comfortable. The day she'd been moved from the hospital, where they'd said they could do no more for her, Jessica had spoken to her cheerfully, like an adult cajoling a troublesome child, while she packed all of Pippa's pitiable hospital possessions into a bag and walked alongside the orderly who wheeled her out to the waiting ambulance. She had no say – *no say whatsoever* – in any of this. She had not been the least bit comfortable. She had been apoplectic with fury at the thought of being incarcerated in a home, when she had years yet to live.

Wrong way to behave. It had driven up her blood pressure and caused a further stroke, a mini one this time. God save her, she hadn't even the release of fury.

Then again, she'd felt for a long time that her life had been underpinned by injustices. For years she'd felt she was living in the shadow of her sister – a beautiful, multitalented sister. Everything Pippa strived to do (badly) had already been done by Evie, only to a far higher degree. Evie took after their mother: petite, blonde, and ethereal. Attractive to look at. Charmingly pleasant to everyone. She moved around with a careless grace and was brilliant in the classroom, regularly achieving high grades with the minimum of study. In comparison with her sister, tall, dark-haired, beanpole Pippa had always felt clumsy, ungainly, and dull. Even her voice was low registered compared with Evie's light, silvery tones.

Prodigy vs prodigal. The slightest difference in the spelling. The world of difference in the meaning.

Jessica arrived at the home from time to time, bringing drifts of a beautiful scent, her hands soft as they held Pippa's. Sometimes Jessica touched the back of Pippa's ears with that beautiful scent or massaged her hands with the soft cream. She sat talking about her job, Paul, Amber, and Adam. Sometimes one of them might be with her. But no matter how hard she tried, Pippa could never make herself speak clearly. And she didn't always notice when Jessica was going, or even that she'd left, until she looked around to find herself alone.

One day Jessica had come with all her family and produced a cake with 'Happy 70th Birthday' on it. It couldn't have been for her – she was only fifty-something, wasn't she? Looking at them, so *alive*, she felt like a piece of wreckage on the periphery and she raged because she was no longer part of their day-to-day lives. They didn't know how lucky they were, able to walk out the door into the sunny afternoon, the ordinary joys of moving around, going shopping, to the hairdresser's, or restaurants and concerts.

Then one day she had a new visitor. Her brain had been a little fuddled that day and she felt angry with herself when she didn't recognise him at first. Not that it seemed to bother him. He seemed to know exactly what to expect from her, and she wondered if he'd visited her before. It wasn't until he began to talk, about the past and what had happened, that she realised who he was. And she realised he was just as angry as she was.

At first she was pleased. Then she realised some of his anger was directed at her. But, he said, living a shadow life, cooped up in the home, was punishment enough for her. And so, his attention was now directed at Evie. As far as he was concerned, she was responsible for wrecking his life, and now he had her in his sights. From where Pippa was sitting, his life wasn't wrecked at all. He told her what he was going to do, how he was going to exact a punishment. She couldn't tell him that he'd got part of the story wrong, and she tried to recall if anyone else was still around who knew the cold, tawdry truth, but as she grappled with this, the filaments in her brain refused to connect.

The next time he called, she wasn't pleased. He mentioned Jessica. He mentioned Amber. After all, they were part of the family too. The family he hated. And now that he knew exactly what had happened, it was time he did something about it.

She had raged and raged – with him, then later with the nursing staff, and with Jessica as soon as she saw her – but no one understood what she was trying to say. No one knew she was trying to *warn* them.

But after what she'd done, this was the greatest punishment of all.

Evie, 1962

'I suppose you'll be spending another summer making eyes at your boyfriend,' Pippa said, as we were packing our bags for the second holiday in Heronbrook.

'He's not – oh, don't you start,' I said, forgetting my decision to stay calm and unruffled in the face of her taunts.

'It doesn't bother me if you do,' Pippa said airily. 'Rachel and her family are coming again. I'll be too busy with her and my friends to notice you two.'

Lucien.

The letters had begun in September, from me to him, written on a pad with the help of a sheet of lined paper underneath to guide my straggling hand. He rarely replied with a letter, sending instead a postcard with my address on the front and a few lines of writing and a small cartoon-like sketch on the back, illustrating his morsel of news: a book he'd enjoyed, music he'd listened to, something that had happened with Granny Kate or in school. There was a phone call at Christmas, me clutching the receiver of the land line in the hall in Drumcondra, feeling as though I was talking to a strange version of Lucien, which made me speak awkwardly and not too sure of how to bring the conversation to an end. I didn't know how interested he really was in the contents of my letters, full of mundane things like Latin homework, hockey on a freezing cold Saturday afternoon, choir practice in the hard wooden stall of the church balcony as we rehearsed for the Easter ceremonies.

And now it was summer again. I liked being sixteen. I felt more grown-up, surer of myself, and I had started to wear some eyeshadow and mascara. I had come through the Intermediate Certificate exams, and I had a great feeling of accomplishment. Quite a few of my classmates were not returning to school in September, going out into the world of work instead. I wondered how the more grown-up version of me would get on with Lucien and if it would be different between us.

I needn't have worried. Any initial shyness I felt melted away as soon as Lucien and I began to chat. It didn't make any difference how grown-up I felt – age didn't matter when it came to us – we were just the same two friends, picking up exactly where we had left off.

It was another summer of sitting under scented pine trees, oaks, and weeping willows, occasional rainy days when drizzle softened the woods outside Heronbrook, a feeling of freedom from the classroom and a forgetting of algebra and history and Latin declensions, my future still shimmering like a wonderful promise on the horizon. Then the beach, where there were many of the same faces from the previous year, Lucien's Croydon cousins returning, Pippa picking up with Rachel and her family again, hanging around with much the same gang when they hadn't got Rachel's young brother and sister hanging out of them. A fish and chip van arrived in the field at the far end of the mobile-home park, beside the hut that sold hot water in dented teapots during the day, and it was a novelty to stroll up to the van some evenings, sharing a bag of salt and vinegar chips as we strolled back, the day drifting to a close, the sea a calm pellucid blue.

'I'm going to be an actress,' I said to Lucien one afternoon as we sat in the sand dunes, me plucking the marram grass, the scent of warm bracken in my nostrils. The tide was out, a silvery line glistening across the horizon, past the expanse of damp, sand-packed mudflats.

'Are you? When did this come about?'

I told him about the afternoon our honours English class had been brought to see *The Merchant of Venice* in a small Dublin theatre as part of our studies for the exams. I had been entranced by it all, an excitement tingling through my veins from the moment we stepped into the theatre. It was an excitement that had only intensified as the curtain went up on the stage, my heart tripping as the performance began. I soaked up every moment of it, imagining myself up there, throwing my heart and soul into someone else's character. We were allowed to troop in backstage afterwards in an orderly line, my eyes out on stalks, absorbing the sights and scents, the actors in their costumes taking our questions. It had sparked something inside me, a heady mixture of nerves and adrenaline. I couldn't believe that people actually got paid for doing this.

'It seems like an exciting job to have,' I went on. 'It doesn't seem like work at all, just having fun, and other people enjoying it too.'

'How would you get started?'

'Acting school,' I said blithely. 'There are two or three in Dublin. I asked the woman who was playing the part of Portia. I'd like to be versatile,' I went on, hugging my knees, staring into the bright horizon of my life. 'I'd study for stage and screen.'

'Screen? Would that mean going to Hollywood?'

'I was thinking more television, but Hollywood sounds amazing,' I said, wondering if such a marvellous thing could be possible.

'I think you'd be amazing,' he said.

'Do you? Really?'

'You're so bright and determined – if you put your mind to it, you could be whatever you wanted. And I'm sure you'd be great on stage or on the screen.'

His encouragement gave me a boost. 'You're the first person I've told this to,' I said. 'I haven't mentioned anything to my parents yet.'

'I'm sure they'd feel the same as I do, Evie. I went to see *Breakfast at Tiffany's* with Granny Kate – I could just see you up there as Holly Golightly.'

'Really?' I felt chuffed. I turned onto my tummy, raising myself on my elbows, my hands plaiting long strands of marram grass. 'My guess is,' I said, 'when we all have televisions, there'll be more films shown, and they'll need lots of actors. People will be delighted to watch plays and films in their own homes.'

'Hey,' Lucien said, 'just stay like that, don't move.'

I was used to this by now, Lucien whipping open his sketch-pad. He'd already told me to never feel self-conscious, that he was just practising some life-drawing techniques. Pippa had seen us the week before, when Lucien was trying to capture my silhouette by the edge of the brook. Unbeknownst to me, she'd been watching from a distance, curious to know why I was sitting so still, why Lucien was staring at me so intently.

'I thought you had to be in the nude for life drawing,' she'd said to me, when I had tried to explain. 'Maybe you've done that already.'

'You're such a pest, Pippa – that's what I'll call you from now on, pesty Pippa.'

Naturally she went whining to Mum about it.

I just closed my ears. Here, sitting in a hollow up in the sand dunes, I was satisfied she wouldn't come across us.

'What about you?' I asked. 'What are your plans for after school?'

Lucien was going into the final exam year. I was expecting him to announce an exciting painting venture, but instead he said, 'I'll get a job somewhere.'

I was so surprised that I whipped around and stared at him. 'What kind of job?'

'I'll be applying to some banks and building societies. It will all depend on my exam results. And I asked you not to move.'

'But—' For a moment I was speechless.

'But what?'

'Aren't you going to be an artist?'

'I already am an artist.'

'I mean – isn't that going to be your main job?'

'How can it be my main job?'

'But, Lucien, you can't not paint.'

'I will paint, but in my spare time. I'll need a job to bring in a weekly wage. I'm not stupid enough to think that painting alone will do that.'

I don't know why I felt so terribly annoyed; snubbed, almost. In a warm bubble at the back of my mind I'd had the idea that, following school, we would both be chasing our dreams into our future lives, but now, to my disappointment, Lucien didn't share the same view. I sat up, my good mood dissolved.

'What's wrong?' he asked.

'What's wrong?' I said, my voice practically choking on the words. 'You can't just get a job. You probably think I should get a job too and act in my spare time.'

He snapped his sketchbook shut. The breeze picked up and ruffled his hair. He pushed it out of his eyes. 'Did I say that?'

I looked away, furious tears pricking the corners

of my eyes as I stared at the expanse of the crumpled grey sea, tasting the salty breeze on my tongue. 'I just thought you were more ...'

'More what?'

'More passionate ... more committed ... more serious about your work.'

'I am passionate and committed.'

'Then you should be giving it all your time and energy. Not settling for any half-measures. '

'I don't settle for half-measures,' he said, a glint of annoyance in his eye. 'I'm surprised you'd think that about me.'

I could see I'd hurt his feelings. I felt hot and embarrassed, unsure how to find my way back to our pleasant, easy friendship. I plucked at the grass, wanting the ground to swallow me up. 'I didn't mean it like that,' I said.

'Just because I can't give it all my time doesn't mean I won't give it my all whenever I get the opportunity,' he said. 'I need to build up my skills and I need money behind me for when I eventually take time out.' To my surprise he pulled me into a loose hug, his smile melting away some of my embarrassment. 'Look, Evie, I always knew I'd have to get a regular job. If it's any consolation, Granny Kate feels the same.'

'She wants you to get a job?'

'Nah, she wants me to stay home and paint. But the money from my parents' estate is almost gone – they didn't have a lot of insurance. Gran is living on a small pension and I'd like to make life a little easier for her. It won't be forever. Someday I'll be free to follow my dreams.'

I was awkward and ill at ease over the next few days after causing our almost-row and Lucien seemed to sense it. He gave me a friendly hug now and again. He teased me gently. He told me that after Granny Kate I was his best supporter. By degrees my embarrassment faded and once more I was conscious of the latter part of our holiday flying in; the less time we had, the swifter it seemed to run on.

I found it harder to say goodbye to Lucien at the end of that summer. I wished him well going into his exam year. On our last afternoon he kissed me goodbye, my first proper kiss and my face felt hot with pleasure. I wrapped up the memory of it in my head – it had to last almost a year.

Evie, 1963

On our third summer in a row at Heronbrook, I had just turned seventeen, Lucien eighteen.

'What was it like,' I asked him on our first afternoon, 'walking out the door of the school for the last time?'

'Great,' he said, blinking at the memory. 'A bit mad, but I never felt as free and easy as I do now.'

'Good.'

He had to wait a few weeks until his exam results came out before he'd get any job offers. We agreed tacitly not to talk about it – I certainly didn't want to cause any upsets between us, and we spent the summer much as in previous years, on the beach and in the sand dunes, Pippa hanging around with the usual gang. She was clearly put out, though, that her friend Rachel had developed in the intervening year and wore a full swimsuit with cups whereas Pippa had hardly anything on top. Her vexation almost cancelled out her one-upmanship over Rachel, who still had to look after her younger siblings on a regular basis.

But nothing she said irritated me because things had changed between Lucien and me. The same mellow sunshine filtered through the woods, creating an iridescent canopy overhead; Lucien sketched, sometimes I read, we chatted and listened to music on his radio. But our lingering hugs and our kisses were new and exciting. I kissed him back, something about it filling me with underlying joy and contentment, as though the world and my life were falling into place just nicely.

Not that I thought we were officially boyfriend and girlfriend. What we had together seemed far too natural for that. I saw it as a lovely practice run for when I'd be a grown-up. I trusted Lucien. I felt secure and content in his company. I knew he'd never hurt me.

Towards the end of the summer, Lucien got his exam results and, just as we were preparing to pack up and leave Heronbrook, he accepted a job as a clerk in a building society in Wicklow town.

'Are you happy about this?' I asked him.

'Sure,' he said. 'I'll have my evenings and weekends free to paint – that's more time than if I were still at school. And I'll be earning money.'

'So long as it's not for too long,' I said.

In September it was my turn to start thinking seriously about the future and I found myself agreeing to do a course in a reputable commercial college after my exams. It guaranteed jobs in the banking and financial sector for its top thirty per cent of pupils. Not that I'd be partaking of any of those. I spoke to Miss Hayes, my English teacher, of my hopes, and she said she'd have a word with her brother, who worked in a Dublin theatre.

'I don't know why you're bothering to study,'

Pippa said, sidling around the door of my room. 'You can easily do a commercial course and become a secretary without any Leaving Certificate. So it's a waste. You're wasting your time.'

'Shut up,' I said, knowing full well that she was jealous of the attention I was receiving from my parents, as they tried to keep things calm for me in the months before the exams.

Lucien spent the autumn and winter settling into work in the building society. He rang one day in December and surprised me by saying he'd come to Dublin and bring me out for a Christmas lunch in Bewley's of Grafton Street. He'd learned to drive and was saving for a car, but he was insured on Granny Kate's Volkswagen Beetle. Months out of school and on the bottom rung of the permanent and pensionable job ladder had given him a polish and maturity. I found myself intrigued by him – he seemed so different to the T-shirt-wearing boy I was used to meeting under the shade of the trees, or the barefoot-with-rolled-up-shorts guy I paddled alongside in the frilly shallows of the sea. But as soon as we started to talk, we could have been back there again, such was the ease between us.

After lunch, we went for a drink – it was my first time to be inside a public house, and while Lucien ordered a pint of Guinness, I had a vodka and orange, which seemed like the height of grown-up sophistication. I asked him if this was what he did on weekend nights with his work friends.

'Hardly ever,' he said. 'I'm painting a lot, using my sketches for inspiration.'

'That's great! Painting what?'

'Mostly you.'

I was surprised by the pang of pleasure that gave me.

Afterwards, he brought me around to a side road where his car was parked. He kissed me then, again, and if an occasional passer-by happened to peek in and see us, well, it was Christmas after all. At Easter, we had lunch in a hotel on O'Connell Street. He wished me all the best in my exams and gave me some practical advice for getting through them in one piece. I didn't tell him about my plans to do a commercial course. That could wait until I was down in Heronbrook, for that special place seemed to be the repository of our dreams and our future selves. It would be a different summer this time, with him working. But he planned to take his summer leave when I was there, and there would always be the long bright evenings and all weekends.

Then school was out and I had the intoxicating feeling that I was just at the beginning of my wonderful life.

Or so I thought.

Evie, 1964

We were on the beach, one evening near the end of our first week of the holidays, Lucien, his cousins, and the boys from the mobile-home park horsing around with a football, me watching, Pippa and Rachel hanging around pretending to be bored, Pippa needling me by wearing a white eyelet blouse of mine she'd sneaked out of my wardrobe. It was too big for her, as she was still rather lacking on top. I decided to have words with her later rather than cause a scene there.

Then Lucien's Croydon cousins jumped for the ball and bumped heads, eleven-year-old Timothy coming off the worst. He was all skinny legs and arms as he folded into himself, shoving his face into the thin crook of his elbow to hide sudden tears. Lucien hurried across the sand towards him, he rubbed his Timothy's head and pulled him into a bear hug and asked him where it hurt. He smiled at me over Timothy's dark head, a warm, indulgent, messy kind of smile.

As our glances met and I saw the light in his eyes, a beam of clear, bright energy coursed through me and cracked me right open. I blinked and blinked again. It was as though up to then I'd only been seeing the world in black and white and it had suddenly transformed into wonderful colour. I breathed in, and although the air tasted much the same, a new vitality ran through me. The still, calm evening, the sky bleached to the palest duck-egg blue, and the light of the sea on the horizon seemed more beautiful than ever.

Lucien organised his cousins in some kind of ball game, and heat scorched my body as he came off the strand and jogged towards me, flopping down on the sand dune beside me, laughing, his wind-tossed hair blowing around his face. I had a sudden urge to reach out and touch the hard length of his legs, to snuggle into his chest, to kiss his face. I'm not sure whether he sensed something had changed inside me when he met my eyes and smiled; I looked away quickly, fearful of what he might see in mine. Not only that, but whatever had happened to me was coming off my body in such waves that they were palpable. My mouth dried up and my legs began to shake.

There had been no such thing as falling in love with Lucien. That was far too tame and timid a description to explain the tide of emotion that bludgeoned me and stripped me back to my core, opening all my raw, vulnerable defences. I knew I could never go back to the old carefree Evie Lawrence, where life was safe and predictable and I slept peacefully and contentedly. Right now life was thrilling but dangerous. I knew that from then on I'd have no real control over my happiness and contentment, because it was all dependent on the man sitting beside me, calling out to his cousins in a jokey commentary, turning occasionally to throw me a grin and include me in the fun.

Later, in the dusk of the evening, he walked me back to Heronbrook, and I stopped him in the shelter of the trees before we reached the clearing. I drew him deeper into the violet shade, wrapping my arms around his neck and pressing my body into his, hearing his sudden intake of breath. We clung together, our breaths mingling. We kissed in a way we never had before. Afterwards, he cupped my face in his hand.

'Dearest Evie,' he said, the spark in his eyes telling me he felt the same about me as I did about him, but had been biding his time. When he left me and I went into Heronbrook alone, I felt as though my right arm had been torn off. I knew I'd be in a fever of agitation until I saw him again, which was both a blessing and a curse.

I spent the next few days trying to look much as normal on the outside, while every cell in my body hummed with an ache and expectation. I didn't want to be consumed like this, my time away from Lucien spent anticipating the next moment I would see him, but when I was with him, life was brilliant and exciting, the sight, touch, and feel of him energising glowing sparks within me.

Pippa asked me straight out one morning what

was up with me – I had a silly new laugh, she said – but I tried my best to glaze my eyes and appear nonchalant. Then at last the day came when Mum had to bring her back to Dublin for a dentist appointment to have a tooth filled. They'd be gone all day, because afterwards they were meeting Dad for lunch and going shopping in Arnotts and Roches Stores. I met Lucien down by the brook as normal and, dizzy with a thrilling expectation, I brought him back to Heronbrook and into my bedroom.

It was awkward initially, the first time for both of us. We laughed and joked and fumble-touched our way around each other's bodies, me looking at Lucien's hard beauty in amazement, but after a few hastily abandoned attempts, interspersed with deep kisses, we finally got there. I'll never forget the first moment of startling discovery as the sore-sweet heat of him filled me up, the look on his face as we tentatively moved together, and I knew I'd never be the same person again.

We took chances – in quiet hollows in the woods, slipping back into my bedroom in Heronbrook when Mum and Pippa were gone to the beach for the afternoon or grocery shopping in Wicklow, Lucien hiding under the bed once when they came back early. He climbed out the window and crept along behind the wall until I signalled that he could make a break for it. I knew all hell would be let loose if my parents suspected I was no longer a virgin.

What we had was so beautiful, I didn't feel I was committing any sin. Instead I felt full of awe and wonder, invincible and glorious, as if I'd discovered the secret to life itself.

One afternoon when Mum, Pippa, and Rachel had gone to the pictures in Wicklow, we talked about our futures. Outside my bedroom the sun was glinting through the trees and turning the brook to a silver dazzle. The shimmering light reflected off the bedroom ceiling like flickering silver foil. Lucien was lying on his back, his skin a pale alabaster. I was full of love and full of life, cocooned in a world of light and beauty. I rolled towards him, my legs coiling easily against the heat of his.

'How are your plans coming along, Lucien?'

'What plans?'

'You said your job wouldn't be forever, that you'd have to work for a while before taking time out for your painting. How soon will that be?'

There was a long pause. 'I don't think I'm good enough,' he finally said.

I turned onto my stomach and raised myself on my elbows. I stared at his face. 'Of course you are. You *are* that good.'

'You're biased, Evie.'

'Don't put yourself down, it's making me cross,' I said.

He had already shown me some paintings he was working on. There were three of them. He'd packed them carefully into his satchel and slid them out with painstaking precision in the privacy of my room, where I studied them, hairs rising on the back of my neck. All of them were radiant with softly lit colours that reached out from the canvas; all of them featured me in the surrounds of Heronbrook: sitting by the brook, standing on the flint-grey stone-curved bridge, lying under the shady trees in dappled sunshine. The figure of the young woman was blurry and indistinct, more an impression, but the wash of yellow in her dress and prism of gold in her hair gave it away. All of them spoke of the peaceful essence of being under the trees, the soft touch of the breeze, the balm of mottled sunlight on your skin, the rush of the brook skipping over stones. They touched all my senses so that I felt I was there again, in those places.

Then in a gentle voice, because I couldn't bear to be even pretend-cross with Lucien, I said, 'I'm not just biased. You're a wonderful artist who deserves to be out in the world.'

'It's a world that prefers brashness and rock 'n' roll, revolution and drugs.'

'It's a world that's opening out to anything and everything. Don't you believe in yourself?'

'Not yet.'

'I believe in you. You deserve to be doing what makes you happy.'

'You make me happy,' he said, pulling me close.

◆

Pippa sensed something significant had changed about me. No surprises, given my constant, barely suppressed excitement.

'You're up to something,' she said, when I took longer than ever over a bath.

I shrugged dismissively.

Another morning, I was alone in the kitchen when Cilla Black's latest record 'You're My World' came on the radio. I felt it could have been written for Lucien and me, and I twirled around the kitchen floor, arms outstretched, pretending we were dancing together. I turned to see Pippa standing in the doorway, silently watching me. She flounced off and slammed her bedroom door.

'You're doing it,' she said to me after dinner the following evening.

'Don't be ridiculous,' I scoffed.

'See? You know what I'm talking about. I know you're doing it ... letting him ...' She went on to describe the sexual act in crude terms but it just bounced off me.

'You haven't a clue what you're talking about,' I said nonchalantly, feeling so magnificent in the wonderful bubble that was me and Lucien that her vulgarity didn't register with me. This irritated her. Her stares across the table grew more calculating. I caught her following me a couple of times as I headed to meet him, and another time she was waiting when we emerged from the woods, watching us with narrowed eyes. We were more careful about the time we snatched in Heronbrook and went deeper into the woods. When I lay with him on the scented pine carpets and saw his face above mine, silhouetted against the flickering trees and a liquid green light, I wanted to laugh and shout at the exquisite joy of it.

An exquisite joy that was soon to plunge to the darkest depths.

Because what happened that last summer in Heronbrook undid us all.

Evie, present day

I slowly become aware that I'm cemented in warmth, unable to move my limbs, powerless to open my eyes, trapped by eyelids the weight of boulders. A far-off bleep continues its rhythmic monotone.

A woman's voice. 'What's that draped over the bed?'

An answering voice, also a woman. 'It's a blanket that regulates the heat and keeps her cosy.'

'Good. So she's comfortable?'

'From her vital signs we can safely say that there are no indications of any kind of distress ...'

No signs of distress? Someone tried to kill me. If only I'd done what Amber asked and called the police sooner.

Where is Amber? She was in danger too. I try to call out, but a weight is pressing heavily on my chest and no words will come. I try to move my mouth but it feels cast in concrete. I don't have the superhuman strength necessary to part my eyelids by even a millimetre.

'I'm probably not supposed to be here this late ...'

'We're allowing one visitor in compassionate circumstances.'

'And these are compassionate circumstances?'

'Yes. Unfortunately, I would say so.'

'Well ... thank you for your honesty, Doctor.'

I hear footsteps disappear, then apart from my scattered thoughts there is nothing – no sensation whatsoever, just the sound of that bleeping monitor.

Think, Evie, think.

Hang on for now ...

Two Weeks Earlier

'Something funny happened this morning,' Amber said on Friday afternoon. 'There was a drone on the laneway when I was coming back from my run on the beach.'

'A *drone*?' Evie put down the book she'd been reading.

'Yeah, it flew up behind me before it went off.'

Outside, rain fell in a soft, fine mist. They were relaxing in the living room, Amber having drawn up two comfortable armchairs to the sliding doors, positioning them so they faced the back garden. Evie sat with her feet up on a footstool, a book in her hand, a glass of water on a small table beside her. The fragrant aroma of fish pie came from the oven.

Amber didn't admit the fright it had given her. She'd just reached the bend in the lane where Evie had been knocked down, where she'd paused for a moment, still trying to figure out how the accident had happened. She'd heard a buzzing noise growing louder, and had glanced back to see the drone hovering in the air above her. She'd had the uncanny feeling she was being watched by it before it lifted up and veered away. Who, though? And why here, right at the scene of Evie's accident?

Back in Heronbrook, questions had swirled

around in her head. The drone had been as creepy as Evie's accident itself *and* the Polaroid Evie had been sent. Amber was growing increasingly curious as to what dark secrets Evie was keeping. On Wednesday, on the phone, her mother hadn't even discounted the possibility of Evie having an enemy. And the long and bitter rift between Evie and Granny Pippa – *I mean, what happened?* – then Barry Talbot's cryptic remarks about a history they never wanted to revisit, a Barry Talbot her mother claimed to have never met – a definite fib – a Barry Talbot who'd also known Pippa, who'd wanted Heronbrook for himself, and who seemed to know all the goings-on in the locality.

The past is another country, he'd said. Yet in moving back to Heronbrook Evie had surely plunged herself right into that past. Had Evie decided to confront history that shouldn't be revisited? Had she upset somebody by doing so? As Amber had gone about the day, she'd wondered how best to broach it with an Evie who'd asked not to be badgered with questions.

She took another sip of wine now. 'Have you seen many drones around here before?'

'Not on the lane,' Evie said, 'but I've seen them on the beach recently.'

'How about the day of your accident?' Amber asked, voicing a thought that had been niggling her. 'Did you see one then?' Had someone been checking out Evie's progress up the lane, waiting for the right moment to strike?

'I could have, but I just can't remember. That morning is all still a bit fuzzy.'

Glancing at her great-aunt, Amber saw her eyes cloud with uneasiness.'I can't help wondering,' she said, 'why did you really move down here?'

Evie's hands shook as she picked up her bookmark and slid it into her book. 'I thought we agreed not to pry into each other's lives?'

Pry? Amber couldn't help thinking that Evie made it sound like there was something delicate to unearth, but the troubled expression on her face prevented Amber from questioning her further. 'Sorry, we did. I'm just curious because ... it's so different to the glamorous world you used to move in,' she finished up lamely.

'I was starting to plan my retirement when it came on the market,' Evie said. 'It had been empty for a while and it just seemed fortuitous.'

'It's a beautiful place,' Amber said, not wanting to press Evie further. 'I find it very peaceful.'

'Without prying,' Evie began, giving Amber a soft smile tinged with interest, 'is the change of scene doing you good?'

She realised her great-aunt had neatly steered the conversation around. But her soft smile plunged Amber right back to the day in the church when she'd first seen Evie Lawrence. An Evie, she now realised, who'd gazed at a young Amber with an expression of sad regret. How distressing that time must have been for her. Whatever had gone wrong between the sisters, she sensed Evie had been through the wars.

Amber realised with a sense of liberation that she didn't fear Evie's judgement of her character. And seeing Evie at her most vulnerable and defenceless was helping her to see that admitting helplessness and being honest about yourself could be a personal strength, a grace of sorts. And far from being a burden on someone else, it could help them to be a better version of themselves – as she was finding out, discovering a strange sense of fulfilment in the day-to-day care of her aunt.

It gave her the courage to be completely honest.

'I came here because I was in a dark place,' she admitted. 'I did something incredibly stupid but I paid unfairly for that carelessness. I was ... to put it mildly, in a bad frame of mind.' Her words hung in the air between them. She was grateful Evie didn't immediately rush in with platitudes or a solution of some kind.

After a while, Evie spoke. 'How do you feel now? Can you see any light at the end of the tunnel?'

Amber looked out to the steady fall of rain cloaking the trees in a hazy curtain. She was beginning to feel strangely at home in Heronbrook, as if she had plugged into its peaceful energy. Close to nature, there was something immensely comforting about the rhythm and unfaltering continuity of it all, her morning runs on the beach and the slow calm of time spent on the terrace, helped along by books and the music Evie streamed in the background, anything from David Bowie to Elton John, from Ralph Vaughan Williams to

Bach. The Wi-Fi was mostly behaving itself and Amber had even hooked up her Spotify and treated Evie to Picture This. Moving around in this place of ancient, quiet beauty, her train wreck of a life didn't seem as significant.

Especially when she was beginning to be gripped by the feeling that, apart from Will and the angst he had wrought, her career up to now bore all the hallmarks of a stifling conventional straitjacket.

'Yes,' she said. 'Being here is helping.'

'I'm glad to hear that,' Evie said. 'While you're here, do whatever you can to look after yourself. And, Amber, don't be hard on yourself for whatever happened. Think of what you might say to your best friend if she was in a bad place and say that to yourself. We all make mistakes. I certainly made a mess of things.' She paused and took a sip of water. 'Whatever you were escaping, I'm more than glad you were around to come to my help. You've saved me from climbing the walls of a convalescent home.'

'That would have been a miracle recovery.' Amber attempted a joke.

Evie smiled and studied Amber's face for a moment, and Amber had the gut feeling she was trying to come to a decision.

'You were asking me about my motives for moving down here …' Evie paused.

Amber waited, hoping her great-aunt might answer some of the questions swirling at the back of her mind.

'One of the reasons I came here,' Evie said, 'is because Heronbrook is where I'd been the happiest I'd ever been in my life. Intense, all-consuming happiness. Like nothing I had ever known before or since. But it was also the place where the rest of my life skidded off the tracks.'

Evie took a slow sip of water and cursed herself. Amber was fixing her with a look of keen interest. She hadn't meant that nugget of information to slip out.

'I'm not going to divulge any sorry details,' Evie said, 'but at the time I was eighteen and passionate about life, and I viewed it in extremes, whether that was crazy joy or incandescent anger. It took me a long time to get over myself and figure out that life is fluid and made up of complex layers of varying shades, and that the past can live in your head and collide with the present. For me, now, some memories are as sharp as yesterday, so actually, Amber, I don't know if I've moved on at all. Or if you ever do.'

'So there's no such thing as gliding gently into a golden twilight?'

Evie snorted. 'I don't think I've ever felt gentle about this life – passionate, angry, even savage sometimes, but never gentle. Coming back here …' Evie paused again.

Amber took a sip of wine and waited.

'It was some kind of pilgrimage,' Evie said, looking for the right words. 'I was hoping that if I allowed myself to remember the happy days they might be strong enough to cancel out the unhappy days and the long, dark nights. And now that I'm at the summing-up stage of my life – at seventy-five, it stands to reason that I've fewer years left ahead and little or no chance to effect any great sea-change – I wanted to find out …' She paused momentarily. 'I wanted to know if it had all been worth it.' She glanced at Amber with a wry smile, 'If that makes any sense.'

'Not to me,' Amber said. 'But what's your verdict? *Has* it all been worth it?'

'I don't know,' Evie said, sighing heavily. 'I doubt if there's a person alive who doesn't have some regret. Everyone must have experienced a pivotal moment in their life when they chose one path over another, and then later, when things disappoint, as they so often do in life, the temptation is to look longingly at the path you didn't take, because that still represents endless possibilities and is free from disillusion.'

'It's sometimes hard to know what path to take,' Amber said.

'I'm sure you have lots of choices, Amber, and remember, not everything is set in stone, especially at your age.' Evie smiled and shook her head. 'Don't mind me and all my ramblings. I'm just streaming my thoughts here without the usual four-ply filter.'

'Well, I got you all wrong,' Amber said.

'What does that mean?' Evie looked at her sharply.

'From things I picked up over the years, mostly in the media – sorry, but you were rarely mentioned in the family – I saw you as the glamorous actor over in London, who then took Irish television by storm.

You were the one relative I knew who succeeded in following her dreams. I can't say my parents did.'

'Didn't they?'

'Dad was out of work a few years ago and it impacted on both my parents. Now they're stuck in jobs they don't particularly like.'

Evie felt a pang in her chest. 'I'm sorry to hear that. I didn't know.'

'They're getting on with things but it's been tough, and then Granny Pippa' – Amber gave a short laugh – 'I used to call her my cross granny compared with Nana Beth. But I thought you were the original free spirit.'

'I thought that too, once upon a time, before it all went wrong. Sometimes I don't know who or what I am any more. So much for the wisdom and enlightenment that's supposed to come with advancing years. That's the biggest myth of all.'

'I'm doomed, so,' Amber said.

'Not yet,' Evie said. 'You have plenty of time to redeem yourself. But I'm certainly beyond rescuing at this stage.'

'What do you need rescuing from, Evie?' Amber asked softly.

'The mess I made of my life.'

'You shouldn't speak negatively of yourself.' Her grand-niece took a few moments to gather her thoughts, surprising her when she did eventually speak. 'I'm sorry to think that you could have some dark nights. When you said … about your life having been worth it …'

'I did say that, didn't I?'

Amber put down her glass and looked at her earnestly. 'Mum always enjoyed *Spencer Row* on the BBC, but she loved *Delphin Terrace*,' she said. 'You've no idea how much she looked forward to it – it was great escapism for her, a chance to relax and put her feet up after a hard day's work. '

Evie smiled. 'That's good to know.'

'And Mum was only one of thousands,' Amber went on. 'I might start watching it myself during the winter nights. And before *Delphin Terrace* you had years in London. So when you think of it, the path you took meant you entertained hundreds of thousands of people over the years. You took them away from their lives for a while, helped them relax and gave them some respite from their problems as well as some joy. That's so important, Evie, that it must cancel out some of that mess you're talking about.'

Evie was silent for a few moments, overwhelmed by Amber's words. Like turning back the pages of a calendar, unfurling in her mind's eye she saw a movie reel of months and years; London, festivals in Liverpool and Edinburgh, her name on the billboards, *Hamlet*, *Romeo and Juliet*, *Blithe Spirit*, *The Mousetrap*, *The Woman in Black* ... hundreds of nights of packed auditoriums, hundreds of upturned faces rising up in a sea of applause, the sound ringing in her ears, flowers on the stage, '*Lawrence brings a fresh edginess to the fragile Ophelia*', '*Her evocative portrayal of Juliet is visceral*'. Then later, the television cameras, a different world but the same escape from reality, into the role of brassy Jo Baxter in *Spencer Row*, before moving to Dublin and Ma Donnelly. Much the same accolades as well as record ratings.

Her hand shook as she lifted her water, her teeth chattering against the glass.

'Sorry,' Amber began, 'I've said too much.'

'No,' Evie said immediately, 'I'm touched by your words. I don't think you know how much they mean to me. Thank you for that validation. We should raise a toast to ourselves even if I'm on sparkling water. Here's to you and me,' Evie said, 'we will prevail.'

'Absolutely,' Amber said, lifting her glass also. 'You and me.'

It was the strangest time Evie had ever raised a glass in a toast, but one of the most meaningful. Just for the moment, she let go of everything, and they sat together in comfortable silence, facing the back garden while the rain continued to drip down gently through the autumn woods outside, slow and gentle, washing everything clean like a blessing.

On Saturday afternoon, when she walked into the foyer of Pinedale Lawns, Jessica was stopped by Helen, a member of the care team, who was clearly agitated to see her.

'What's wrong?' Jessica asked, her heart somersaulting.

'I'm so sorry, Jessica,' Helen said. 'You've had a wasted journey. I can't let you through to your mother. Didn't you get the message?'

'What message?'

'All visiting is cancelled for now. We've had a small outbreak of the vomiting bug. Rest assured, your mother is fine – you need have no worries about her. We're taking all necessary precautions and have a robust action plan in place to prevent its spread.'

'It's not even winter yet,' Jessica said, realising her comment was totally inane, but her sudden alarm had subsided, leaving her blank.

'My sincere apologies for this inconvenience,' Helen said. 'You should have been notified. I'll have to see where that fell down. Please know we're making strenuous efforts to eradicate this and are in the process of a deep disinfection of all rooms and communal areas. The bug seems to be contained to one or two rooms in the south wing.'

Her words rolled over Jessica's head, while her

brain struggled to catch up. Now that access to her mother was being refused, Jessica felt a cold sense of loss tugging at her heart. She hoped her mother wouldn't miss her or feel upset when she didn't show up. She didn't like the thought of her sitting isolated in her room, feeling confused, unwanted, or alone. For all her failings, Pippa had had a raw deal in life, thanks in some part to Evie's behaviour. Not that Jessica blamed Evie – she knew on some intrinsic level that she had enough on her plate without weighing it down further with old family resentments.

All the same, with both of them in a vulnerable situation at the moment, Evie was the one recuperating in the comfort of her own home with Amber on hand to look after her, whereas Pippa was confined to a lonely nursing home room and a fading mind.

It was all so sad.

'You'll let your brother know, won't you?' Helen said.

'My *brother*?'

'About the visiting restrictions? It would be a shame if he had a wasted journey too,' Helen said chattily. 'He told me he regretted not being able to visit his mother that often.'

'I doubt if that will be a problem for Jamie,' Jessica said, bristling slightly.

'I'm talking about Simon,' Helen said.

'Simon? He hasn't been here in a couple of years.'

Helen gave her a cagey look. 'But – um, yes he has,' she said.

'I doubt that,' Jessica said tartly. 'It must have been Jamie.'

Which was a surprise to her. He'd called in soon after arriving home from New York, accompanying Jessica because he couldn't face it on his own. Never again, he'd said afterwards, distinctly shook up by the shrunken, incapacitated sight of his mother. So upset that he'd had to go down to the pub local to Laurel Lawns afterwards to get the taste of it out of his mouth, dragging Paul along with him, not that Paul had needed much persuasion. Surely, though, if Jamie had braved the nursing home without her, he would have been only too delighted to boast about his self-sacrifice, expecting to bask in the warm glow of Jessica's approval.

'He told me he found it difficult to come home from Hong Kong on a regular basis,' Helen said, 'but seeing as he was in Dublin on business he dropped in, oh, twice in the one week, maybe about two months ago? Although it could have been three? Times flies, and visitors are coming and going so much it's hard to keep track of them all.'

This was very odd. 'Had you met Simon before?' she asked, a horrible possibility dawning on her that someone had set out to impersonate her brother.

'No, I'm only here a year, and he said he hadn't visited in a long time, due to work and other commitments. He said he'd forgotten the run of the place, but he came through reception.' She shrugged, as though coming through reception set the seal on his validation. 'He was quite attractive, youthful and charming.'

Jessica wanted to snap that being attractive, youthful and charming scarcely legitimised anything. Her twin brother could be described in those terms and they were not, Jessica sometimes fretted, a close-knit family, but Simon would never have come to Dublin, let alone visited their mother, without seeing Jessica and giving her plenty of advance notice.

'I showed him to Pippa's room,' Helen continued. 'He was really appreciative. Who else would be visiting your mother anyway?' she said defensively, as though she suspected something was amiss.

'How was my mother when Simon called?' Jessica asked, keeping her concerns to herself for now. 'Did she recognise him?'

'Not in the beginning, but later when I was bringing in tea, she seemed to have some flicker of recognition, because she got excited when he said he was leaving soon. I was glad he got some reaction from her. He seemed pleased enough.'

'How long did he stay?'

'I suppose … about half an hour? It was lovely for your mother to have such a fine man calling. I don't think she wanted him to leave.'

'Why not?' Jessica asked.

'As I said, she got excited.'

'But was she happy-excited or upset-excited? There's a difference. Like, did Simon's visit do her more harm than good?'

'I think it was a mixture of both. It took me a while to settle her afterwards. Is everything all right, Jessica? I'd hate there to be an issue with this. Sometimes families—'

'No issues at all,' Jessica said, deciding not to raise any alarms until she had this checked out for herself.

It was a good nursing home for the most part, Jessica conceded, putting up her umbrella against the drizzle as she walked across the car park, the breeze sending whirlpools of damp leaves around her boots. Well-run, with attentive staff, it was brightly lit and spotlessly clean. In the porch, a keypad code was needed to gain entry through the main doors. The code was changed regularly, with visiting relations kept informed. It *was* possible to claim to have forgotten the pin code and gain entry. Jessica herself had done that a couple of times. Reception had the names and contact details of immediate family members. Visitors had to sign in and out, so there would be a record of so-called Simon's visit. It would also be possible for someone to sign the attendance book and pass themselves off as another person, especially if that someone knew the man they were impersonating wasn't a regular visitor to the home.

But only family would be aware of that detail,

surely. And whoever had impersonated Simon would know he was running the risk of Jessica being informed about her mother's charming visitor by a chatty assistant. Which meant he hadn't cared about that, once he had seen Pippa. A Pippa who'd had to be settled afterwards.

There had to be a reasonable explanation, she told herself, breathing slowly to dispel a surge of unease. She was at a loss to know who would have gone to those lengths to see her mother. And, given the five years that Pippa had spent in Pinedale Lawns, why now?

When Jessica arrived home, Paul was in the kitchen, having coffee. He was wearing chinos and a light blue sweater. She knew by his slightly damp hair that he wasn't long out of the shower. He asked after Pippa, but Jessica didn't mention her concerns, afraid that with her thoughts so scattered one conversation might lead to the very one she wanted to avoid at all costs.

'You're just in time,' he said.

Jessica racked her brains and came up blank. 'For what?'

'I was supposed to be meeting Adam in town for the second half of the City match. But he can't make it after all. Why don't you come in with me? We could have a drink and go for a bite to eat afterwards. It would be good for the two of us to do something different.' He spoke casually, as though he'd made a routine suggestion, but his anxious face told a different story. It was a long time since Paul had made an impromptu offer like this.

She had a sudden longing for a carefree Saturday afternoon, strolling up Grafton Street, popping into a pub for a drink or two, deciding at the last minute to stay on for some food, maybe another drink. The kind of thing they used to enjoy.

'I can't,' she said.

'Why not?'

'I've shopping to do.'

'Shopping? I thought you went last night?'

He was right. She'd gone to Penneys in Dundrum Town Centre for a new pair of work trousers, using the excuse to stay out of the house as long as possible.

'Those trousers I bought ...' she grasped at straws, 'they're the wrong size.'

'You could do that another time,' he said, giving her a half-hopeful, half-perplexed smile.

'Look, Paul,' she said, putting down her bag, going over to the kettle, 'we'll do town another time, OK?'

'If you don't want to come with me just say so,' he said. He picked up his cup and threw the rest of the coffee down the sink before going out the door.

Fuckity-fuck. Jessica gripped the kitchen counter, breathing deeply.

The long-awaited reply from the bank had come yesterday – she'd been lucky to grab it from the hall before Paul had arrived home. It had been more or less as she'd expected. The bank had absolved themselves of all responsibility ... blah, blah ... she hadn't taken reasonable precautions ... they had fulfilled their duty of care ... constantly issuing warning notices about phishing scams, advising customers to never input their bank details or pin numbers on foot of an email or text. This was their final response in the matter.

Cosying up with Paul in a pub was the last thing she needed right now.

Jessica headed upstairs, plucked a freshly

laundered bath sheet from the hot press, and went into the shower, hoping her tension might ease with the help of a generous dollop of lemongrass-scented gel. Afterwards, she put on navy leggings and a cerise top before going down to the kitchen and sitting at the island counter.

Only then did she feel calm enough to call Jamie.

'Hey, sis, how are you? What's up?'

She came straight to the point. 'Did you by any chance visit Mum recently?'

'What? Are you joking?' He sounded flabbergasted. 'I was in there with you once and it's something I've no wish to repeat.'

'That's not nice, Jamie.'

She'd had to confirm it, but his response was just as she'd expected. Something pulsed at the back of her head, but instinct bade her to keep her worries from him. *Old habits.*

'Hang on,' he said, 'have you any idea how I felt seeing Mum in such a state with her drooping face? Most women of her age are still out there, enjoying a good life. Going shopping, getting their hair done, nice meals out …'

It was a long time since their mum had enjoyed life, but Jessica didn't bother to comment. Jamie was right in one sense.

'Instead she's stuck in that home,' he went on, 'sitting around in frumpy clothes. I'm finding it upsetting.'

He was finding it upsetting? Jessica wanted to retort.

'And all that shite is draining away our inheritance,' he said, 'thanks to the package she's under.'

'I bet that's the part you're finding the most upsetting,' Jessica said. 'I don't need to hear this. Where were you and Simon when Mum was ill? I did the best I could in the circumstances.'

'Yeah, sorry, sis, you're right,' Jamie said, his apology rather grudging. 'Any word from Amber?' he asked, changing the subject. Typical Jamie.

'She's fine,' Jessica said. 'I spoke to her on Wednesday.' She was relieved that Amber hadn't been back to her since with more probing questions.

'Did you pass on my message?' Jamie said. 'She never called me.'

'I expect she's busy looking after Evie.' Jessica swept stray crumbs on the counter top into a small pile. The remnants of Adam's toast, she guessed. 'Why are you so interested in talking to her?'

'I was hoping for some kind of insider report as to what life is really like in Heronbrook. How long will she be staying there?'

'I don't know.'

'Surely her high-powered job is missing her? Or her boyfriend?'

Jessica bit her lip. Amber was still keeping radio silence on the reasons why she was now suddenly on leave, with acres of free time on her hands, never mind the absence of her boyfriend. Will, if she recalled his name correctly. 'I'm sure Amber has all that covered,' Jessica said smoothly.

'You might think I don't know what you're up to, dropping her in there, but I have my suspicions.'

'What suspicions?'

'Evie must be loaded,' Jamie said, a hint of belligerence in his tone. 'I know she has an apartment in Blackrock rented out. And the land her house is sitting on must be worth something. You could knock that down and build half a dozen luxury apartments, like they've done up the far end of the woods. You can't deny that some funds would be useful to both of us. I'm sure the wicked witch would happy to share a bit with her long-lost family.'

'For God's sake, Jamie.' Jessica lost her patience. 'You're being ridiculous. And you seem to know an awful lot about Heronbrook as well as Evie's affairs.'

'Be honest, Jessica, wouldn't you just love to break away from that financial treadmill you're on?'

'Don't talk rubbish,' she said, annoyed that he'd managed to glean some knowledge about the state of their financial affairs from his time in Laurel Lawns. Although, her stomach clenched, he didn't know the half of it. Neither did Paul, which was far more critical. 'I'm not listening to any more,' she said. 'I'm ending the call now.'

'Wait, did you hear about the painting?'

'What painting?'

'A couple of months ago an original Lucien Burke sold privately in London for a tidy sum.'

Jessica stiffened. 'Who told you that?'

'I've known since just before I left New York. I saw an article in a culture magazine hanging around in the bar. Apparently there are three known paintings, a Heronbrook landscape series, and his work has suddenly become a collector's item, so now they're worth a few bob. One of them has been acquired privately but it didn't say where this painting originated or who bought it, but the other two are being actively sought—'

'Why didn't you say something before now?' Jessica interrupted.

'I was biding my time.'

'How come I don't believe you?'

Jamie ignored her question. 'Thing is, there's supposed to be a fourth, a portrait of some kind, the last of his work, and it's rumoured to have been painted in Heronbrook itself, back in the sixties, but it hasn't been seen since. Anywhere. What's the betting it's still there somewhere?'

'I can't believe you've kept all this to yourself.'

'I was waiting to see what way the land lay. You don't sound surprised, dear sis, which makes me suspect you knew about this already. I've been on to Simon, but he isn't aware of it. Neither is he interested, he said. Too busy cultivating his Chinese stocks, I expect. But you have Amber in pole position.'

'Is this the real reason you came home from New York?' Jessica said. 'To sniff out an elusive painting that might exist?'

'I wish.' Jamie laughed sourly. 'Far from it, dear sister. Far from it.'

'That sounds interesting. Are you going to enlighten me at last?'

There was a pause. 'Never mind,' Jamie said. 'I'm wanted out front. Bye.'

Jessica went to the fridge, and lifting out a bottle of white wine, she poured a generous glass. The late-afternoon drizzle had lifted and shafts of orangey September sunshine reflected off the houses behind them and lay in oblongs across the shiny worktops. The kitchen, in that moment, looked warm and peaceful. And safe. She sighed heavily, relaxing into the moment for a precious few seconds. After a while she began preparations for the evening meal, knowing she wasn't particularly hungry. She knew all about that fourth painting, but she'd no intention of revealing that to Jamie.

The Glenmaragh View was an inviting-looking one-storey timber-framed building, set back from the road, bedecked with hanging baskets and a line of flowering containers spilling over with blooms just edging past their summer best. Colourful bunting strung outside flapped and curled in the breeze, along with chalkboards announcing that day's specials. Wooden tables and benches were set up to the side. Amber parked the Kia, choosing a spot as close as possible to the entrance.

'Are you sure you're up to this?' she asked Evie. 'It's no problem if you want to change your mind. I could get a takeout for our lunch?'

'No thanks,' Evie said, 'this is great. I'm looking forward to being out and feeling a little normal again.' She had already expressed delight when Amber had helped her into a pair of black slacks, instead of her tracksuit bottoms, and a pair of patent-leather, flat-soled boots. The bruises on her face were fading, but she'd covered any signs of them with thick foundation.

Amber helped Evie out of the car, Evie doggedly steering herself and her crutches across to the entrance.

Inside, the ceilings were low, the café accessible through the shopping area, where mahogany shelving and cabinets held displays of locally produced crafts: candles, diffusers, items of jewellery, coloured prints and handmade postcards, books, jars of preserves, knitwear, and crocheted scarves, all aimed at the passing tourist trade. To Amber, it had a tired, disinterested air, as though the merchandise itself had become bored from lying around too long. She wondered just how much trade passed through here, although its proximity to the garage was a help. A fresh coat of paint and a little creative thinking could have brightened it up. They walked through to the café, the aroma of freshly brewed coffee floating around along with the hum of conversation from several occupied tables. It was quite busy, she thought, for Monday lunchtime.

Evie headed across to a table by the window. A young waitress was clearing it, her eyes widening when she saw who was approaching, and she took a step back, almost dropping her tray.

'Careful now,' Evie said, lowering herself gingerly into a chair, allowing Amber to place her crutches to one side. 'Can't have you breaking the crockery. Tess might dock it from your tips.'

'Ms Lawrence ... oh ... em ... I'll let her know you're here.'

'There's no need to disturb her if she's busy.' Evie smiled. 'My niece and I have just popped in for lunch. But if she's free it would be nice to see her. Can we have a menu?'

'Of course,' the waitress said, resting her tray on a nearby table while she fetched two menus.

'We were lucky to get this table,' Evie said, nodding out the window after they had ordered – an omelette for Evie and a caprese salad for Amber.

They were facing the back of the Glenmaragh View where, beyond a small meadow, the mountains rose in a steep gradient in front of them, the dark and jagged sloped face exposed in a series of ancient serrated slate and granite rocks. 'That's the Glenmaragh Peak,' Evie said. 'Impossible to climb, I believe.'

'There's a challenge for you, Evie, when you're recovered,' Amber teased.

They were halfway through their food when Amber noticed a woman bearing down on them, superiority and importance reeking from every line in her body. In her early sixties, she was thin, angular and beautifully dressed in a plain-cream blouse, green skirt and high heels, a chunky silver pendant at her throat.

'Evie!' she said, pulling up a spare chair and sitting on it. 'Darling! I couldn't believe it when I heard you were here. How are you keeping? Are you making a good recovery? Doing well, I hope?' Without waiting for Evie to reply to her barrage of questions, her bright blue eyes swivelled to Amber, bulging with an imperious interest that soured her stomach.

Evie sat up straighter. 'Tess, darling!' she said fulsomely. 'How wonderful to see you – I've been waiting to thank you in person for saving my life.

This is my niece, Amber, who's staying with me for the moment. Amber, meet Tess, my saviour and knight in shining armour.'

From the way Evie reacted to Tess, Amber guessed she was in full actress mode. No surprises there. If you were feeling any way fragile, Tess's in-your-face dominance was something to be avoided.

'I'd hardly call myself that,' Tess said with a coy bashfulness that even Amber could see was fake. 'Lovely to meet you, Amber,' she went on, extending a limp hand. 'You have a look of your mother about you.'

'I do?' Amber was disconcerted. 'I didn't know you knew my mother?'

She half-expected Tess to say she knew Jessica from her childhood, that they'd perhaps grown up near each other in Bray, even though there was at least a decade between them. Instead Tess frowned and turned to Evie. 'It was Jessica you were with at the charity thing, wasn't it, when you were talking to Barry?'

'That's right,' Evie said. She didn't give anything away in her tone of voice, Amber noticed, like, for instance, that Jessica and Evie hadn't seen each other for years before that.

'What event was this?' Amber asked. She recalled her mother talking about seeing Evie a few months ago – where, it now appeared, her mother had also met Barry, contrary to what she'd told Amber. Why hadn't she simply admitted it?

'It was a fundraiser for care homes and centres

in the region. Evie was one of the guest speakers.' Tess smiled. She turned to Evie. 'And you were both caught on camera with Barry.'

'We were?' Evie looked startled.

'Yes, the *Wicklow Weekly* ran a supplement the following week covering the event, and there were lots of photographs. Didn't you know?'

'I remember posing for a photograph with Jessica but I didn't realise it was for a newspaper.'

'You needn't worry, Evie, it was a lovely photo of you both,' Tess said. Then she leaned forward as though she was about to impart very important gossip. 'Matthew Casey was there too,' she said, pausing, and Amber knew she was waiting for a reaction of some sort from Evie. When none was forthcoming Tess went on, her eyes bright like a bird's as she watched Evie carefully. 'He came to support the event because his sister Rachel had just died. Cancer. She'd only been ill for a few months. She'd still been living in Manchester but she came home to a hospice in Dublin for her last few weeks. She was a friend of Pippa's, I believe.'

'An old childhood friend,' Evie said. 'As far as I know they never kept in touch after' – she paused – 'when we stopped holidaying down here,' she finished up, sounding excessively polite.

'You mean after Leah's accident,' Tess said.

Evie made no reply.

'The end came quite suddenly for Rachel but her family were with her,' Tess said, seemingly satisfied she'd had all the reaction she was going to get from Evie. She straightened up. 'Anyhow, I'm delighted to see you out and about. I was only too glad that I came along in your hour of need. You didn't have to send flowers, but thanks for them all the same.' She glanced around the café, as if to make sure she wasn't within earshot of others before saying in a low voice, 'You still don't know who was responsible?'

'No, ' Evie said soberly. 'I guess I was in the wrong place at the wrong time.'

'Unlucky for you. I heard a couple of characters have been hanging around along that stretch of the beach, lighting fires in the sand dunes, leaving litter behind them, messing with drones – even poaching. They must have no gainful employment. At least you have Amber to keep you safe,' Tess said, glancing meaningfully at Amber.

'Why, do you think I'm in danger?' Evie asked.

Tess laughed. It sounded forced to Amber. 'Not at all,' she said, 'but there's safety in numbers and, let's face it, you are a little vulnerable at the moment.' Her gaze fastened on Evie's crutches.

'I won't need them for much longer,' Evie fibbed, exchanging a quick glance with Amber.

'Fair play to you.'

'You're doing a good trade here, I see,' Evie said, glancing around the café.

'Just about. There was a time last year when I thought we might go under, but the home baking has proved to be successful. Although I don't always feel so cheerful about it at six in the morning when I'm donning my apron to roll out pastry and Barry is still snoring in bed. Still, this is my one and only baby, of which I'm extremely proud.'

'It's a lot of hard work,' Evie said.

'Tell me about it.' Tess gave her a crooked smile and rose to her feet. 'I thought Barry and I would have been heading off into the sunny Costa del Sol by now to enjoy a well-earned retirement. Only it didn't quite work out.' There was a short silence. 'I'd better get back to my office. Baby or no baby, the dreaded paperwork is a chore.' She patted Evie's shoulder. 'I'm covering this lunch.'

'Not at all, I'm paying and I'm treating Amber.'

'Not this time. If you want to support our little business, maybe you could put something out on social media? Or perhaps you, Amber? A nice little Instagram post? It would be good marketing for us – Evie Lawrence, recovering from her accident, enjoying the best that the Glenmaragh View has to offer, a sort of follow up from the newspaper article. We might get a little trade boost before the quiet winter months.'

'Sure,' Amber said, not bothering to explain she was off social media for the foreseeable. Until she got Will out of her head, no matter how long that took.

As they walked across the car park, they met Barry getting out of his Mercedes.

'Good afternoon, Evie,' he said in loud, false-jollity tones. 'And good afternoon to you too, Amy.'

'It's Amber.' From the gleam in his eye she had the feeling he knew her name but had been trying to disconcert her.

'Well, then good afternoon, Amber, my apologies.'

'Come off it, Barry,' Evie said. 'You wouldn't know an apology if it jumped up and hit you in the face.'

He grinned. 'So, you're getting back on your feet – not much harm done by the look of you.'

'I hope you're not disappointed,' Evie said. 'It seems like my demise has been postponed for now.'

'That's good news, Evie, at least I know Heronbrook is in safe hands while you're still around.' He laughed again and strode into the café.

'I take it you're bosom pals – not. You and Tess, I mean,' Amber said to Evie as she drove down the hill from the café. Evie looked spun out, she thought, a thin film of sweat on her brow.

'Was it that obvious? I thought I deserved a gong for my acting. I don't know how I kept a straight face when she spoke of donning an apron at six in the morning, unless she's putting it on in an attempt to get the snoring Barry's attention.'

'Evie!' Amber smiled and shook her head. 'Does she resent the way you whipped Heronbrook from under her husband's nose?' Something Tess had said was nipping at the edge of her thoughts, but she couldn't quite put her finger on it.

'I don't know. You heard him saying he's not interested in it any more. I think he's just gotten tired of life. They never had children but from what I gleaned from my bridge friends, Tess stays with Barry because she'd lose out financially if they separated. He stays with her for convenience. Tess has put up with a lot from Barry over the years, but she gives as good as she gets, if you follow me.'

'Oooh, sounds like some drama in this quiet backwater.'

'Quiet backwaters can hold simmering passions,' Evie said eventually.

'And are you going to elaborate?' Amber asked.

'It wasn't me and Barry,' Evie said. 'That's all I'm prepared to say.'

Amber indicated for the turn off for Heronbrook. Had Evie rejected Barry's advances? Was that part of their old history, long flowed under the bridge? Another piece of the puzzle she was trying to unravel? And how come he still seemed familiar to her?

She swung down the lane towards Heronbrook, twisting through the trees, braking suddenly when she saw several crows on the narrow roadway in front of her pecking at a mound of a dark orange and red substance. 'What's that?' she said.

Evie looked out through the windscreen. 'Oh my God. It looks like a dead animal.'

'Stay here,' Amber said, turning off the engine and jumping out of the car. Cawing wildly, the crows wheeled up into the air in a flutter of dark wings, like cloaks. It was a dead fox, and to judge by the state of the body it had been run over some time ago. Looking at what the beautiful animal had been reduced to, Amber was gripped with nausea. She went back to the car and filled Evie in.

'I'll ring the council the minute we get home,' Evie said. 'They'll look after it. Have you enough room to get by?'

'You mean without going over it again?' Amber said, shivering. 'I think so.'

She eased the car forward, managing to avoid the pitiable animal by partly driving into the ditch, glancing down at it as she cleared it with room to spare. Back in Heronbrook, as soon as Evie had phoned the council, Amber made strong coffee.

'You look like you need this, Evie,' she said, noting her great-aunt's pallor, 'you're very pale. Are you feeling OK?'

'I got a bit of a fright, that's all,' Evie said, not meeting Amber's eyes. 'I'll be fine.'

Gripping her mug, as if she was steeling herself in some way, Amber said, 'You don't think I caused that, do you? Earlier, when we were leaving here?'

'No way, Amber,' Evie said. 'We would have known – we would have seen it in front of us and felt the impact. I'd say it was hit on the main road and limped down here until it could go no further.'

'It didn't look to me like it could have limped anywhere.'

'That has to be the only explanation,' Evie said. 'I'm sure there was more damage caused by other animals or birds. Let's not talk about it any more.' Her tone, to Amber's surprise, was rather curt. Evie was a lot more shaken than she was admitting.

'I'm going to cover it with something,' Amber said, leaving her coffee. She brought a couple of black sacks up the laneway, disturbing the crows again and throwing the sacks over the carcass. She went into the ditch, picking up stones and windfall twigs, scattering them over the sacks to secure them.

Evie was right about one thing – the animal was sizeable enough for a hit to be noticed. But she was mistaken if she thought the fox had somehow hobbled down from the main road. From the condition of it, and the lack of dried blood surrounding the carcass, it looked to Amber as though the fox had been run over elsewhere and placed here deliberately.

She wasn't even going to try telling that to Evie. She would just have to keep her eyes and ears open, and find out what was going on.

They were out on the terrace on Tuesday, Evie feeling a little drowsy, when the loud beep of a car horn interrupted the calm of the afternoon.

'You're not expecting anyone, are you?' Amber said, sitting upright.

'No,' Evie said, 'are you?'

'No way,' Amber said, 'none of my friends even know I'm here.'

Evie's heart dipped. Did Amber not have friends who cared enough to ask after her? Or had whatever rocked her world been so destructive that Amber was keeping them at arm's length? 'It's no problem if any of your friends want to call,' Evie told her. 'You could bring them out here for coffee or whatever, and I'd keep out of your way.'

'That won't be happening,' Amber said, getting to her feet as the beep sounded again.

Her grand-niece was back a moment later, with a man in tow.

'Evie,' she said, 'this is Jamie, come to see how we are.' Amber didn't look particularly happy to have him there, and it didn't take Evie long to figure out why.

'Well, this is a nice little set-up,' her nephew said after they'd greeted each other. His gaze roved around the terrace, causing Evie to view it with fresh eyes: the assortment of patio flowers still throwing out some colour and scent and small shrubs of variegated green, all set against the landscape of the woods. She realised she felt rather contented in that moment, despite the resentful energy she sensed emanating from Jamie. Evie hadn't seen him in over twenty years yet she would have picked him out in a crowd – that square jaw, the cow's lick, the jaunty set of his shoulders, just like his father, but the pale-blue eyes so like Pippa's. As were the negative vibes radiating from him. Someone else who always saw the glass half empty.

'I see why you haven't called me,' he said to Amber, a muscle working in his face. 'You're having far too cosy a time.' He nodded at the small table holding her book and a retro crystal wine glass, one of a set that Evie had insisted she use.

'I'm not sure about that,' Evie butted in. 'I'm rather a slave driver, and I have Amber at my beck and call all the time. This set-up didn't magic itself into being.'

'Magic indeed – I thought you had put some kind of spell on her to make her forget all about the outside world.' He flicked a slightly impudent glance at Evie.

'I'm not the wicked witch your mother thinks I am, Jamie,' Evie said, holding his gaze, quietly triumphant when his slid away from her. 'Yes, I know what she's thought of me all these years – your brother, Simon, was only too pleased to enlighten me at my mother's funeral – but I'm actually a far worse sorcerer than you could imagine.' She winked at Amber before turning back to Jamie. 'Will you have coffee? A drink?' she asked him. 'Amber will look after you. I'm good at issuing orders but I like to think I'm a fair boss – isn't that so, Amber?'

There was a flicker of a grin on Amber's face. 'I suppose you are.'

'Amber's good at knowing what side her bread is buttered on,' Jamie muttered.

'I should hope so,' Evie said, eyeing him again. 'It's a basic prerequisite for surviving in this world. There are far too many predators out there, ready to take advantage of you.'

'There certainly are,' he said. This time he held her stare as he sat down. 'Sure I'll have a beer then, if there's one going. I'm driving and due in work later but a quick one won't do any harm.'

'I promise not to put any arsenic in it,' Amber said, disappearing into the kitchen.

Good for you, Evie silently applauded.

Amber returned a moment later with a chilled beer and a glass with ice in it. Jamie didn't bother with the glass. He necked a good third of the bottle before he sat forward and asked, a note of concern in his voice that Evie sensed was fake, 'Jessica told me you were almost killed. It must have been a shock. Did the police ever find out who tried to run you down?'

'I haven't heard if they did.'

'It was a laneway near here, wasn't it?' Jamie said. 'It looks like such a safe, secluded place. You wouldn't think any harm would come to you in this neck of the woods.'

'I guess it's as safe here as anywhere else in the world.'

He rose to his feet and strolled down to the garden to the brook, looking around him before coming back up. 'Have you got security cameras?' He craned his neck, checking out the rear of Heronbrook. 'You have, I see,' he said, sitting down again. 'I take it they're working.'

'They're in perfect working order,' Evie said. 'And they've been serviced recently, as have the monitored alarm and the strategically placed laser beams. They'd stop any intruder in their tracks.'

Out of the corner of her eyes, she saw Amber giving her a half-smile. The only time she'd seen laser beams in action had been in a movie, but she'd been talking to her that morning about calling the alarm company. There was a faulty sensor somewhere so the alarm wasn't setting correctly, and she wanted it fixed.

Her momentary contentment evaporated, replaced by a wave of apprehension. She needed to ensure that Heronbrook was as secure as possible because it seemed her ill-wisher had set out to terrorise her again. She knew she'd been deliberately targeted the minute she'd seen the dead fox on the lane the previous day because Ma Donnelly had had a dead fox placed in her bed soon after she'd been sent the offensive Polaroid. Chilled with foreboding, Evie had found it impossible to relax the previous evening. Now, as she sat out in the warm afternoon, it was easy to reason that the hit-and-run had given her mindless begrudger the perverse idea of frightening her by copycatting Ma Donnelly's series of intimidating incidents. In the two years she'd been living here, nothing like this had happened before. The perpetrator could go bugger off, Evie decided, once Amber was safe. The last thing she wanted was her grand-niece feeling threatened.

'Laser beams?' Jamie said, interrupting her train of thought. 'That sounds like a robust security system, so long as you're not taking the piss out of me.'

'And why should I do that?'

'Let's face it, Evie, name-calling aside, there was no love lost between Mum and you.' He leaned back in his chair and stretched his legs out further. 'From what she said, you took the piss out of her big time.'

'I'm well aware of Pippa's view of me,' Evie said stiffly. 'Which is why I really appreciate Amber being here.'

'I'm a bit happier about Amber being here if you're so secure, and it'll help keep your valuables safe.'

He was baiting her – so like Pippa, once upon a time. 'Oh yes, I'm guarding them closely,' Evie said. 'All of them.'

There was a silence, broken only by birdsong.

'Isn't this lovely all the same?' Jamie said eventually. 'A beautiful terrace and a little family reunion. I should have come back from New York sooner.'

'What prompted you to come home?' Evie asked.

'I don't know why everyone is so interested in my homecoming motives,' he said.

'It was a big change for you,' Evie said. 'A big life change is usually precipitated by some kind of epiphany.'

'Or a crisis,' he said, looking at her with another impudent glance, before his gaze slid to Amber. Amber wasn't contributing much, Evie noticed. She sat quietly, her eyes watchful but giving nothing away.

'America's loss,' Jamie went on. 'I no longer have any inclination to shop in New York or head to Disneyland. And good ol' Ireland has a lot to offer, stuff I'm only just appreciating now. Family for one.' He grinned at her before taking another slug of beer.

'You might find this surprising, but I agree with you on family,' Evie said.

'Good,' Jamie said. 'How are you feeling now? What kind of recovery can you expect?' he asked.

'I'm great, thank you,' Evie said. 'I'm seeing the physiotherapist later this week for an assessment. Then next week I hope to drop down to one crutch, which means I won't need as much minding, which means Amber can go home.'

'I'm not in any rush,' Amber said.

'Not even to run back to Will?' Jamie said swiftly.

In the act of topping up her wine, Amber's hand shook so that the liquid slopped on the table.

'Sorry. I hope I didn't put my foot in it,' Jamie said.

Liar, Evie wanted to say. Jamie didn't look sorry at all. Was Will the guy responsible for Amber's life collapsing? If so, it was terribly cruel of Jamie. He might resemble his father physically, but his attitude and demeanour could have been mainlined straight from Pippa. Behind his belligerent front, she saw a dreadfully unhappy man. How much did he know about Pippa's dark secrets? Had she enlightened him at any time? Probably not. She wouldn't want her son to think any less of her. She wondered if Amber had made any connections, considering the way she'd been quietly studying Jamie. He'd tried to unsettle Amber quite deliberately, and Evie didn't want him here, invading her territory with his bad vibes.

'You don't know your niece very well, do you, Jamie?' she said. 'I haven't known Amber very long but I can see that she's not the running kind.' She fixed him with a withering stare, in her best Ma Donnelly manner. Then she was afraid she might have spoken out of turn, only relieved when, in her peripheral vison, she sensed Amber relaxing slightly.

The tension in the air calmed a little when Amber began to chat to Jamie about the pub in Naas, the nightlife. Then, later, he asked to use the bathroom.

'Feel free,' Evie said. 'Amber will show you where it is.'

'Not at all. I'm sure I can find it,' he said, rising to his feet.

Her grand-niece's gaze followed him as he walked through the terrace doors into the house. When there was no sign of him returning, Amber picked up the bottle of wine, draining the last of it into her glass. 'I'll get some more,' she said, disappearing inside.

Was Jamie taking the opportunity to snoop around? He'd seemed interested in the house and its security; he'd even strolled down to the brook with a swagger as though he owned the territory. Was he imagining how it might feel when Evie was no longer around? He'd also seemed quite interested in her accident, hadn't he?

She wasn't on the set of *Delphin Terrace* any more, she reminded herself. There, all her soap opera family had been prime suspects when it came to her character's murder. Yet the real family she'd been estranged from for years were suddenly connecting with her now. It was Jessica who had made the initial approach to her at the charity event, and had immediately come to her rescue when she'd been hospitalised. Then Amber had come to her help, happy to bury herself here and attend to Evie's needs. Now Jamie, a man fizzing with resentment, had found his way to Heronbrook.

Evie closed her eyes. Her imagination was running away with her. She was tired, her brain fuddled from the painkillers she'd taken earlier that day. After a moment, she became aware of angry voices coming from inside, too far away for her to make out the words: Jamie and Amber in a heated exchange.

Amber arrived in the kitchen just in time to see Jamie coming out of Evie's bedroom. 'What were you doing in there?' she asked, her voice low in case it carried out to Evie.

'No harm in having a quick look at the witch's lair.' He grinned.

She was infuriated by his attitude as much as she had been side-swiped by his mention of Will's name earlier. 'Why don't you fucking get a life?' she said, surprised at her vehemence.

'Ooh, Amber, taking sides now, are you?'

She stared at him.

'You're on the wrong side of the family divide. You mother won't be happy. She can't stand Evie any more than I can.'

'You know my mother's not like that,' Amber snapped. 'She has nothing but respect for everyone. I don't know what happened in this family or what Evie has done to deserve your snarkiness. I wouldn't mind but she's spent most of her life in London, and you've spent half of yours in New York, so she's never been part of your life in any way.'

'I don't know what happened in the family either,' Jamie said, rubbing his jaw, 'but I do know Evie is to blame for turning my mother into a raving alcoholic. Mum told me herself, years ago. Watch your step around her, that's all.'

Amber turned her back to him. 'I'm going outside.'

'Just one thing, and I promise I won't mention Will again.'

She wheeled around. 'That was shite of you.'

'Sorry about that,' he said. She was surprised to see he looked genuinely contrite for a moment. 'I know only too well when love hurts.'

'Oh, do you now?' She lifted her chin, challenging him to say more.

'Ah, here, let's both calm down. I need to ask you something.'

'Like what?'

'Have you seen any paintings stashed away?' he asked. 'Originals. In the style of a Monet, impressionist, oil on canvas?'

'No, what are you taking about?'

'Could be landscapes of Heronbrook. Or a portrait. If you saw them, you'd know. They're worth a few bob. It's rumoured that one of them was painted in this house but has never been seen out in the world. What's the betting it's still here, somewhere?'

'Is that what this visit is really about? And your talk of security alarms? What are you up to?'

Jamie looked as though he was at a loss for a moment. 'It's not what you think ...' He paused. 'Oh, forget it, it's no big deal.'

'Good,' she said, stalking out of the kitchen.

Jamie followed her outside, but only to say his goodbyes to Evie, telling her he might pop down again, now that he knew what a lovely welcome he'd get.

'Call ahead first,' Evie said. 'We could be out gallivanting now I'm on the mend.'

'I can do that once I have Amber's mobile number,' he said, grinning at her. 'You'll have to give it to me before you let me out through the gates. You've locked me in.'

Amber gave him her mobile number. She watched him drive out onto the lane and stood for a moment in the golden sunlight, relieved to be rid of his unsettling presence.

When she returned to the terrace, Evie smiled at her gently. 'I'm not sure which of us Jamie was trying to wind up the most,' she said in a warm voice. 'Hopefully we'll be out somewhere the next time he decides to call. I'm not going to be caught out like a sitting duck again, waiting for his verbal pellets.'

'Neither am I,' Amber said.

Jamie's mention of Will had thrown her into a tailspin. Her days in Heronbrook had enclosed her in a sort of bubble, like a protective bandage covering a wound, but she'd known the ache was there underneath, waiting to be tackled as soon as she had the energy. Jamie had got it wrong, though. It wasn't love that had hurt: it was her pride, her self-respect, her reputation that was badly injured.

Things like this weren't supposed to happen to Amber Lennox.

And, she decided, Will Baker wasn't going to get away with it.

She felt a little more relaxed on the terrace that evening, sitting alongside Evie, who had her legs raised on a rattan storage pouffe. There was a residue of heat in the air after the day – unexpectedly warm for September – and Amber had switched on the twinkly lights that were wrapped round the balustrade and threaded through the potted shrubs. Both of them read until the sun sank low in the sky and shadows began to descend. A light drizzle began to fall.

'I don't feel like going in just yet,' Evie said. 'I'm far too comfy here. And there's something about the air this evening that's just beautiful.'

'There is,' Amber said. 'I'll put up the canopy.' She got up and pressed the lever so that it slid out to cover the terrace before it locked into position. The scent of freshly dampened foliage rose into the air. A veil of misty rain floated across from the east, silhouetted against the autumnal trees like spidery lace, shimmering like rainbows where it caught the last of the slanting sunlight. Something stilled inside Amber, shutting off her internal critical chatter. In a moment of gentle awareness, she had the sense that colourful, textured life was expanding in front of her, and it was far more immense than the tight dark box she'd consigned it to. A tiny prism of hope rose inside her.

'Can I talk to you about me and the stupid mistake I made?' she said. 'I can't tell my parents, I don't know how to, but I need to get it out somehow.'

'Of course, my dear, but—'

'I'm not looking for advice. I just feel that, here, it's safe for me to take it out of my head, and it might help me to clear my thoughts and figure out a couple of things.'

Like why her, and what had she ever done to Will Baker? She would find him. And then she would ask him.

'I've always felt the same about Heronbrook,' Evie said. 'Even though we had a terrible … event, ultimately it's a good place, soothing for the spirit.' Evie smiled at Amber. 'Rest assured, whatever you want to say will stay here.' She nodded at the wine. 'Would you like to open another bottle?'

'Actually, no,' Amber said, wanting a clear head for this conversation. 'I'd rather have some water.'

'I'll have some too,' Evie said.

Amber went into the kitchen, returning with two glasses and a jug of water, glinting with ice cubes and slices of orange. Then when she was settled, she told Evie about Will, right from the morning she'd first met him in the foyer in Russell Hall up to the last time she'd seen him, the Wednesday evening just before everything came crashing down.

She'd gone out to Dundrum that Wednesday afternoon to work remotely. She was busy gathering together all the submissions for the big tendering project she was working on, preparing an initial report, telling Will there could be no sex until she had a certain amount of work completed. He'd waited patiently and had been unexpectedly tender, insisting she had long soak while he made a start on the evening meal. He'd even drawn her a geranium-scented bath, lighting a matching scented candle, and had a pile of freshly laundered bath sheets ready and waiting. Later that night, when her taxi arrived to take her home to Laurel Lawns, he'd kissed her lingeringly, sending her off feeling wrapped in a warm glow.

She'd clutched at that feeling the following morning when Fionn stopped by her desk and told her he'd got the job he'd interviewed for.

'Your days in Healy's are numbered,' she'd said, forcing a smile.

'They are. And I'm heading off on holidays first thing in the morning.'

She'd forgotten. 'Remind me again where you're off to?'

'Two weeks in Greece – early morning flight to Athens, then a boat to an island.'

'With Sadie, I guess.' Amber had been surprised at how sour she'd felt.

'I'll only have a week left here after that.'

Amber blinked, bringing herself back to the peace of the drizzly rain falling gently on the garden at Heronbrook, the scent of lavender in the twilight, soft shadows caused by the garden lights.

'I was delighted for Fionn,' she told Evie, 'but I knew I'd miss him from Healy's. On Friday morning, I texted Will about lunch, but I wasn't worried when he didn't reply. He'd told me he'd be very busy with a work thing. Then when I got back to the office after lunch—' Amber had to take a deep breath to steady herself as the memory of it exploded painfully inside her. 'I was only sitting down five or ten minutes when two guys from business security walked straight up to me. They asked me to move aside. Then they picked up my laptop and my mobile phone and took them away.'

She poured more water into her glass, gulping it so fast that an ice cube slid into her throat. She glanced at Evie, whose face was wreathed in concern.

'What exactly did that mean, Amber?' she asked gently.

Amber pulled her velour throw closer around her shoulders, burrowing into it before continuing. 'I didn't know in the beginning – I thought someone was playing a prank ... I was looking around at everyone, ready to laugh. The whole floor was distracted by what had happened, then gradually phones began to ring, monitors blinked, people turned back to their desks. Back to the normality of their lives. I had the unnerving feeling that they were distancing themselves from me,' Amber said, her voice catching a little. 'Even Nicole and Kim, friends of mine, were staring at their screens as though they held the secrets of the universe. Then I was called to the CEO's office, where my line manager was sitting along with three or four department heads.' Amber took another deep breath and tried to stop her teeth from chattering. 'And that's where everything went really mad.'

'Take your time,' Evie said.

'My line manager was white-faced,' Amber said. 'He sat hugging himself. I thought someone had died. Everyone looked in a state of shock. The chief accountant was pacing around, yelling orders into her phone. The CEO—' Amber gulped. She'd always had a positive, mentor-like relationship with Margaret McEvoy. 'She was staring at me as though I was some kind of alien monster, in between firing questions at the legal guy, and that killed me. The legal guy was tapping furiously on his laptop, throwing me filthy looks.'

'Oh my goodness,' Evie interjected.

'Long story short,' Amber said, her voice shaking, 'it turned out the confidential report I was preparing on the submissions for Healy's request-for-tender had been released on a circulation list to each of the competing bidders. The report included each bidder's full proposals and fees, as well as critical details relating to their business, all highly classified and sensitive information that Healy's were obliged to keep strictly private. Not only that,' Amber went on, looking directly at her great-aunt, 'but it went out under my email address. Healy's had been alerted just after lunch.'

Evie's jaw dropped, and her hand flew to her throat. 'No. Good God, no, Amber!'

'The CEO asked me if I understood the enormity of the damage I had done,' Amber said. 'What were my motives? What had possessed me? Had anyone put me up to this? Any rival firms? Did I realise how serious this was? That the bidders could take legal action against Healy's for lack of trust? That it hugely discredited the firm? I was asked to explain it all. I was blindsided. I couldn't think straight for a while.' She hung her head. 'And then I realised what must have happened.'

Evie reached across and patted her arm. 'Oh Amber, how desperate for you. What do you think went wrong?'

Amber lifted her head. 'There's only one person who would have had the opportunity to send that report through my email,' Amber said. 'Because I handed it to him on a plate. Will.'

'Will?'

'Yep. He must have accessed my report when I was in his apartment. It was the only time it could have happened. Foolishly, I didn't always lock my screen.' Her voice broke momentarily. 'It locks automatically after a few minutes,' she said, 'but he would have had time to copy stuff, and I'm sure all the times we sat together working, he must have been watching me inputting my email password.'

The memories scorched her brain … the times he'd coaxed her into the bedroom, leaving her there ready and waiting while he nipped back into the kitchen for wine or bubbly … or the condoms he'd put away in the kitchen cupboard instead of his bedside locker. The times he'd sent her into the shower and, just on Wednesday evening, insisting she had a bath. She was almost as outraged at herself for being so careless as she was at Will for engineering the whole thing.

'I tried to explain about Will and it was just excruciating.'

'Christ. Did they believe you?'

'I don't think so. I was stumbling over my words and my face was hot, they were checking things as I spoke and looking very dubiously at me. My line manager left the room and came back a few moments later, he could have been trying Will's office, but he just murmured something to the CEO, both of them staring at me as though I was some kind of disgusting slime.' Amber shook. 'It was the worst experience I've ever had in my life. A total nightmare. The upshot was that my contract was terminated immediately for grievous breach of protocol.'

'You have to be joking.'

'I wish I was. Word had gone around like wildfire. When I was escorted back to my desk, no one spoke to me. No one looked at me. I could hardly stand upright but I had to watch while they emptied my desk drawers and put the contents, along with my briefcase, into storage boxes for security to check along with my mobile phone. As it was, they went through my bag and took my security pass before seeing me down to the foyer and off the premises. Even Rob, the guy on reception, looked as though he couldn't believe his eyes. I kept waiting for someone to say they had made a mistake. I kept thinking that if I pinched myself, I'd be back out having Friday lunch with colleagues and none of this madness would have taken place. When I landed outside on Baggot Street, I thought I was in some kind of mad parallel universe.'

'That was terribly cruel, Amber,' Evie said. 'A dreadful thing to happen. Do you think you were the target, or was it directed at Healy's and you just happened to be the fall guy?'

Amber bit her lip, glad that Evie, while genuinely concerned, wasn't blinded by an excess of outraged emotion the way her well-meaning mother might have been. 'That's exactly what I need to figure out. If it was the firm Will wanted to discredit, using the tendering request, it would have been easy enough to find out I was involved in that by asking around the office gang over a few drinks. If it had been me he was after for some reason,

I'm sure accessing any of my work files would have done the trick – anything to do with financials in the context of a building conglomerate is bound to be sensitive. But why me?'

'Can you think of any reason why he would want to target you personally?' Evie asked gently.

'Not a thing,' Amber said. 'So I can only guess that Healy's was the target.'

'And does that make it a little less upsetting if it wasn't about you?'

'It makes me furious, and my stupidity makes it humiliating and soul destroying. Not securing your work is a mortal sin in my job. Any job, come to think of it. My reputation is fucked, pardon my French, never mind my self-esteem being on the floor. In the first few days after I was fired, I felt so – so horribly dark.'

'I'm not surprised. It must have been a dreadful shock. When your life is upended in the way yours was, it takes time to absorb the blow. You have to be gentle with yourself.'

'Being here with you, helps. My social media blackout was an absolute necessity. Mum doesn't know what's going on, or Dad, beyond they're not to give out my new mobile number to anyone. They have to know something major is up, and I'm sure they're worried sick, but fair dues to them, at least they're giving me space. Or else' – she laughed mirthlessly – 'they're afraid to ask.'

'I'm sorry that you've had such a distressing

experience, Amber,' Evie said. 'I don't know how to make things better other than to say you're welcome to stay here as long as you want. Even after I've recovered, don't feel you have to go home. Don't feel you have to face anything just yet. Take all the time you need. Have you been in touch with Will since? Or he with you?'

Amber bit her lip. 'So, yeah, that's the thing … Will seems to have vanished, disappeared off the face of the earth.'

Evie fixed the cushion behind her back. The drizzle had stopped, the breeze riffled gently through the trees, and the sky above was deepening to indigo. Soon the stars would come out, twinkling in the heavens. All was calm and tranquil except for the disturbing story Amber had just shared.

'Will vanished?' she said. 'I didn't think that was possible nowadays with social media and Mr Google.' She kept her voice even. No need to let Amber know how shaken she felt at the lengths someone had gone to to ruin her career. She was glad her grand-niece had felt able to unburden herself. She liked to think Heronbrook and its surrounds was a place of sanctuary. She was also gratified that Amber felt she could trust her with the truth.

She was good for something.

'I haven't seen Will or been able to contact him since that Wednesday evening,' Amber said, pausing to take a gulp of water. 'His number was on my confiscated mobile, which included all my contacts. I'm not like Mum with her address book going back centuries and updated regularly. When it happened, I was far too shocked and humiliated to hang around near the building to see if Will appeared. I drifted downtown. Everywhere had that Friday-afternoon feeling and it sickened me. I was coming up to St Stephen's Green shopping centre when I bumped into Jamie. I invited him home with me but as soon as I got home, I parked him with a beer and took the landline up into my bedroom. I rang Russell Hall reception and asked Rob to put me through to Will's office, and this is where it went crazy.' Amber paused.

'How so?' Evie asked.

'"Will who?" Rob said to me.' Amber stared blankly ahead. 'They were his exact words. "Will who?" It was like – God, I got such a pain inside. Things went from bad to worse as I spoke to Rob about Will Baker, the guy I was fully convinced was a new tenant on the fourth floor. You see, Evie,' Amber looked at her, her beautiful eyes clouded with a hurt that wrenched her heart, 'it turned out there was no Will Baker setting up his business on the fourth floor. Or on any floor in Russell Hall. No one of that name occupying anything in the building, not even a shoe cupboard.'

'But that's—'

'Yeah. Mad. When I thought about it, I'd never been up to the fourth floor – I'd suggested it once but Will had said he was busy. I met him a couple of times in the foyer for lunch, but on the way back afterwards, he made excuses not to come into the building – a meeting elsewhere, dry cleaning to collect. Otherwise I met him for drinks or dinner at a venue, everything arranged by text. The afternoons I went out to his apartment, he had his car already waiting out front of the building, for my convenience, he'd said, but obviously he hadn't got access to the Russell Hall car park.'

'The prick!'

'I checked Will's LinkedIn profile page, but that was gone. No profile. Nothing. And no sign of the Will Baker I knew anywhere online … I drove out to his apartment in Dundrum on Saturday morning. I had to tailgate someone to get into the building, but although I waited at his door for ages, there was no sign of life in Will's apartment. I went back out on Sunday and Monday – same thing. I called the reception at Russell Hall again but Rob said there had been no sign of the guy I'd been asking about. I knew for definite then that Will had set up some kind of trap and I'd fallen right into it.'

'And he had done a runner.'

'Renting a Dundrum apartment for the guts of four weeks at least wouldn't have come cheap. It made me wonder if he'd been hired by a rival firm with money to burn to destroy Healy's reputation. I don't think' – she gave a little half-laugh – 'the derailing of my career is worth that much to anyone.'

'So are you going to pursue him any further?'

'Absolutely. He's not getting away with this. There has to be a trail somewhere. Maybe the management company in charge of the apartment has his personal details, unless he conned them too.'

'He might own it himself and is just lying low at the moment.'

'Possibly. It was barely furnished, apart from the bedroom. I found that surprising but he said his stuff was being freighted from Rome. He had it all covered.' Amber dropped her head into her hands. 'I've been such a fool.'

'You're not a fool,' Evie said gently. 'From what I see, you're a kind and warm-hearted woman who happened to cross paths with a calculating and devious man. I know I said I'd never dream of giving you advice, but I've changed my mind – as is the prerogative of a person of advanced years. Well, any age, come to think of it.' She paused.

Amber waited.

'You made a mistake in not securing your work,' Evie said. 'It had unfortunate consequences for Healy's, but for your part, that's all it was, a mistake, an error of judgement. Show me the person who claims to have never made one, and I'll show you a liar. What happened was regrettable, but not bad enough to ruin your life. Will was the monster, not you, setting out on purpose to harm you and Healy's. How were you supposed to know?'

'Looking back, there were times …' Amber hesitated. 'I remember, in the bedroom, the set-up and the way he acted seemed almost a little staged.'

'He must have been very cunning and cold-hearted to have planned all that. How were you supposed to recognise that maliciousness when you haven't a devious bone in your body? You were the trusting one, having a bit of fun, like most people your age. What big sin is that? No harm in enjoying some good sex.'

Amber smiled faintly.

'I suggest you go back over everything, if it's

not too painful. Will is bound to have slipped up somewhere, dropped a clue, maybe, as to where he came from or what his intentions were. Maybe if you wrote an account of it all, something might strike you as odd. It would also be a useful document to have for any further discussions with Healy's.'

'Good idea,' Amber said. 'They said I'd be hearing from them in due course.'

'But no matter what happened, Amber, you have a choice. You can keep on going over and over it in your mind, painting yourself blacker and blacker, worrying at it, like ploughing the same old ditch, making it deeper and darker. Or' – Evie strove to inject a positive tone into her voice – 'you can say OK, I made a mistake, but I'm not going to let it wreck what's true and good about my life, or ruin my future happiness.'

'Are you speaking from experience?' Amber said.

'From bitter experience,' Evie admitted. 'I was … caught in a situation, different circumstances to yours, but I let it define the rest of my life. I was deeply in love … at the time it was as if we were the only ones who existed in our world, so wrapped up in each other that we didn't pay heed to what was going on around us. Then I made a dreadful mistake. After that, I turned my back on happiness and the person I loved more than life itself.'

'Oh dear.' Amber shook her head.

'So I don't want to see you beating yourself up about this once-off error of judgement. Don't let it tarnish the rest of your life,' Evie said. 'I wish I had been kinder to myself and kinder to other people too. I wish I had been able to move beyond my mistake. By the time I gave myself permission to, it was too late. I denied myself and another person the love we should have shared because I was too hard on myself.'

Although she was trying to rescue Amber, Evie found it cathartic to voice what had been festering in her heart for so long. The spoken words released something inside her. They swirled away from her, drifting gently like the autumn leaves that slipped off the trees and flowed like copper discs in the brook.

Early on Thursday morning, Amber felt renewed as she headed along the track through rain-laced woods, inhaling the sweet, earthy scents, crossing the stone bridge over the brook, then down to where the woods thinned out and she met the laneway to the beach and the salty sea breeze.

She took off her trainers and socks and ran along the damp strand. There were few people about, dog-walkers, runners like herself, strollers, all silhouetted against the metallic grey of the silver-tipped sea and soft-grey humps of clouds. By the time she came back to Heronbrook, the day had brightened, sunlight filtering through golden, russet trees, running in long fingers across the terrace and gleaming on the purple spikes of lavender. Soaking it up, she felt an urge deep in her heart like faint music she couldn't yet fathom. She didn't know what lay ahead for her, but she knew there would be life after Healy's. And after Will.

Later, in the evening, while Evie was resting in her room, Amber finally downloaded apps to her phone to connect with her email and social media. Time to get back into the world. Taking a deep breath, she logged into her personal email account, steeling herself as she opened it. She ignored the promotional and social in-boxes, going straight to her primary account.

Nothing whatsoever from the Healy Group or any of her office colleagues.

Nothing from Will.

She scrolled through the list of unread messages, spotting emails from her college friends Megan and Julie, checking in with her because she hadn't been active on social media in a while and she hadn't responded to their texts – which she hadn't received, as her iPhone was still commandeered by Healy's.

And most recently, two emails from Fionn. The first one, sent earlier that week, expressing outrage. That she hadn't bothered to contact him. That she hadn't trusted him enough to tell him what had happened. That she'd let him find out in the crappiest way possible when he'd wondered why her desk was empty on his first day back in the office after his hols. How *dare* she treat him like this? Thankfully it was his last week there. That if she had wanted to make a major fuck-up of her career, he had to hand her the platinum award for outstanding excellence in the field. That was a joke. *Of course* he knew a mistake had been made. But. Why. Hadn't. She. Told. Him?

The second email, sent yesterday, full of apologies for his rant. Could she please get in touch with him? Otherwise he'd have to call in person to Laurel Lawns looking for her to set his mind at rest.

Her heart flooded with relief. He still had her back. Maybe Kim and the rest of her lunch-break gang were ignoring her, but not Fionn. She got up and boiled the kettle, making a cup of tea, grabbing a biscuit, and bringing them back to the table. Without thinking about it too much, she sent off a quick email to say she was alive and well and spending some time looking after her great-aunt, but away from everything digital for a while. She sent the same reply to her friends. She was touched when Fionn responded almost immediately, telling her not to stay away for too long or he would come looking for her so he could give her a real life hug, that whatever had happened, he was most definitely on her side, and she was to give him a shout anytime she wanted to talk.

Give him a shout ... wanted to talk ... in spite of herself, Amber found herself smiling at this mixed message, along with the row of smiley faces and a virtual hug gif. She responded by giving him her mobile number, telling him where she was staying.

She then googled the *Wicklow Weekly* newspaper, and she sent an email requesting a copy of the supplement edition covering the May fundraising event, saying she could call into their offices to collect it. Maybe the photo of her mother with Evie and Barry might jog her mother's memory of the man she claimed not to know. The man whom Evie seemed to think knew everything that was going on in their neighbourhood, with whom she shared old 'water under the bridge'.

Taking a deep breath, she put Will's name into her browser: Will Baker. William Baker. Will Baker, Rome. Nothing came up to match her Will. She searched property company websites for apartments to rent in Dundrum to see if his was listed now that he had apparently vacated it, but she drew a blank there also.

Write everything down, Evie had said. Something might strike her as odd.

She looked around the living room to see where she might find some paper – a spare notebook, perhaps. Even some blank A4 paper that Evie might have for her printer. Evie had offered to open an account for her on her laptop, and she would take her up on that, but for now paper and pen would do to marshal her initial thoughts.

Evie's laptop was on a shelf on top of her DVD player. Her compact printer was beside that, and underneath were shelves holding linen-look storage containers. She slid out a couple of them. One was full of lever arch files labelled accounts and tax returns; another held plastic folders of paperwork and old magazines. Amber pulled out a third storage container. It was much lighter than the others and, whatever way she pulled it, it came out of the cubbyhole completely, toppling onto the floor so that something enfolded in layers of bubble wrap and tissue paper fell out, most of its protective covering becoming dislodged. Her scalp prickling, she picked it up and eased off the remaining covering.

It was a painting, and it glowed. About A4 size, it was a framed watercolour impression of a young woman lying sideways across a bed. The colours shimmered like soft jewels. The woman's porcelain face was luminous, the light of love shining out of her eyes, her cheekbones a delicate shade of rose. Her mouth was slightly open, as if in an intake of surprised breath, lips pink and dewy, then the lines of her body curved down past generous breasts and a small belly, and flowed to dark shadows between her thighs. One hand was thrown up above her head and rested on the pillow; the other held onto a rumpled sheet covering her legs. Her long blonde hair was swept across the pillow, tendrils framing her face.

Amber's breath caught in her throat.

'Ah. I see you've found it.'

She wheeled around; Evie was standing in the doorway, supported by her crutches. Amber's heart squeezed in agitation. Then she didn't care that she'd been caught snooping. This find was far too significant and explained so much that she wasn't concerned about Evie's possible displeasure. Not that her great-aunt looked displeased. Her whole stance was one of resignation.

'Is this what I think it is?' Amber said, her senses swimming with an innate knowledge, her eyes flying to the inscription on the bottom.

'It's a Lucien Burke,' Evie said, manoeuvring herself into the room.

'Yes, that's what the inscription says. It's incredibly beautiful. It looks like …' Amber paused.

'What does it look like?'

'This woman looks like she's just had the most amazing sex.'

'Yes, you're right. She just had.'

'But—?' Amber was puzzled.

'But what?'

'How come …?' Amber's gaze rose to Evie's face. 'This is you, isn't it?'

'Yes. Once upon a time.'

'How come … When *was* this?'

'We met years ago, as teenagers, right here when we came on holidays. We became lovers when I was eighteen.'

'So that time when you said you loved someone more than life itself, it was Lucien you were talking about?' Amber said, a catch in her chest.

Evie sighed. 'It's a long story; it started when I was fifteen, the first summer we came to Heronbrook …'

They sat at the table and Amber listened, totally absorbed in Evie's words as she opened up to her about the summers when she had been fifteen, sixteen, seventeen, and her developing love story with Lucien.

'Gosh. I don't know what to say,' Amber said eventually, her head whirling with the images Evie had conjured up.

'Lucien and I thought we were invincible,' Evie said, staring at the jug of wildflowers on the table as though she was seeing something else. 'Then one terrible afternoon, back in 1964, there was a tragedy of sorts, and there were desperate consequences in the years ahead. But, Amber' – she looked at her with a soft expression in her eyes – 'if you make some fresh coffee, I'll tell you about that also. At the very least it might stop you from making the same mistakes I did.'

Evie, 1964

Afterwards, the terrible afternoon that splintered our lives lived on in my memory like a series of disjointed images. The afternoon that divided my life into the 'before' and the 'after', the bedrock of that life shearing apart as easily as damp tissue paper.

There had been no sign that an ugly fate was awaiting us in the quiet of Heronbrook, although the factors that came together and resulted in a meltdown had been simmering under the surface for quite a while, hidden in plain sight. Hidden in the way Pippa had begun to begrudge the years I had up on her.

I was revelling in the summer, but fourteen years of age was a dull watershed for her: the excitement of reaching her teenage years and starting secondary education already in the past; the future of permissible romance and alcohol still seeming a long way away, when every year seemed to take a decade. At eighteen, I had a lot more freedom, as well as Lucien.

It was unexpectedly warm that afternoon, all the windows in Heronbrook opened to allow the air to circulate, the doors in the living area opened onto the terrace, where we had breakfast that morning. My mother was going up to Dublin – an electrician was coming into Drumcondra to do some rewiring, and she was going to her hairdresser to have her perm done. She'd be gone all day. Pippa would be spending her day down by the beach with Rachel Casey and her family and the usual gang. Heronbrook would be free. I felt full to the brim of dazzling sunshine, and an inner glow because Lucien was coming over that afternoon.

'I'm going to paint you in the nude,' Lucien had said the night before, when I'd told him we'd have the house to ourselves for a few hours. Every cell in my body tingled in anticipation.

Pippa guessed something was up. It must have been written across my face. If only I had been less transparent, our lives would have taken a different course entirely.

'It's not fair,' she said to me before she left for Rachel and the beach.

It had been her constant refrain over the years, but more so that summer.

'What's not fair?' I asked.

She stuck out her bottom lip, the petulant expression I'd come to know so well settling on her face. 'You, here, with Lucien,' she said.

When she'd suspected I was sleeping with Lucien, she'd told me she hoped I'd get pregnant, that it would serve me right. But I never told her that Lucien was taking care of that; a friend of his had a brother who regularly brought condoms down from Belfast and sold them at a profit. I wasn't so stupid as to allow myself to get caught out, not when I had so many dreams to fulfil. Right then, at that moment, I was full of mild exasperation for a sister who wouldn't leave me in peace.

'Don't be so stupid.' I tossed my head, trying to appear nonchalant and hide the excitement in my eyes.

'I'm not being stupid, I know what you're up to. I'll be stuck on the beach with Rachel, minding her whiny little sister and brother. What fun is that? *And* in your cast-off swimming costume that doesn't even fit me properly.'

She had a point. Although the pink swimming costume she was talking about had hardly been used, Pippa was a late developer, her barely-there bust a huge disappointment to her, compared to the curvy, generous proportions I'd been endowed with by her age.

'I wore lots of hand-me-downs as well,' I reminded her. Rig-outs that had come my way over the years courtesy of my older cousin Myra. My parents preferred to spend money on our education and culture rather than new wardrobes.

'So, yeah, so mine are third hand.'

It was a disgruntled Pippa who went off to meet Rachel.

And an Evie who felt as though fireworks were exploding inside her when she opened the door to Lucien.

In the hallway, I threw my arms around him and I pressed my body against his. I locked my bedroom

door in case Pippa came home early from the beach
and pulled the curtains closed so that light drizzled
through, bathing us in a silvery glow.

'I want you to remember this,' he said, when we
were lying on the bed and he was deep inside me. 'I
want to see it in your face when I paint you.'

I tightened my insides around him and watched
the haze of desire softening his eyes, smiling at
him as I moved beneath him. Afterwards, he sat
with his sketchpad and I held a pose on the bed,
the coverlet arranged low about my hips. Lucien
had brought his radio and he switched it on so that
I could listen to some music while he worked. He
looked up from his pad every so often to examine
my body, and the concentration in his narrowed
eyes had the effect on me of a laser beam. I felt
voluptuous and seductive and full to the brim with
womanly powers. Oh God, how much I took it all
for granted – the sheen of our youth, the vigour
of it, that we would always be this strong and
invincible, and the blind, juvenile confidence that
we could have whatever kind of life we wanted
with a click of our fingers.

'Stranger on the Shore' was playing softly on the
radio when the knock on my bedroom door startled
me.

'I know you're in there,' Pippa said. 'With Lucien.'
Then after a short pause, 'Doing dirty things.'

'Go away,' I said, instinctively drawing up the
coverlet, even though I knew she couldn't see me
through the keyhole.

'I'm going back down to the beach. Rachel and I are going for a long walk.'

I leaned across and increased the volume on the radio.

Pippa's voice came again, high pitched, fast, talking about Rachel and her baby sister Leah, her words barely audible against the music and interspersed with smothered high-pitched giggles. The last of her words were garbled and, finally, there was the sound of her footsteps on the terrace outside, then silence.

But the mood was broken.

'She's a little brat, my sister,' I said crossly, sitting up in bed.

'Relax, she's gone.'

'I'm going to kill her when I see her.'

'No. You're going to lie back now and let me finish.'

'I'm not in the mood.'

'Aren't you?' He grinned at me and lunged forward, and I squealed when he wrenched the coverlet off me and kissed me hard. He got back onto the bed and I threw myself backwards, loving the feel of our skins sliding together and the hot, sweet thrust of his body. I turned my bad mood with my sister into an energy with which I loved him, coiling my legs around his hips. Afterwards I lay back, replete, and he got off the bed and took up his pencil again.

'Now,' he said. 'Stay exactly as you are.'

It must have been almost an hour later when

I got up, threw on a dressing gown, and opened the door to go out to the bathroom. An hour later when I opened the door to the catastrophe beyond. The first thing I saw was an empty pushchair, placed right outside my bedroom door. I tried to move it, but I had to release the brake first. Pippa playing childish tricks on me, I decided grumpily.

I was coming out of the bathroom when Pippa came bursting through the house, her face twisted, blotchy and ugly, tears pouring down her cheeks. She jumped on me, attacking me with her flailing fists, hitting my chest, my face, my arms.

'She could be dead and it's all *your* fault.' She wept uncontrollably, hitting me wherever she could.

Something icy cold trickled down my back.

'What are you talking about?'

'Leah,' Pippa gulped, her eyes red, her mouth contorted as she continued to cry.

'What happened to Leah?'

'I left her here, I *told* you,' Pippa cried. 'She was asleep. In her pushchair. Then she woke up and went to the beach and … and … and now she could be *dead*. It's *your* fault for not minding her.'

The icy-cold feeling reached up into the back of my neck. I didn't understand what Pippa was saying, and I grasped at the images her words were making: Leah asleep in the pushchair, the sound of muffled laughter outside my bedroom door, me increasing the volume on the radio, Pippa's words lost in the sound of laughter and music.

'You left her *here*?' I said, trying to make sense of it all.

'Yes, I *told* you.'

I looked at the empty pushchair, pushed to one side in the hallway, the pink straps in a muddle in the seat. I felt the edges of a nightmare biting at me.

'What are you saying?' I asked, trying to stave it off, this black thing that was becoming more monstrous with every word of Pippa's.

Lucien came out of the bedroom. He had dressed hurriedly, his jeans fastened with the zip undone, his T-shirt thrown on inside out. I met his eyes. Saw what was in them. Knew he had heard Pippa's words and joined them up to make sense before I could grasp the horrendous reality. Knew by the shock on his face that our perfect idyll was over.

◆

It all came out later that day, my mother arriving back in a whirlwind of anxiety, with her tight new perm and new crimplene dress, having heard talk when she'd stopped off in the shop in Glenmaragh about the ambulance and the Casey girl. My father summoned from Dublin, both of them talking to me and Pippa, separately, getting our sides of the story. My parents beside themselves with shock and heartbreak; the muttered aside from my mother, *We'll talk about Lucien later*, her deep disappointment in me running under the immediacy of her concern for Leah and the Caseys.

Earlier that afternoon, Maureen Casey had had to bring her six-year-old son Matthew to the hospital, after he'd stepped on broken glass and gashed his foot, leaving three-year-old Leah in the care of Rachel. When Leah fell asleep in her pushchair, Pippa said she had persuaded Rachel that it would be a great prank to leave her with me—

A prank?

After all, said Pippa's pouty face, I was the one lounging around at home with nothing much to do, except have lots of intercourse with Lucien, thinking I was great – it would do me good and serve me right to see what it was like to have to care for a small child, and they wanted to go to the far end of the beach where Barry Talbot and his mates were hanging out, without being dragged down by a small child.

My father was unable to talk to me or meet my eyes. That killed something else inside me. My mother had lots to say, all of it delivered in a tone of sad bewilderment that I had never incited in her before.

'Didn't you think to check on the child, even once?'

'I didn't know she was there.'

'But Pippa told you.'

'I didn't hear her telling me that.'

'Why not?'

Pippa, all blustering indignation as she neatly

deflected responsibility: 'I did *so* tell you. I was sure Leah would wake up after a while and start to cry, that she'd disturb you, and you'd have to mind her. How was I supposed to know that she could slide her reins down her arms and climb out? If you'd been minding her properly, it wouldn't have happened.'

Then all the maybes and if onlys ...

If only the back door hadn't been left open on account of the heat, with enough of a gap for a three-year-old to get through.

Maybe if little Leah hadn't already been to Heronbrook with Rachel a few times, so she knew how to get to the beach ... Maybe if she hadn't had the determination to tag along with the parade of bucket-and-spade-and-lilo-wielding families who were coming out from the mobile-home park for the afternoon session on the beach.

If only the beach hadn't been so crowded that afternoon that no one noticed an unaccompanied toddler making her way to the sea, through hordes of children and parents and barking dogs splashing in the shallows, sending up spray after spray, and swimming rings and buckets of water for moated castles, until one mother noticed a small child face down in the water, and screamed, and wrenched her up, racing with her up the sand dunes to the nearest bungalow to phone for an ambulance, two red setters bounding alongside her as though it was a game.

Leah Casey hadn't died, but she'd been deprived of oxygen long enough to sustain damage to her brain and cognitive functions, which would stay with her throughout the rest of her life. The Caseys blamed Rachel – after all, she was her sister and she'd been careless with her.

My parents blamed me and Pippa; I being the elder, and an adult, and therefore the more responsible one, carrying the larger proportion.

And whatever Lucien and I had shared was indelibly tarnished.

Evie, 1970

In 1970, six years after that last holiday in Heronbrook, my parents decided that, with the dawning of a new decade, enough time had gone by to make it OK for our family to go on holiday together again. They decided to join the new band of Irish tourists heading for the sunshine and beaches of Majorca, on holidays that had become packaged, affordable, and popular in recent years. My mother told me of the plans on a cold evening in early February. I was standing at a payphone in the draughty hall of a London house in Clapham, where I had a tiny bedsit with a shared bathroom on the third floor.

'I hope you'll join us,' my mother said. 'I'll write to you with full details and, if it suits, you can go to a travel agent and book the same hotel. We're going for two weeks in early September, and if you could join us for even one week, it would be great. Your father has said he'll pay.'

'There's no need for that. I do have some income.'

'Your father wants to do it. He wants us to have one more holiday together, as a family. It could be our last chance before you and Pippa have friends or families of your own to head off with.'

I got it. My father was making an attempt to

paper over the cracks of Heronbrook and transfer a fresh new holiday into the family memory bank in the hope it might obliterate the one that had left a dark shadow. I was twenty-four by then and Pippa was twenty. I didn't bother telling my mother I had few friends to go holidaying with and I'd already decided I was never having a family. My self-punishment for helping to cause little Leah Casey's accident. That I had done so unwittingly was no consolation.

'Is Pippa coming too?' We'd never been close, but an arctic coolness had hardened between us after the terrible afternoon at Heronbrook, neither of us willing to rise above it.

'Yes, of course.'

I stared down at the peeled linoleum floor of the hallway where the faint scent of stewed vegetables hung in the air and the sound of canned laughter came in staccato bursts from the television in the ground-floor flat. The hall door was flung open and Sasha from the second floor burst in, wearing an oversized, purple, faux-fur coat open over a white leather miniskirt, bringing in a blast of cold air along with her boyfriend, both of them reeking of a joint as they passed by. Almost three hundred miles and an eternity from the peace of the woods, and the music of the brook, and Lucien's love. I wondered if it was time to follow my parents' example and put things behind me so that we could act like a normal family once again. At that time, I was playing a supporting role but also doing understudy for a main role in *Gwendoline's Fan*, a Regency comedy running in the Cameron, a small theatre in the West End. It was coming to the end of its run in August so the timing seemed fortuitous.

I knew I'd join them. Even for a week. It would satisfy my parents, break some of the ice with Pippa, and help dilute the anticlimax that I'd realised can hit when a play comes to the end of its run, which is one of the scariest places to be if there is no work on the immediate horizon. This was living the dream, I reminded myself. Although a lot of the time, moving around London, going to and from the theatre, out to after-parties, or shopping on Oxford Street, I felt I was acting a part both on- and off-stage.

Then in May, Verena, the actor I was understudying, suddenly quit for personal reasons – in other words she fell pregnant – and I was offered her role in *Gwendoline's Fan*. I decided that fate was smiling benignly on our family at last. This was my chance to glitter and shine. If I gave it my best shot, my career could finally take off. Judi Dench, Francesca Annis, and Glenda Jackson were the rising stars of the day and I wanted to be among them.

Two days after I'd taken over the role, Lucien phoned me. Granny Kate had died.

◆

We hadn't been there much for each other in the years after Heronbrook. The part we'd played in

Leah Casey's accident had driven a wedge between us, neither of us able to find a way through the thick wall of remorse, humiliating embarrassment, and self-flagellation in which we were held fast. I couldn't think about what we'd been doing that afternoon, any more than Lucien, without remembering how we'd been cavorting across the bed, luxuriating in each other's body, while little Leah had slipped out of her reins and toddled out through the terrace doors and down to the sea. Lucien had said after that day that he'd never pick up a pencil again or indulge in such a frivolous hobby. I'd told him not to be so ridiculous. His art was as important as breathing to him, and he had a right to breathe.

I had started commercial college the September after the accident, which slightly assuaged the chill between me and my parents, learning typing, shorthand, good etiquette, and table manners, being steered towards a secretarial job. I was expected to be grateful for this job until such time as I found a man (Lucien being deemed totally unsuitable after the sinful way we'd behaved), giving up my job on marriage and settling down to funnel my creative abilities into running a comfortable home and maintaining a well-fed and properly serviced husband. I had no intentions of going in that direction, but I couldn't see the way forward.

Lucien and I were at an impasse when we met in Dublin that Christmas for lunch in a café on

O'Connell Street. It was raining outside and the windows were fogged up with condensation, the damp air heavy with the smell of frying food. The Beatles were singing in the background, a jaunty tune about feeling fine, but both of us were anything but fine – awkward and ill at ease, the strain between us new and frightening. I'd had my long blonde hair restyled in a hairdresser's on St Stephen's Green; it was shorter and more mature. Watching the stylist slice into it with the scissors, I had imagined he was cutting away a chunk of my past. Lucien hadn't mentioned it.

'Are you painting?' I asked.

'No.'

'Why not?' Using my paper napkin, I swiped grains of sugar off the Formica table with more force than was necessary.

'I told you I'm finished with all that.' His voice was thick with irritation.

'Still?' Our gazes locked.

There was a silence.

'What a waste,' I said, angry with him for not picking up his pencils again, but most of all angry with what had happened that afternoon to cause him to abandon them, and furious with myself for unwittingly setting the train of events in motion.

If only I'd listened to Pippa.

'Don't attempt to understand,' he said.

'You're not even trying,' I said hotly. 'That's what I don't understand.'

'Evie—' His voice caught with emotion.

At the sound of it, the back of my head pounded with rage and disappointment at the sorry place we'd found ourselves. 'Well, if you won't chase your dreams, I'm determined to go after mine,' I snapped.

We parted on a bad note in the wet December afternoon. Even though I was heart sore watching him turn up the collar of his coat and walk away, the rain pelting his dark hair, I decided it was the least I deserved.

After the commercial course, I got a job in a solicitor's office on Parnell Square. I had kept in touch with Miss Hayes, my English teacher, whose brother worked in a Dublin theatre, and he gave me an intro into an amateur dramatic company. Determined to prove myself, Tuesday nights saw me descending a rickety staircase in Dorset Street, down to a draughty basement, with a mishmash of talented and not so talented wannabe actors and a director who thought he should be cutting it on Broadway. Still, after a few months of taking tuition and practising various roles, I secured a small part in a production of *Tolka Row*, the play that preceded the television series, which the company took to competition level the following spring, landing a commendable place in an amateur dramatics festival.

Over the next year I found myself being cast in better roles in the Dublin amateur dramatics circle. I was still barely talking to Lucien, and that stung me, but, fuelled with a hot-headed determination, and despite my lack of significant experience, I began to make plans for London in stubborn pursuit of my dreams. It was where it was all happening. My parents only allowed me to go when I found digs in a Catholic boarding house in Kilburn and a job doing filing and typing for a jewellery company. Miss Hayes and her brother gave me references and letters of introduction to a couple of London-based directors.

Even so, when it came time for me to go, in the spring of 1967, I felt torn in two. I had half-hoped that Lucien would come with me – the razzmatazz of London might not have been so conducive to his art, but a fresh start might have given him inspiration. At the same time, I mocked my fragile hopes. I didn't see how we could ever be together; Leah's accident would always come between us. He wished me well when I met him for lunch, this time in a grill room on Abbey Street. We were both subdued, thanks to the strain and discomfort of the previous three years, and my chicken tasted like rubber.

'You never know,' I said, testing him to see what he'd say, 'you might find a lovely girlfriend in your insurance company.'

'I'll be waiting for you,' he said.

I looked at his face, scanning the image onto my brain to take out and linger over in London. 'How can we be happy together after what happened?' I said, voicing the ceaseless words in my head. 'Besides, I'll be in London, and you'll be in Wicklow.'

'I can't leave Granny Kate, but I hope you'll come home from London and take Dublin by storm after you've gained more experience,' he said, pushing his teacup aside. 'Thing is, Evie' – he leaned across the table towards me – 'no matter how pitch black life can seem, time can heal, so I hope that we'll be able to find some way of being together.'

I guessed he was talking about his experience with losing his parents. 'We'll see,' I said unconvincingly, an overwhelming sense of loss sweeping over me. We didn't say goodbye. Or have a farewell kiss. Before we parted, at the corner of Abbey Street, he touched my face and I rested my cheek in the palm of his hand.

In London, I felt homesick and stripped of my skin in that strange, frantically busy, brightly lit city, with the constant phalanx of shoppers, the rushing underground, big black cabs, and red double-decker buses. It took me three years of sweeping the stage, making tea, organising costumes, speech and drama classes, walk-on parts, half a dozen lines in a bit part, and practising, practising, practising, until I finally landed that supporting role in *Gwendoline's Fan*. In the meantime, a tiny bedsit in Clapham and acres of freedom had replaced the Catholic boarding house, and I had given up the full-time office job in favour of a part-time job serving breakfasts in a Piccadilly hotel. Lucien and I kept in touch with occasional phone calls and less frequent letters. And now, into the maelstrom of our lives, came another loss: this time, Granny Kate.

♦

'It was a heart attack,' Lucien said on the phone. 'I came home from work and found her in her armchair.'

My stomach twisted at the image of Lucien finding his beloved granny like that. At the same time, my head grappled with the fact that even though I knew he was virtually alone in the world at this sad time, I couldn't go home.

'I'm terribly sorry to hear that,' I began.

'You're terribly sorry?'

'Yes, I'm sorry to hear Granny Kate has died, and I'm sorry, Lucien,' I softened my tone, 'but I can't be there with you.'

'You're not coming home for the funeral?' His voice rose. 'You're the only person I want, Evie.'

His words were a knife in my gut. Much as I wanted to be around to console him, I felt it wasn't right for me to be there. I still believed we had no future and that our love was tarnished, and the more I wallowed in that pain, the more I felt it was some sort of reparation for my neglect of Leah Casey.

As well as that, I had just been given my golden opportunity. How could I walk away from it? I clung to that as an excuse, rather than reminding Lucien right now of the cold, hard fact that we were finished.

'I feel really bad about this,' I said, 'but it's the worst possible time for me to leave London.' I explained about my starring role, the golden opportunity I couldn't afford to turn down, hoping there might be a glimmer of understanding from him, but I knew I was talking into a void.

I was with him in spirit the day of the funeral, imagining the proceedings in County Wicklow. When I was getting ready for the theatre, instead of immersing myself in the character of Gwendoline, I wondered how Lucien was coping now that Granny Kate had joined his parents in a graveyard on the side of a Wicklow hill. As the curtain came down that night, the applause seemed to come from far away, the upturned rows of faces in the auditorium blurry and indistinct. Instead of revelling in the post-performance high, I felt wretched, as though I was coming down with the flu. In the following weeks I wrote to Lucien, once, twice. I sent a Mass card. He never acknowledged anything. I phoned the house in Wicklow and the call rang out. I wrote again, explaining how busy I was in the theatre, asking if he could come over to London for a short visit, I really wanted to see him.

Then as the weeks went past, everything we'd been to each other swelled and burgeoned inside me, softening my hard remorse. I looked for him in the London streets, the shops, and the underground, hoping that by some miracle he might come to visit. I counted the weeks until the play was over, the applause every night making me feel empty instead of fulfilled. I knew then that realising my dreams meant nothing to me at all unless I had Lucien to share my life with.

My parents came over for a weekend, staying

in a hotel, coming to the show on the Saturday evening. While they were pleased with my achievement, their pride in me having been dented after Heronbrook, it was an empty victory. I didn't bring up the subject of Lucien or Granny Kate because that might have led to Wicklow and Heronbrook. Neither did I ask after Pippa. She had gone straight to work in ladies' fashions in a department store on Grafton Street. I had spoken to her briefly on the phone when I called home one evening and she had said, laughingly, that she was in great demand and far too busy to spare the time to come to London to see me on the stage.

Now, two months after Lucien's phone call, I decided that after the holiday with my parents, I would take a break from London and go home to see Lucien, talk to him, visit the grave with him, help him go through Granny Kate's things. Be a shoulder for him to cry on. Love him as much as I could. See if we had any future. Hope that maybe we had.

I didn't know then it was already too late.

Evie, 1970–1974

Majorca. My first holiday in the sun. I arrived the same Saturday evening as my parents, joining them for the first week of their holiday. Pippa wasn't coming out until the following Wednesday, so we would be sharing a room with twin beds for three nights. I didn't relish the thought of that, but I knew that it was the least I could do for my parents, to maintain some semblance of family unity.

The constant grip of the heat, the moment I stepped off the plane, thrust me into another world – permanently blue skies, the scent of suntan lotion, the spicy aroma of fried meals in the hotel restaurant, the nightly scents of blossoming flowers threaded through wrought-iron trellises, the warmth allowing us to sit outside in the evenings on spindly furniture and sip glasses of sangria and Bacardi and Cokes – my mother enjoying the novelty of it. But it was the love songs, floating out across the evening air, that seared my heart with thoughts of Lucien: The Beatles and 'Something'; the Carpenters, 'Close to You'; Simon and Garfunkel, 'Bridge Over Troubled Water'. I had heard them on my transistor radio back in my London bedsit, but here, mingling with evocative Spanish dancing, the click of castanets, and the romance of the evenings, they spoke to me with new meaning.

I would have this week with my parents and then go to him. I couldn't wait.

Late Wednesday evening, the hotel garden bathed in flickering lamplight, the sound of Procol Harum and 'A Whiter Shade of Pale' drifting in the air, I was sitting on the edge of my seat, knowing that Pippa's arrival was imminent and my relative peace would be disturbed. I saw her coming towards us, weaving through the flower-lined pathways. She was wearing a soft green maxi-dress, her dark hair loose around her shoulders. There was someone with her. A man. Tall. For a wild moment I thought it was Lucien, and my heart quickened. It was as if my ceaseless thoughts of him had finally summoned him up.

Then I knew. It *was* Lucien. Following Pippa across the twilight garden towards us. My mind was gripped with a thousand questions. Had he followed me here? Read my letters? How did he know I was missing him so much, especially here, where the air was tinged with love and romance? My heart crashed around as I half-rose to my feet.

And then ... and then I saw Pippa take his hand and pull him forward. Had she brought him to me? Had Pippa really done this huge favour for me? I grasped wildly at this, wanting it to be true, hoping against hope she had done this, but hope flickered when I saw the cold, hard reality of this moment sliding across her face. Her smile, cat like. Triumphant. Her arm, now linked through his, marking her territory for me to see. Lucien's failure to meet my eyes. His discomfiture as he looked at my parents. My mother and father, their puzzlement plain to see. My mother, throwing me a look of concern.

Then Pippa, wearing the biggest and cattiest smile I have ever seen on her face as she slid her hand down over her abdomen so that I saw the slight swell in her belly.

I got up and walked away, my legs wobbling, my hands clenched into fists. It was the only way I could to prevent myself from giving in to the tremendous urge I felt to punch my sister right in the middle of that smile, and right in the middle of her softly burgeoning belly.

'Wait! Evie, wait.'

Lucien's voice. He was coming after me. Pain sliced through me, my chest, my stomach, so that I almost doubled over. I ignored him. He caught up with me halfway across the garden. I felt his touch on my arm and a spasm shot through my body.

I whirled around. 'Don't touch me,' I said, my teeth gritted, the words forced through a throat that had become swollen with my bleeding heart lodged there.

'I'm sorry,' he said, his hands hanging uselessly at his side.

'Sorry?'

'I didn't know you'd be here. I didn't want you to find out like this. I was going to tell you myself ...'

'Is *that* what you're sorry for?'

'Yes – no, not just that. Oh, Evie … it was an accident, but she was … Pippa was … she was around when I had a bad time after my grandmother. She came to the funeral …'

'I wonder how she knew about that.' I stared at him, trying to absorb some of this black pain, knowing I hadn't yet fathomed the dark immensity of it.

'I hadn't seen her in a while. She was some kind of connection to you … We got talking … then she was upset when she found out she was—'

'Don't bother with the violins, I can just see it all,' I said, bile rising in my throat as I imagined them in bed together.

Pippa to the rescue. Pippa seizing her opportunity to comfort Lucien when Evie was out of the picture. Pippa there to bind him to her for all time, now that a baby was on the way. I knew Lucien would never turn his back on a child of his. Pippa would have known that too.

'Evie—' He put his hand on my arm.

I hit it away. 'Don't you dare. Don't you ever touch me again.' I summoned the best of my acting ability and stared at him, mustering as much hate in my eyes as I could manage. 'You're welcome to my sister. But don't talk to me ever again.'

He didn't. Not for a long time.

Pippa used the excuse of being almost five months pregnant to have a small, rushed wedding. According to my mother, my absence was neatly explained by the short notice of the ceremony and a few choice comments about the swift trajectory of my career on the London stage. My mother must have found it difficult to be torn between her warring daughters, never mind having us at such odds with each other, particularly when Pippa and Lucien's twins, Jessica and Simon, arrived and there was no adoring auntie around to complete the happy family picture. Not that my mother took sides.

The only thing that saved me at the time was her quiet solicitude. It poured out from her phone calls and letters. It was in the gentle way she tiptoed around me on her occasional visits to London, and my far less frequent trips back to Dublin – only when I was assured that Pippa wouldn't be around. She let me know as tactfully as possible that Lucien had sold Granny Kate's house and used the proceeds, along with a mortgage, to buy a family home in Bray, near the sea-front. He'd also got a better job in an insurance company on Dame Street.

I still held an image of him sitting in the dappled sunlight by the brook, pouring his heart across his sketchpad. I couldn't see him stuck at a desk in an office with a view of a busy street, where an opened window meant a blast of traffic-fumed air and the squeal of brakes. But with small babies, a wife, and a mortgage, he had no choice.

My heartbreak found its way into my performances, lending them an authenticity that resonated with my audiences. I poured my anguish and jealousy along with my battered heart into every portrayal, finding that I was totally wrung out at the end of each performance. There were after-show parties in heaving clubs in Soho and Islington, and in jam-packed flats on the Holloway Road, electric moments when a skinny David Bowie arrived, and George Harrison turned up with Eric Clapton. Noise and music, 'My Sweet Lord' and *Dark Side of the Moon*, shrill, over-bright laughter bouncing around somewhere outside of me. Men, sex, gin, vodka, and Bacardi, everything empty and mechanical.

My only escape from it all was the stage.

Four years after Pippa and Lucien's marriage, my lovely father died suddenly in his sleep, and only then did I appreciate what Lucien must have gone through with the loss of his grandmother, never mind his own parents. The cold, hard ache, the pain in your chest, shielded slightly with numbed disbelief, but you felt it, behind the wall of shock, a great tsunami of grief, like a rattle of nails ready to pounce and embed itself into you when you were at your lowest ebb. I was the one Lucien had looked for in his time of need but I had failed him. No wonder he'd run to the open arms of a ready and willing Pippa.

I went home for the funeral, remaining as civil as I could towards Pippa, ignoring Lucien completely, making sure I was never within reach of him, yet conscious of his gaze following me around, conscious of mine seeking him out, wanting more than anything to fall into his arms and weep for the loss of my father. Wanting to tell him how sorry I was not to have been there when he'd lost his grandmother. Time had healed nothing at all. The sight of him scored through all my senses, but I couldn't weaken, not even for a moment, and especially not when I saw him with his beautiful daughter and son. They were brought to the hotel where we had lunch after the burial. I saw the caring way he looked after them, organising food, bringing them outside for a walk in the fresh air, allowing Pippa time to talk to friends and relatives, being just the type of attentive father I had imagined him to be. When I saw his arm curving around Pippa later, and witnessed the ease with which she leaned into him, my stomach heaved.

I met him in the hotel corridor just before I left for the airport, both of us stopping short of each other, close enough to see faint new lines fanning from his eyes, eyes that held a soft concern, and I was unable to breathe for a moment with the urge to touch his face and trace it gently with my fingertips.

'Evie.'

'Lucien.'

'I'm sorry … for your father, for everything.'

'So am I,' I said, my voice cracking as I backed away.

I felt like the loneliest person in the world as I moved through the throngs in the airport terminal. Mixed with the loss of my father was the fresh loss of Lucien all over again – all that we had been in the past, and what we might have been in the future.

Evie, present day

I am tempted to slip under the waves of exhaustion, away from the soft beep of the monitor to where a deep and silent chasm awaits. It would be so easy to let go and sink soundlessly to the depths.

I see us all as we were then: Pippa, Rachel, and Barry Talbot – and Lucien, and the bleak look in his eyes when the full ramifications of the incident became apparent to him.

Lucien, who's waiting for me in Heronbrook. Isn't he?

I catch the resin scent of the pine trees drifting around me and the soothing balm of deep, purple lavender. It transports me to afternoons on the terrace, the sun's rays through the trees, the swirl of relaxing music, summer blooms spilling over terracotta pots. I hear the brook gurgling along, tipping over the weir.

I hear a voice telling me to go to Lucien.

One Week Earlier

It was Friday lunchtime, and Evie had almost finished a bowl of vegetable soup before Amber made any reference to their conversation of the previous evening.

'What you spoke about,' she said slowly, 'all that family history, you and Lucien ... my grandfather ... I had no idea.'

'Was there not even a whisper from anyone?' Evie asked. 'Even Pippa?'

'No, not a word.'

Evie digested this in silence, spooning her soup. Then she said, 'I can't blame Pippa for wanting Lucien – he was ... just so lovely.'

'I never knew him,' Amber said, breaking open a crusty roll.

'He would have loved you wholeheartedly,' Evie said, knowing that truth with every fibre of her being. *You look like him, the way you smile, I see his reflection in your blue eyes, you carry his beautiful spark*, she wanted to say. There was another brief silence. Somewhere in the trees outside, a bird sang out, the sound clear and perfect.

'I can understand now what made Pippa behave as she did,' Evie said after a while. 'I was a bit condescending with her from time to time, even on our holidays when I was becoming involved with Lucien. I loved being the eldest, the first to have more freedom and do new things. As a child, I was prettier than she was, I was popular in school, more able for the work. Our parents loved us equally, but we had different relationships with them, Pippa was always … as a child she was petulant, seeing grievances where there were none, envious of anything I had. And then, at the end of it all, I can't say that Pippa led a long and happy life either.' Evie sighed. 'I was crippled with guilt. I ran away from it all, over to London.'

'Sometimes running away is good in the short term,' Amber said.

Evie put down her spoon, her appetite gone. 'I agree,' she said, 'but in my case I was a bit of a drama queen. I thought I was making a grand gesture, sacrificing myself to atone for my big, negligent sin by turning my back on everyone, including Lucien. I took the risk of going over to London without properly establishing myself in Dublin first. It was like I was on a mission of self-destruction. However, London worked out for me eventually. I worked hard, got a couple of lucky breaks, and I had more success than I could have dreamt of. But it was an empty success without Lucien by my side. I felt I didn't deserve happiness with him after what had happened. I was so hard on myself. On both of us.'

'Granny Pippa must have known she caused the whole thing by not alerting you properly about Leah in the first place. What a burden to be carrying at fourteen.'

'It's not something she ever admitted,' Evie said, fidgeting with the salt cellar, 'but, yes, I've often wondered how Pippa felt. It left a scar at the heart of our family and it's not something we talked about. My father was too upset; my mother sided with him for the sake of peace and never mentioned it. But it was always there, running under everything. How could we fully enjoy family celebrations, thinking of the Caseys and the trouble we'd caused?'

'God. What a sad mess,' Amber said.

When she finished her soup, she rose from the table, picking up Evie's bowl along with her own, and made coffee for both of them. Sitting back down, she looked keenly at Evie and said, 'And tell me, what happened to the Caseys?'

'My parents tried to talk to them the following day, and a lot of the mobile home park residents tried to rally around them, but they were beside themselves with shock and wouldn't have anything to do with anyone. They went home later that day. From what I heard, they laid the blame fully on Rachel.'

'Oh?'

'They had trusted her to take care of her little sister. I don't know if they were aware of the part Pippa and I played in Leah's accident. Apparently Rachel had been fooling around with Barry Talbot, which she'd been strictly forbidden to do. We left Heronbrook before the end of the week and never went back. I heard years later that Barry Talbot had kept in touch with Rachel. He was mad about her, but she kept giving him the runaround. I heard she was soured by what had happened to her sister. Understandably, of course. Still, they went on to become engaged and then days before the wedding she called it off. Barry was devastated.'

Amber stirred her coffee slowly. 'You're joking. More drama.'

'Rachel went to England and became a nurse. She never married. I can't remember the last time I heard anything about her, until Tess told us the other day that she'd died a few months ago. Leah is still alive and being looked after in a care home. It's sad to think that she and Pippa have ended up in much the same way. Pippa was so sharp and spiky – it's hard to imagine her freedom curtailed like that.'

'She was never happy,' Amber said. 'My mother shielded us from her a lot, visiting her by herself, then trying to lighten the mood whenever she was in Laurel Lawns.'

'You could go deep into this and ask if her anger was an unconscious result of some kind of suppressed childhood guilt,' Evie said. 'Because we never really spoke about it, that afternoon went unprocessed. That term didn't even exist then. Nowadays there would be counselling available.' Evie sipped some coffee and glanced outside at the September afternoon, trying to centre herself in the moment and escape from sad, old memories. How peaceful it looked with the sun falling across the terrace and sparkling on the brook.

'Life was different then,' she continued. 'A lot of uncomfortable things were swept under the carpet. It was tougher in some ways.'

'I don't think my mother knows any of this,' Amber eventually said.

'Probably not,' Evie said.

'If she does, she never breathed a word to me. She never got on that well with Granny Pippa, not that she ever confided anything about that either,' Amber continued hurriedly. 'In front of our family she was loyal to her mother, but growing up you see these things, you hear the end of a sharp conversation, you see the difference in other people's family relationships ...' She paused. 'That's me putting it as diplomatically as possible in the interest of maintaining a semblance of family solidarity.'

'You're being very diplomatic.' Evie smiled. 'Anyway, it was all a lifetime ago.'

'There's something I wanted to ask,' Amber said.

Her grand-niece seemed a little hesitant. 'What is it?' Evie asked encouragingly.

'Could I have a look at the painting again? It's just ... It's beautiful and there's something about it that seems to ... I dunno ... click with me,' Amber said.

Evie smiled. 'I'm glad you feel like that about Lucien's painting. And ...' – she paused for a moment – 'I have to tell you about the others.'

'What others?'

'There should be three more, dating back to

the sixties. They went missing. I thought they were gone, and then – it was mad, Amber – I was watching a BBC programme earlier this year, about a heritage castle in the Cotswolds, and lo and behold, I saw what looked like one of Lucien's paintings on display in the hall. Long story short, one of my UK contacts put me in touch with an art dealer, and he hunted it down and arranged the sale of it to me. It's being held safely in storage in London and he's searching for the other two.'

She picked up her mobile and scrolled through it, her hand shaking a little as she showed Amber an image on the screen – Lucien's painting of her standing on the curving stone bridge in the woods.

'Oh, gosh,' Amber said, 'that's you, back then, isn't it?'

Evie nodded.

Her grand-niece stared at the image for a long time, before looking across at Evie, her blue eyes vulnerable, her gaze making Evie's throat catch.

'I can't explain it properly,' Amber said, her voice thin, 'but like the portrait of you, it makes me want to cry, it's so beautiful. It makes me want to …' She gave a half-laugh. 'I'm probably mad but, oh Evie, I'd love to be able to do something like this myself … the colours … the glow … the soft imagery … I find it so moving.'

For a long moment, Evie felt the shadow of Lucien gracing the room.

Life goes on. And in the most serendipitous way. She felt sudden tears in her eyes.

Amber sat up straighter. 'Sorry, I've said something wrong.'

'No, you haven't,' Evie said, smiling gamely. 'You reminded me of your grandfather, that's all.' *That's all?* It was everything. 'Have you painted before?' she asked.

'I was good at art in school,' Amber said, 'but I dropped it when I was sixteen and took up economics instead, thinking it would be a better fit for college and a career. My art teacher wasn't impressed. I worked my butt off at economics trying to prove myself right and ended up getting maximum points in that subject.' Amber made a funny face.

'It's never too late to dream a new dream,' Evie said, conscious that her words held meaning for herself also. 'You've surprised me, Amber, but in a lovely way. I might think I'm old and cynical and full of withered bitchiness and tired of life, as I often feel these days, but now and again life can surprise you – it flickers through your veins once more, reminding you of what it's like to be vital and alive.'

'I guess if anything at all is still flickering through your veins it means you're still vital and alive,' Amber said.

Alive for now, Evie thought, suddenly recalling the terror of the hit-and-run. She stared out at the deciduous trees in the woods, shedding leaves of russet and gold against the deep green of fir and pine, a sudden and chilling premonition running through her that she might not be around to see them budding next spring.

Amber's mobile rang Just before lunch on Saturday.

Fionn.

'I'm outside,' he said.

'Outside?'

'Yeah, I'm outside the gates to this quirky little house surrounded by the most fantastic, ancient trees that are telling me they've been around a lot longer than I have.'

'I don't believe you.'

'Aren't you going to let me in?'

If she'd wondered what kind of support he was willing to give her, seeing that she had effectively derailed her career, she had no doubts now. With a heart that suddenly felt lighter, she went out to the door with the fob for the gates. Fionn Heffernan drove in and parked his car. Wearing a dark-green T-shirt and jeans, and stuffing his car keys into his jeans pocket, he walked across to her and put his arms around her. She buried her face in the crook of his neck, and even though it felt surprisingly good, she began to shake.

'Hey,' he said, gently rubbing her back. 'It's fine, I've got you.'

She stood in his embrace for several moments until her shaking subsided. Then dry-eyed – because she was too fraught for tears – she stepped back and looked at him. 'I guess you're still talking to me?'

He grinned. 'Just about.' Then his face softened as he gazed at hers. 'I couldn't believe what I'd heard when I went into Healy's on Monday. What the hell happened? No one will tell me the details. There was a presentation for my last day yesterday, and I wanted to tell them all to stick it.'

'I hope you didn't – I don't want you getting involved in my crap.'

'Jeez, Amber, from the bit Nicole was telling me it sounds crazy. How could Healy's believe you capable of damaging their business?'

'I'll tell you exactly what happened. But first, you have to meet Evie.'

'If this is the wonderful place she calls home, then I can't wait to meet her,' he said.

Evie said she was delighted to meet a good friend of Amber's, and he was welcome to Heronbrook, so long as he came in friendship. Fionn assured her that Amber could always count on him for friendship and support, whereupon Evie said it was just lunchtime and he was to join them if he was prepared to muck in and help out.

'I'm good at making cheese and tomato toasties,' he said.

'Toasties? When do you think you might improve your culinary skills beyond your student offerings?' Amber teased.

'A tomato and cheese toastie sounds perfect to me,' Evie said.

'I guess that gives me no choice,' Amber said.

'Not if you know what's good for you,' Evie said, winking at her behind Fionn's back.

After a light-hearted lunch, Evie announced that she intended to do a few of her horrible exercises, then have an afternoon rest, so it would be best if they made themselves scarce and she'd entrust her grand-niece to Fionn for a couple of hours. Perhaps Amber could show Fionn around Heronbrook, the woods, the brook, and down as far as the beach?

He grabbed a black jumper from his car, and as they strolled out under the trees and along the track to the lane, Amber told Fionn everything about Healy's and her suspicions about Will, finding it easy to get the words off her chest. By the time they reached the end of the lane and crested the sand dunes, where the silvery expanse of sea came into view, she had brought him up to date.

'I'm surprised at Healy's not investigating further before ending your contract so abruptly,' he said. 'How could they think you sabotaged them? You've had an impeccable record for years.'

'This was a real fuck-up. Securing your work is a basic rule even a newbie would be expected to know. As I was talking to them about Will, I think they were checking out his details but I only realised afterwards that they wouldn't have been able to trace him any more than I could, and they must have thought I was inventing him. So it looks like I really stitched them up.'

'Can you think of any reason Will wanted to mess you around?'

'No, not one. I guess I was in the wrong place at the wrong time. I haven't been able to contact him since. His number would have been on my mobile that security confiscated. But if he was that devious about putting up a smokescreen, I'm sure he used a burner phone and that account is deactivated by now.'

'Have you thought about chasing him through the apartment? There has to be a record of his identity – you don't just pick up the keys without providing some kind of documentation.'

'I'm getting on to that now. I was literally running away when I came here – looking after Evie was a lifesaver. Much as I dread the thought of confronting him, he's not getting away with it.'

'I'll do a bit of digging around. We can't have that wanker getting away scot-free.'

'He won't if I have anything to do with it, but I don't want you being dragged into my stupidity.'

'I'm through with Healy's so it won't be a conflict of interest. Security have finished going through your things. Rob told me yesterday that he has a couple of boxes in the store room for you and could I let you know. I offered to take them but he has to sign them out to you.'

'I'll get them next week.'

They turned at the headland and walked back up the beach, the breeze now in their faces, both of them drawing in gulps of the bracing, salt-scented air.

'What's next for you, Amber?'

She kicked at a small hillock of sand and looked out at the horizon. 'Good question,' she said. 'My reputation is shot to pieces, but, Fionn, I'm not sure I want to go back into that corporate life again. There were times when I found it stifling. There are a few things I want to think about and I'm in no rush anywhere for now.'

'Take your time.'

'How was your Greek island?' she asked.

'Good – great, actually. I stayed in a hut near the beach, with a lovely tavern up the hillside, and a shop down a dirt track that sold fresh crusty bread each morning. I walked, I swam, and I read – no Wi-Fi, just the sea and the sky, the sunshine, and fresh air, fresh food, and delicious white wine. It takes a full day to get there, but it's worth it.'

'Sounds like my kind of bliss. How did Sadie like it?'

'We're no longer an item.'

She stopped in her tracks and looked up at him, shading her eyes with her hand against the pale September sunlight. 'Don't tell me it's off again?'

'Off for good this time, Amber,' he said, 'over and out, *finito*. We split about two weeks before Greece, so I went ahead on my own. Best thing I ever did.'

'Two weeks *before* you went? You were still in Healy's – why didn't you tell me?'

He stared out to sea for a moment, the breeze tossing his hair, and then looked back at her with a half-smile on his face. 'I didn't really have the chance.'

'I get you,' she said. 'I was too wrapped up in Mr Baker. I'm so sorry I didn't notice that things had gone kaput.'

'There wasn't anything to notice.'

'Still, though, I could have brought you out for a drink to commiserate.'

'Celebrate, more like. It had become a habit and the closure was a relief.'

She slanted him a glance. 'Did anything in particular bring it to an end?'

'Well, I did,' he said, 'when I realised I wasn't looking forward to two weeks on a digital detox island with Sadie. She was as relieved as I was when I called halt. She'd far prefer the buzzy nightclubs of Hersonissos, she said, cocktails till dawn, that sort of thing. Whereas me, I was up at dawn most mornings just to swim in the sea.'

'That's good, then, isn't it? No broken hearts.'

'Just a tiny dent, but I'm over it.'

He smiled at her and Amber was filled with a peculiar lightness, as though part of her world had righted itself. They walked back up the beach, coming out through the sand dunes onto the rutted tarmac laneway, grasses and ferns tumbling out onto it, the sea-salty air infused with their warm scents. Overhead, drifts of cotton-wool clouds slid slowly across the blue bowl of the sky, steered by the slight breeze coming up off the sea.

'It's a bit like that Greek island here,' he said. 'A total chill-out away from the rat race. You have the sea and then the woods and the brook – I didn't think places like Heronbrook existed.'

'It was the gatehouse to some ancestral pile that's long gone. It's a great little retreat.'

When they came to the bend in the lane, Amber told Fionn the details of Evie's accident. 'She was lucky she was found by a local woman,' Amber said.

'And then you were around to give her a hand.'

'Yeah. Funny, now that I think of it. Evie's accident happened the day before I was sacked—' She stopped short, wondering why that hadn't registered with her before now. Both of them in the wrong place at the wrong time? Both their lives turned upside down? Sheer coincidence? Not that the two events could be related in any way. She'd nothing in common with Evie beyond a family tie. Still, she had to shake off the feeling of a ghost walking over her grave.

Fionn had coffee before he left, sitting out on the terrace with her and Evie, saying it was well for them now that they were ladies of leisure, able to relax and enjoy the beauty around them all day long. Afterwards, Amber saw him out, wishing him all the best in the new job he was starting on Monday. She felt at a sudden loss, sorry to see him go, but was glad he gave her a warm hug before he jumped into the car.

'I'll call you next week,' he said through the open window. 'Can I pop down again?'

'Yeah, sure,' she said, hiding the dart of pleasure his words gave her.

'He seems like a nice young man,' Evie said, back out on the terrace.

'He is,' Amber said. Something in Evie's eyes caused a soft blush in her cheeks, and she lifted their empty mugs rather clumsily off the table.

'I just said "nice", that's all,' Evie said.

'I know, he's a good friend. That's all.'

'Good friends are the gold dust of life,' Evie said. 'Although in Fionn's case I'd add huggable, hunky, sexy, let me see … beddable—'

'Evie!'

Evie was right, though, Amber decided, stepping into the kitchen – now and again life surprised you.

Amber picked up the keys to the Kia and checked the table. Coffee in a flask, ready for Evie, a glass of orange juice and a bottle of water. Evie sitting there, reading the newspaper.

'Are you sure you'll be OK?' Amber asked.

Evie looked up from the newspaper. 'Are you not gone yet? Or are you back already?' In a softer voice, she went on, 'You can change your mind at any time. You're in charge of you – nobody else is. I'll be fine, don't worry.' She picked up the fob for the gate. 'Look, I'm on one crutch now and I can even see you out.'

'I'll be back in time to bring us out for a nice lunch,' Amber said.

By the time Amber turned the Kia out onto the merging lane of the motorway, most of the Monday morning commuter traffic had cleared. She passed a garden centre that looked like a lovely spot to bring Evie for lunch. Her great-aunt's words reverberated in her head – she was in charge of herself – and a curious calm overtook her as she drove through the autumnal countryside, bathed in golden September sunshine.

About an hour later, as she approached the city centre, she was conscious that her hands were gripping the steering wheel in a vice-like hold. Calling in to Russell Hall to collect the contents of her desk had seemed like a good idea the previous night, when she'd been fortified by a glass or two of wine. It would show she was moving on with her life. But, crucially, there might be something there that would lead her to Will. She was within sight of Russell Hall when a car pulled out, leaving a handy parking spot for her. She threw back her shoulders and marched into the building exactly as Evie had coached her the previous evening.

'Act regally and confidently,' Evie had said, getting up and demonstrating how to stand to attention despite her crutch. 'Pretend you're wearing a beautiful crown on the top of your head. It got me through many a wobbly moment,' she'd said. 'People tend to take you as you portray yourself. No one will know if you're feeling a little queasy on the inside.'

In the foyer, Rob looked up and smiled. 'Amber! You're back to see us.'

First hurdle over. 'I came to collect my things?' she said. 'I believe they're ready in the store room.'

'Ah.' Rob grinned. 'You were talking to Fionn. Good stuff.' He touched some buttons on his console and took out a set of keys. He disappeared down a short corridor behind the reception desk and came out several moments later with two storage boxes.

'These have your name on them,' he said, sliding them across the desk. He passed over a pad for her signature. 'Do you need a hand?'

'No, thanks, I'm parked outside.' The boxes were sealed, she noted.

'How have you been?' he asked. 'We've missed your smiling face.'

'We?'

'Yeah, me and Nicole and Kim.' His eyes gave nothing away and she wondered how much he knew of her summary dismissal, how much he remembered of her phoning back to enquire, futilely, about Will after she'd been escorted off the premises. 'You were one of the nicer ones,' he said, 'not like some of the robots that march through here as though a smile might crack their faces. And now Fionn is gone too, another of the good guys. I saw your fella, by the way,' he continued, a concerned look in his eyes. 'The fella you were asking about – Will.'

'Oh, right,' she said, sounding casual even though her heartbeat quickened.

'He was coming out of a hotel in Ballsbridge with an older guy, could have been his father. He wasn't looking where he was going and almost bumped into me.'

'When was this?' Amber asked.

'Last Wednesday. I was bringing herself out for a meal for her birthday.'

'Did he recognise you?'

'Is he still your guy?'

'No,' Amber said emphatically.

'He just looked right through me, Amber. I'm mostly invisible to those privileged types, even though I looked after him.'

'In what way?'

'The first day I saw him, I remember he came right up to the desk, looking for you. I said I'd just seen you going out for coffee. He told me he wanted to surprise you so he said he'd wait. He asked me to give him the nod when you came back in through the door. That was the day you spilt the coffee. It only struck me afterwards that although he'd talked to me like he was a friend of yours, how come he needed me to give him a signal when you arrived in?'

'I see,' Amber said.

'That was OK, wasn't it?' Rob asked, looking anxious.

'Sure. Did he ever show you any ID?' Amber asked.

'Nah. He never came up to the desk after that. Why?'

'Nothing, Rob,' she said, sliding the boxes into her arms, 'it doesn't matter now.' What was the betting that if Will had produced ID it would have been fake? And if it hadn't been the spilt coffee in the foyer, which must have been deliberate, he would have found some other way of getting her attention. She knew now he'd deliberately arranged to connect with her, although she still didn't know if he'd been mounting a personal or business attack.

The fucker.

Saying goodbye to Rob, she walked out of Russell Hall, her irritation mounting. She just about managed to stay within the speed limit on the drive back to Heronbrook. However, once there, she was conscious that she felt a lot lighter than she'd felt leaving it earlier that morning.

'I'm glad I went and slayed that dragon,' she said to Evie. 'It gave me a tiny boost.' She didn't bother to relay what Rob had said about Will. One step at a time.

'Good for you,' Evie said.

Amber made coffee and went through the boxes containing the contents of her desk: stationery, pens, spare tights, birthday cards that she'd received in the office, detritus from another life, one she didn't want to rush back to. The same with her briefcase: more stationery, an old lanyard ribbon, along with a takeaway menu for a new restaurant in Baggot Street and a flyer for a chill-out spa in a Wicklow hotel, which she'd obviously shoved into a compartment in her briefcase. Any documents or notes relating to Healy's were gone, and her phone had not been returned. She closed the boxes. Nothing here to lead her to Will.

It was too early for lunch, so she checked her emails.

Sarah O'Brien of the *Wicklow Weekly* had replied to her. There were no spare copies of that particular supplement available, she said, but they were happy to attach a copy of the photos taken on the night. All she had to do was to open the link included in the email. The photographs were under copyright but were available in print for a small fee. Amber clicked on the link and scrolled through the succession of images that opened up on her phone.

Most of them were of groupings of people she didn't know, a copyright notice stamped in watermark across the centre of each one. Then one image popped up. Her mother and Evie, along with Barry Talbot. Seeing her mother like this felt like the way you catch yourself off guard in a mirror and don't recognise yourself for a moment. Jessica Lennox looked beautiful. Her hair had been freshly styled, and she was wearing a red dress with laced sleeves. White gold jewellery glinted on her fingers and wrists and at her throat. It wasn't a posed photograph. She was caught informally on camera talking to Evie and Barry, a smile wreathing her face. So much for claiming ignorance of Barry.

There was a posed photograph later in the roll, both Evie and her mother standing close as they smiled for the camera, glasses of bubbly held aloft, Evie looking equally beautiful, her white hair shot through with a soft pink wash, her softly curved face with its beautiful cheekbones dewy in the light. One to frame, most definitely. Then another: Tess Talbot with her husband Barry – both of them posing as if they were standing on the red carpet at Cannes, Tess's head tilted at an angle, Barry's chest puffed out. Then an informal one of them sitting at their table, along with a striking-looking man that Amber guessed to be in his early sixties. He was bald, with an arresting-looking face. Amber stared at the man, unable to shake off the feeling that she'd met him somewhere before.

Another one of this man talking to Barry, both of them standing up at their table, Tess sitting down, looking up with something in her eyes that Amber could only too well identify: lust. But Tess wasn't staring at her husband; she was looking at the other man.

Amber studied all four photographs before saving them to a folder on her mobile.

The garden centre off the motorway was busy on Monday lunchtime and Amber had to circle around, looking for a convenient parking spot for the Kia.

'The lovely weather has everyone out,' Evie said. 'Maybe this wasn't a good idea after all.'

'It was a great idea,' Amber said stoutly. 'I'll drop you off as close as I can to the entrance, then I'll go park somewhere.'

'We could pick up some autumn bedding before we have lunch,' Evie suggested. 'The summer displays are past their best.'

Amber couldn't help feeling a lift as they strolled in the sunshine through colourful displays and mingled scents of outdoor bedding, Evie with a crutch under her right arm, her left hand on the trolley that Amber pushed. They selected trays of pansies, violas, and primroses and fresh peat for the terracotta pots.

'You'll have to do the necessary with these,' Evie said. 'I'm excused.'

'I knew you were a slave driver behind it all.' Amber grinned. 'You'll have to instruct me, though, I've never planted stuff before.' She paused at the containers holding displays of flower bulbs. 'How about some bluebell bulbs? They're gorgeous.'

'There are loads in the ground already,' Evie said, 'drifts of them running down the sides of the garden, as well as daffodils and snowdrops. They look fabulous in springtime against the trees.'

Inside the shop, Amber selected cream candles for the lanterns and a beautiful blue hurricane lamp along with some butterfly solar lights before they went to the till. She made sure Evie was sitting comfortably in a table by the window in the bright, airy café before she brought the purchases out to the Kia, returning to queue at the self-service. Presently, she came over to their table with a tray bearing glasses of water and plates of quiche and fresh crusty bread.

Amber waited until they were having coffee before she took out her phone. 'I've some photographs to show you, Evie,' she said, passing over her phone.

Evie stared at the images. 'Where did you get these?'

'The *Wicklow Weekly*,' Amber said. 'Tess Talbot mentioned them the day we lunched in the Glenmaragh View, and I contacted them to see if they had any copies available. Tess was right. The one of you and Mum is beautiful.'

'It certainly is,' Evie said.

'Who's the other guy with Barry?' Amber asked.

Evie studied him. 'I don't know,' she said. 'A business acquaintance, I expect. I love the one of me with Jessica,' Evie went on. 'I'm sorry about all the time your mother and I have lost, but if the *Wicklow Weekly* was available in the nursing home, and it more than likely was, I hope my sister never saw those photos – they would drive her mad.'

Amber glanced at the picture again. This time, something about Barry caught her in the throat – something familiar about his eyes. 'You mean the one of you with Barry Talbot?' she asked Evie, taking a stab in the dark.

'It was never me and Barry,' Evie said, 'but some old secrets are better kept that way, especially if they're not mine to reveal.' She gave Amber a meaningful look.

Amber decided in this instance it was best to keep her suspicions to herself. They left soon after, Evie waiting by the entrance to the café while Amber went up to the far end of the car park to bring the Kia around. She popped the alarm, opened the car door, took off her cross-body bag and tucked it under the seat. She was just about to jump in when something struck her as odd. She stepped back and surveyed the car. She'd missed it on her approach, busy admiring the greenery and plants in big dividers in that part of the car park. Now, with a flash of panic, she saw that the front tyres on both sides of the Kia were completely flat.

One flat tyre would be a nuisance. But two together, Amber realised chillingly, had to be a deliberate act of viciousness.

Jessica had had a long and tiring day at work, patients disgruntled because their usual doctor, the friendly Dr Walsh, had been called away on account of the death of a close relative, and she'd had to explain time and time again that the locum, Dr Byrne, was just as competent. She wasn't particularly in the humour for a trip to Pinedale Lawns after her evening meal, and even Paul was surprised when she'd told him where she was going.

'What's this in aid of?' he asked. 'You don't normally visit on a Monday.'

'I can visit whenever I feel like it,' she said, unable to prevent herself from sounding snappy. She was avoiding talking to him as much as possible, feigning tiredness and pretending to be busier than she was, fearful of blurting something out and upsetting him with the amount of money missing from her bank account. How many weeks' net salary did that come to? So far she hadn't told him about her mother's surprise visitor, any more than the vomiting bug in the care home, or that this evening's trip there was an attempt to find out who'd been visiting her mother.

It hadn't been Jamie – the way he'd sounded, as if this was an absurdity, had saddened her. Not even her younger and favourite son wanted to see Pippa. Yet, you reap what you sow, and Pippa had alienated all of them with her destructive alcoholism. If it had been one of her far-flung cousins, acting out of a sense of duty, they would have called Jessica first. Furthermore, they would never have used Simon's name.

She'd phoned Simon, although she knew it was highly unlikely he'd come to Dublin, let alone visit the care home, without seeing her. 'I hope to be over next spring,' Simon had said, 'and I'll definitely see Mum then. I appreciate you have the bulk of the visiting and the general looking after her. It's been a while since I showed my face.'

'Yes, it has.'

'Is everything all right?' Simon had asked. 'Jamie behaving himself now that he's home?'

'Just about. You know Jamie.'

'I hope he settles down a bit,' Simon had said. 'You don't need him in your hair.'

'No. I've enough going on at the moment, thank you.'

She replayed the conversation in her head as she drove out of Laurel Lawns towards the motorway for Bray. Simon was the one person she probably could have confided in about her fraught financial situation. Simon only visited Dublin from Hong Kong intermittently. She hadn't visited him in recent years on account of her stretched funds, as well as their busy lives getting in the way, but, as his twin, she was a lot closer to Simon than Jamie. Weeks could go by before they'd talk, but they always seemed in tune with each other and easily picked up wherever they'd left off.

The car park of Pinedale Lawns was practically empty. 'Is Helen around?' Jessica asked, coming through the foyer. Over at reception, Muriel was manning the desk.

'You're not supposed to be here, Jessica.' Muriel looked up with a slight reproach in her eyes. 'I'm sure you were informed that visiting is off-limits, thanks to the vomiting bug. We haven't given the all-clear yet. Your mother is doing fine, rest assured. She's still eating well, which is positive.'

Positive for what, Jessica wanted to ask. Still, at least Pippa was allowing herself to be properly nourished and not pining too much for her daughter.

'I know,' she said. 'I haven't come to see my mother – I want to talk to Helen.'

'She's around somewhere. I'll call her for you,' Muriel said, pressing a button on her console. 'Can I help you with anything?'

'Maybe you can,' Jessica said. 'I want to update my mother's visitors' list. One or two family members said they'd pop in to see her, but I'm not sure she'd want to see them, if you get my drift.'

'I can do that, no problem,' Muriel said, pulling across her keyboard.

'And my brother Jamie is now back in Ireland. I have new contact details for him.'

'He was over in New York, wasn't he?' Muriel said, scrolling through some documents on her screen. 'That's strange …' Muriel took off her glasses, replaced them, and tapped her keyboard.

'What's wrong?'

'I can't find your details. The document must have been misfiled.'

'How would that happen?'

'I presume the last person to access it saved it in the wrong folder.'

'Can you find out when that was?' Jessica asked.

'If I find the document, I can …'

A door swung open behind them and Jessica turned around in time to see Helen coming towards her.

'Jessica, you were looking for me?'

'Hi, Helen, I'm back again about Mum's visitors, updating the list, and … while I'm here, could you take a look at these photos and see if you remember either of them calling in to Mum recently?'

Jessica took out her mobile and brought up her photo gallery, where she'd pinned photos of Simon and Jamie, wanting to rule them out completely.

'I remember him coming in,' Helen said, pointing to Jamie, 'but I don't think I've ever seen the other guy. Nah. I'd remember him, he's quite attractive.'

'Thanks, Helen.'

'Here it is.' Muriel's voice broke into her thoughts. 'Pippa Lawrence Burke. The document was saved under Lawrence instead of Burke – wasn't that your mother's maiden name?'

'Yes. Do you know when it was misfiled?'

'Hold on a minute.' Muriel clicked on her mouse and tapped the keyboard before reading details off her screen. 'It was last accessed and printed on the eleventh of June.'

'Printed?'

Muriel looked discomfited. She gazed at her screen. 'That's what the file properties appear to say ... Maybe someone needed to cross-reference your details.'

'And who might that be?' When there was no answer from Muriel, Jessica continued, 'Any idea which of the staff in here would have accessed that?'

'It could have been any of us,' Helen said, looking pointedly at Muriel. 'It's normal procedure that all reception staff and supervisors can access contact details in case of emergency. Each member of staff is aware of their responsibility with personal information. I'm sure it was only accessed for a legitimate purpose.'

'Just remind me what details you have exactly?'

'Um ...' Muriel checked her screen. 'You're the main next of kin – we have your name, address, mobile, email. Spouse mobile also – that's Paul, isn't it? And Amber's next on the list in case you and Paul are uncontactable, email and mobile ...'

Jessica didn't bother to say that Amber's mobile had changed. 'What about my brothers?'

'Jamie Burke and Simon Burke – we have them down as living in New York and Hong Kong respectively.'

'So let me check that again,' Jessica butted in. 'A document with our personal information was accessed and printed on a date in June.'

'It was obviously required for something,' Helen said.

'We don't have Simon's or Jamie's mobile or email,' Muriel said. 'And we still have Jamie recorded as living in New York. Do you want to update that?'

'Certainly not at the moment. Not when there are doubts about the security of your information,' Jessica snapped.

'Rest assured I'll talk to all the staff at this end, Jessica,' Helen said smoothly. 'It was obviously a clerical procedure of some kind, but I'll have it checked out.'

'The date it was accessed, the eleventh of June,' Jessica said, steeling herself for the answer, 'did my mother have any visitors that day?'

'I'll have a look,' Muriel said, turning to the visitors' book. She riffled through several pages before stopping at one and running her finger down the entries. 'Yes,' she smiled brightly, as though to convince herself and Jessica that all was in order, 'that was the day your brother Simon called in.'

Evie had just finished her breakfast on Tuesday morning when the police called, unannounced, to Heronbrook. Garda O'Reilly seemed to be a new recruit, judging by the dazzling glare of his pristine high-viz jacket and his unblemished, laser-sharp cap. Garda Sergeant Byrne had already talked to Evie in the hospital, but today her calm manner and staunch confidence that her hit-and-run assailant would be caught seemed somewhat diminished.

'Our investigation has stalled,' she said. 'We've checked dash-cam footage and traffic cameras on the motorway, but there's no sighting of anyone on a motorbike within the timeline of your accident. Is there anything else you remember? Any other detail that might help?'

'I can't think of anything new,' Evie said. 'If there's no sighting on the motorway, the cyclist must have taken the road through Glenmaragh up into the mountains.'

'We've checked CCTV in the village,' Garda O'Reilly said. 'There's nothing on that either.'

'You see, Ms Lawrence,' Garda Sergeant Byrne said, 'this might suggest that the cyclist knew exactly what they were doing. The perpetrator clearly avoided the cameras, which suggests there is a possibility they had the route worked out in advance. In other words, the incident could have been planned.'

'Are you saying you think it was deliberate?' Evie said.

'I'm doing a full review of the case,' Garda O'Reilly said. 'Has anything else happened that seemed a bit odd?'

Evie looked at the young man and his fresh face. She imagined him poring over the reports with the energy and conscientiousness of a new recruit and felt jaded. Before she had a chance to reply, he tilted his head to one side and asked her about her car.

'What about my car?' she said.

'You had a problem yesterday with your tyres, I believe. I was in Glenmaragh garage getting coffee this morning and they told me about it. Why wasn't it reported to the police?'

'This isn't part of your review, is it?'

'It might need to form part of the investigation. Is there any reason why you haven't notified us?'

'I haven't had the chance yet,' Evie said. 'We were out most of yesterday afternoon. We had to speak to the garden-centre manager and wait for the garage to send out a tow truck, and by the time a member of the garden-centre staff kindly brought us home, we were exhausted. Weren't we, Amber? Anyhow, I thought tyre slashing would be filed under anti-social behaviour,' Evie continued, without waiting for Amber to respond. 'The garage said we'll have it back shipshape by tomorrow, so no harm done.'

Garda O'Reilly gave her a sceptical look that belied his inexperience. He checked his notes before fixing her with beady eyes. 'Ms Lawrence, do you think you might have any adversaries who would wish you harm?'

'Me? An adversary? Look at me.' She gave a half-laugh. 'I mean, who'd be bothered?'

It took her a while to convince the diligent Garda O'Reilly that she was quite sure she had no adversaries, and that *of course* she'd call him if anything else struck her. She was aware of Amber watching the proceedings quietly, taking mental notes, no doubt. After they left, her grand-niece busied herself with the laundry and popped out for some fresh bread and milk, using her own car, waiting until they were finished their lunch and sitting out on the terrace before she brought the subject up.

'Evie, about earlier today,' she said, 'did you mean what you told the police about having no enemies?'

'No more than anyone who has reached my age, I expect. We all ruffle a few feathers along the way,' Evie said, struggling to sound light-hearted. 'That young garda thinks he's on the set of *Delphin Terrace*.'

'Why should he think he's on the set of *Delphin Terrace*?' Amber asked.

Evie bit her lip. 'Well, it's just—' She shrugged. 'I bet I'm his first case. When he gets a few more under his belt, he'll soften his enthusiasm.'

'And you don't think your car was personally targeted?' Amber asked.

'I don't see why — it has to have been an opportunist attack. Living in the peace of the countryside doesn't prevent those petty crimes from happening — cars get burgled, windows get smashed, and the likes of a dead fox on the road is also a normal enough event.'

'I didn't mention the dead fox,' Amber said.

There was a short silence. 'Nor did I,' Evie said, 'otherwise the young guard would have blown it out of proportion in his enthusiasm. As for yesterday, thanks again for your help.'

She felt cold as she stared out across the garden. She hadn't seen the damage to her tyres. When Amber had returned with the bad news, she'd insisted Evie wait in the café while she chased down the manager to make a report. He'd promised to check the CCTV covering the grounds, admitting that most of it was trained on the entrances to the garden centre and café, and not on the area in which Amber had been parked. Evie had been chilled to the bone when they'd eventually arrived home. She'd insisted they both had a brandy for restorative purposes, and when the mechanic phoned later, after his examination of the tyres, reporting that they'd been slashed, she'd felt a wave of panic gripping her.

Much the same thing had happened to Ma Donnelly, the last upsetting incident, just a week before her final episode had aired.

'Are you sure you don't think it was anything more sinister?' Amber pressed.

'Like what?'

'I can't help thinking about what happened at the end of your holidays in Heronbrook. Could one of the Caseys have a grudge against you?'

'I understand where you're coming from,' Evie said. 'The incident with Leah had difficult consequences for my family, but the outcome was far more horrendous for the Caseys. I doubt if anything from the past is coming back to bite me. I've been living in Ireland for over twelve years now. Surely if someone was out for revenge – for want of a better word – they would have got to me before now? It would have been more damaging when I was actively working and had more to lose.'

Amber didn't look too convinced. 'I suppose. How about Barry Talbot? Would he have it in for you?'

'Why him?'

'Because you thwarted his plans to get his hands on Heronbrook? And you told me his fiancée jilted him at the altar, and she was the Casey girl who was blamed for not taking proper care of her sister. He could still hold a grudge about that.'

'Again, Amber, it was so long ago. Barry moved on and had a good life. He can be full of puff and hot air, but you heard him say he's no longer interested in Heronbrook. And I don't think he's the type to be bothered holding a grudge. He's seems too laid-back.'

'Well, someone is certainly messing you around. It would be best, I think, to put it all in the capable hands of Garda O'Reilly.'

'Leave it for now, Amber,' Evie said. 'I haven't the energy for him yet.'

It was only partly true. When she'd spoken to Amber the previous Thursday evening, she hadn't told her everything. Pippa's marriage to Lucien hadn't been the end of their story. There had been more, later, in London. The last cruel act before the curtain came down after both of their lives had been devastated, and Pippa and Evie had had their final, bitter argument, during which Pippa had warned her to stay away from her family.

Problem was, Evie hadn't kept her part of the bargain when she'd reconnected with Jessica at the charity event. Not that she thought for one moment her own sister was out for revenge. But it was both mystifying and perturbing that now, after two years living in Heronbrook, someone was harassing her. Had Pippa confided in someone, years ago, about her threats? Someone who cared enough about her sister to threaten Evie, seeing as Pippa was now incapable of that?

Furthermore, she knew, sadly, that Pippa's children would have good reason for wishing her ill-will if they knew about the final act that had caused the sisters' rift. And now that she was beginning to enjoy some kind of reconciliation with the family, especially her new and surprising connection with Amber, it would be all the more painful and difficult to reveal it.

A clutch of icy-cold fear had gripped her yesterday when she'd realised that they must have been followed to the garden centre deliberately. They had probably even been under surveillance by the malicious tyre slasher as they'd shopped and moved into the café. Yet the main reason she'd felt chilled to the bone was that Amber was now being included in the targeting. And the main reason she hadn't come clean with the diligent Garda O'Reilly was because she knew she'd have to come clean with Amber first.

And that's what she was dreading.

Amber drove into the car park of the Glenmaragh View just before lunchtime, reversing her car into a spot close enough to the entrance. She ordered a selection of fresh sandwiches and pastries to take away, and a coffee to have on the premises while she waited for her order.

And then she asked for Tess. She took her coffee across to a table and presently Tess came over to her, a flour-dusted apron covering a cobalt-blue dress.

'Sorry for disturbing you,' Amber said.

'You're not disturbing me,' Tess said, glancing down at her apron, implying that Amber had clearly interrupted her in the middle of some Very Important Baking. From what she could see, the dress Tess was wearing seemed rather too stylish for working in a kitchen, her navy high heels too impractical for the same purpose. She wondered if Tess had another appointment planned for later. Or an assignation, considering what Evie had said about her giving Barry as good as she got.

'I want to talk to you about my aunt,' Amber said, 'in particular the morning of her accident.'

'What a dreadful thing to happen.' Tess's face was full of solicitude. 'I'm so glad to see she's making a good recovery.'

'Did you see anything unusual that morning? Anything at all?'

'No, nothing,' Tess said.

'Even a drone, perhaps, when you were down on the beach? Or a motorbike parked in the car park?'

Tess shook her head. 'Sorry, Amber, I'd love to help you, but I've already told the police I saw nothing unusual. Is there a problem?'

'We're still trying to figure out exactly what happened and who might be responsible.' Amber had found herself coming up with mad conspiracy theories, one of which was Barry being responsible for Evie's accident, frustrated that his retirement plans hadn't worked out, pretending to Evie, and indeed his wife, that he was no longer interested in Heronbrook. Perhaps Tess, in coming to Evie's rescue, had inadvertently foiled his attempt to scare her. Or she could have discovered what Barry had been up to and effected some damage limitation. Her head in a whirl, Amber had decided it was best to start at the beginning in her efforts to find out what was going on.

'I'm double-checking everything,' Amber said. 'The family, and Evie, appreciate that you came along when you did, otherwise things could have been so much worse.'

'I was only too glad to be of help. And now, if you'll excuse me,' Tess said, rising to her feet.

Amber took out her mobile. 'Just one more thing,' she said, as if it was an afterthought. 'I have some photos to run by you.'

'Yes?'

'They're from the charity event.' Amber scrolled through her mobile, opening the image of Tess with the two men by the table. 'Do you know who this other man is?' she said, showing it to Tess, wondering if Tess would recognise the naked lust written across her face as she'd stared at the man.

Tess looked at the screen and looked back at Amber with a neutral expression. 'Yes, that's Matthew Casey.'

'Matthew Casey?' Of the Casey family Evie had spoken about? Amber's scalp tightened. If anyone had a reason for a grudge against Evie, he certainly had. 'Who's he?' she asked, feigning innocence.

'He's a self-made millionaire, one of Wicklow's success stories but a bit of a recluse – he doesn't normally show his face at these events. I mentioned it to Evie the day she was here for lunch.'

'I remember that now,' Amber said smoothly. 'His sister was a friend of my grandmother Pippa's. And you know him?' she couldn't resist adding.

'We're related ... second cousins ... something like that,' Tess said dismissively.

Cousins? From the way Tess was gazing at Matthew in the photograph, she wanted to be something more than that.

'Why are you asking?' Tess went on, a hint of mocking curiosity on her face.

'Evie thought she recognised him, but she wasn't sure,' Amber said, hoping she was getting away with her fib. It wasn't that Evie had thought she'd known him, it was that Amber had had the unshakeable feeling she'd met him before, somewhere significant. Although she was scarcely mingling in circles that included reclusive millionaires. 'So he lives in Wicklow?' she remarked casually, as though she was making conversation, as she popped her mobile into her bag and stood up.

'Yes, somewhere off the beaten track,' Tess replied, equally offhand.

Both of them headed back up the restaurant, Amber collecting her order wrapped in a carrier bag.

'Give my love to Evie,' Tess said. 'Tell her I'll pop out with some freshly baked treats later in the week.'

'Sure.'

Amber went out to the car park, putting the carrier bag into the boot before getting into the car. She had just tucked her handbag under the passenger seat and fastened her seat belt when she looked up to see Tess coming out of the café and walking purposefully down to the far end of the car park, something in the woman's urgent gait and her stylishly groomed appearance alerting her. Tess was wearing a cream jacket over her blue dress, a designer bag dangling off her shoulder. The picture of a woman going somewhere, scarcely on her way home after an early morning start. Amber was satisfied that she hadn't been seen by Tess, half-hidden as she was by two chalkboards. Through the gap between them, she saw Tess jumping into a silver BMW before accelerating out of the car park.

Amber followed her. There was a small crossroads

in the village, the left turn leading back down to Heronbrook, the right to Wicklow town and the Talbots' house on the hill, and she was just in time to see Tess going straight through the crossroads and up a narrow road that led away from the coastal routes, into the mountains.

She thought of what Tess had said about Matthew Casey living off the beaten track, as well as the way she'd looked at him in the photograph. Even though Evie was happy there could be no link between her hit-and-run and little Leah Casey's accident, Amber couldn't resist following Tess.

The narrow road was forest-lined, twisting up steep inclines, and in her peripheral vision were glimpses of luxury houses tucked back amid beautifully tended gardens. She followed the silver car at a distance around zigzag bends where the forest cleared at intervals, giving Amber brief views of steep purple terrain that fell away into green lush valleys. The route straightened out for a stretch and Amber dropped back slightly, gaining a little speed when a signpost indicated another corkscrew bend up ahead, anxious to keep Tess in view. She had to focus on the twists and turns, conscious of a large drop down into a valley, but when the road straightened out again, there was no sign of the silver car. Amber hit the accelerator, expecting to see Tess's car around the next bend, but when she had driven fruitlessly for another mile or so, she had to admit defeat.

Back in Heronbrook, gut instinct prevented

Amber from mentioning her wild goose chase to Evie. After lunch, when Evie went for a rest, Amber asked if she could use her laptop on the pretext of typing up a report of her summary dismissal. Her search would be easier on the larger screen.

'Of course,' Evie said. 'Work away.'

Amber's browser searches brought up links to a few articles about Matthew Casey. What she read confirmed what Tess had said about his reclusive lifestyle. Casey rarely gave interviews. He'd made a lot of money selling off an internet security company he'd founded, moving on to private equities and various property and financial deals. There was a list of his various chairmanships, a mention of a daughter and a son, Patrick and Jennifer, but nothing about a wife. He lived in a remote part of County Wicklow – a house called Temple Raven, which he'd snapped up ten years ago for less than half the original asking price when the bottom had dropped out of the housing market.

Temple Raven. It was easy to find it on Google Maps. From Glenmaragh, the route went deep into the mountainy heartlands of west Wicklow, the same route Amber had taken earlier. Zooming in, she saw that she had overshot a laneway that led to Temple Raven close to the corkscrew bend where she'd lost Tess.

Then, feeling a bit uncomfortable for using her laptop like this, Amber googled Evie, using an incognito window so Evie wouldn't have any record of her search.

Something in the way her great-aunt had mentioned Garda O'Reilly being on the set of *Delphin Terrace* had aroused her curiosity. She clicked on a link to an article about Evie's character's death, reading about the huge boost it had given the ratings. Then she scrolled further to find out Evie's character had been fatally injured in a hit-and-run following a campaign of intimidation. A wave of fear slammed into Amber's chest as the article detailed the events that had led to the fatal accident. They were all too similar to what had been happening to Evie of late, including the Polaroid of the scan with the offensive message. In Ma Donnelly's case, a dead fox had been left in her bed and all her tyres had been slashed.

What the actual ...? Why had Evie kept this vital information from her? And why the hell hadn't she mentioned it to the police?

Another link caught her attention, and she clicked into the article. It was an interview Evie had given to a journalist in a Sunday newspaper when she'd first returned to Ireland. Amber's interest sharpened when Evie was asked about the reason she'd abandoned her role of Lady Macbeth and her West End stage career almost overnight.

Overnight? Amber read on, her head tingling. The high-profile role in the sell-out run would have cemented her star status, the journalist had said. Were the rumours that she'd been taken suddenly ill true? Evie's reply was fudged and, reading on, Amber saw that her great-aunt had steered the conversation to six months later, when the BBC came looking for her to play a cameo role in *Spencer Row*, and when Evie had seen the script at a production meeting, she'd asked if she could test instead for the part of Jo Baxter, the abrasive, uncouth wife of the main criminal character.

The rest is history, the journalist had stated.

Amber sat back absorbing this information. Something had happened to Evie back in – she checked the dates in the article – December 1990 that caused her to crash out of her best role to date. There was something significant about that date, Amber realised. She sat for several moments until it came to her, a frisson running through her when she realised it had something to do with her grandfather. Fingers trembling, Amber deleted her search history and closed the lid of the laptop. No matter how difficult it might be, she would have to talk to Evie about London in 1990. And she had to talk to her mother. Apart from the hit-and-run, Jessica didn't know what had been going on with her aunt. Amber fired off a quick text to her, suggesting a visit to Laurel Lawns.

But first up, Evie's safety was a priority. For all her casual protestations to the contrary, there was no doubt her great-aunt had a vicious enemy. No harm, Amber decided, in paying a little visit to Matthew Casey.

The pub in Naas where Jamie worked was busier than Jessica had expected when she walked in on Tuesday evening. She'd asked to meet him, surprised when he'd said he could only see her during his break.

'You must be a busy man,' she'd said. 'Or have you a woman on the go?'

'Are you joking? Not after the last time.'

'What happened the last time? I didn't know you'd been unlucky in love.'

'Are you coming out or not?' he'd said. 'We've a party coming in at eight o'clock so I'll be needed.'

'I'll be there.'

It meant she'd had to jump in the car and head straight down to Naas as soon as she came home from work, telling Paul she'd sort out dinner when she returned home. Nowadays, her life seemed on a constant merry-go-round of one juggle after another, including the strained finances. Paul hadn't been too impressed, asking her outright why she needed to head down to Naas to see Jamie so urgently. She'd made an excuse to fob him off.

'Quite a change, sis, you turning up here,' Jamie said, pulling out a chair opposite her, having brought over glasses of still water and a bowl of nuts.

She'd chosen to sit in a corner, away from the general melee and out of range of the television screens. Too late, she realised she was half-trapped in there with Jamie and his air of belligerence facing her down.

'What's the big occasion?' he asked.

'Does there have to be one?'

'Come on, this is scarcely a social visit. What's up?'

Jessica gave him a measured look. 'A man has called into the nursing home to visit Mum, at least twice. The thing is, he's telling the staff he's Simon. But it's not him.'

'When did this happen?'

'The first visit that I know of was in June of this year.'

He helped himself to some nuts while he looked at her with narrowed eyes. 'What's going on?'

'I don't know. It's weird, though. He didn't want us to know his identity, but it didn't bother him that we might get to hear of his visits.'

'That's mad.' Jamie sat up straighter all of a sudden.

'It might be nothing,' Jessica said, 'but, still, why pretend to be Simon?'

'He didn't want to be identified?' Jamie suggested.

'Well, obviously, but why? Have you any idea who it might be?'

'*Me?* No.'

'There's something else,' she said. She told him about Pippa's next-of-kin document being accessed and printed on the same date as the visitor had called. 'I thought it was a bit too coincidental,' she said. 'Short of lining up the nursing-home staff and giving them a grilling, there's no way to know if it was an administrative procedure or if the details were actually passed on to anyone else, which could make it a breach of data privacy.'

The more Jessica had thought about it, the more her head had throbbed. Had the information been handed to whoever was impersonating Simon? It was significant that he had called in on the day it had been accessed. Yet what use were their personal details to anyone? Whoever had impersonated Simon must have known he lived in Hong Kong before they'd called to the nursing home. Yet what about her email address falling into a stranger's hand? The email address that had been used to scam her out of a lot of money? She tried to tell herself she was over-reacting but it was impossible to rein in her anxieties.

'It's a major fuck-up if that's how someone got their hands on my New York address.'

'What do you mean?' His eyes shifted away from her.

Something crawled in her chest. 'Did someone get your address who wasn't supposed to have it? You'd better tell me.'

'I dunno,' he said, shrugging.

'Right then, play it your way.' She picked up her bag, pretending to leave. 'I've things to do.'

'I got something,' he said. 'In the post. In New York.'

'Like what?'

'Hang on a sec,' he said, getting to his feet. 'I

have it in my room. Hey, why don't you come up with me? I don't fancy having this conversation in the bar.'

'That sounds ominous,' Jessica said.

'It is,' he said.

Apprehension gripping her, she picked up her glass of water and followed him across the floor, through a code-activated side door and up a flight of stairs.

Jessica didn't know what she'd expected of Jamie's bedsit, but not this – an anonymous room holding a double bed and wardrobe, a small table and two chairs, and, at one end, the tiniest excuse for a kitchen she'd ever seen, with an overhead press, a space holding a kettle, toaster, and microwave, and a small sink, looking like they'd been shoehorned into place, everything so meagre.

Was this the sum total of her brother's life?

'I have the use of the shared bathroom on the landing and the kitchen downstairs,' he said, as though he sensed her surprise at his surroundings.

'Is this all your – everything you have?' she said, indicating the single wardrobe and the books on the bedside locker. He hadn't brought much in the way of belongings to Laurel Lawns, but Jessica had assumed that her brother's possessions were being shipped from New York and had since been redirected to Naas. Or maybe it had suited her, caught up in her own busyness, not to delve too much into his life.

'I like to travel light,' he said, fixing her with a defensive look that dared her to contradict him.

She saw a dog-eared photo on his bedside locker, and the sight of it ambushed her. She also had a copy of it, a family photo taken years ago on the esplanade in Bray, her father with toddler Jamie sitting on his shoulders, twelve-year-old

Jessica and Simon standing beside him, all of them squinting into the sunlight in front of an expanse of sea gleaming like crushed tinfoil. A stranger had taken it, Jessica remembered, her mother in bed with one of her headaches, her father bringing them out for seafront chips and ice-cream cones as a treat.

Jamie took an envelope out of his locker. 'You'd better sit down,' he said.

Jessica did as he asked.

'Have a look,' he said, sitting beside her, handing her the envelope.

Jamie's New York address was typed across the front of the envelope, which had been airmailed from Ireland. She pulled out a card with the photo of an ugly grinning monkey on the front. A message had been typed out on a separate piece of paper and affixed inside: 'I KNOW WHO YOUR REAL FATHER IS – DO YOU?'

Jessica studied it for several moments, trying to grasp her spinning thoughts.

'You don't look too surprised,' Jamie said. 'Did you know about this?'

She ignored his question, unsure how to answer it. She replaced the card in the envelope and said, 'Is this what brought you home?'

'No way, not this piece of crap. Is that all you have to say? You still haven't told me if you knew about this. So, Jessica, is my father actually my father or what?'

'Why didn't you show it to me before now?'

'See? You're still avoiding my question. For all I know you could have sent this card.'

'*Me?*'

'You could have been fed up being the only one in Dublin and available for Mum. Maybe you were trying to stir the shit.'

'For God's sake, Jamie, I'm in enough shit as it is without stirring up any more.'

'Are you? What kind?'

She had spoken without thinking clearly. She took a deep breath. 'The usual – mortgages, bills – anyhow, I didn't send this.'

'But you know something about it – like who my real father is.'

'I don't,' she said, deciding that a white lie was the best option for now. 'You must have got a bit of a shock. It's a shock to me too,' she went on truthfully, alarmed that Jamie had received this in the post. 'What are you going to do about it?'

'It wasn't that much of a bombshell,' Jamie said, sighing. 'I think I've always known on some level that we've different fathers.'

'What makes you think that?' Jessica asked. 'Dad never treated you any differently to me or Simon.'

'No, he didn't, and big respect to him for that. I heard them arguing a few times years ago, mostly Mum arguing with Dad – or not my dad,' he said, sounding resigned. 'I heard one or two things she said, something along the lines that he was a fool if he thought all her children were his. Another time

I heard him saying that he loved all the children equally and she called him – God ...'

Jessica waited quietly.

Jamie rubbed his face. 'She called him a big fucking dope for being so gullible.' He met Jessica's gaze. 'I asked her, you know.

Just the once, before I went to New York. I asked her if I had a different father to you and Simon.'

'And?'

'She went bananas. She threw something at me – a glass, a plate – and said I had been another one of her stupid mistakes. I don't know if she meant my birth was the mistake, or if the affair was a mistake. She refused to talk about it after that. I put it all behind me when I went to New York. I wasn't going to let it mess up my life.'

'And did it?'

'No. Being away from it all was a great chance to reinvent myself. It was just what I needed. I managed to forget all about it, until now. But, look, this has to prove that Mum had an affair and I have a different father.'

'This card doesn't prove anything,' Jessica said.

'Come on, Jessica, you were older than me, you must have heard far more rows.' He raised his eyebrows questioningly. When Jessica made no response – what could she have said anyway? There was some truth in what Jamie was saying – he continued. 'Mum felt unloved and unwanted. You don't have an affair unless something is wrong with your marriage. And there *was* something wrong. You know Mum, she was so single-minded, there's no way she would have strayed unless she was terribly unhappy. I heard her shouting at my supposed dad on more than one occasion, something about knowing she was always only second best. Then I heard her asking him how did it feel to know he was second best in bed.'

Jamie hadn't overheard anything that Jessica hadn't heard, and his words plunged her back there, sending a wave of pain through her.

'It was all right for you,' Jamie said. 'You escaped early on.'

'Escaped? Did I? I'd hardly call getting pregnant and rushing into marriage with Paul an escape.'

'That's what it seemed like to me. A convenient way out for you, too busy setting up your own life to have time for Mum or me. I was – what, twelve when you got married? – I was left with her, watching her life fall apart slowly but surely. Mum often spent the day in her dressing gown, her hair in bits, the smell of drink on her breath. I'd come home from school to no food and no heating. Her friends stopped calling – even my friends were too embarrassed to drop by. You've no idea how much I hated what happened to our family.'

Jessica stayed silent.

Jamie picked up the card and tapped the edge of it off the table. 'I'm not going to do anything about this for now,' he said. 'If whoever sent this wanted to shock the living daylights out of me, they didn't succeed. If it happens to be true, it means someone out there knows and wants to fuck me over. And if whoever fathered me sent it as a weird way of making contact, I'm sure I'll find out sooner or later. If and when I come face to face with him, I'll be so angry that I'll be tempted to inflict some serious injury on him.'

'Hey, Jamie, calm down.'

'I don't feel like calming down. Where was he, in my mother's life? Why didn't he hang around? Why didn't he look after her, take care of her, when she was left all alone?'

'Look – you don't know if any of this is true,' Jessica said.

'And why wasn't Evie there for her, when Mum needed a sister? That bitch didn't give a shite.'

'You don't know what was really going on in Mum's life.'

'Sounds like you do, in which case you had better enlighten me.'

Jessica wavered for a moment. She took another sip of water to prevent herself from blurting something and to give herself some precious time to think. She had a good idea who Jamie's father was, and she also knew the extent of the role Evie had played in causing her mother's unhappiness. But absolutely no good would come from her telling Jamie now, and whatever way she explained it, he would twist it to suit himself. He was like his mother in that regard – seeing only his side of the story and no one else's. On the one hand she couldn't blame him, he'd had a rough ride through childhood and adolescence, but so did lots of people, and over the years, she'd tried to encourage him to forget about old hurts and mould a life of his own, just as she had done. Now that wretched card had upset everything.

'Look, Jamie, what I'm trying to say is none of us knows what's going on behind closed doors.'

Jamie sat back and crossed his arms. 'By the way I did call in to the home to see Mum, just in case she had any comprehension at all.'

'You called in without me? When?'

'I showed her the card,' Jamie said. 'I held it up to her face. I asked her if she knew who my father was. But I got nowhere with her.'

Jessica was shaken. As much by the vehemence in Jamie's tone as the fact that he had lied to her. 'Why did you lie to me when I asked if you had visited?'

'Did I?' he said. 'If I remember, I said it was something I'd no wish to repeat.'

'Oh, you're clever,' she said. 'What else are you twisting with your choice of words?'

'I didn't pass myself off as Simon,' he said moodily.

'You told me earlier you didn't come home because of that piece of shit.' She pointed to the card. 'So it has to have been something more significant. Any chance you might tell me about that? Let me know what's really going on?'

He stared into space for several moments. Then he shook his head and laughed. 'No way, dear sister, no way. You're best left in blissful ignorance before I ruin whatever is left of your poor opinion of me.'

'It can't be that bad,' she said.

'Want to bet?'

He refused to be drawn on it. He stood up, saying his break time was over and that she would have to leave.

It was typical Jamie, she decided as she got into her car. She'd gone to see him to talk through one problem, and he'd presented her with another. She drove home almost on autopilot, wondering why he'd left New York and what was going on in his life that was so bad.

Amber slowed her car when she came to the crossroads outside the Glenmaragh View. The bunting was fluttering away as normal, but the car park was empty, the shop and café now closed for the evening. She turned up into the mountains, taking the route into west Wicklow, where long golden darts of sunshine flashed through the autumn trees and clusters of burnt-orange leaves twirled around in the verges.

She'd made an excuse to Evie to cover her absence; she was paying a quick visit to one of her college friends who lived outside Wicklow town. 'Just as a way of reconnecting,' she'd said. 'I won't be too long.' She felt bad for fibbing to her great-aunt, but Evie would have been anxious and worried if she'd known about her mission to find Temple Raven and talk to Matthew Casey.

She took the same route she had earlier that day, making sure to watch for the corkscrew bend. The right-hand turn for the road to Temple Raven was barely discernible and easy to miss, but she saw it in time, the road there even narrower, the tops of the trees meeting overhead as she drove along. After a while, when she realised she had to be close to Temple Raven, her chest tightened and she found it difficult to breathe. If she got cold feet, she decided, she could simply turn around and go home.

In her anxiety she overshot the house, slowing to

a halt after she'd passed a set of high wooden gates mounted between two impressive pillars, the name Temple Raven etched in one of them. She had to drive half a kilometre further on before she could turn around, which she did breathing as slowly and calmly as possible. Then she pulled into the small inlet in front of the gates and got out. The air was chillier up at this height, but the breeze purer. She saw the keypad at the same time as she saw the tiny telescopic glint of a camera lens set into the pillar. Feeling as though she was outside of herself, watching on, she pressed the buzzer. Presently there was the sound of a click and a woman's voice spoke. 'Can I help you?'

'Hello,' Amber said. 'I'd like to speak to Matthew Casey? My name is Amber Lennox and I'm the grand-niece of Evie Lawrence.'

'Is he expecting you?'

'No, but this shouldn't take too long.'

'What is it in connection with?'

'It's private and confidential.'

There was silence at the other end and she had the feeling she was being watched on a security camera somewhere inside the house.

After a minute the woman spoke again. 'Can you give me some indication of what this is about?'

At least she wasn't being sent away. But there was no point pretending she was there for a picnic. She took a deep breath to calm her quivering nerves. 'I need to talk to Matthew Casey about my aunt's hit-and-run accident.'

After a short pause, the woman's voice came again. 'Mr Matthew Casey will see you, but he's free for five minutes, no more.'

Amber felt her senses on high alert as the smooth gates began to glide apart. She jumped into her car and drove up a curving grey cobble-locked driveway bordered by beech hedging, and around a swathe of manicured velvet lawn, rimmed with beautifully landscaped trees and a profusion of flowering shrubs drenched in evening sunshine. She arrived at the front of an imposing bungalow with dormer windows, where the driveway opened out into a wide sweep and a section of it went on around to a large double garage. As she stepped into the porch, the hall door opened, revealing a middle-aged woman wearing a cream blouse and black trousers.

'Please follow me,' she said, in a mannerly tone. She led the way through a marble-floored hall bedecked with beautiful mirrors and hung with photographs and portraits, doors closed on each side, denying Amber a peek inside. At the far end of the hall, she turned around by a wide staircase and led Amber into a big study that held deep-blue velour sofas, two walls lined with perfectly arranged bookshelves, and a large neat and tidy desk, behind which a man sat with his back to her. He was looking out through floor-to-ceiling windows that afforded a spectacular view down into a Wicklow valley, with the pine-forested curve of the mountains to one side. September sunshine lay across the autumn landscape in columns of golden light.

'Wow,' she said, the word coming involuntarily.

The man swivelled around in his deep leather armchair and faced her. He was wearing a pair of jeans and a dark blue jumper. Matthew Casey. If he had seemed striking in the *Wicklow Weekly* photograph, he was even more so in the flesh. He had a vibrant energy that rolled off him in waves and an undeniable aura of power and affluence. Sharp intelligence shone out of his grey eyes as he looked at Amber. She wondered why the photograph of him had seemed familiar. She was satisfied she'd never met him before. He was not a man you would easily forget.

'Beautiful, isn't it?' he said. 'It's something I never tire of.'

'Can I get you anything before I leave?' the woman asked him.

'No, thank you, Irene,' he said, his voice polite. 'Unless Ms Lennox would like tea or coffee? Some water?' he went on, looking impassively at Amber.

He was obviously going to grant her longer than five minutes but Amber shook her head. 'No thanks.' She didn't trust herself holding a container of any kind of liquid, her hands were so shaky.

'Well then, Irene, you might as well head off for the evening,' he said.

'Sure, Matthew, everything is prepared,' Irene said. 'The casserole will be ready in five minutes.'

She gave Amber a look that said she'd want to make herself scarce by then.

'Sit down, Ms Lennox,' he said, as soon as Irene had left the room, indicating an armchair to one side of his desk. And then in an even voice he said, 'What brings you here?'

'My great-aunt – Evie Lawrence – I'm staying with her in Heronbrook, close to Glenmaragh, while she recovers from a hit-and-run,' Amber said, having rehearsed the words in advance. 'She was knocked down by a motorcyclist on a laneway near the beach. The police appealed for witnesses. Did you know about that?'

'Ms Lennox,' he said neutrally, 'I lead a busy life and the minutiae of what goes on in Wicklow doesn't cross my radar.'

'The police are investigating if the hit-and-run was deliberate,' Amber said. 'And now Evie has also had her tyres slashed, just this week, and there were other threatening incidents. It's most peculiar.'

'How can I possibly be of help with this?' he said.

'The police have asked Evie if she has any enemies.'

'Enemies?' He shot out the word, giving her a cold look, and all her nerve endings jangled.

What did she think she was doing here?

'I believe you and my great-aunt go back a long way,' she said, deciding to put it up to him. 'You have … history between you.'

'Are you implying that I could have had something

to do with these incidents?' he said in an arctic tone of voice.

It was exactly what she had been beginning to think. This man sitting in front of her had every reason to hate Evie's guts because of what had happened to his sister all those years ago.

'I'm trying to establish if anyone had a grudge of any sort against my aunt,' she said.

'You hardly suspect me?' he said, staring at her with a slightly insolent look.

She didn't reply, holding his stare. Silence grew and swelled. Amber held her breath and steeled herself for some kind of explosion as he continued to observe her carefully. And then everything tilted when he laughed as though Amber had cracked a good joke.

'I think you do suspect me, Ms Lennox. What a preposterous idea!' He granted her a superior look that raised her hackles.

'Is it?' she said, going in all guns blazing in her attempts to get to the truth. 'You have good reason to be hostile towards Evie Lawrence and her family for what happened to your sister.'

His eyes glittered. 'Has she sent you to question me?'

'No,' Amber admitted. 'She doesn't know I'm here.'

'Excuse me a moment,' he said, looking horribly calm as he rose to his feet. He walked out of the room, leaving Amber alone.

Her stomach heaved with apprehension. What the hell did she think she was up to? She had come up here, linking Matthew Casey to Evie's intimidation in her efforts to get to the bottom of Evie's problems but she was totally out of her depth. She'd absolutely nothing to back up her statements, beyond a gut instinct. Yet suppose she was right? Suppose Matthew was responsible for Evie's accident, almost killing her? It would mean he was totally ruthless and she'd put herself in danger.

Where had he gone? She listened hard, but there wasn't a sound breaking the thick silence. She imagined the worst – the cold steel of a knife being pushed against the back of her neck, or a bodyguard arriving to 'take care' of her. He looked like the type to have a bodyguard. She was probably being watched even now, and she stared around the room, looking for evidence of a camera lens. There could be anything hidden in the bookshelves, she decided. Her gaze darted around his desk: an expensive-looking laptop, a selection of thick cream stationery and pens, and neatly arranged paperwork and documents that she scanned, trying to make sense of them upside down.

Something tugged at the edge of her mind.

She was tempted to take out her mobile to get a quick photo of the documents when she looked out the picture window to the valley stretching below. If anything were to happen to her she could kick and scream all she liked, but up here, in the remotest wilds, no one would hear her. Her body could be thrown down into that valley and never found again. No one apart from Irene knew she was here, confronting a potential adversary of Evie's.

How foolish she'd been.

She got to her feet, wanting to escape. Then he walked back in and she froze.

'Sorry about that,' he said mildly. 'I had to turn off the oven.' Then, observing her, 'you weren't leaving, were you, Ms Lennox?'

'I think I'm wasting my time,' she said.

'And mine,' he said pointedly. 'But we haven't finished our conversation yet.' It was an order, and he sat back into his leather chair, looking unperturbed. 'You were implying I could be responsible for what has befallen your aunt?'

'I'm looking at all possibilities,' Amber said, sitting rigidly on the edge of her seat, ready to make a run for it.

'That is some tale you have invented,' he went on. 'But I'd like to assure you that if I'd ever felt any antagonism towards Evie Lawrence for what happened to Leah, I can guarantee you she would have known all about it long before now.'

'You mean you don't hold any ill will towards her? I find that hard to believe.'

'It's not that difficult,' he said crisply. 'I have no feelings whatsoever towards Evie Lawrence.'

She was beginning to sense a core of hard steel underneath Matthew Casey's exterior.

'Let me explain, Ms Lennox,' he said. 'Our

family was never the same after Leah's accident. My parents never spoke of that day – it was a forbidden subject but it hung over us like a cloud. I was six years of age at the time. I wasn't sure what exactly had taken place other than my parents blamed my older sister Rachel for not looking after Leah properly. It was a huge burden for Rachel to bear. In subsequent years, my parents devoted a lot of time and energy towards managing Leah's needs, so much so that Rachel and I barely got a look-in.'

Amber nodded her head. This was what she had imagined: a family torn apart, a heartbroken brother out for revenge. His next words surprised her.

'It didn't bother me,' he said. 'I got on with life, Rachel less so. It was easier for me because I could hardly remember a time when Leah hadn't needed care. It had the effect of spurring me on. I turned to my studies and worked hard to catch my parents' attention and win their approval. A lot of my contemporaries left school at fifteen, but I stayed on and was the first in my family to go to college, where I graduated with first-class honours.'

He sounded to Amber like he was boasting. Still, she realised with a tiny dart of compassion, he had accomplished a lot, after what must have been a very difficult childhood.

'I am a successful man, Ms Lennox,' he said, his voice a quiet monotone. 'Maintaining that level of success is what drives me. It was only in the spring of this year, when Rachel unfortunately became ill and spoke about our childhoods, that she told me she'd been fooling around in the woods with Barry Talbot the afternoon of Leah's accident, something she'd been forbidden to do, and that it was the Lawrence girls who should have been taking care of my sister.'

'So you always thought your sister was responsible for Leah's accident, until earlier this year?' Amber said.

There was a short silence. Then he gave Amber a cold look, ignoring what she'd said. 'Rachel was responsible insofar as she allowed Leah out of her sight. Rachel is now dead. Fact. My parents are long dead. Fact. Leah is being looked after. Fact. I lead a busy and fulfilling life,' he went on, a hard edge to his voice. 'There's no room in that life for harbouring a grudge against a seventy-something woman, and I haven't the slightest interest in endangering her life. I don't need that kind of silly, juvenile power trip. So I suggest you take yourself and your shabby little accusations out of here,' he said, his eyes hostile, 'and be thankful I'm not suing you for defamation of character.' He stood up, signifying the conversation was at an end. 'I'll see you out,' he said.

He escorted Amber out into the hall. She caught an aroma coming through a door that was now slightly ajar. The kitchen, she guessed, glancing into a large, brightly lit room with floor-to-ceiling windows giving on to the valley, an oak table with a bowl of roses in the centre, and two place settings including crystal wine glasses. Matthew marched up the hall, opening the door wide and closing it behind her the minute she stepped out onto the porch. Holding her head high, she strode across to her car, unable to shake the uncomfortable feeling that she was being watched. She looked back at the windows but there was no sign of anyone.

She drove back to Glenmaragh and Heronbrook. Matthew Casey seemed to have been telling the truth, but now that she was free of her challenging encounter with him and her head had cleared a little, she realised that something had chimed like a faint alarm bell in her subconscious during the time she'd been sitting in Temple Raven, but frustratingly, that's where it stubbornly remained.

He might have protested his innocence, but Amber had the nagging feeling Matthew Casey was still in the frame.

Evie loved this time of the evening when the sun was going down and the garden was bathed in cool softness and shadows. The air was layered with the call of the birds and rich scents drifting up from the plants and soil, everything all the sweeter in the golden wash of the approaching sunset. Perhaps when Amber returned from visiting her friend they would sit outside for a while.

Her mobile pinged, a new email notification. She opened the app – it was from Jessica. She couldn't remember Jessica emailing her previously – had she even given her niece her address? But there wasn't any text, just an attachment. Evie opened it and something squeezed the air out of her lungs.

The attachment was a clip from an episode of *Delphin Terrace*. It showed the last few seconds of her soap opera character's life, just after the collision. Ma Donnelly lay by the side of the road, the camera zooming in on her pale face, her eyelids fluttering before they finally closed. The camera zoomed out to focus on the trail of thick red blood pouring from the back of her head. The scene was eerily hushed except for the sound of a bird singing, and then the rousing music of the *Delphin Terrace* signature tune broke in and the final credits rolled.

She closed her email and, fingers trembling, called Jessica, who answered straight away, a hollow ring to her voice.

'Hi, Aunt Evie? In case the line is bad, I'm driving. How are things?'

'You're driving?'

'Yes, I'm on the way home from seeing Jamie in Naas.'

'So you wouldn't have sent me an email just now?'

Jessica laughed. 'I know I try to multitask but I'm not superwoman. Are you sure it was from me?'

'I'll have another look.'

'Amber texted something about coming up to Laurel Lawns this week,' Jessica said, 'maybe tomorrow evening? I presume you'll be coming with her? It would be lovely to see you.'

Evie gave a noncommittal answer before ending the call. She replied to the email, receiving an 'undelivered' notification. Then she closed her eyes and sat in the cool silence of the kitchen. She would have to send Amber home, where she'd be safe from whoever was menacing Evie.

Despite her own anxiety, she couldn't help noticing that Amber was distracted when she arrived home from visiting her friend, a taut smile fixed to her face when she greeted Evie. It didn't take long for her grand-niece to come out with what was bothering her.

'We need to talk,' Amber said, sitting down at the table opposite her, her chin in her hands, giving her a level look. 'I know someone is harassing you in much the same way that your *Delphin Terrace* character was intimidated. The hit-and-run ... the dead animal ... the tyres.'

'How did you find out?'

'I googled you,' Amber said, her blue eyes half-apologetic, half-challenging, as if daring Evie to chastise her for this. 'I also saw the nasty message you were sent on a Polaroid,' Amber said, softening her voice, 'purely by accident, the first morning I was here.'

'I see.'

'I find it worrying, Evie,' Amber said, looking at her steadily. 'I can't understand why you haven't mentioned all this to the police, apart from not being honest with me.'

'I have my reasons,' Evie said.

'We'll come back to those in a minute,' Amber said. 'There's something else I want to ask you about, to do with our family.' She gave Evie a smile that was a blend of sadness and concern. 'What exactly happened in London in 1990?'

Evie's heart quivered at the sudden memory. 'Why are you asking this?'

'I read in an article that you walked away from a high-profile play because you were ill. Did that have anything to do with my grandfather? He was in London then, wasn't he? I remember Mum telling me that when I asked where he was... She said he was there in 1990 when ...' her voice broke.

Evie closed her eyes.

Amber took a deep breath. 'Sorry, look, I'm trying to find out what happened. I think I deserve the truth. It was six months before you returned to work.'

'I wasn't pregnant,' Evie said, 'if that's what you're thinking.'

'I don't know what to think,' Amber said,

running her hand through her hair, blinking hard in a way that jolted Evie.

'I'll tell you about Lucien in a moment,' she said, taking a deep, steadying breath. 'You're right, you deserve to know. But what you said about the harassment – I got an email this evening, when you were out. There was no text, just a short clip attached of the closing moments of the final scene I played in *Delphin Terrace*, when Ma Donnelly was killed in a hit-and-run.'

'God. That's creepy. But you must know who sent it?'

'That's the thing ... at first glance I thought it was from Jessica. That's the only reason I opened it. I rang her but she was in the car driving from Naas. Then on closer inspection I realised that the email address looked like it could be Jessica's, but some of the vowels were replaced by digits. I replied to it but I got an "undelivered" notification. Whoever sent it to me must have deleted the account straightaway.'

'Who'd have your email address?'

'Lots of people – acquaintances, and journalists, other actors in London and from my time on *Delphin Terrace*,' Evie said. 'The hit-and-run could have been entirely coincidental, but when someone read about it in the press it might have given them the hare-brained idea to spook me. People do horrible things for no good reason other than a few power trips. Maybe they didn't like my character. Maybe they're annoyed she was killed off. Maybe they don't like me, they're jealous of my success. It could be someone who's confusing fantasy and reality. There are plenty of wretched people out there ready to attack, especially if you're in the public eye.'

'I still think it's a matter for the police.'

Evie fidgeted with her mobile. Then she gave Amber a straight look. 'Problem is,' she said, 'I don't want the police digging into my past looking for possible motives – that diligent Garda O'Reilly for example.'

'Why not?'

'They could uproot an old family skeleton, and the problem with that is it would look like Pippa's family have every reason to be hostile towards me.'

'You mean us?'

'As well as that,' Evie said, 'what's the betting it would get plastered across the tabloids by a gossip-hungry media? I don't want that happening. I don't care about me, but it wouldn't be fair on you or Jessica.'

'It can't be that bad,' Amber said, giving a half-laugh.

'I only told you part of the story,' Evie said. 'You don't know the rest of what played out between me and Pippa and Lucien. You were asking about London in 1990 – if you knew what happened there, you wouldn't want to know me. But much as I don't want to shatter my lovely new connections with you and Jessica,' she said, her voice a little wobbly, 'I don't want you getting caught up in someone's warped idea of fun. What I have to tell you will, I hope, send you home and far away from me.'

Evie, 1975–1980

London was an exciting place to be in the 1970s, a colourful decade of change, creativity, and general upheaval. I went to loud parties in stuffy clubs where I met artists, photographers, musicians, DJs. Feeling eviscerated inside, I drank too much, didn't eat properly, skimming along the surface of things, keeping my energy for my work. Somehow, with the aid of thick panstick, a costume, and often a wig, I managed to transform myself night after night into whoever I was supposed to be. The stage was an escape, the only way to paper over the bruises in my heart.

My mother visited me every three or four months, her conversation carefully vetted to include some references to Pippa and her children, designed to make me feel included in the family. She rarely mentioned Lucien. I popped home two or three times a year. Occasionally my visits were rudely interrupted by Pippa, arriving into Drumcondra with children and Lucien in tow, claiming to have forgotten I was visiting. I know she did it on purpose to flaunt them in front of me.

I told myself that I only longed for Lucien because I had been thwarted by my sister, that whatever we had been to each other would have fizzled out in time – we were too young to be soulmates, each other's north star, lovers for life; but when I saw him on those occasions, it scalded my heart and unsettled me for weeks. We never spoke. I ignored him and Pippa as much as possible, directing my scant conversation to my mother, a granite-faced Lucien equally monosyllabic.

I wondered how suffocated he felt, sitting in his airless office with a view of passing traffic. I thought of the boy who'd sat under the trees and I wondered if the beating heart of him was still there under the straitjacket into which he'd allowed life to thrust him. My one crumb of comfort was that at least he was still alive and on this planet, and as long as he was still here, the future was open to some possibilities.

I knew Lucien was still working in Dame Street, and once, when I was home in Dublin to visit my mother and waiting at a bus stop in Westmoreland Street, I saw him coming towards me with a colleague, both of them clutching briefcases, heading to a meeting somewhere. My heart flew into my throat. My blood roared in my ears. I jammed on my sunglasses and shrank into the crowd waiting at the bus stop. His stride faltered and stopped. Had he sensed he was being scrutinised? In that moment I could see he looked tired, slightly worn. I wanted to hold his face in my hands and kiss away the tiredness. I wanted to lie with him all night long. It was still there, everything I had felt for him. I told myself I shouldn't be having these feelings –

he was Pippa's husband, father to her children, he slept in her bed every night. I watched as he glanced further down the street. Then he said something to his colleague and turned back towards Dame Street. My gaze fastened on the back of his head, the sight of it so dear to me, until I lost him in the weaving crowd of pedestrians.

When they were just over eight years married, my mother told me that Pippa was pregnant again. The news hit me like a sledgehammer. What had I expected? They were husband and wife, *of course* they were sleeping together. I was stupid to think otherwise. This time Pippa gave birth to a boy, Jamie, and I visited Dublin less frequently, making sure to avoid her.

The following year, one Sunday afternoon as I headed for the departure gates in Dublin airport, I met Lucien on the concourse in a heart-stopping moment.

'Evie,' he said, his voice hoarse.

'What are you doing here?' I asked, my head sparking. Was he London-bound like me? Going somewhere on business? Otherwise he should be with Pippa. My mother had told me Pippa and Lucien would be calling over that afternoon, after I had left, to plan the twins' birthday celebration – an annual event I was always absent from.

'I've been watching for you,' he said. 'I knew you were flying back to London this afternoon.'

'I'm surprised at you,' I said, my heartbeat quickening, furious with the way the sight of him almost dissolved me. 'What would Pippa say? Aren't you supposed to be with her now, visiting my mother, playing happy families, and making plans for your children?'

'I managed to get out of that. I needed to see you.'

I couldn't bear to look at his eyes. My gaze fastened on the boarding gate I'd be going through in a moment. 'It's a bit late for that now,' I said. 'You're married to my sister. You've made your bed and you can go lie in it.'

'Oh, I have and I am.'

'Don't remind me.' *Please don't remind me you're sleeping with her, being intimate, rejoicing over the life you've made together.*

'It's not what you think. I'm paying for my mistake. And so is Pippa.'

'I'm sure she is,' I said disparagingly.

'She knows I was never truly hers.'

'You both seem to be making the best of things, from what I hear.'

Then he surprised me. 'I saw you in town, last year, at the bus stop.'

'Did you?'

'I *knew*, Evie. I sensed you, and then I saw you. I had to turn back and pretend you weren't there because otherwise ...'

'Well?'

'Otherwise, Evie, I would have pulled you into my arms, even if my colleague was looking on, ready to report it all back to Pippa. She was pregnant with Jamie at the time.' His next words surprised me. 'Even though I'm fairly sure Jamie isn't mine because' – his voice broke – 'we don't … hardly ever.' He swallowed. 'Pippa sometimes strays from that bed.'

I felt a flicker of unease. Much as I resented their marriage, the idea of Pippa being unfaithful to Lucien was a hollow victory. How messy was life.

'That's none of my business whatsoever.'

'I choose to ignore that, just as I ignore her drinking and the occasional nights she goes out with her friends and doesn't come home. And I do that out of guilt because I never really loved her and to keep the show on the road, especially for Jessica and Simon. And little Jamie, who is part of our family regardless.'

I shrugged. 'None of this explains what you're doing here.'

'See, the airport is different, Evie. It's full of people saying goodbye. We won't be noticed in the crowd.'

His lips brushed mine, sending a shock through me. Then he pulled me into his arms, and – oh, my treacherous heart – I gave into it, for long, delicious moments. His mouth crushed mine and I kissed him back as deeply as he kissed me, absorbing every glorious second, telling myself I had to store this up for the empty days ahead.

Then I wrenched myself away and ran without looking back.

Evie, 1980–1990

The 1980s in London were nowhere near as drab as life in Ireland. There was a lot of social rebellion, mirrored in the angry punk music that proliferated over the airwaves. I began to shun parties, tired of the sight of tables overflowing with glasses and bottles, tired of glass-eyed people falling into them, too drunk to see the mess. I poured my energy into my career. I moved twice, a bedsit in Wandsworth, then a small flat in Shepherd's Bush. While I didn't scale the heights of such luminaries as Helen Mirren and Maggie Smith, I won an Olivier award for the role of Portia in *The Merchant of Venice*, an accolade I found particularly bittersweet.

But then there was something about the dawn of 1990, a ray of hope and optimism that flickered softly in the air like a freshly lit candle. We were within sight of a whole new millennium. I was coming up to my mid-forties, but not the kind of forties my parents had experienced. The post-war babies were singing a different tune, buying wholeheartedly into the notion that the forties were the new thirties. I moved from Shepherd's Bush to a more spacious apartment in Holland Park. When my mother told me quietly that she'd heard Leah Casey was now settled in a comfortable care home, I immediately made anonymous donations to fund a sizeable activities budget. I sometimes found my name linked with men in the tabloids, even if we'd just been for lunch, usually accompanied by vastly exaggerated gossip. No matter how much I enjoyed a few dalliances, my heart remained in Lucien's keeping. The first time I heard Sinead O'Connor's 'Nothing Compares 2 U', the hairs rose on the back of my neck, so much did the emotion of it all resonate with me.

London turned into fairyland for Christmas, and in 1990 the city was even more magical as the festive season approached, thanks to falls of snow throughout December coating everything in filigree white lace. It was magical for me too, as I had just landed my biggest role to date, the role that could elevate my career and launch it into the stratosphere - Lady Macbeth. Then I dreamt of Lucien one night, the dream so vivid that, on waking, I half-expected to see him in my bed, in the bathroom, at my breakfast table. When he wasn't, the emptiness and sense of loss were so painful that for the next few days I couldn't get him out of my mind. I imagined him in the audience, his upturned face smiling at me, his eyes seeking me through the crowds between us. I pulled my heart out of the depths on the stage that week, hearing the longing for him in my voice, feeling it shine through my face and eyes, so that by the end of that week, when I came off stage, I was totally flatlined.

And when he appeared in my dressing room after the performance on Saturday night, for those first few moments I was convinced that my imagination had conjured him up. Even as we greeted each other – awkwardly, to say the least – I was convinced I was having that conversation in my head, just as I had played and replayed conversations with him in my mind, many times over.

'How did you know where to find me?' I asked.

'It's not that difficult to check out the London theatre listings,' he said.

When he came closer, so that I could see newly silvering hair at his temples, fresh lines around his eyes and mouth, I knew he was here at last. But instead of feeling impelled to run into his arms, it was if someone emptied a vat of ice-cold water over my head and down the length of my body: I became chilled to the bone, my teeth chattering, my arms hugging myself through the thin material of my dressing gown. Then I flew at him, hitting him wherever I could, my hands raining blows on his cheeks, his neck, his arms, his chest. 'What took you so long?' I cried, my voice raw.

'Evie ... please ...'

'I've been waiting and waiting ...' My arms flailed in vain as he caught them, holding them tightly, drawing me close, folding me into him, against his overcoat. His breath on my cheek, the scent of him, the pure solidity of him, poured into my parched cells like vital, life-giving water. I fumbled with the buttons of his coat, opening them, pushing it aside so that I could burrow right into him, against the soft texture of his jumper, the solid wall of his chest, heat, warmth, and his beating heart.

We went to my flat, hurrying through snow-covered streets, once inside barely pausing long enough to undo hooks and pull zips and tear out of jeans and jumpers and shove away cotton and lace before we pressed against the heat of each other. After that first, urgent coming together, he drew back, resting his weight on his elbows, and stared down at me. I wanted to hit out and rail at him again; this, with him, felt so right and so joyful that it seemed nonsensical it had taken so long, or that we had deprived each other of so much because of an accident. Instead, I leaned up so that my mouth touched his, my fingertips fluttered against his cheeks as I deepened the kiss. We made love again and again, slow, unhurried, delicious. I savoured every moment, each sensation, each breath. Like parched earth, I needed to be saturated by the touch of his fingers, the warmth of his flesh against mine, the bliss of his body curving around me.

I awoke around three in the morning, my body weightless, the whole of me replete. It wasn't fully dark, London never is, but now the bedroom curtains were outlined by a glow of light from the snow-covered street outside. I saw the shape of Lucien asleep in the bed beside me. The sound of night-time traffic on the main road outside broke in, an ambulance siren in the near distance before it faded. Somewhere beyond this room life was going on as normal. Somewhere beyond this room and across a sea, Pippa was asleep, unaware that Lucien was lying with me.

Pippa. The name rose in my consciousness like a faint breath before it floated back down to the dark depths, easily and effortlessly.

When I woke again it was daylight, and Lucien was awake, lying on his side, staring intently at my face.

'Good morning,' I murmured.

'It's a beautiful morning,' he said, scooping me into the hard heat of his body. I closed my eyes, shutting out the world and the London daylight streaming across my bedroom, the better to imagine we were back in Heronbrook once more, in a room with watercolour reflections and birdsong, and the music of the brook, when the world was young to us and nothing had gone wrong.

Afterwards, when we were resting in a nest of warm, messy sheets, he said, 'I finished it.'

'Finished what?' I asked, relishing in the luxury of coiling my legs around his, of putting out my hand to rest on his chest.

'The portrait of you.'

'When?'

'Just recently. I was away in Cork, at a conference, in a hotel overlooking the river, and I brought it with me.'

Something quivered in my heart at the thought of Lucien needing to be away in the blandness of a functional hotel room to find space for his art.

'It doesn't do you justice,' he said, his hand cradling my cheek.

'Ah, here,' I said, smiling, 'I'm sure it flatters me

immensely, especially if it was me as I was – how many years ago?'

'Twenty-six,' he said. 'I've counted every one – it's a lot to make up for,' he said smiling. 'I have today free, then the seminar tomorrow and Tuesday.'

He'd mentioned, late last night, that he was in London with three of his colleagues to attend a seminar in the UK headquarters of the insurance company. He'd flown over on Saturday afternoon to attend the opening reception, which he'd skipped, coming to the theatre instead. I'd let his words float over my head. Now, though, it was the first time real life punctured the bubble of joy in which I'd floated since we'd left the theatre last night. I didn't want to know. I never wanted to be parted from him again. Why couldn't we just stay like this, in this bed, in this flat, for as long as possible? I didn't want anything to come between us. He had to go back to his hotel, he said, for a change of clothes and a check-in with his colleagues about Monday's agenda.

'I'll be back in an hour or so, two hours max,' he said, over coffee. 'What time do you have to go into the theatre at?'

'I don't have to go. I can call in sick and my understudy will stand in.'

'I was hoping you'd say that,' he said. 'I can stay the night and go back to my hotel in the morning. A cab's picking us up at eight thirty to bring us to the seminar venue.'

'Your colleagues must be wondering where you are.'

He grinned. 'I mentioned something about seeing family.'

Don't look too far ahead, I urged myself, as I showered and dressed after he'd left. Don't overthink this. Just for now, don't imagine what he might say to Pippa when he goes home. Just for now, don't dare think of Jessica and Simon, and young Jamie. When I went out into the snowy day, shopping in a local supermarket – fresh rolls for lunch, steaks for dinner, some wine, a bottle of vodka – I pretended, just for a while, that this was my life with Lucien and Pippa didn't exist. Knowing he'd be back to my apartment in less than two hours seemed far too wonderful to be true. And all the empty years in between Heronbrook and now collapsed into one another when he walked through the door and I flew into his arms once more.

There was lunch, bed in the afternoon, a dinner we cooked between us, wine, and chatting on my sofa as we left the curtains open to the softly falling snow, buttery yellow in the street lights. I couldn't stop looking at him, touching him every so often, his hand, his arm, his shoulder. I didn't ask him if he was happy, when it was clear he was conflicted. Neither did he ask me. We spoke of everything except the smoking grenade in the room between us.

Pippa – does she make you happy?

Your job – it is satisfying you at all?

When do you make your precious art?

What do we do now?

I didn't need to ask if I meant anything to him

when I saw it in the way he looked at me, spoke to me, kissed me. I saw it in the painting of me that he'd completed. He'd brought it to London to gift to me. The portrait was small, not more than ten by twelve inches, but he'd caught the total love and unwavering trust in my eyes as I stared calmly at him. It had to have resonated with something inside him to have been able to capture it as he did. I was back there in that moment once more, eighteen all over again, that gaze intent on my body, the rest of my life sitting in the palm of my hand like a promising bud.

'There were other paintings, weren't there?' I said.

'Yes, I had three completed.'

'Where are they now?'

He dropped his head. 'I don't know,' he admitted. 'They were in my room in Granny Kate's, but they were auctioned off along with the contents of the house when I sold it just before Pippa and I got married. They were supposed to have been removed first, but someone somewhere got their wires crossed. I'm not sure where they went.'

Pippa, I guessed. Making sure no trace of our love remained.

It was hard to accept it had been over half of our lives ago. I rose from the sofa to get more wine before I went back down the road of regret and recrimination. Lucien reached out for my hand, sensing my mood. I put it all behind me, sat down on his lap, and kissed his face, bringing myself back to the here and now and the feel of his skin under my mouth.

Nothing else mattered right then.

'I heard that Heronbrook might be coming on the market sometime next year. I'm going to buy it for us,' he said.

'Can there be an "us"?' I asked.

'There will be. There has to be. I have something to tell you ... Pippa was talking to me – she was drunk one day and what she said changes everything.'

'Tell me now,' I said.

'Tomorrow night, my beloved. You won't like what you hear, so let's leave it for now and not spoil tonight. Just know that my marriage is over. I don't like disrupting the children's lives and Jamie is still so young, but we'll sort something out. When I get the chance to buy Heronbrook, I will. It will be ours alone. I'll wait for you to come, for whenever you're finished in London, or whatever we manage to work out no matter how long it takes.'

Warm in the knowledge that we had a future of some kind to look forward to, I couldn't have made love to him more passionately than I did that night, responding to him with every cell in my being. I stayed awake for a while, watching Lucien sleep the relaxed sleep of the totally defenceless, counting his breaths, allowing my hand to rest on his chest where I could feel his heartbeat.

In a way, it's just as well we don't know what terrible things fate can have in store. Counting down Lucien's breaths would have been horrendous.

Evie, 1990

When the phone rang that Monday at lunchtime, I had no premonition. I had already called the theatre to say my stomach bug hadn't yet cleared, and it would be Wednesday before I'd be back on stage – slightly aghast at how easily the lies slipped from my lips.

But it was Pippa, and she was incoherent.

A terrible fear clawed at the back of my mind. How had she found out so quickly? But instead of screaming at me for sleeping with her husband, I heard fumbling as she passed the phone to someone else, then a woman spoke, whose voice I didn't recognise.

'Hi, I'm Elizabeth, Pippa's neighbour,' she said. 'There's been an accident. With Lucien.'

My scalp tightened and froze.

'He's in London at the moment …' I heard murmuring, a strangled gasp: she was obviously conferring with Pippa '… a work thing.'

'What accident?' I asked. Whatever clawed at the back of my mind was dark and demonical.

'In London, this morning.' I heard her next words as if from far away. 'There was an accident on the road. Lucien is dead. You're the only one in

London that Pippa knows. She needs you to go to the hospital and find out what's going on.'

'What hospital?' I asked. The sooner I got there the better. The better to end this nightmare. Lucien couldn't be dead, not when we'd made love so warmly that morning, and he'd thrown me a kiss as he ran, late, out the door, saying he'd see me that evening; not when we had so much to talk about, so much love to give to each other ... Looking at the messy bed-sheets and the dent of his head in the pillow after he'd left, I'd already decided that we had to find some way to make it work between us.

It couldn't be over. He couldn't be gone.

But he was. When I saw him lying so still and so lifeless, something died inside me like a flower-bud being slashed away from its life-giving stalk. The breathing, walking, laughing Lucien was gone. I'd never talk to him again, never see the light of love flare in his eyes, never be kissed, or hugged, or held close by him, or feel his breath on my cheek. Never again meet him under the trees by the brook.

I went through the cruel, relentlessly hard motions of the next few days, meeting his shocked colleagues in the hospital, hearing about the accident. Running late, he'd come rushing out of the hotel with his briefcase, across the road to where the cab waited, already positioned to whisk him and his colleagues to the seminar venue. Lucien, not paying enough attention to the oncoming traffic, losing his footing on a hillock of slush in the centre of the road, falling back awkwardly into oncoming traffic, his three colleagues sitting waiting in the cab, watching in horror.

I met my grief-stricken sister, along with Jessica and Simon, both coming up to twenty years of age, off a flight in Heathrow. They'd flown over with Lucien's manager, and they stayed at the hotel along with him and Lucien's colleagues. I was grateful Pippa and her children hadn't expected to stay with me. I needed some time apart from them during the next fraught days while the repatriation of Lucien's body and the funeral in Dublin was arranged. I needed valuable breathing space to learn to cope with the pain that was cleaving me in two, and find ways to hide the true depths of my grief during the hours I had to be there for my sister, in body if not in spirit. She was the person most entitled to kick and scream and weep relentlessly in the throes of loss and shock, not me. She was the chief mourner everyone deferred to, and rightly so. I, the sister in London who had rarely been home, was the person they expected to be strong for her sake.

Back in Dublin, I stayed with my mother in our family home in Drumcondra. Ruth Lawrence was about the only person who had any inkling as to how I felt. I was grateful for her practical support, the tacit empathy that I sensed coming from her. On an icy-cold day, a week before Christmas, Lucien was buried in a graveyard in Bray surrounded by housing estates. I would have cremated him and scattered his ashes at Heronbrook, in the dappled shade under the trees. Inside me, behind a wall of shock, I knew my foundations were crumbling, but I had to hold on until this nightmare time was over. I could weep all I liked when I returned to London.

Two days after the funeral, Pippa arrived in Drumcondra and marched into the sitting room, demanding to speak to me. Alone. It was clear from her tone of voice she wasn't looking for sympathy for her newly acquired widowhood or to cry on my shoulder. My mother raised curious eyebrows, but Pippa's belligerent demeanour alerted her enough to absent herself, mentioning something about cheese in the local supermarket, even though the temperatures had dipped and it was freezing outside.

My mother was no sooner out the door, down the tiled path, and out the gate than, drawing off her leather gloves but without waiting to remove her thick woollen coat, Pippa flew at me and slapped me across the face.

'He was with you, wasn't he?' she snapped.

'What do you mean?' I asked, feeling the sting on my cheek but not giving her the satisfaction of rubbing it.

'I fucking know he was fucking you, don't bother to pretend.' She slapped me again. 'I was wondering,' she said, her voice raw, her eyes darting all over the place in fury, 'when I heard he was going to London. I was wondering if he'd sleep with you. You were in bed together, you dirty slut, don't bother to deny it.'

I didn't reply. I stared out into the darkening December evening, past the slumbering, stalky winter garden and over to the red-bricked terraced houses across the road, where lights were being switched on in hallways like ours and Christmas trees twinkled from cosy sitting rooms. Another day drawing to a close. Another day sliding past in a world that had become terrifying without Lucien in it.

'How *dare* you,' Pippa screeched, incensed by my lack of reaction. She went for me again, extending her clawed hands, looking as though she was prepared to gouge out my eyes. I raised my arms protectively until she eventually backed away, her initial anger subsiding.

'I heard all about it,' she said, hissing the words out, her voice ragged and hoarse. She jabbed her index finger towards me. 'His colleagues thought I might find it of some consolation that he'd spent little or no time in the hotel because he was catching up with family. They thought I might find it of *some* consolation that he hadn't slept in his hotel bed.' Pippa stared at me, watching my face. 'He didn't appear for breakfast either morning, and when he was late for the cab, one of them knocked in for him. Lucien was throwing stuff into his briefcase but his bed hadn't been slept in. When his colleague joked about him being out on the town, Lucien said he'd spent the night with family. I mentioned something about him having cousins in Croydon – not to save you, you whore, but to save my face.'

There was nothing I could say. I had no defence to offer. But I didn't attempt to apologise. Pippa would never understand the depth of compelling love that had flared between us. Neither did I feel guilty about sleeping with Lucien. It had been an essential healing of the arid emptiness that had sat at the centre of both of our lives for so long. But I did feel a crippling guilt about delaying him that morning so that he'd rushed across the road in heedless haste. Which Pippa zoned in on.

'It's your fault,' she hissed, 'that he was running for that taxi. Your fault that my children are left without a father.'

I didn't bother to tell her I'd live with that guilt for the rest of my life.

'Even before all this, you wrecked my marriage,' she stormed.

'Hang on, Pippa,' I said, a pounding in my ears, unwilling to let that one go. 'You wrecked my life, leaving young Leah Casey in my care the way you did.'

She looked at me triumphantly, as though she'd been waiting to have this out for years. 'I did not,' she sneered. 'You ignored me as usual that afternoon, like you always ignored me, as though I was a nuisance to be batted away.'

'Is that how you've squared your conscience? You deliberately left a child in a vulnerable situation, you were careless, you endangered her—'

'Not half as much as you did. If only you'd listened to me that day.'

'You must have known there was a chance I couldn't hear you. You created the conditions—'

'Fuck's sake – you didn't listen to me, as usual. You were too busy fucking Lucien. But you wrecked your own future with him. You were the one who went to London, and when his grandmother died and he needed you most, you stayed away. You put your career before him. If you'd come home then he would never have looked at me.'

Pippa wasn't telling me anything I hadn't already spent endless hours agonising over.

'He would never have looked at you,' I said, 'if you hadn't thrown yourself at him and deliberately got pregnant.'

'I paid the price because you were always between us,' she said. 'Like a witch. Lucien was never happy with me. You spoiled him for me. He didn't understand me or my needs.'

'Was that your excuse for playing away?' I asked, thinking of what Lucien had told me about Pippa not coming home some nights. About the child he didn't think was his. And there had been a man, I remembered through a haze of pain, at the funeral, an old friend from Wicklow. He'd introduced himself when he'd commiserated with me over my brother-in-law's death. I'd caught him and Pippa staring at each other from time to time.

'And does Jamie know?' I asked, taking a stab in the dark, apologising silently to my eleven-year-old nephew, who was surely innocent of this, but knowing I'd aimed correctly when Pippa's hard expression faltered for a split second. 'Lucien said he had something important to tell me that changed everything,' I said, hating the way I was admitting we'd been together by default, by needing to know what he'd meant. 'He didn't get the chance to tell me. Have you any idea what it was?'

Pippa's face changed. It became stiff as a mask, her eyes taking on a calculating look. There was something in her stare that turned my stomach. The calculating look in her eyes hardened to contempt. 'That's for me to know and you to find out – which you never will.'

Inside, I wanted to weep. My sister and I were two grown women playing tit for tat like foolish children, driving a wedge further between us at a time when we should have been united in grief. 'Look, Pippa,' I said, 'I know you're sad and heartbroken. Is there any way we can put all this ... aside for now and help each other through this?'

I knew by Pippa's hard, set face that that was never going to happen. 'Fuck off, Evie,' she said. 'I want you to remember something. I was Lucien's wife of twenty years. We had a happy marriage. I'm beyond devastated that he's gone and nothing will bring him back. As far as everyone is concerned, Mother included, he never saw you in London, and he was never with you, full stop. He was mine. *All* mine. He was faithful to me. I'm not going to have my widowhood tarnished or ridiculed by the abominable way he spent his last weekend, thanks to you, never mind your offensive idea that I was unfaithful. And this is *my* grief, not yours. I don't want you piggybacking on this. I don't want you or anyone else to think for even one moment that you share any part of it, any part of him. Having fucked my husband and humiliated me, the least you can do is stay silent on this and fuck off out of my life for good.'

I understood, then, what she wanted. The role of the grieving widow would give her a free pass to bask contentedly on the receiving end of a wealth of sympathy and kind condolences, whereas a wife wronged, whose husband had spent his final weekend in the arms of his lifelong love, would have to endure other people's pity and curious glances, not to mention those spurious friends who would have gloried in her situation – a humiliating situation that I had helped to cause. I couldn't help feeling sympathy for her, as well as acknowledging that I now had more sins on my conscience.

'Is that it?' I asked, calling on all my acting skills to feign indifference. The sitting-room curtains were still open, and out on the street, dancing flickers of snow began to fall, turning to yellow and burnished gold in the glow of the street lamps. Even in the moments that I watched, the light fall thickened until the snowflakes were whirling around, dusting the blackened silhouette of the garden hedge. I wondered if the snow was blanketing Lucien's freshly dug grave, and a painful spasm sliced through me. I would never be able to grasp that he was now sleeping underneath, forever oblivious to the world going on above him, oblivious to the changing seasons in Heronbrook, where the dancing waters still flowed. A world with me and Pippa so thoroughly alienated.

'I never want to lay eyes on you again,' Pippa raged, her voice shaking. 'I want you to stay the hell away from me and my family. I'm not going to breathe a word to anyone about the way I was humiliated, but if I hear that you've come near my children, or that you've uttered one word, one hint, one whisper, about the weekend you had with *my* husband, I'll kill you with my bare hands. Got that? I'll kill you and I mean it.'

Just before she marched out of the room, Pippa spat in my face.

I listened to the slam of the hall door and knew we could never recover from this.

Evie, present day

Maybe now is the time to take that deep dive down ...

I feel the lightest touch on my hand, like the kiss of a feather. I become aware of another hand resting gently over mine – and my downward spiral jolts suddenly, like a fish that has jerked at the end of a played-out line.

There is something niggling me about Amber. Is she alive? Is she safe?

If only I'd called the police sooner. By the time I realised what was going on, she was as enmeshed as I was.

What was going on? It slides away from my mind, just out of reach.

There's something about Barry Talbot slipping through the back of my mind. I hear him shouting at me ... he's pulling me ...

And Will ... Will?

I'm too tired right now to think ... I hear the soft bleep as the monitor measures out the seconds of my life so I know I am still alive.

They say the hearing is the last to go ...

Two Days Earlier

Jessica felt herself being dragged out of the warm cocoon of sleep by a far-off noise. When she realised it was her mobile, she was instantly awake. She reached across to her bedside locker and grabbed it. One o'clock in the morning. Therefore this call didn't bode well. Her mind grappled with a slipstream of possibilities – her mother, Evie, Amber – bracing herself for whatever fresh calamity had befallen them, mentally re-juggling her day ahead – what day was it? The early hours of Wednesday – to facilitate whatever new demands this might place on her.

A woman. Calling on behalf of Adam. *Adam!* The kind of phone call that sat like a permanent cold dread at the back of her mind once her children had been old enough to leave the house independently.

'What happened?' she asked. 'Who are you? Where is he now?'

'He's fine,' the voice at the other end tried to reassure her. 'I'm a nurse in accident and emergency—'

Paul clicked on the lamp. 'What's up?' he asked.

She frowned and shook her head, trying to follow the thread of what the nurse was saying. When the call had finished she relayed it to Paul. 'It's Adam.

He's OK. He's in A&E, they're keeping him in overnight for observation.'

'What happened?' Paul threw back the duvet, got out of bed, and reached for a pair of trousers.

'He was waiting for a taxi home and he was mugged. He has a knife wound on the side of his neck and he hit the back of his head when he was pushed to the ground, which is why they're keeping him in, but he's OK. If you can be OK after you've just been mugged.'

'Christ.' Paul went into the en suite, throwing a column of light across the bedroom floor before he closed the door.

All of a sudden Jessica felt overwhelmed. She sat on the side of the bed shaking like a leaf, feeling as though she was staring into a fresh new abyss that she was incapable of crossing. When Paul came out, he stopped in his tracks. 'Are you OK?'

'No,' she said. 'I just feel … I can't take any more. I feel scared,' she blurted.

'Hey.' Paul came across and wrapped his arms around her. 'You heard the nurse, he'll be fine. He's being looked after. It's OK.'

It's not just Adam, she wanted to say but the words wouldn't come. *It's the past few weeks … it's everything.* She couldn't remember the last time she'd allowed herself to be held in his arms like this and she relaxed for a moment.

'It won't take us long to get there,' Paul said. 'Get dressed and I'll put the kettle on for a quick coffee. You can drink it in the car.'

By the time she came downstairs he had two travel mugs filled with coffee ready to go. The housing estate was shadowy and quiet in the light of the car headlamps as Paul reversed out of the garden and left the cul de sac, heading for the roundabout and main road beyond.

'Something about this reminds me of years ago,' he said, as they drove through a shuttered and quiet village, 'those two early morning runs to the hospital when you were in labour. Remember?'

'Don't remind me,' she said.

'Ah, but they were special,' he said. 'Driving through the night, knowing our babies were about to come kicking and screaming into the world.'

'You're quite ... reflective tonight,' she said, wondering what had brought on his reminiscing, guessing it was something to do with being called to the rescue, being needed, both by her and Adam. But he was right. Despite her painful contractions, those car journeys they had shared, motoring along quiet streets full of hope and anticipation, had made her feel as though they were enclosed in a special world of their own on the brink of a wonderful discovery.

'They were good, though,' he said, 'the old days, when the kids were small and we were omnipotent.'

'Do you miss those days?'

'Yes, don't you? We were able to fix their problems and difficulties, it gave me a sense of achievement, whereas now ...' He stopped at traffic lights, the red light beaming out onto a street deserted except for them. 'Now I sometimes feel I'm surplus to requirements,' he said.

Jessica wavered between surprise that her husband was suddenly being so forthcoming in expressing his feelings, and anxiety as to whether it was something else that was being unloaded upon her, some perceived gap in Paul's life that she was supposed to try and fill.

He took his hand off the wheel long enough to touch hers for a moment. 'I'm not looking for sympathy, Jessica, neither am I moaning. It's good that we've raised the kids to be independent – that's what you'd hope for. I'm just talking out loud about how I feel and I'm glad you're listening, even if you are' – he threw her a quick, rueful glance – 'a rather captive audience.'

'Right,' she said, feeling at a total loss.

They reached the hospital, Paul driving down into the underground car park, both of them hurrying to A&E, Jessica's chest tightening with a formless panic. She let Paul take the lead, explaining who they were, allowing him to go first when one only person at a time – and ten minutes, no more – was permitted through to the area where Adam was on a trolley.

Paul was back minutes later, his face calm and relaxed, telling her not to be worried, that all was well, fetching a bottle of water and some chocolate from the vending machine for her to bring through. And then it was Jessica's turn to brave the bedlam.

At first she thought she'd landed in a scene straight from *Casualty*, with a flurry of blue-coated staff milling around under blazing fluorescent lights, dodging various pieces of equipment that were being wheeled around, a nurse's station that was cluttered with staff and clipboards, phones ringing, monitors bleeping, a huge whiteboard where a nurse was scrawling details in red pen into a vacant box. She saw a hand waving at her from a trolley lined up against the wall – Adam. She swallowed any motherly hysteria that might be bubbling away as she weaved her way over to him, mindful of other patients on trolleys in varying stages of distress, as well as the staff trying to do their jobs in this frenzied environment.

'What happened? Although you look OK – the other guy must have got off worse,' she said, trying to infuse her voice with light jocularity when she really wanted to weep. Adam's face was pale, dark circles under his eyes, and there was a bandage covering the right-hand side of his chin, stretching down to his neck. Inwardly she shivered, thinking of how close that blade must have been to his artery.

'I don't know what happened,' he said, his voice low and drowsy. 'I was jumped on, in Portobello, from behind. I just felt the knife against my neck and I threw my phone and wallet as far as I could, like Dad told me.'

'*Dad* told you?'

'Yeah, if anyone ever pulled a knife or tried to

mug me to fling my stuff as far away as I could – the mugger would chase that and give me a second or two to get away.'

Thank you, Paul.

'And that's what I did,' Adam said. 'I lobbed my phone and wallet over the wall of a front garden, but ...'

'But what?'

'He didn't go after them immediately. He nicked my neck with the blade and said something peculiar.' Adam frowned. His eyes hazed over in tiredness. 'Something like "your turn now". My turn? I've no idea what he meant.'

'Did you tell the police?'

'Yeah, a taxi driver saw the tail end of it and called the guards and an ambulance. So here I am.'

'Why didn't you call us as soon as it happened?'

'Look, Ma, can you imagine if I'd rung you and said I was in an ambulance? That would have freaked you out. I knew it wasn't life or death. And anyway I'd no phone.'

'Did you get a look at your attacker?'

'No. He was tall and had a deep voice. The taxi driver said he was dressed in black, wearing a hoodie over a balaclava. He leaped over the garden wall, grabbed my stuff, and disappeared down an alleyway between the houses.'

'Would you recognise the voice again?' Jessica asked, appalled that Adam had gone through this trauma, and that his assailant would probably get away scot-free.

'I doubt it. I was too shocked. And it was distorted through whatever he was wearing. Anyhow, I'll be home tomorrow. They'll call you when I'm ready to go.'

♦

Jessica was never so glad to feel the walls of her home enclosing her. Compared with the frenzy of the hospital, all was calm and cosy. Not dull at all, she thought, looking into the sitting room as she passed it, her eyes roving around the familiar walls, the framed photographs telling the story of their lives, the soft untidiness of the bookshelves. She went into the kitchen, the heart of the home, and saw the shadows of their grown-up children imprinted there, the fun arguments around the dinner table, the noticeboard a repository for the agenda of their day-to-day lives. Adam would be back sitting at the dinner table tomorrow, grumbling about being starving or moaning about the emptiness of the fridge, and she would welcome and soak up the normality of it. He had been so lucky not to have sustained a more serious injury.

'It's good to be home,' Paul said, shrugging out of his jacket and hanging it in the cloakroom. 'It'll be even better when we have Adam back tomorrow.'

'Yes,' Jessica said, swallowing hard. 'I know it's late,' she went on, 'but would you like a nightcap? I need to get the taste of hospital out of my mouth.'

'Good idea,' he said. 'Gin? Or a whiskey?'

'Gin,' she said, 'please.'

She'd felt irritated with him in recent months, before that irritation had faded in the light of her own stupidity. But that hadn't been fair of her. So what if they were merely plodding along for now, going through the motions of life, the dull routine from Monday to Friday measured out in clean shirts, socks, and underwear? So what if the weekly menu was samey and uninspiring? There was a lot to be said for the ordinary, undemanding but familiar creature comforts.

She was halfway through her gin and tonic when she knew she couldn't pretend any more. 'I have something to tell you, Paul,' she began.

'No, Jess,' he said, putting his glass of whiskey on the low table. 'Please don't. Please just let us carry on as we are.'

'But we can't. At least, I can't any more.'

'I wish you wouldn't.'

'Wouldn't what?'

'Say what you're about to say.'

'But you don't know what I'm going to say.'

'You're having an affair ...'

She stared at him, speechless at the utter absurdity of these words. 'An *affair*?'

'I can't blame you if you are ... The way I've been behaving over the last couple of years.'

Her head spun.

'You've been so distant,' Paul continued, 'so ... unreachable these last few weeks. Turning away from me. Making excuses to go out at odd times to the nursing home, even to your brother. I've been quietly terrified that you were about to pull the plug on our marriage. I can't say I blame you. I know things haven't worked out the way you were expecting. I know I've turned into a boring old fart with a joyless job, but—'

She shook her head. 'Oh, Paul, you have it all wrong,' she said, amazed that it was possible to live with and sleep beside someone and yet have no idea of what was going on in their life. 'That's not what it is at all.'

'What is it, then?' he said, his face tired and worn looking.

'I've been terribly stupid,' Jessica said, her voice choked as she broke down. 'I've made a huge, crappy mistake that I really, really regret. I lost us a pile of money.' She looked at the concern etched all over his face, and starting from the beginning, she told him what had happened.

His concern was for her, not the vanished funds. They would deal with it together, he said. Her problems were his problems. His love for her was far bigger than any temporary financial hitch. Not once did he breathe a word of annoyance with her or lay any blame at her door. They would take this as far as they could, to the Financial Ombudsman, he said. She had supported him in his hour of need and listened without complaining to his grumbles, now she had to let him fully support her.

She wondered why she hadn't told him before,

but she knew it was because she'd always felt she had to be the strong and responsible one. Growing up, she'd always tried to fix things between her mother and her brothers, and she'd gone on to feel she had to be Mrs Fix-it within her marriage and for her family. A script she had written entirely by herself, for herself. But it was a script that wasn't set in stone.

Afterwards, he held her tightly in bed and kissed all her tears away.

Amber was unloading the dishwasher when her mum phoned mid-morning, filling her in on Adam's mugging. She went over to where Evie sat in a chair by the terrace doors, listening to a podcast. Evie removed her earbuds and Amber sat beside her and put her phone on speaker so Evie could join the conversation.

'He's grand now,' her mum said, after they'd expressed outrage and solicitude on his behalf. 'He's being discharged after lunch and Paul will collect him.'

'Is Dad not in work today?' Amber asked.

'No, neither am I,' her mum said. 'We're skiving off, both of us.' Behind her upbeat tone, she sounded tired and upset.

'Going to lavish all your attention on Adam?' Amber said with false cheer.

'Of course,' her mum said.

'What on earth is happening to this family?' Amber said unthinkingly.

'What do you mean?' Her mum's voice was sharp.

She belatedly remembered that her mum still wasn't aware of the way she'd lost her job or the harassment against Evie. But this wasn't the right moment to broach either of those subjects. Not over the phone, and with Evie listening. 'I meant Evie with her hit-and-run,' she said, 'and now Adam being mugged.'

'Seeing as we're off work today,' her mum said, 'why don't you and Evie call up this evening?'

Amber looked questioningly at Evie, who nodded at her. 'Yes, sure, we'll do that,' she said.

'It will be lovely to have you both here,' her mum said. 'Come for dinner. How are you feeling now, Evie?'

'I'm great,' Evie said. 'Amber's been a star.'

'I know she is,' her mum said. 'We're so proud of her.'

'Mum!' Amber said, suddenly feeling close to tears. It was time they knew about Healy's and her messed-up life. After the call, she finished emptying the dishwasher, and then she made coffee, putting out fresh soda bread, butter, and strawberry conserve.

'You hardly think there's a link between Adam's mugging and me, do you?' Evie asked, stirring her coffee and looking at her worriedly.

'Not at all. I just spoke off the top of my head,' Amber said, spreading jam on her soda bread, then giving Evie a forced grin, reluctant to upset her any further.

What was happening within the family was strange ... Evie and her intimidation, the way Amber's own life had crashed off the rails recently, now Adam being mugged. Could a family unit really be all that unlucky? So many disparate incidents, yet when you added them together you'd swear someone had a vendetta against them. Even Jamie's coming home unexpectedly from New York after so long, and with no proper explanation. Amber realised with a sudden clarity that he had to be hiding something.

'Actually, Amber,' Evie said, 'I'm relieved you're still talking to me after the other night. Although I'm not sure you should still be here.'

'Of course I'm still here and talking to you,' Amber said. 'I couldn't have any hard feelings towards you for being with my grandfather with the way things were between you. Besides, it was years ago. Ancient history.'

Nonetheless, Evie's surprise revelations were still swimming around in her head. She'd known that her grandfather had died in London in 1990, but she wasn't sure if Jessica had any idea that her father had spent that final weekend with Evie. Not unless Granny Pippa had told her, and according to Evie, Granny Pippa had been determined to keep her husband's unfaithfulness to herself.

'I'm so sorry it ended the way it did,' Amber went on, 'and I think the promise Granny Pippa extracted from you must have been the absolute pits, having to hide your grief.'

'I don't know if Pippa realised what she was doing,' Evie said, 'but I found keeping silent horrendous. It was the loneliest place in the world. I wanted to scream and cry and look for comfort as much as she did. I missed Lucien so much. It was one thing when he'd been married to Pippa, at least I knew he was alive, but now he was gone, and with that, all hope. I couldn't go back on the stage after that. My heart was too shrivelled. Thing is, Amber, if that newspaper supplement with the photos of me and Jessica was hanging round the care home and Pippa saw it, it would send her into a rage,' Evie said. 'Even by talking to Jessica that time, I broke my promise to her, never mind the way we looked so well together, compared with the situation she's in.'

'I won't be spilling the beans, but I doubt if Granny Pippa has the wherewithal to recognise anyone any more,' Amber said.

'You'd be surprised,' Evie said slowly. 'The human brain is an amazing organ. Vital sections of it could be perished, yet other parts functioning just as sharply as ever, if not even more finely attuned. What date did the photographs appear in the supplement?'

Amber picked up her mobile and checked her emails. 'The third of June.'

'My hit-and-run was weeks later, so there's hardly any connection,' Evie said, finally helping herself to a slice of soda bread.

'Did you think there might be a link?'

'Not really, I was adding two and two and making a hundred.'

'By the way,' Amber said, hoping she sounded nonchalant, 'I showed the supplement photographs to Tess Talbot when I collected our lunch yesterday. That guy sitting at the table with Tess and Barry is none other than Matthew Casey.'

'Matthew Casey?' Evie exclaimed. 'Let me have another look.'

Amber passed her mobile across to Evie.

'I'd never have recognised him,' Evie said, studying the image, 'although I haven't seen him since he was about six years old. A lifetime ago.'

'That's what you have to remember, Evie,' Amber said. 'It was all a lifetime ago.'

She was relieved she'd said nothing about her reckless trip to Temple Raven. Evie had enough going on without worrying about her grand-niece's risky foray into that remote part of the mountains. Besides, it meant she could continue to do some quiet digging of her own, without alerting Evie. An odd sensation about Temple Raven still persisted at the edge of her mind – Matthew Casey wasn't off the hook yet.

'I understand how you feel about the police,' Amber said. 'But if one more peculiar thing happens, I'll call them myself and get Garda O'Reilly back here. If he unearths any family skeletons, Mum and I will be able to handle it. And even if something ended up in public, so what – it would only have a short lifespan. So don't worry on our behalf. Your safety is more important.'

'Thanks, Amber. I'm sure it's all over by now. Nothing else untoward happened to Ma Donnelly.'

'Here's hoping,' Amber said, a shiver running down her spine, deciding not to remind Evie that Ma Donnelly had been killed in the end.

'The motorways are great,' Evie said, when they exited off the M50 and swung down towards Templeogue and Laurel Lawns on Wednesday evening. 'When we travelled to Heronbrook in the sixties, the journey seemed to take forever.' She sounded like she was gabbling. Then again, she was nervous, never having been in Jessica's house before. As well as that, her grand-niece had been slightly on edge on the journey up from Wicklow so the atmosphere in the car was taut.

They'd had a late lunch that afternoon, after which Amber had asked to use Evie's laptop – she was continuing to work on the account of her dismissal, she'd said. Evie had gone back to bed for a rest and left her to it. Now Evie wondered if compiling her report had put that strained look on Amber's face.

They came to a roundabout and Amber took the first exit. 'You might as well know,' she said at last, 'I'm going to tell Mum and Dad about Will and the way I was fired from Healy's. I'm sure they've been worried. I'm trying to work out what to say – a censored version of what happened with Will. I was using your laptop today to try and trace him, among other things.'

'Oh dear, I hope it doesn't combust,' Evie said. 'He sounded like a right Beelzebub to me. Did you have any luck?'

'No,' Amber said, 'I need to do a bit more checking around.'

A sense of welcome relaxed Evie and her nervousness dissolved as she stepped carefully into the Lennox home, Jessica and Paul both making a huge fuss of embracing her. They had a comfortable home – a vase of yellow carnations on a hall table, a glimpse into a sitting room that had a flat-screen television, packed bookshelves, and rows of family photographs in assorted frames on windowsills and cabinets, along with miscellaneous souvenirs from holidays abroad; then the big, airy kitchen, a crammed corkboard with a busy-looking calendar on a side wall, a sofa beside shelves holding books and a music system, house plants providing pops of colour against shades of yellow and cream; the sight of an overflowing clothes-horse in the utility room to one side. She had to pass up on sinking into the comfortable sofa, explaining that she needed to sit upright for now, so Paul made sure her crutch was within easy reach as she sat at the kitchen table, which overlooked a neat back garden. A tall, dark-haired young man whom she guessed to be Adam arrived in, his face pale, a bandage covering the side of his neck. He was fussed over by Amber, hugging him, reaching up to ruffle his hair. 'Adam!' she said. 'I can't believe what I heard. Thank God you're OK. Tell me everything.'

'Hey, give us a chance,' he said, extricating himself from her arms. 'I haven't even met Aunt Evie yet.'

The introductions were made, Evie telling Adam that the apple hadn't fallen far from the tree, he was so like his father.

'Not sure about that,' Paul joked. 'I was married and a father at his age, but Adam's having far too good a time partying the weeks away.'

'Hey,' Jessica interjected, 'I thought we had a good time in those early years. I thought you were happily married to me.'

'I was, darling, of course.'

Evie watched the way they moved around the kitchen in seamless unison, plating up a chicken casserole, setting out salads and breads on the table, and organising wine with the ease of a long-married couple used to working in well-practised tandem. Sitting at the far end of the table, Amber's faced was creased with concern and her attention was focused on Adam as he told her all the details of his mugging. An ordinary family, but with the everyday family love and unity that is beyond price. Evie was under no illusion that any of their lives were perfect or devoid of stresses and strains, but still, fair dues to Jessica for bringing this off, considering the upsetting childhood she'd had with her mother's alcoholism and her father's untimely death.

Lucien would have rejoiced had he been part of this – the thought came unbidden. He would have loved even more to have met his beautiful grandchildren.

Pippa should be here, enjoying this.

'Does Pippa manage to get out of the home at

all?' she asked Jessica quietly, when Amber, Paul, and Adam were chatting about a Netflix documentary.

'Not in recent years,' Jessica said. 'We tried to take her out and bring her here on a couple of occasions, but it was a disaster. Mum was just too incapacitated. It only upset her.'

'I almost went to see her,' Evie admitted.

'You did?'

'Soon after I met you in Wicklow I had the urge to see Pippa again, but I was too nervous. I was afraid that if I went in to see her looking hale and hearty and living a full life, with the ability to walk out the door again into the lovely day, it might upset her big time.'

Jessica sighed. 'It's all so sad,' she said. 'I wish there was more I could do.'

'Let me know if I can ever help with anything,' Evie said, 'or if it's worth my while trying to see her again.'

'I will, and thank you.'

Later, when the food was eaten and cleared, and they were nibbling on cheese and biscuits, Amber glanced down the table at Evie, as if for a little encouragement, before quietly announcing that she had something to say.

'What's that, love?' Jessica asked, studying her daughter's face with an expression of concern.

'I'm sure you've all guessed I'm out of a job and not seeing Will any more,' she began.

'It didn't take too much to work that out,' Adam said with a cheeky grin.

'Adam!' Jessica frowned warningly at him before turning back to Amber. 'We didn't know what was going on, love. You don't have to tell us anything unless you feel up to it.'

'It's OK, Mum,' Amber said. 'The two things are related, and you're not going to be proud of me.'

'We're always proud of you, Amber,' Paul said.

Amber shook her head and took a deep breath. 'It's easier to tell you all at once. My contract with Healy's was terminated for a grievous breach of confidential work practices. I was a little careless, so I'm not entirely blameless, but for some reason, which I'm still trying to figure out, it seems as though Will set me up and took advantage of my carelessness so that he could sabotage my position in Healy's and my career.'

It was clear to Evie that Jessica and Paul, and even Adam, were stunned by Amber's admission. They all sat up to attention, as though Amber had just announced she was harbouring an atomic bomb somewhere.

'What?'

'You're joking.'

'Jesus Christ.'

'Enough of the profanity,' Jessica said to Adam, before casting a glance at Evie.

'Don't mind me,' Evie said. 'Will is a first-class bollocks as far as I'm concerned.' She delivered this in her best thespian voice, which earned her a grateful look from Amber and a mimed fist bump from Adam. Both Jessica and Paul began to talk at once, tripping over words in their concern for their daughter.

'Hang on, everyone,' Amber said, putting up her hand. 'I'm not going into all the details, but I admit that I did something terribly stupid, which was a disciplinary offence. However, it seems Will set me up, and I'm determined to get to the bottom of it, so if that creep ever happens to show his face around here, you can tell him I'm on to him.'

'And if he shows his face in Heronbrook, I'll be ready for him,' Evie said with gusto.

'Have you any idea why he might have done this?' Jessica asked.

Amber gave her mother a long, conspiratorial look, and Evie wasn't surprised when Jessica swiftly engineered it so that she and Amber would stay in the kitchen to organise the clearing of the table, while Paul brought a chair suitable for Evie into the sitting room.

'Paul is going to show you the video montage of family photographs he compiled for my fiftieth birthday,' Jessica said to Evie. 'You'll be able to catch up with our various adventures over the years.'

Evie didn't miss the glance Paul gave his wife, as though it was the first he'd heard of it.

'Sounds good to me,' she said gamely.

Jessica was relieved that Paul immediately understood she wanted to talk to Amber alone, asking Adam to bring through a fresh glass of sparkling water for Evie. She flashed him a grateful glance. Any new-found relief she'd felt after unburdening herself to him had been dented at the dinner table when Amber had stunned her with the news about Will and her dismissal, and now it was punctured further as she and Amber cleared the table and loaded the dishwasher while Amber ran over the bare facts of her dismissal.

'I'm not going into all the gory details,' Amber said, placing the wine glasses on the countertop. 'But I think Will set out deliberately to entrap me. Thing is, I can't trace him now.'

'What do you mean?'

'His bio is deleted off LinkedIn, then I found out he never had an office in Russell Hall, and he's gone from his apartment in Dundrum.'

'That's crazy, Amber. I'm really sorry to hear about all this. You don't deserve it – you've worked so hard in your career.' Jessica gave her a hug, rubbing her back.

'It's not over until I find him and have it out with him. I'm putting together some kind of account for Healy's. I'll never work there again, and they won't give me a reference, but maybe there's a way of lessening the cloud I left under. I told Evie I'm not in a rush back to the corporate life, so you might as well know that too.'

'Whatever you want or need, Amber, whatever you choose to do, know that your dad and I are behind you all the way. Talk to me any time.'

'Thank you.' Amber kissed her cheek. 'But as well as all that, Mum, I'm seriously beginning to think that something weird is going on in the family,' Amber said, swirling some cutlery in the basin of sudsy water. 'Weird things have been happening to Evie. She thinks it's probably a mad fan, but it could be something more sinister.'

'Do you mean apart from the hit-and-run?' Jessica asked, feeling a cold tingle at the base of her neck.

Amber nodded slowly.

'What things?' Jessica listened, freshly aghast, as Amber ran through them. 'Then to cap it all,' Amber said, 'someone sent her an actual video clip of her final moments in the drama and Evie opened it because she thought it was from you.'

'I didn't realise that,' Jessica said slowly. 'Evie only asked me if I'd sent her an email, which I hadn't.'

'Evie said it looked like it came from you when she glanced at it. But between Evie, what happened to me, and now Adam's mugging, I think it's kind of freakish.'

And me, Jessica wanted to say. *I've been victimised also*. And what about Jamie, with the card that was sent to him in New York? A stab of anxiety gripped her and she took her time scraping the remains of food off the serving dishes, trying to look as neutral as possible, unwilling to distress Amber further.

Then Amber dried her hands on some kitchen roll and produced her phone. 'I've photos from the *Wicklow Weekly*, Mum, taken at the charity thing when you met Evie.'

Jessica stared at them in silence.

'That's Barry Talbot beside you and Evie,' Amber said pointedly.

'You asked me about him before, didn't you?' Jessica said, managing to sound casual. 'I'd forgotten his name,' she fibbed, 'but I remember him now.' She waited to hear what Amber might have to say about Barry, but instead she continued to scroll through her phone.

'There he is with his wife, Tess, and that other guy is Matthew Casey.'

'Matthew Casey? Should I know him?'

Matthew Casey. The Caseys. She knew, of course she knew.

'He's a wealthy man, living in the depths of Wicklow,' Amber said. 'Without betraying Evie's confidence, he has ancient history with her and Granny Pippa, from when they spent their summers in Heronbrook. Evie told me about it herself. And it's not a good story. It was a bit of a tragedy, actually.'

That was one way of putting it, Jessica decided, recalling what she knew.

'I thought there might be a link between him and

Evie's misfortunes,' Amber said. 'Evie doesn't know because I didn't want to worry her, but I googled where he lived and called to his house yesterday evening.'

Jessica's head whirled. 'You *what*? Seriously, Amber, that mightn't have been your best idea.'

'Probably not, but I didn't get anywhere. He said he'd absolutely no interest in Evie, never mind our family. He's far too busy maintaining his mega-successful life to be bothered. Too busy plotting his next move in the expansion of his empire, if you ask me.'

'Can you send me those images? There are a couple of things I want to check out,' Jessica said.

'What things?'

'Just send them to me, Amber. I'll let you know if I get anywhere.'

'But you agree with me, don't you? It's all a bit peculiar.'

'It's strange all right,' Jessica said, a fresh chasm of anxiety opening up inside her. 'Are you sure you and Evie are OK down in Heronbrook? Those incidents should be reported to the police.'

'They called the other day about the hit-and-run, and they know about the tyre slashing. Evie doesn't want to involve them any further and she doesn't think there'll be any more intimidation, but I'll be ready to call them if there is. And if I do, I'll talk to you beforehand.'

'Keep me updated. On everything,' Jessica said. 'Call me every day.'

And as if the evening couldn't have become more stressful, Jessica and Amber were no sooner back in the sitting room watching the rest of the video montage when the doorbell chimed. Jessica looked out the window. Jamie was at the hall door, hunched into his jacket, looking like he was spoiling for an argument.

Shit. 'It's Jamie,' she said, speaking to no one in particular. 'He's a bit late for food, although I didn't exactly invite him.'

'I was talking to him this afternoon,' Adam said. 'I texted him about what happened to me and he rang me back. I might have said that Evie and Amber would be here this evening.'

Thanks a bunch, Adam.

Paul paused the video while Jessica opened the hall door. Practically ignoring her, Jamie strode into the sitting room, aggression radiating from him.

'So here you all are, quite the happy little family.' He flung himself into an armchair, his hands resting on the arms, fingers drumming on the edges. 'And Aunt Evie, back in the bosom at last.'

'Jamie, Aunt Evie's our guest. What's up with you?' Jessica said, feeling as though a loose cannon had just rolled into the room.

'I have a question. I wonder who can answer it,' Jamie said, looking around the group. 'Ah, Aunt Evie, you might be able to enlighten me.'

'What is it?' Jessica asked.

He ignored her, looking belligerently at Evie. 'So who's Barry Talbot, when he's at home?'

Afterwards, Jessica marvelled at the way she managed to stay cool and unflappable on the surface, considering how her stomach coiled even tighter with the permanent tension she seemed to be carrying these days. She was grateful that Evie rose wonderfully to the challenge, thanks in some part, Jessica decided, to her stage training.

'Barry Talbot is a neighbour of mine. Why are you asking?' Evie said calmly, as Jessica held her breath. 'Do you know him yourself?'

'I've never met the man,' Jamie said. 'But I heard talk of him lately and I thought he might have something to do with you?'

'Well, he has,' Evie said pleasantly. 'His wife, Tess, is the person who found me after the hit-and-run and called the ambulance. And by the way, it's really lovely to be in the bosom of the family,' she said, smiling warmly at Jessica. 'Family is everything.'

'Yes, it is,' Jamie said. His antagonism had cooled a little, and to Jessica he looked lost and subdued, something in his eyes reminding her of the young schoolboy who'd been so upset when she'd left home to get married.

'Can I get you a coffee, Jamie?' she asked. 'How about some cheese and crackers?'

'Just coffee is fine,' Jamie said.

'I'll get it,' Paul said, wanting no doubt to escape the stressful atmosphere for a moment.

Jamie gestured towards the television. 'Don't let me interrupt your cosy family viewing.'

He seemed to have dropped the subject of Barry Talbot but Jessica sat on the edge of her seat as they all settled back down to watch the end of the video. She was conscious that they looked on the surface as though they hadn't a care in the world, including her. Yet she felt it fizzing underneath, the tension, and she just wanted to lie down for a long time in a cool, dark space. Evie and Amber left soon after, Evie expressing her gratitude for the lovely evening once again, Amber saying she'd call her tomorrow, but there was no sign of Jamie making a move, and when the others had left, with much hand-waving and exhortations to drive safely, he asked if he could speak to Jessica alone.

'We can go into the kitchen,' she said, realising the fraught evening wasn't over yet.

He paced the floor for a minute before pulling a card out of his pocket, flinging it across the island counter. 'This arrived, today, at the pub in Naas.'

This card had a picture of a gorilla on the front. Jessica opened it and read the message within. Like the previous message, this was typed on a sheet of paper and stuck inside.

'WHO'S BARRY TALBOT? ASK EVIE LAWRENCE.'

'I bet he's my father,' Jamie said. 'But I didn't understand the connection with Evie until she said he's a neighbour of hers.'

'You can't be sure of anything – could be

someone playing a huge joke,' Jessica began, feeling she couldn't pretend to be the strong one any more.

'This guy ... I've checked him out online, and a lot of the details fit – the age, he's Wicklow based, I've seen his Google photo, and I look a lot more like him than my supposed father. I bet Mum had an affair with this Talbot guy. He's also married, so that's probably why he didn't want to know me, afraid to rock the boat with his wife. That's if Mum told him about me in the first place. Maybe she didn't. Maybe she was happy to pass me off as her husband's son and stay in her marriage while letting him witness the evidence of her unfaithfulness on a daily basis.'

'What are you going to do?'

Jamie rubbed his face and looked out into the garden. 'I don't know. I need time to think. I don't know who's sending me these cards – the first one arriving in New York, but then this one arriving in Naas means they know I'm back from there.'

His Naas address hadn't been on the nursing home file, Jessica realised, her thoughts churning. 'Who knows your new address?'

'Just the immediate family – and Evie too, a couple of mates, that's all. I haven't been home long enough to pick up many old friendships and a lot of my mates are scattered now.'

She felt a stab of dismay when Jamie slumped forward and put his head against the patio door. 'Bloody hell, Jessica, even though I've had a gut feeling about this for years, I feel all over the place now that it's been put up to me. I don't know who's taking the piss or why they want to cause trouble – fuck's sake, things are wrecked enough already.'

'Wrecked? What are you talking about?'

He stared around at her, his eyes pained. 'Look at me – living in a dingy bedsit with no real prospects. How am I going to improve my life? How will I ever afford a home of my own? I know I sound narky and bad humoured a lot of the time, but I can't seem to help it. The years just seemed to go by, without me thinking too much of the future, and now it's too late. I'm sick of the way my life has turned out.'

'Is that why you left New York?'

He didn't answer her question. He wouldn't meet her eyes. 'The thing is, sis, I'm afraid of turning out like Mum – permanently unhappy with myself and the world.'

Jamie's words dismayed her so much that Jessica had to sit down. 'Why on earth do you think you'll turn out like Mum? You're not an alcoholic, unless you have a problem I'm not aware of. But, Jamie, there's always hope. It's not too late – you've plenty of good years ahead. You can turn your life around if you really want to. We can talk about this.'

He paced the floor. 'I'd just like to have an ordinary kind of life. A home. A family.' He wheeled around to her. 'You don't know how lucky you are.'

'Lucky? My life involves a lot of hard work,

Jamie, and in fact, I've had a crap week – first Adam, then Amber—' She stopped.

'I'm sorry about Adam, that was horrific, but what's wrong with Amber?' he asked.

'She told us this evening. She didn't swear us to secrecy so I'm sure it's OK to tell you. That guy she was with – Will – he turns out to have been a nasty piece of work. He seems to have set her up and sabotaged her job in Healy's by compromising some of her confidential work. Her contract was terminated. With immediate effect.'

'Holy shit. Why target Amber like that?'

'I want to kill him for what he did. And she can't trace him now – he seems to have vanished.'

'What a wanker. That's strange, though.'

'And then Amber told me that someone has been harassing Evie, copycatting the things that happened to her character in *Delphin Terrace*. This started after the hit-and-run. Amber's ready to go to the police …'

She realised Jamie was staring into space, a hunted look on his face.

'What is it?' she said, his stance making her light-headed.

'I have to go. I need to talk to Amber. When will she be back in Heronbrook?'

'In less than an hour, I expect, if they go straight home. What's wrong?'

He was already walking towards the door. 'Text her, will you? Tell her to expect my call later and to please answer it.'

He barely said goodbye to Paul and Adam, hurrying up the hall and out to his car as though he were trying to escape a burning house. Jessica closed the door after him and went down to the kitchen, relieved that Paul and Adam were absorbed in a sports programme. She sloshed some wine into a glass, going back over her conversation with Jamie. The minute she'd mentioned Evie's incidents and the police, his face had changed. She picked up her mobile, hesitating over her text to Amber. Was there any point in alerting her to Jamie's reaction? In the end, she told her to expect a call from Jamie, that he needed to talk to her and it had something to do with Evie.

She thought about what he'd said in his bedsit about leaving her in blissful ignorance. What had he done that could ruin her opinion of him? Then, afraid to think any more, about Jamie or what was happening in the family, she sat and watched the shadows darken in the garden outside until everything was blanketed in the soft, purply night.

Amber sat at the table in Heronbrook, scrolling through websites on Evie's laptop, a pen and notebook beside her. Her mobile buzzed. Jamie. After her mother's mystifying text, she'd been expecting his call. She was glad that Evie had just gone to bed, saying she'd had a lovely and enjoyable visit to Laurel Lawns, but she needed an early night.

'Jamie? Hi.'

'Amber ...' he began, his voice subdued. 'I don't know where to start.'

'Mum said you wanted to talk about Evie,' she said, sensing his dejection. 'I'm not sure how much she told you about the terrifying things that have been happening, but if it continues, I'm going straight to the police. So if there's anything at all you know—'

'Fuck's sake, you don't think I've anything to do with that? What do you take me for?'

'Hey, you made it clear you can't stand Evie, and you were prowling around here on the lookout for a painting—'

'You've got the wrong end of the stick,' he said soberly. 'I was looking for Lucien's painting because I was interested in it, that's all. Interested in his work and wondering why he gave it up. I know so little about him. I was, what, eleven when he died? I've nothing from my childhood home beyond a couple of photographs. Sometimes it makes me feel rootless.'

Amber was speechless for a moment at this unexpected admission. Then, 'What brought this on?'

Jamie sighed heavily. 'Forget it, it's for another day. I called you to talk about Will.'

A thud in her chest. 'What about him?'

'Jessica told me about Will and your job in Healy's,' he said bluntly.

'Did she now.' Amber hadn't been expecting that, not that it made much difference, she thought tiredly.

'I got talking to her after you left. I was telling her about – well, never mind. She said you think Will stitched you up. And now you can't trace him?'

'That's true,' she said, defeated, as she stared at the blank screen of the laptop, the cursor blinking.

'Guess what, Amber,' he said in a sour voice, 'we have a few things in common.'

'Like what?' Amber asked, suddenly alert, sensing already she would not like this.

'The reason I came home is because I was more or less deported from New York.'

'Deported?'

'Yeah, thanks to my lovely girlfriend.'

'What lovely girlfriend?'

'She shopped my illegal status to the authorities. Then she vanished into thin air.'

'I don't understand.'

'I'll start at the beginning,' Jamie said.

Amber listened, pinpricks of panic shooting around the back of her mind, as Jamie skimmed through the details, sounding as bitter as if it had happened yesterday.

He told her about Emer, who had walked into the bar where he worked at the end of June. She was petite, blonde haired, blue eyed. She sat nursing a gin and tonic before ordering another, her expression so downcast that he'd asked if she was OK, realising from her accent that she was Irish. She'd said she was from Dublin, and she appeared to have been stood up that evening. When she became a little upset, Jamie fetched her tissues, and when she said she'd been expecting to go for a meal with her boyfriend, he brought out some food for her.

'I had a couple of drinks with her when I knocked off,' he said, 'and that was the start of it all. We got together pretty quickly – we couldn't get enough of each other.'

'No need to elaborate, I get the picture,' Amber said.

'Emer seemed to be really into me, like no other woman ever was before. I fell hard for her, her sparky attitude, the way she came on to me like she adored me. She seemed so genuine and natural. Holy shit, Amber, I couldn't believe my luck. I thought things were picking up for me at last, that my life had changed for the better. It lasted all of three weeks, but I still don't understand why she fucked me over.'

'What did she do?'

'One minute I was flying high, the next I was caught by Immigration and Customs Enforcement

for violating immigration laws and being undocumented. I was invited to leave New York
immediately or spend time hanging around a
correctional facility, waiting for the inevitable. So I
came home.'

'Were you undocumented all this time?'

'Yeah, well, I'd outstayed my student visa by
a couple of decades, but, hey, I was working and
paying social security. The cops didn't tell me who'd
stitched me up, Emer did.'

'She actually admitted she'd shopped you?'

'Eventually, in a text, just before I left. I had
called and called her, but she didn't answer her
mobile. Then I got a text from her asking how much
I liked my surprise. She was sorry, not-sorry I was
being booted out of America, but it was just the way
things were.'

'You're joking.'

'I wish. The next time I called her I got the
message that her mobile was no longer in service.
And I haven't been able to find her online since. The
Emer I knew doesn't exist. I've never felt so down
or humiliated in my life – talk about coming home
with my tail between my legs. I couldn't believe it
when Jessica told me about Will. It seems like we've
both been messed around.'

Amber felt a tingling in her head as the
similarities sank in. She stared out at the darkening
garden, seeing her own reflection in the plate-glass
door, her face drained of colour in the glare from
the laptop. She took a slow breath then picked up

her pen. 'How long were you with Emer when you admitted your illegal status?'

'Not long,' he said, subdued.

'How old was she?'

'Mid-thirties.'

'What was her full name and where did she work?' She scribbled down details as he spoke.

'Emer Wade. She said she worked on one of those fashion magazines. I guessed it was a pretty glam job, but she didn't seem hard-polished glam herself. Just nice and friendly.'

'Were you ever in her apartment?'

'No, she told me she was sharing with a couple of bunny boilers – her salary didn't stretch to her own pad. We met in cafés or she came to the pub. Then it would be back to my place, but never hers.'

'Did she give you any personal information at all?'

'I don't know if it was all a made-up sob story, but she mentioned her father. She didn't have any time for him, she said. He made her childhood miserable, he was such a cold—'

'Unfeeling disciplinarian?' Amber hazarded a guess.

'More or less. How did you know?'

Amber's heart knocked against her ribcage. It was just how Will had described his father. 'Did Emer say anything about having a brother?'

'No, but one night when she had a few drinks too many she said that even though she'd no time for her father, it didn't stop her enjoying the comforts of his palatial home whenever she was back in Ireland. He wasn't short of a few bob, she joked. He lived in a luxury home in the remote wilds somewhere and his wine cellar was well stocked. But she could have been making that up too.'

'Hang on a minute, Jamie,' Amber said, trying to slow her agitated breathing. Like the pieces of a jigsaw coming together, she thought of the affluent Matthew Casey living in remote luxury. She remembered the flyer for the Wicklow spa that she'd found in her briefcase. What were the chances she'd scooped it up along with some papers off the counter in *Will*'s apartment, and not the office? It could mean that Will had been spending time in Wicklow. *Fuck it*. On the laptop, she googled Matthew Casey again, this time checking out links until she came to one that listed his children. She took a note of their names, Patrick and Jennifer. She called Jennifer's name out to Jamie and told him to google it.

'I'll have to end the call first,' he said. 'I'll come back to you in a minute.'

She typed Patrick and Matthew Casey into her browser, her stomach somersaulting when a few pictures came up and Will Baker's face smiled back at her. She searched further but, like his father, Patrick William Casey, to give him his full name, didn't have much of an online footprint. Privately educated at a midlands boarding school, he'd studied economics and technical finance in a German college before joining his father in the business. He was currently based in Dusseldorf, strengthening their European platform.

Well, he's lurking in Dublin at the moment. And I must have been chicken-feed to him.

Then with a clarity borne of anger, she remembered something else. The documents lined up on Matthew Casey's desk that she'd tried to read – one of them had borne the letterhead of a Dublin-based property-management company specialising in exclusive lettings. She'd come across the name when she'd been searching for rentals in Dundrum. What was the betting Matthew Casey held Dundrum apartments as part of his investment portfolio? And his son had temporarily helped himself to one? Though surely an outfit as powerful as the Caseys wouldn't have needed to use the likes of Amber Lennox to sabotage Healy's? Did that mean it wasn't Healy's they had been after, but her? Less than five minutes later, her mobile rang again.

'I don't fucking believe it,' Jamie said, his voice shaking with rage. 'That's her, the bitch. She's working in New York all right, but in some elite hedge-fund firm. I bet she has her own swanky penthouse apartment she was afraid to let me see. I would have rumbled her lies straightaway. What the hell is going on, Amber?'

'I don't know but I'm going to find out.' It wasn't just about sabotaging her, she realised coldly. There was something bigger playing out here.

'We're busy at the pub with funerals and parties for the next couple of days,' Jamie said, 'so I can't follow this up straightaway. But I need to talk to Jessica. I'm sure she's wondering why I ran out of the house earlier tonight. I've been too humiliated to tell her what happened.'

'Leave everything with me, Jamie,' Amber said. 'At least until the weekend. There are a couple of things I want to check out before I unload all this onto Mum. I'm really sorry about New York, but you *will* come back from it, and you weren't stupid, you just came up against a devious bitch,' she said, recalling Evie's words to her. 'Hey, at least you're home, with family who love you and want you.'

'Thanks, Amber.'

Even though it was late, she texted her mum to say she'd spoken to Jamie. His call had had nothing to do with Evie, she said. He'd been commiserating with Amber over Will because a girlfriend had let him down in New York and he knew how much it stung.

'Poor Jamie ☹' Jessica texted back. 'Why didn't he tell me?'

'He was embarrassed and didn't want to talk about it,' Amber texted. 'He was trying to console me. He's fine now,' she fibbed. She added a thumbs up emoji. The less her mother knew for now, the better. Otherwise her mother would insist she call the police. But she wasn't going to do that until she found Will and spoke to him herself.

Amber got up and poured herself a glass of water. There were too many strands still to untangle, but there had to be a link involving the Caseys between

Evie's accident and intimidation, herself and Jamie, perhaps even Adam. A link that stretched back to the summer in Heronbrook when everything went into free fall for Evie and Lucien.

How could she tell Evie she suspected that her sad past had reached out to the present day, drawing them all into the same battle? It would break her heart. Jamie knew nothing of the events of that summer. Neither did her mum, as far as Amber was aware. And that's the way it would stay for the moment, she decided.

She recalled what Will had told her of his 'unfeeling disciplinarian' father. Matthew Casey seemed to be utterly comfortable in his own skin and utterly relaxed in his own home. Well, he was bound to be, given his considerable wealth. It was disturbing to think he could have dragged his own children into taking such a savage and sordid revenge against Evie and her family. She recalled the table set for two in Temple Raven that evening, the crystal wine glasses ready. No doubt Patrick, as well as his equally obnoxious sister, was happy to disregard his father's coldness in order to partake of board and lodgings in his luxury home?

On Thursday morning, she told Evie she was going shopping in Arklow. She left sandwiches ready for her in the fridge in case she was delayed, glad that Evie could now operate the coffee machine single-handedly. She took the road up to Temple Raven just after midday, rehearsing what she would say depending on the reception she got, ignoring the nausea in her stomach. She parked in front of the wooden gates and pressed the buzzer. Once again a woman's voice came across the intercom.

'I want to see Patrick William Casey,' Amber said. 'It's urgent. He might be staying here, but if not, his father should have some idea of his whereabouts.'

'There's no one at home today who can help you,' the woman said.

'Irene? You are Irene, aren't you?' Amber said. Without waiting for an answer she went on, 'I'm determined to talk to Patrick and find out why he scuppered my career. I want to know why my family is being subjected to some very distressing events.'

'You've had a wasted journey,' Irene said.

There was no way of knowing if Irene was telling the truth, Amber realised. 'In that case I'm going to come back here tomorrow and park in front of these gates, and I'm going to block them until I get satisfaction.'

'I don't think Mr Matthew Casey will be pleased with your ultimatum, Ms Lennox. I suggest you leave before I call the police and inform them of your harassment.'

'I intend to go to the police myself and inform them of Mr Casey's harassment of me, his criminal behaviour, and his suspected involvement in Ms Lawrence's hit-and-run. I'll be back here tomorrow. I expect to talk to him then.'

Sitting on the terrace with Evie that afternoon, she made a pretence of reading a book. Everything seemed much as normal, the sun sending golden prisms through the trees and sparking off the surface of the brook, birdsong filling the air, both of them wrapped in thick, comfy hoodies. Amber looked at the words jumping up and down in front of her, knowing everything had changed and that she'd started a course of action there was no coming back from.

'I won't starve,' Evie said on Friday morning. 'There's leftover pasta in the fridge that I can have for lunch. I'm well capable of heating it in the microwave and carrying it to the table. That only takes one hand.'

'I'll be back before then.' Amber pulled on her parka and picked up her bag.

'I'm glad you're meeting a friend for coffee,' Evie told her, 'especially now that I'm a little less helpless.'

'But no bending down under any circumstances, even if the Wi-Fi goes on the blink.'

'Do you think I'm going to jeopardise my recovery now?'

'Not deliberately, but you might try to do more than you should. I don't want you undoing all my hard work.'

'Right. Off you go.'

Amber was gone only fifteen minutes when the doorbell chimed and Tess Talbot's voice came though the intercom, telling Evie she was outside. Good manners and a feeling that she still owed her a debt bade Evie go to the hall door and invite her in. Tess stood outside the gates, wearing dark jeans and a pale-blue jumper, and she held a tinfoil-covered basket in her hands. Evie saw the bumper of a silver car parked outside on the lane. She picked up the fob off the hall table and opened the gate, calling out to tell Tess she could park in the driveway.

'No worries, it's grand where it is,' Tess said, walking up the driveway as soon as the gap in the gates permitted.

'This is a nice surprise,' Evie said, as Tess stepped into the hall.

'Good,' said Tess. She held up her basket. 'I told Amber I'd drop in with some pastries, and I thought today would be a good opportunity. Then I was worried you might not be able to answer the door, but I see you're able to get around fine on one crutch.'

'Another two weeks and I hope to be rid of this,' Evie said, leading the way down to the kitchen.

Tess put the basket on the table and peeled off the tinfoil, revealing a selection of lemon curd pastries, pear and almond tartlets, and chocolate éclairs.

'My goodness,' Evie said. 'They look positively sinful.' She was torn between pleasure at Tess's thoughtfulness and wondering what exactly her gossipy neighbour wanted.

'Well, it is Friday – nice to think of it as a day for treats,' Tess said. 'I insist you sit down and relax – I'll make the coffee or tea, whatever your poison, although I guess it's too early for wine o'clock.' She opened her bag and took out some napkins. She set them down on the table and busied herself at the counter, putting on the kettle and lifting mugs off the mug tree.

'I'll have coffee,' Evie said. 'You just have to

pop a gold capsule into the machine and it does the rest.'

'Grand,' Tess said. 'I'll have tea.'

Presently Tess brought the tea and coffee over to the table, and she fetched plates and cutlery for the pastries, arranging them in front of Evie, leaving the napkins within easy reach. She sat down with a flourish, looking as though she was settling in for the morning.

'I'm certainly being spoiled,' Evie said, 'but it's me who should be spoiling you.' She helped herself to a pastry.

'Not at all, it's my pleasure. You've a wonderful aspect from this room,' Tess said, staring out the window, 'right down to the brook. It looks so peaceful.'

'It is, nothing beats sitting on the terrace once it's not too cold.'

'You're a lucky woman,' Tess said. 'You have the woods and the beach close by, and civilisation isn't that far away either. I can't believe I've never been in Heronbrook before.'

'Haven't you? Did you not have a look-see when it went on the market?'

'No, I leave all that stuff up to Barry. Mind you, if I'd taken more interest I might have snatched it back from under your nose, instead of letting you gazump him.' She lifted her eyebrows and glanced at Evie with the hint of an impudent look. She helped herself to a chocolate éclair, cutting off a small morsel of it before popping it into her mouth.

'That's not quite what happened,' Evie said, beginning to wonder if she might regret this interruption to her peaceful day.

'Isn't it?' Tess frowned. 'He told me you usurped him at the final hurdle.'

Evie laughed. 'I don't think so. My purchase was straightforward – I wasn't even aware Barry was interested until I had signed and sealed the deal.'

'Weren't you?' Tess looked at her steadily, before looking away. 'That fecker might have pulled a fast one on me, pretending you had gazumped him. I had the feeling he was losing his mojo, getting too lazy and slack for anything that might resemble work. Feck's sake. I'll be sorting him out soon.' She gave Evie a cryptic look before laughing. 'It's so beautiful here that I'm jealous. You'd think at my age I'd have more sense.'

'Age might cause a decline in the body but it doesn't diminish the capacity for passion or emotion,' Evie said. 'Anyhow, I thought Barry was only interested in knocking this house down.'

'You're right.'

'That's what I thought – however, Tess, you still have the nearby beach and the woods to enjoy, and they're both free.'

'When I said you're right,' Tess said, correcting her, 'I meant what you said about passion and emotion. They can be a curse.'

'Only if misdirected.'

'Or if they're not reciprocated.'

'That too, I suppose,' Evie said. Silence fell, and Evie didn't know if she was imagining it, but it seemed to her it was strained with unease of some kind. 'Why don't we take ourselves outside?' she said, wanting to dissipate the tension.

'I thought you'd never ask,' Tess said.

Her smile, Evie thought, was a little too sweet and satisfied.

Amber took a deep breath when she arrived at the corkscrew bend in the narrow road in the heart of west Wicklow. Meeting a friend for coffee, she'd told Evie. It had been the easiest way to cover her absence. She hadn't slept much the night before, and the only thing that had sent a ray of warmth through her that morning was a text from Fionn to say he'd be down the following day. As she ventured up the narrow mountainy road, anxiety charged around her body. How long did she think she could park outside Temple Raven, blocking the gates, until she managed to see Patrick, or get his contact details if he wasn't staying there?

However, just as she pulled in front of them, the wooden gates slid open. She drove up the curving driveway, sensing she was under surveillance of some kind, and this was further confirmed when the front door opened as she walked towards it. She stepped into the hall. There was no sign of Irene, but the guy who'd called himself Will Baker was standing there, wearing a soft denim shirt, his hands dug into the pockets of his dark chinos, his eyes glinting sardonically.

'Aren't you the little clever clogs,' he said. 'How did you find me?'

Any nerves she felt at the sight of him dissolved under a wave of pure anger.

'What were you playing at?' she snapped.

'Pretending to be my boyfriend and wrecking my career? I want an explanation, Patrick William.' An angry blush swept up from her neck and stained her cheeks.

'Who said anything about me wrecking your career?' he said, nonchalant. 'You did that to yourself.'

His words had the effect of cold water hitting her face. 'The hell I did. You can't bluff your way out of this. You know exactly what you did to me, you prick,' she said, her voice wobbling with rage.

He shrugged carelessly. 'And by the way, thanks for dragging my father into it,' he said. 'He rarely knows what's going on in my private life.'

'He must have had some involvement?'

'My father couldn't give a shite what's going on, once I don't do anything to dent his bank balance.'

He walked across the hall with an easy gait, indicating that she should follow him. He led her into a beautiful reception room overlooking the front gardens, where thick pile rugs sat atop a parquet floor, a display cabinet held an array of glittering crystal glasses, and three sumptuous crimson sofas sat at angles to each other in front of a marble fireplace. A magnificent chandelier hung from the ceiling, set into a delicately crafted ceiling rose. The walls were adorned with an eclectic selection of original art, and in a far-off corner of her mind she realised she'd love to have examined the paintings had the circumstances been different. Right now she felt like pulling out the contents of the cabinet and smashing the crystal against the wall. She refused to sit down, too distraught to sink into the depths of a sofa, where she'd feel at a disadvantage. She remained standing, gripping the back of a sofa as she confronted him. He didn't sit down either. He stood lounging against the display cabinet, his arms folded in front of him, as though he hadn't a care in the world.

'I know what you did,' she said heatedly. 'You leaked highly sensitive information about Healy's tender to competing bidders through my email account. You're the only one who had the opportunity, because I stupidly left my account open when I was in your bed, in your apartment. Enticed there. By you. On purpose. Talk about corporate and personal sabotage. I want to know why you set me up. What did I ever do to you to deserve this? And your sister, I believe, pulled a similar kind of stunt on my uncle in New York.'

He ignored her questions. He took his mobile out of his pocket and checked it, glancing at her mockingly as he shoved it back in.

'For fuck's sake, answer me,' Amber hissed, incensed.

'You had the misfortune to be born into the wrong family,' he said. 'As had I.'

'What do you mean?'

'Have you any idea what it was like to be the son of Matthew Casey?' His voice was indifferent, as though he wasn't expecting a response from her. 'My father was only interested in one thing – making money. Making lots of it. Proving himself. Being better than anyone else at what he did. Growing up, we were to all intents and purposes locked up in golden cages lest any disaster befall us. We were shipped off to boarding schools, which we hated. As teenagers, we couldn't go on sports trips with our classmates, or on mid-term travel breaks, or even discos. We were effectively locked down.'

'My heart bleeds but locked down in luxury sounds like a life of privilege to me.'

'He didn't love us. He never hugged us, read stories to us, got down on the floor to play with us. He didn't know how to love. He was just as emotionally distant with my mother. She had enough and took off with another man when I was twelve, making such a clean break that she left me and my sister. We were lucky to see her once a year.'

'That's no reason to intimidate my family. It has nothing to do with us.'

'It has everything to do with your family,' he said, his rising voice showing the first sign of emotion. 'I always knew my aunt Leah had suffered serious brain damage as a young child. But I didn't appreciate the way it tore the family apart until I was in my teens. My grandparents found the tragedy almost impossible to deal with – there were no resources available back then to help them manage Leah's needs, never mind their own emotions, and it shattered their lives.'

'I know about that,' she said, feeling cold.

'Then when I was at college,' he said, 'I had a talk with my aunt Rachel and found out that my father was a victim of that shattered family in his own right. As a child, he'd been left to fend for himself, vulnerable in a school classroom of almost fifty kids – too many to be looked after properly – wearing his defenceless status like a label around his neck in front of the more abusive so-called teachers – I don't need to spell it out. He knew his parents had enough to deal with without him bringing home more trouble, and the only way he could cope was to close himself off, bury himself in his books. He was determined to pull himself free and leave that life behind him. By the time he was finished school, any softness he might have had, any empathy, had been beaten out of him.'

'That was tough,' Amber said, 'but it's no reason for you and your sister to do what you did to me and my uncle. But far more serious was my great-aunt being knocked down on the lane. What have you to say about that?'

He ignored her question. 'We thought that Rachel had been responsible for Leah's accident,' he went on. 'It was never spoken about. Then earlier this year, before she died, our small family was together for once when my father, my sister, and I visited her in the hospice. Rachel spoke about that day and that's when we heard that Pippa and Evie Lawrence were, between them, the ones to blame.'

'Evie told me about that herself,' Amber said. 'It was terribly tragic, and she regretted it hugely, but it's no reason for you to go around causing mayhem.'

'The Lawrences' actions that afternoon wrecked our family. Why should they get away scot-free?' He glanced down at his shoulder and, straightening up a little, brushed a speck of dust off his shirt. 'An eye for an eye, as it says in the Bible.' He slouched back against the cabinet and continued in a bland voice. 'Rachel died at the beginning of May, seventy years of age. She'd been lonely for most of her adult life. Aunt Leah has spent the last thirty years in a home, not having any quality of life. As a result, my father is a cold-blooded, distant man. Then my sister and I heard that both your mother and Evie Lawrence were spotted at a charity event, looking like they were enjoying the high life. *And* that Evie had actually moved back to the scene of the crime two years previously to enjoy a relaxing retirement. Now, that didn't seem right to us.'

Amber simmered with fury at the impertinence of his casual attitude. It was also fury directed at herself for allowing him to upset her. This guy wasn't worthy of her thoughts, he wasn't worthy of the slightest ounce of her energy. The knowledge freed her and came with such clarity that she was blindsided momentarily.

'What you and your sister have done,' she said, striving for control, 'apart from being criminal, is taking revenge to a whole new level.'

'Criminal?' He laughed. 'We had a score to settle but we just exploited your weaknesses. I've been in Ireland for the last four months laying the groundwork for a new financial enterprise, so it stopped me from feeling bored. My sister was living in New York, so it was serendipitous. And for me, highly enjoyable. Not criminal at all, in fact.' His eyes flicked salaciously over her body and her stomach lurched.

'You bastard.'

'Pippa is already paying for her sins,' he went on, his arrogance infuriating her. 'I dropped in on her, you know. I introduced myself and told her what I had planned. I don't think she was too happy. But you were careless, you wrecked your own career; Jamie was illegal, he brought it on himself; Evie – too bad she was in the wrong place at the wrong time; your mother—'

'What about my mother?' Amber snapped.

'You mean she didn't tell you?' He grinned.

'What are you talking about?'

'Ask her what happened, oh, let me see, in early August? She did something stupid. Maybe she hasn't come clean about it yet.'

'You fucker,' Amber said. 'My mother did nothing to harm you or your family.'

'Nor did your brother but that's not the point.'

'Not Adam,' she said. 'He was *mugged*. Dear God, you really are an evil bastard.'

'Nope. It's simply payback time for the Lawrence family.'

'You're nuts,' Amber said. 'Both you and your sister. Whatever about me and Jamie, Evie's accident was vicious. She could have been killed. How can you live with your conscience, knowing that?'

'You hardly think I was personally responsible for her accident?' He looked mildly affronted. 'I wasn't driving that bike. The plan was just to shake her up a little.'

'You *were* responsible if you helped to plan it, you scumbag. How did you know she'd be there at that particular time? Was it a drone? I saw it on the laneway one day – was that you?'

'I don't know anything about a drone,' he said.

'Don't act innocent. Are you happy now that you've caused so much havoc?' Amber said, trying a different angle.

'My sister and I feel somewhat vindicated.'

'Then why are you still tormenting Evie?'

'You have that wrong. I'm not still tormenting her.'

'You are. You sent her a video, just recently, a clip of her accident. The hit-and-run was bad enough without running a dirty campaign to intimidate her after that.'

'I didn't send her any such thing,' he said, giving her a cold look, 'and I don't know what campaign or intimidation you're talking about.'

'Of course you do. Her tyres didn't slash themselves, and there were other things … you needn't try and wriggle off the hook, you ignorant bastard.'

'I haven't a clue what you're on about,' he drawled. 'I know nothing about slashed tyres or drones or video clips, and you've overstayed your welcome, Ms Amber Lennox.'

She was confused by his denial of Evie's intimidation, then his use of her name thrust her back to the first day she'd met him. She'd sensed, even then, that he possessed an arrogant streak. Theirs had been a superficial relationship, more of a sexual charge on her part, responding to an excitement he'd switched on inside her. A wave of fatigue washed over her. Her sleep had been broken for several nights as she'd tried to make sense of things, and now that she had come face to face with 'Will', her heightened emotions of the last few weeks were beginning to crash spectacularly. She would have to get out of here soon.

'How did you find us?' she asked, something else that had been nibbling at her thoughts. 'How did you know I was Pippa's granddaughter and that I worked in Russell Hall? And Jamie in New York?'

He grinned. 'I thought you would have had that sussed already. It's easy to find people nowadays on social media once you know where to start.'

'How did you know where to start?'

He shrugged. She thought of what he'd said about the charity event, how her mother and Evie had been talking to Barry Talbot, hadn't they? He'd presumably gone back to the table and relayed the conversation to Matthew Casey.

'What part did you father play in all this?'

'Nothing. I told you he doesn't give a shit about anything at all, his children included, unless it impacts on his bank balance or property portfolio, and we have the Lawrences to thank for that.'

'I bet that doesn't stop you from enjoying the benefits of that bank balance,' she said.

'As far as I'm concerned, this little episode in my life is over. I'm back to Germany next week.'

'We'll see about that,' Amber said. 'I'll be making a statement to the police as soon as I talk to my family.'

'Good luck with that,' he sneered. 'It'll be your word against mine – you won't be able to prove a thing.'

'Won't I?' she said with more bravado than she felt. 'Don't be surprised if you find yourself being called in for questioning on a charge of attempted murder.'

'I didn't attempt to murder anyone. Your aunt was just supposed to be frightened. I'm not a total monster.'

'My aunt was almost killed,' she said. 'Watch this space.' And tossing her head for good measure, before placing an imaginary crown on top, she stalked across the thick pile rugs and marched out the door.

Her legs were shaking and there was a mist in front of her eyes as she walked over to her car and drove out the driveway, the gates parting smoothly to allow her to exit. She knew she needed to calm down before seeing Evie, to get the taste of Patrick and his chilling behaviour out of her mouth. She needed to tell Jamie what had happened. But first she needed to talk to her mum as a matter of urgency. For all his horrible treatment of her, his cold sneering and

casual attitude, she sensed he was telling the truth
about Evie's accident. He might have planned it, but
she couldn't imagine him getting on a motorbike
in order to inflict damage on a seventy-five-year-
old woman. He would have hired someone else to
do the dirty work, someone who had apparently
veered from the plan to shake up Evie a little. And
even though he'd chillingly mentioned her mother
and Adam, he'd claimed ignorance about the nasty
campaign against Evie. Which meant whoever had
instigated the other incidents against Evie, and
whoever had driven that motorbike and tried to kill
her, was still out there somewhere.

But soon after she negotiated the first corkscrew
bend in the road, Amber could go no further. Her
stomach convulsed with nausea and sweat prickled
across her face and neck. Her hands and legs began
to shake uncontrollably. Delayed shock. Hitting
her with the force of a sledgehammer. As soon as
she could, she pulled into the small off-road space
afforded by the entrance to a pedestrian forest trail
and stopped the car.

Amber had left the keys in the lock of the terrace door from earlier that morning, and the bolts top and bottom had been left open, so it was easy for Evie to turn the key and slide back the door, allowing the cool air, the birdsong, and whisper of the trees to rush in, calming her a little and easing her tension.

'I'll get this organised,' Tess offered, grabbing some kitchen roll and going out ahead of her to wipe down the outdoor table. 'Will I bring out fresh coffee for you?' she asked, glancing into Evie's cup.

'I'll get it,' Evie said, reaching for her cup with her free hand, needing to do something to show she wasn't helpless.

'Sit outside and relax, I'll sort it,' Tess said in a voice of such insistence that Evie found herself subsiding into a rattan chair while Tess busied herself in the kitchen. She brought out the place settings, arranging them on the table, followed by the basket of pastries, napkins, and fresh tea and coffee. She picked up a tongs and, selecting a lemon curd pastry, put it on Evie's plate. 'Why don't you try one of these?' Tess said, a little peremptorily.

'Bang goes my diet, but in this case it's worth it,' Evie said, trying to lighten the atmosphere. 'I hope to be back to a decent level of fitness soon and able to exercise properly.'

'You certainly had a better outcome than Ma Donnelly,' Tess said, selecting a lemon curd pastry herself, her knife flashing as she sliced off a piece. 'Your accident, I mean. At least you didn't die.'

'Yes,' Evie said. 'Although there were moments on that laneway when I wasn't sure if I'd make it or not.'

'That must have been frightening for you.'

'It was and it wasn't,' Evie said, taking a large gulp of her coffee, unwilling to admit how terrifying it had been.

'How do you mean? Did you feel as though you were back on television and it was only make-believe?'

'So you watched *Delphin Terrace*?'

'Oh, I never missed an episode, but it didn't hold the same interest for me after they killed you off in such a spectacular fashion.' She flashed Evie a cold smile. 'And the lead up to it was something else,' Tess said, her mouth curling as she continued to look steadily at her.

'Yes, it was,' Evie said, realising there was a distinctly unfriendly look in Tess's eyes.

She wanted her gone.

'It must have been tough to have to put up with that kind of crappy ending, especially after your glory days.' Tess sliced off another piece of her pastry, using the knife to spread the curd a little more evenly.

Evie finished her coffee, hoping Tess would take the hint that their break was over. 'I think I got more out of my career than most people would,' she said.

'You did, didn't you?' Tess looked at her steadily once more, but now there was no hiding the antagonism in her eyes. 'On the pig's back, you were, living the high life. Not like some of us here in Wicklow.'

'Are you trying to get at something, Tess?' Evie had to ask. 'I don't understand your attitude.'

'No, you don't. How could you? Too busy queening it in your ivory tower, too busy strutting your stuff on television screens all across England and Ireland, being fêted as an infamous gang moll, or should I say matriarch, long after a lot of us have become invisible members of the human race. Flaunting yourself with socialites half your age, accepting accolades and awards as if they were your due at a time when the rest of your contemporaries were being put out to grass.'

'It sounds like you have a problem with that.'

'Too right I do – bitch.'

Bitch? Even as her senses were jolted by Tess's insulting rudeness, Evie felt a slight lassitude creeping over her. She was feeling unusually tired this morning, just when she needed her wits about her to get a horribly abusive Tess out of Heronbrook. But it was only when she saw Tess glancing with satisfaction at the dregs that were left in Evie's coffee cup that she knew something was terribly wrong.

There were days when Jessica could have sworn her mother understood every word out of her mouth and this was one of them. She sat in her usual chair, while Pippa sat in hers, and Jessica held her hand and chatted to her as though Pippa was perfectly lucid.

'I don't always come on Fridays,' she said, forcing herself to sound cheerful and upbeat for her mother's benefit. 'But I'm on a day's leave today.' For some reason she'd felt the need to check on Pippa, given the week it had been with all the family upsets.

Thankfully, Adam had made a rapid recovery and announced his plans for attending his mate's party in Rathgar, where he'd be staying overnight. Amber's news had shocked her, but surprisingly enough she seemed quite settled in Heronbrook with Evie, both of them getting on far better than Jessica had expected, to judge by Wednesday night. She'd already called Jamie but he hadn't answered the phone, sending her a text in reply to say the pub was very busy and he'd call her back soon. Happy that her family would be OK for one night, she was going into town for a cheap and cheerful meal with Paul that evening, in an attempt for them to reconnect as husband and wife. Then tomorrow morning, she'd decided, she was going to arrive down in Heronbrook, unannounced, to talk further to Amber, and try and get to the bottom of whatever was going on with the family.

'Paul and I are going to try out a new restaurant this evening,' she told her mother. 'It's on Camden Street, and it's casual Italian,' she said, chatting about the menu, conscious that she was prattling on in a deliberate attempt to keep any thread of conversation away from Evie's visit to Laurel Lawns, which she knew would be the equivalent of lighting a fuse to a powder keg, as far as Pippa was concerned.

When she was getting up to leave she thought she saw moisture in her mother's eyes. Tears? Surely not.

'Are you OK, Mum?' she asked, not expecting any kind of reply.

Pippa made a funny noise, between a shout and a howl.

'I don't have to leave just yet,' Jessica said, sitting back down. There was silence from Pippa as Jessica chatted inanely about her week in the GP clinic. Presently she sensed that her mother's brief lucid window had gone.

Out at reception, Henry was on duty, and Jessica asked for Helen, waiting for her for several moments. As soon as she appeared in the hall, Jessica scrolled through her mobile to the pictures Amber had sent through.

'Mum's visitor – the guy who said he was Simon – I want to check something with you, Helen. Is this him? The guy on the left?'

Helen stared at the picture of Barry Talbot before shaking her head. 'No, definitely not,' she said. 'He was a lot younger than him.'

Younger? Jessica let out her breath. She'd been half-convinced her mother's visitor must have been Barry. She barely had a chance to figure out who else it could have been when Helen looked more intently at the image.

'The other guy,' she said, 'I'm sure I've seen him before ... or maybe someone like him ... he seems a bit familiar.'

He probably was, Jessica thought, closing over her phone. Although Matthew Casey kept a low profile, he popped up occasionally in the media. 'Thank you, you've been most helpful,' she said.

She walked down the driveway, crisp autumn leaves underfoot rattling in a gust of wind, and was almost halfway across to her car when she was called back. Muriel was standing in the doorway.

'What is it, Muriel?' she said, retracing her steps.

'I followed up that query you had on the visitor information list,' Muriel said. 'There was a bit of a mix up with dates.'

'How was that?' Jessica asked, following her back into the hall.

'The sign-in page in the visitors' book had the wrong dates. Some idiot had written June eleventh instead of June twelfth at the top of the page that morning. Can you believe it? I can show it to you, if you like?'

'No, it's fine. So that means that Mum's visitor

called the day after the contact details were accessed?'

'Yes. The list was accessed on the eleventh and your mother's visitor was here on the twelfth. There was also a legitimate reason – sort of – for checking your details.'

'And what was that?' Jessica asked.

'You won a prize with a raffle ticket you'd bought at the charity event, a gift voucher. One of the event organisers needed your name and address to send it to you because your mobile number was blurred on the ticket stub. She knew your mother was one of our residents, so when she was dropping in with some bouquets left over after the event, she asked for your details. Grace was on reception that day and remembers that Tess was in a tearing hurry and suggested it would be quicker to print off the page on file rather than typing out the details on a separate page.'

'Tess?'

'Yes, Tess Talbot.'

Jessica had forgotten all about that. The One4All gift voucher for the grand total of twenty euro had arrived in mid-June. The card had been used towards grocery shopping the following week. Outside, back in her car, she rested her head on the steering wheel and rubbed her temples. Although far from best practice, there was no need to worry unduly if Tess had been the receiver of the information – her aunt's neighbour and the very person who had come to her rescue.

Tomorrow. She would talk to Amber then and try to get to the bottom of it all after her date night with Paul. She switched on the ignition, turning to a cheerful music channel on the car radio, before she accelerated out onto the road.

'Did you put something in my coffee?' Evie asked, conscious of a sudden fatigue weighing down her limbs and clouding her mind.

'I might have,' Tess said, eyeing her with disdain.

'Just what are you up to?'

'I'm righting a few wrongs,' Tess said.

'What kind of wrongs?'

'Me, for example. I've been living in someone's shadow for most of my marriage. I didn't realise you were responsible for that until earlier this year.'

'I don't know what you're talking about.'

'You ruined so many lives, you and your sister. Wrecked people's chances of having a normal life with your careless stupidity.'

'I'm sorry, I don't—'

'I should never have married Barry Talbot – he only ever wanted Rachel Casey,' Tess said, the words tumbling out as though coming from some pent-up place inside her. 'But you and your sister effectively ruined her life, and mine into the bargain, because I've been compared with her for most of my marriage. For instance, she was much better in bed than I was, apparently.' Tess's mouth twisted in annoyance.

Ruined Rachel's life? Tess was right, and for a moment Evie had nothing to say. The sins of the past can have a long reach.

'And as if that wasn't enough to put up with, your sister then went and slept with my husband. Talking about rubbing my nose in it. I know, so don't bother to deny it – I've seen the proof. I knew Barry had been seeing someone after I had the second miscarriage – that was another failing of mine, my inability to provide him with children. I didn't know for certain who he was cheating with at the time, although I suspected Pippa. It was well known on the social circuit in Bray that she was unhappy in her marriage, drinking too much, lusting after other women's husbands. Naturally, word filtered back to me through the grapevine. Talk about shitting on your own doorstep. A slapper – that's what the golf club ladies called her. Then a few years ago, we were over in New York on holidays and we met Barry's nephew and a bunch of his ex-pat friends for drinks, and there he was, lo and behold, bold as brass, Jamie Burke. And I said to myself if he's not Barry's son, then I'm not Tess Talbot.'

'Does Barry know?'

'I don't know. I never mentioned one word. I didn't want to tell him he had a son by that bitch and remind him that I couldn't give him one. I didn't want to rock the boat on my marriage. Barry's so cute about money I would have ended up scraping a living. I had it out with Pippa, although that didn't go down too well.' Tess gave a short laugh. 'Still, it was way past her payback time.'

'Payback time?'

'I gave her a stroke, didn't I? Literally. Outside the post office.'

'You were with her that day?'

'I couldn't resist tackling her. She'd gotten a taxi into town, too drunk to drive, and was staggering along the pavement on the way to her hairdresser's.'

Evie felt a huge stab of remorse at this unexpected glimpse into Pippa's sad life. How low had her sister fallen before her stroke?

'Although she brought most of it on herself with her lifestyle,' Tess said.

'What did you do to her?'

'I asked her if Barry knew he was Jamie's father. I knew by her face that I'd guessed correctly. I told her she'd never be free of me, that I'd be waiting and watching to pay her back. She even denied me that. She keeled over right in front of me. I made myself scarce, hurrying back to my car that was parked down the street.'

Tess was almost boasting, Evie thought, with a sickening lurch.

'I watched as people called for help,' Tess continued. 'After a while the ambulance came for her and she was whisked away to her brand-new life.'

'I think you had better go,' Evie said, struggling to stem the wave of fatigue that threated to engulf her. 'I'm not listening to any more filth out of your mouth. Amber will be here soon and she doesn't need your vitriol.'

Tess gave her a funny glance. 'Will she now?'

She recalled something Tess had said when she had first arrived, about wondering if Evie would be able to open the hall door. Because it meant, didn't it, that Tess had known she'd be on her own in the house. On top of the wall of tiredness beginning to blanket her, Evie felt a new trepidation squeezing her chest.

J essica was just approaching the motorway outside Bray when her phone rang, cutting out the stream of music. Amber.

'Hi, Amber,' she said, 'I'm in the car on my way back from the nursing home.'

'I've seen Will,' Amber said, her voice slightly shaky, 'or rather Patrick William.'

'*What?* How did that happen?'

'He's staying here in Wicklow at the moment. His father is Matthew Casey, the man who had history with Evie, and to cut a long story short, Mum, both Will and his sister were involved in a vendetta against the family. Will arranged for Evie's accident, he wrecked my career, and his sister, Jennifer, messed things up for Jamie in New York – that's why he came home.'

Distracted by her daughter's outpouring, Jessica pulled in to the hard shoulder and switched on her hazard lights. 'This is crazy stuff, Amber. I find it hard to believe.'

'I know. I've been up to the Caseys' house. He was staying there. I … I …' Amber made a funny gulping noise.

Jessica's heart flooded with love and anxiety. What had she been thinking, wanting to run away from her life and reinvent herself? If this week had taught her anything, it had reminded her that she had two wonderful children she was so lucky to share that life with. They meant the world to her. Along with Paul, they were more important, more precious, more fundamental to her life than any stupid, transient mistake. 'Where are you now? Are you OK?'

'Yeah … well, sort of. I'm parked by an entrance to a forest trail. I was so … panicky after I saw Will,' Amber said in a thin voice, 'that I had to stop and calm down before I go home to Evie. She won't be happy with what I found out, and I'll have to see if she's OK with me telling the family about what caused it all before I go to the police. I'm definitely calling them now even though I know she'll be upset.'

'Evie is made of sterner stuff – she'll cope. It's you I'm worried about right now. I'm sorry to hear you had to face that creep. You probably shouldn't be driving.'

'I've opened the window to let in some air,' Amber said, 'and I've a bottle of water.'

'Drink it slowly.'

'I'll explain it all later, Mum – but it's weird, between them, he and his sister were behind the weird things in the family, even Adam—'

'*Adam?*'

'Yes, and he mentioned something about you …'

Good God. A flash of fear tightened in Jessica's chest, almost suffocating her. Conscious that Amber was already upset, she strove to sound unruffled. 'We'll have a good chat about that later,' she said.

'I'm still trying to work out how he knew about us.'

'What do you mean?' Jessica asked.

'Like, that I was your daughter and Pippa's granddaughter? How did his sister even know Jamie was over in New York? The day you were at the charity event, where you met Evie, and that guy Barry Talbot came over, was he asking about your family? Did our names come up in the conversation? Or were you talking to Matthew Casey at any time?'

'No, I never met the Casey guy. I only spoke to Evie and then Barry, when he joined us for a few minutes. Evie could well have mentioned I had a grown-up family when she introduced me to him.'

'I think Barry has to be the link somehow. Otherwise, how did the Caseys know about us and where to find us?'

'You didn't happen to tell Will at any time that Jamie was back home and that he got a job in Naas?' Jessica asked, a piece of the puzzle falling into place.

'I might have when I was chatting to him about my family. I was seeing him when Jamie moved to Naas. Why? Did something else happen to Jamie when he moved down there?'

Jessica forced herself to take a slow, deep breath. 'Nothing for you to worry about,' she said.

'The thing is, Mum, Will said he didn't know anything about Evie's tyres being slashed or any of the other incidents, and he seemed to be telling the truth, which could mean that whoever did those things is still out there.'

A sliver of foreboding crawled up Jessica's spine. 'Tell you what,' she said to Amber in the calmest voice she could muster so as not to panic her any further, 'don't drive until you feel up to it, but call me as soon as you're back in Heronbrook.'

'OK, Mum.'

Tess had to be the link, Jessica suddenly knew, thinking of the family contact details obtained from the nursing home.

Tess Talbot, wife to Barry.

Barry, who'd had a brief affair with Pippa.

Barry, who'd fathered Jamie.

Tess, who'd been sitting beside Matthew, Patrick Casey's father, at the charity event.

How could she go home, without checking out the ramifications of this? She had to talk to Tess, and perhaps Barry. Her scalp pricking with tension, Jessica checked Google Maps. She knew from Amber that the Glenmaragh View, Tess's café-cum-craft shop, was near the crossroads in the village – she'd been there for lunch with Evie. She pulled out into the stream of traffic, but instead of crossing the bridge to take the motorway home, she headed south for Wicklow.

◆

The shop area of the Glenmaragh View was quiet but the café section was busy considering it wasn't the main lunchtime period just yet. People out for brunch, she decided, noting a few tables down one side were occupied by women who looked like they belonged to a club of some kind. Badminton, she guessed, eyeing racquet bags lined up by the wall alongside their tables. She stood a slight distance from the counter, checking out the staff moving about, noting that none of them resembled the Tess Talbot in the pictures Amber had sent her. A young assistant came across to her, a menu in her hand.

'Can I get you a table?'

'No thanks, I'm here to speak to Tess Talbot,' Jessica said.

The assistant frowned. 'I'm not sure she's around.'

'Would you check please? It's urgent.'

The assistant went behind the counter to chat to an older colleague, who came over to Jessica. 'I'm sorry, Tess isn't available to talk to you. She's extremely busy in the office this morning and is not to be disturbed.'

'Look, Maura,' Jessica said, checking her name tag, 'I've come from Dublin, I'm Evie Lawrence's niece, and if Tess knew I was here I'm sure she'd talk to me.'

'I'm sorry,' Maura said, 'we're under strict instructions not to disturb her. She has a large volume of accounts to file, but I'll take your name and mobile and give her a message as soon as she's free, although it's likely to be the afternoon.'

Jessica had no option but to give her details, thinking wryly that Tess had them already. 'I'll wait around for a while in case Tess happens to become available,' she decided.

'As you wish, but it could be a long wait.'

Jessica ordered tea and a scone. She sat at a table, positioning herself within clear sight of the counter and the staff door behind it, conscious of sidelong glances from the staff. Good. She hoped word of her presence filtered back to Tess. It might entice her away from her desk. There were questions that needed to be answered and the minute she came through that door, she'd be ready for her.

Evie repeated her words, trying to think through her lethargy. 'You had better be gone before Amber comes back.'

Tess gave her a malicious grin. 'Really? I'd say she's still in Temple Raven being royally screwed by Will.'

'Will? What do you know of him?'

'His full name is Patrick William Casey. Patrick to his friends and family. Don't you know he's Matthew Casey's son?'

'What?' Amber's Will was Matthew Casey's son? In spite of feeling sleepy, she was filled with a terrible apprehension.

'And that Matthew and I are second cousins?' Tess went on remorselessly. 'Our mothers were cousins but as close as sisters in the housing estate where we grew up. Matthew pulled out all the stops when it came to honouring Rachel's life after she died. He laid on dinner and a free bar for the select funeral-goers – naturally, Barry had insisted that we went. But he doesn't know I had a long and interesting talk with both Patrick and his sister that day. And that's when I found out that you'd played the biggest role of your life when you'd neglected little Leah Casey that afternoon.'

'I'm well aware of what I did,' Evie said, a stab of remorse puncturing her lassitude.

Tess carried on. 'Biggest role in terms of the impact you had on the lives of so many people over the years, including mine. And Pippa had a part to play as well. Unfortunately, Patrick and his sister saw the way I was looking at their father, but they kindly informed me that I was wasting my time, that Matthew doesn't do relationships of any kind, thanks to his harsh upbringing. Such a waste of a fine-looking man. So that's another little pleasure you've denied me, Evie.'

'Now you're being ridiculous.'

'You might think that, but I don't. Years of a bad marriage have frustrated me, hollowed me out, sucked all the joy out of my life. I'm not getting any younger and there's nothing worse than looking back and knowing it's too late for lots of things.'

'Am I to assume you were behind the hit-and-run?'

'You're clever. The three of us were behind it. On account of your age, Patrick just wanted you frightened up a bit. But I gave more detailed instructions to the motorcyclist.'

'And the rest of the stuff? My slashed tyres, for starters?' She was beginning to feel gripped by a mixture of helpless drowsiness and stark terror.

'Well, that's where I diverged a little from the plan. The Caseys weren't interested in the finer details of what happened to your Ma Donnelly character.'

'So you were responsible for the rest of ... the activities.'

'Yes, and it was fun. Patrick and Jennifer only wanted the main event with you and members of your family.'

'What members of my family?'

'All of them – Amber, Jamie, Jessica, and Adam. We upset all of them, one way or another. The way your bad deed upset the Caseys.'

'How dare you,' Evie said, fighting her lethargy as she struggled to get to her feet. 'Get out of my home. Immediately.'

'Oh, Evie' – Tess grinned – 'you're not on *Delphin Terrace*. You can't threaten me.'

'Can't I?' Evie said, picking up her crutch. 'If you don't leave immediately—'

'You'll what? Sock me one?'

'Too right I will,' Evie said, making a supreme effort to swing her crutch in spite of her dizziness, aiming for Tess.

'How dare you,' Tess growled, pulling the crutch from Evie so roughly that she overbalanced, falling sharply on her injured hip. Pain bloomed and her vision swam. Tess loomed over her, a fuzzy image staring down into her face.

'Oh dear,' Tess said, 'too bad you took an overdose of sleeping tablets with your coffee. I'll put what's left of the package on your bedside locker so they'll know, afterwards, what you did and how many you took.' Her foot nudged Evie's supine body along inch by inch until she was lying at the edge of the terrace. Then with another nudge, Evie felt herself falling off the terrace and landing on the grass below. It wasn't a big drop, less than two feet, but she landed on her injured hip and fresh slices of hot, sharp pain reverberated throughout her body.

Tess pushed and nudged her along, every movement sending searing pain racing through her. She heard Tess's disjointed voice floating overhead. 'Too bad you lost your balance and fell, but it was really rotten luck that you got disorientated and rolled into the brook.' Tufts of grass brushed her face and the scent of warm earth filled her nostrils as Tess shoved her body towards the brook.

Tess was still talking. 'As soon as Heronbrook comes on the market again, I'm going to insist that Barry buys it. With planning permission, the land will be worth a tidy sum. Then I'm going to divorce him. He's gone so soft now he's useless – I'll be able to take him to the cleaners and back again. The Caseys will give me a few tips. I've already set the cat among the pigeons.' Tess cackled. 'I'd say Jamie Burke will soon be hunting down his real father, and I'll be the wronged and innocent wife. It should net me a fortune and Barry won't have a leg to stand on.'

Evie heard the rush of the brook as she was edged closer and closer. Never had the sound seemed so melodious or the pungent scent of earth and the lacy canopy of trees overhead so perfect.

Amber, where are you? Please don't arrive home right now in case Tess has any tricks up her sleeve for you. Please stay away. I don't want you getting hurt in any way. I love you, your mixture of spikiness and vulnerability. You don't know how beautiful you are. I'm sorry I never told you these things or spoke to you from my heart. Why do we fill our daily chatter with the inconsequential and mundane, and leave the most important things unsaid?

She tried to resist, to gain some kind of traction, but it was impossible. She was out in space, suspended between the bank and the brook – *Amber, where are you?* – and then she was falling down, the cold waters of the brook wrapping icily around her, before she hit her head off a jutting stone and everything went dark.

Her coffee had gone cold. Jessica debated with herself as to whether she'd order another one. The group of women were leaving, picking up cardigans and jackets, bags and racquets, bobbing in and out of each other as they bade farewell and made arrangements to call, to visit, to see soon. They straggled out of the café leaving tables scattered with crumbs, empty plates and cups, scrunched-up napkins, and a huge vacuum in their wake.

Barry Talbot strolled in, wearing jeans and an anorak, stuffing car keys into his pocket.

Jessica recognised him immediately and waved at him.

'Jessica!' he said, coming over to her. 'It is you, isn't it? Lovely to see you here.'

'It's good to see you too, Barry,' Jessica said. 'Actually, I'd like to talk to you about a couple of matters.'

He drew out a chair and sat opposite her, smiling genially. 'Fire away.'

'It's about Evie Lawrence and the hit-and-run that could have killed her,' she said, watching him closely.

'Dreadful thing that,' he said.

'I also want to talk about an intimidating campaign that someone has been running against her.'

'What campaign?' he asked, looking genuinely puzzled.

'It has been aimed at Evie and our family. It's affected me, my brother Jamie, as well as Amber and my son Adam. Do you know anything about this?'

Barry Talbot's jaw dropped. His jovial smile vanished. He gave Jessica an incredulous look. 'I know about Evie's hit-and-run, and I'd heard that her tyres were slashed, but as for the rest ... I haven't a clue what you're talking about.'

Jessica leaned closer across the table. 'Are you sure?'

He recoiled, as if she'd stung him. His eyes narrowed. 'Fuck's sake, Jessica, pardon the French, but what are you trying to imply?'

'If you're really unaware of this, I'd like to talk to your wife.'

If anything, Barry looked more shocked. 'My *wife*? What's Tess got to do with this?'

'That's what I'm trying to find out. She could be implicated in the attempt on Evie's life, but apparently she's too busy in her office to talk to me and cannot be disturbed, according to the staff.'

'I'm not surprised she won't talk to you, hurling serious allegations about,' he said, rising to his feet so swiftly that he rocked the table. 'We'll see about this,' he said, glaring at her. 'You've no right to come in here with your bullshit. I'll get this sorted immediately.'

He marched across the café, behind the counter, brushing by the assistants and barging through the staff door. Less than a minute later, he strode back through the doorway and began barking questions at Maura, taking out his mobile at the same time to make a call. He wheeled about, frustration written across his face, clearly not getting any answer, staring at his phone in annoyance before he shoved it back into his pocket and stared out through the window.

Jessica picked up her handbag and went across to him. 'What's happening?' she asked.

'None of your business,' he said, his face guarded.

'She's not there, is she? Tess?' Jessica hazarded a guess. 'And she's not answering her phone either.'

Barry pursed his lips and raised his eyebrows. 'So what?'

Something icy slithered through Jessica's head. 'I've been sat here waiting for her,' she said angrily. 'I want to know why she obtained personal data about me and my family from my mother's care home.'

'She what?'

'I want to know what she did with that information,' Jessica ploughed on, 'and, further-more, if she had anything to do with Matthew Casey's family sabotaging both my daughter's career and my brother's life in New York, never mind swindling me and attacking my son, apart from Evie being almost killed.'

'They are some fucking accusations.'

'I'm not making them up. Matthew Casey's son has just been telling my daughter of the role he and his sister played in this debacle, but they had to get family information from someone in the first place. I heard today that Tess got our personal details from my mother's nursing home without our permission. Furthermore, Evie has been intimidated on different occasions over the last few weeks, but the Caseys appear to be unaware of those incidents. I need to talk to Tess. It's urgent.'

Barry looked defeated. 'I don't know where she is. I came in here looking for her too. She was supposed to be here all morning. Wherever she went, she took my car.'

Jessica pulled out her phone and called Evie. The call rang out. She tried again, with the same result. 'I need to check in on Evie,' she said to Barry. 'She's not answering her phone. What's the quickest way to Heronbrook from here?'

The urgency in her voice finally got through to him. 'I'll drive you,' he said. 'I have Tess's car outside.'

Jessica kept calling Evie as Barry drove down the hill and through narrow country lanes, hoping the alarm bell ringing loud and clear in her head was a false one. An oncoming car travelling back to Glenmaragh at speed passed them with inches to spare. She heard Barry curse.

'What's wrong?' she said.

'That was Tess,' he muttered tersely.

Barry turned right onto a narrow track marked with a dead-end sign and soon stopped outside high walls inset with wrought-iron gates and a pillar bearing the name plaque Heronbrook. He jumped out of the car, Jessica following him. He pressed a buzzer in the keypad mounted on the pillar, but there was no response.

'Have you got the code?' he asked.

'No, I don't.'

He pointed to an object on the ground between the gate and the house. 'That looks like a gate fob but it's out of reach.'

He paced around for several moments and pressed the buzzer again.

'What now?' Jessica said, a cold dread creeping up inside her.

'We could go around by the lane and through the woods and get in the back gate, it's lower, but this is quicker.' With difficulty, he grabbed hold of the gates and slowly hoisted himself up, swinging a leg over the top and balancing himself and his rear end precariously until he swung his other leg over and dropped down on the far side, almost falling as he landed. She watched him hurrying up to the hall door, pressing the bell, getting no answer. He ran back towards her and, picking up the gate fob, pressed it before disappearing around the side of the house.

There was a click and a creak and at last the gates parted slowly. As soon as there was a big enough gap, Jessica squeezed through and followed Barry's route around to the back of the house, hurrying past a shed out to a beautiful garden that sloped down to a stream. Barry was lying on his stomach, bent over the stream. He had taken off his jacket.

It was covering a figure lying by the edge of the stream, part of her body submerged. His hands were holding Evie's head up away from the water, the gash in the side of her head visible to Jessica.

'She's still alive,' he panted, his face red with exertion and the effort of supporting Evie. 'I'm afraid to move her too much. Call an ambulance.'

Jessica phoned the emergency services. She took turns with Barry holding Evie's head, calling to her unconscious aunt. Apart from that, there were no sounds save for the chirp of the birds, the running of the water, and the whisper of the breeze through the trees. It was so peaceful and quiet it was hard to imagine anything untoward happening there.

It seemed a long time until she heard it, an ambulance siren travelling through the distance, the sound ripping across the peace of the morning, at odds with the calm, still air.

Pippa stared out at the patch of green fuzz. Today was not one of her good days. Today was one of the days when her memory was jumping all over the place, images pulsing and fracturing like fragile glass before coming back and slotting together like the segments of a kaleidoscope.

She had a memory of a woman walking into the room, infusing the static air with her beautiful scent, and sitting between her and the patch of green fuzz.

Jessica ... the name drifted into her consciousness.

Jessica had spoken, had taken her hand. Had looked at her with warm concern. After a while the woman had left, and it was like something beautiful had gone out of the room. She could see the patch of green again, more leaves drifting down in a silent dance to rest gently on the surface.

Had that been today, or yesterday, or a year ago? She had lost count of the days and the weeks and the months, but she knew when one season ended and another began. She remembered the pictures of them from the blackboard in school. Right now the grass was strewn with leaves, crispy orange and russet and red ... Later, it would be covered with a white layer of frost, stiff, like icing sugar ... then velvet green again before being studded with tiny daisies and the yellow buttercups – the buttercups her father used to hold under her chin, which he said were just as beautiful and perfect as the most pristine rose.

She knew her colours. Ochre, vermilion, emerald, burnt sienna.

She saw them, lined up, tubes in a paintbox ... the sets she'd bought Lucien every so often, hoping he would use them to create his magic again.

She traced the jagged edge of memory through the frail synapses of her brain into the well-worn, well-visited maze of her feelings. The ones where she'd hoped she could love him enough to entice him back to his sketchbooks. The disappointment when he'd thrust them away unopened, telling her he had lost all interest.

The hollow inside her when she knew she had done that. Deprived him of his essential fulfilment and the world of his beautiful artistry. The anguish when she knew he might have married her, slept with her, devoted his life to his children, but he was only a shadow of the man he could have been, a faint reflection of the artist who had been full of potential, until she had killed it.

The feelings of self-disgust and self-hate that had corroded her heart.

She blinked. Drew a shaky breath. Stared outside, imagining the taste of fresh air. The leaves outside reminded her of the trees, but she was glad she didn't have a proper view of them from her chair because they would remind her of other trees ... trees in Heronbrook – that name slid easily into her head. As did the terrible thing she had done to Evie, to Lucien, to everyone.

She would never forgive herself. There was no

one who could forgive her because no one knew the truth. Only Lucien had found out what she'd done, because she'd told him one day, and then he was dead.

Why hadn't she seen how lovely she was at fourteen? Why hadn't she seen the fledgling beauty in her face and body? Why had she compared herself unfavourably with others? Putting herself down in her own head, being her harshest critic, her own worst enemy, for not being bright and clever and beautiful like Evie? Or popular with the boys like Rachel?

Why had she resented Evie so much instead of loving her as a sister and enjoying the closeness and warmth it could have brought to her life? To both their lives? She hadn't appreciated then that it was crazy to look at the beauty of a dandelion clock in full bloom and call it a weed compared with other growing things, or to compare a daisy with a buttercup, or a buttercup with a rose. She hadn't appreciated that she was bright and clever and beautiful in many different ways to her sister. But just as equal. By the time she had made that discovery, after months of looking out onto the patch of green fuzz, it had been too late.

Too late. Two of the saddest words in the English language. Too late to say I'm sorry, too late to say I love you, too late to make amends. Too late to say I wronged you, it was all my fault …

Pippa, 1964

The woods are full of secret things. They are alive with noise: the rustle of small animals scurrying through foliage, the snap of twigs in the undergrowth, the scratch and buzz of insects, the call of birds fluttering through the branches. The soft coo of a wood pigeon.

She is tired from pushing the pushchair up a laneway drenched in summer-afternoon sunshine. She's glad the child has gone asleep, lulled into a doze by the heat of the day and the rhythmic movement of the wheels as they came up the lane and onto the uneven track that leads through the woods towards Heronbrook.

Through the branches of the trees, there is movement, someone coming ... two people ... flashes of a pink T-shirt and a white one, a tanned arm, the glint of blonde hair in a patch of sunlight, murmuring voices, a tinkle of laughter. They pause, half-hidden by foliage, and they come together in a long, hungry kiss.

She checks the child. Still asleep. She puts the brake on the pushchair and moves a little closer to the couple, sliding down the bank, pushing through the branches, crouching down into the ferny undergrowth, peeping out from behind the trunk of a tree. She now has a view of both Rachel and Barry, side on.

She envies them this closeness, this familiarity. She aches for it. She watches, mesmerised, unable to tear her eyes away, wetting her finger and putting it to her lips, trying to imagine what it feels like to have a mouth pressing against hers. But it just reminds her she's to go back to the dentist for another painful filling. She puts her hand to her own still developing breast and tries to imagine how it might feel to have a boy's hand on it. Oh, to be that close to someone, to know about these things … to *do* them. She feels left behind, excluded, like a silly and stupid schoolchild who hasn't a clue, and Rachel has moved beyond her and entered a secret temple she is not yet allowed to venture inside. There is a hard ache in her stomach, a squeezing in her ribs, and something exploding behind her eyes.

After a while they move away, flashes of colour as they run through the trees before they disappear from view. Pippa stands up, brushing scraps of undergrowth off her legs. Her hands are shaking, her legs trembling, her body seared with an unidentifiable ache. She turns and scrambles back up the bank.

When she reaches the pushchair, the child is gone.

Sickening terror grips Pippa. She stands frozen to the spot for a moment, and then she retraces her steps, back as far as the lane, looking down to where it rounds the bend before it passes the caravan park in the final run down to the sea. There is no sign of a small chubby toddler with a pink gingham dress and white slides in her hair. How long was she gone? She couldn't say. The child could have wandered off anywhere or even, more likely – a fresh wave of fear grips her – wandered down to the brook. She runs back to the woods, her heart thumping, her teeth chattering as everything races through her head and she sees how horribly it could all play out.

She is to blame. *She* is the one at fault. *She*'s the one who'd be put to shame, even though she wasn't the shameful one who was kissing her boyfriend in the woods, teasing and tempting him, stoking the fires of hell and damnation, according to Mother Agnes. And she isn't the one who has actually gone to hell by lying in a bed in Heronbrook with her boyfriend, allowing him to see her naked body and to do unmentionable things to her, things Pippa can only imagine, things that make her feel hot and uncomfortable, and put a funny ache in her tummy.

Rachel will never talk to her again, and Pippa can't bear to lose another friend, not even her summer-holiday friend. Even though Pippa had felt resentful that Rachel had more or less dumped Leah on her, to give Rachel a chance to get off with Barry, Pippa knew it was a favour Rachel was grateful for, and it ingratiated Pippa with her at a time when Rachel seemed to be drifting away from her.

Her parents will never forgive her. Golden child Evie, who was already the fairest of them all, would be even more golden in their eyes, whereas she'd be the one who brought terrible shame on the family.

An idea blooms in her head, fully formed.

She can change this around completely.

She releases the brake on the pushchair and, half-lifting, half-pushing it, she hurries as quietly as she can up towards Heronbrook, where Evie's bedroom curtains are drawn. Her tummy clenches in a spasm as she imagines what she might be doing to Lucien inside on the bed. What he might be doing to her. She wants to cry. The difference in their lives at that moment and the unfairness of it all fills her with sad rage. She opens the terrace door to the living room and lifts the pushchair in, wheeling it right through into the hall, placing it outside Evie's closed bedroom door. She calls out to Evie, laughing as though it's a joke, telling her about Leah being in her pushchair and that she's going to the beach, deliberately garbling her words, even though she knows they can just about hear her over the music.

And just as she hopes, just as she'd expected, Evie calls out, telling her to go away and leave her alone.

'I'm going,' she says. 'I'll leave you in charge.' She stumbles over her words, forcing more laughter as though she is making a huge joke. She slips out through the terrace door, not closing it completely, making sure it is open by a gap of less than a foot.

Then she runs free as fast as she can, her heart in her throat, leaving the woods with an even darker secret rippling through the trees.

Evie, present day

It would be easy to slip away, to relax, to let go. My body is so weighed down, it doesn't seem possible to carry on. I'm not sure how long I've been here. Time has all at once expanded and collapsed.

The early years in Heronbrook are as fresh as yesterday in my mind. All the times I lay with Lucien, when we were young and full of vigour, under the shelter of trees, on a blanket of soft ferns, in a room filled with silvery filaments of light. I see him that last December morning in London, turning to me for the final time – although I didn't know that then. I feel his love wrapping around me, I see the light in his eyes.

'When I get the chance to buy Heronbrook, I will ... I'll wait for you to come ...'

He kisses me, a long, lingering kiss that echoes across all the long and lonely years. A long, lingering memory that prompted me to buy Heronbrook and move there.

My pilgrimage in honour of him.

It's been so long since that snowy London morning in December, yet it could be yesterday, so warm is the feeling of his mouth on mine. All I have to do is let go and I will be with him again. Then I catch a memory of Amber's smile and the beautiful light in her eyes – so like Lucien's – before it slides away like a gossamer wisp.

Wait – don't let it slide away. There's something about Amber, something that's important to both of us ... something that made me realise life goes on in the most surprising way.

What is it?

Think, Evie. Hold on.

I am being pulled forcibly upwards, through heavy, pressing water, up from the depths of the green-grey ocean, breaking across a surface that is so unusually warm I could be drifting in a hot, sunlit sea.

On Sunday afternoon, Amber came through the double doors from the intensive care unit and into the waiting area where her parents and Fionn were sitting.

'It's no use,' she said. 'I've been doing my best, but there's no improvement at all with Evie.'

Fionn wrapped his arms around her and rubbed her back. 'You don't know that. There's still time.'

'It's been forty-eight hours, the most critical time,' Amber said.

She was grateful that he'd come rushing to support her, as soon as she'd called him from the hospital on Friday evening. He'd joined her parents and Adam in the waiting area, while Amber had continued her vigil by Evie's bed, coming through occasionally to talk to them and grab a coffee. Both nights, when Adam and her parents had gone home to snatch a few hours' sleep, Fionn had stayed in the waiting area, eventually insisting on bringing Amber down to his car, where both of them had snoozed for a while. That morning, as soon as Amber's parents had arrived at the hospital, Fionn had brought her on a quick trip to Heronbrook, where Amber had recorded the sound of the brook on her mobile and taken cuttings of pine trees and lavender spikes, in an effort to rouse her great-aunt. 'You need a break,' her mum said. 'You've been here practically non-stop since Friday evening.'

'There was no reaction at all, Mum,' Amber said. 'I know they're saying she might still be able to hear and smell, so I've talked and talked, I played the recording of the brook even though my mobile is supposed to be switched off, I waved some pine branches and lavender stems in the air ... and nothing. Although maybe I was making things worse by reminding her of it all. If only I'd gone straight home from Temple Raven this would never have happened.'

By the time she'd composed herself enough to go back to Heronbrook after seeing Patrick, the ambulance bearing Evie off to hospital had been turning out of the lane and the blood in her veins had turned to water.

'You can't blame yourself,' her mum said. 'You couldn't possibly have looked after Evie any more than you did. Look at me, I was sitting over coffee in the Glenmaragh View. If only I'd thought of going to Heronbrook first.'

'I hope that bitch Tess rots in jail,' Amber said.

'I'll go in to Evie for a couple of hours,' her mum said. 'You go off and have a break.'

'Fionn,' her dad said, 'you're under orders to bring her somewhere nice for some food.'

'Don't leave here until I come back,' Amber said.

'We won't.' Her parents spoke in unison.

'Two hours. I'll be back in two hours.'

◆

The cool September air flowed over her face as they walked through the hospital car park. Fionn took her hand in his and she welcomed the warmth of his touch, not letting go until they reached his car, where she sank into the passenger seat and closed her eyes.

Concussion. Evie had severe concussion caused by the blow to her head when she hit it off a rock as she fell into the brook. She could have drowned, but Barry had got to her just in time. The ICU staff said that she was hanging on to life by a thread. Was she wrong, Amber agonised, not to let her slip quietly away? Was it stubbornness or selfishness on her part that she didn't want Evie to leave on her watch? How could she blame Evie if she wanted to free herself of this world and go to her soulmate?

She didn't think she was hungry until Fionn brought her into the restaurant off the motorway where Sunday lunch was being served. He ordered for them both and held her hand across the table until their food arrived. She'd already told him, during breaks from intensive care, about the Caseys and Patrick, and their harassment of the family and Evie, Fionn totally shocked but doing his utmost to soothe her anxieties.

Barry had appeared in the hospital on Saturday afternoon, a subdued, downcast Barry who looked as if his world had fallen apart. Tess had attempted to sneak back into her office in the Glenmaragh View on Friday as though nothing was wrong, telling Barry she'd just been dropping pastries off in Heronbrook when he'd challenged her about seeing her on the lane. But under the weight of his fury and sad disappointment, she'd cracked.

She'd known from Patrick that Amber would be missing for a couple of hours on Friday morning, although Patrick hadn't been aware of her intentions towards Evie any more than he'd known the full extent of her campaign of harassment. The contact details that she'd obtained from Pippa's nursing home and passed on to the Caseys had been the starting point of it all. Not that Tess had got her hands dirty. She'd engaged the services of a small-time crook, a former delivery driver to the café, who had developed a drug habit. Apart from the Polaroid image and cards to Jamie, which Tess had organised, he'd been responsible for everything else, including Evie's accident, using a motorcycle belonging to a mate of his and a drone to check movements on the lane.

The police were still questioning Tess, Barry had said. They'd be releasing her pending a more detailed investigation. They had spoken to Patrick Casey, who'd had to surrender his passport and be available for further questioning. Amber and her mother had both spoken to the police on Friday night, agreeing to go to the station to make detailed statements on Monday. Later that Sunday morning, just as Amber had returned from Heronbrook, a shocked Jamie had arrived up from Naas. Jessica had told her afterwards that they'd had a long talk in the hospital canteen, after which Jessica had called Simon, to bring him up to date.

It was still far from over, and Amber felt swamped with exhaustion and tension.

Now, as if sensing she needed some distraction from all the trauma, Fionn chatted about his new job for a while. Amber ate most of her roast beef and vegetables, and by degrees, the chill that had been in her bones since Friday thawed a little.

Fionn ordered two coffees. 'You couldn't be doing any more for Evie,' he said. 'And from what I saw, you couldn't have looked after her any better in Heronbrook. No one could have guessed that Tess was waiting for her opportunity. She was the villain, not you.'

Amber summoned the ghost of a smile.

'So no matter what happens to Evie,' Fionn said, 'I won't let you beat yourself up about it.'

What she saw in his eyes sent a glow to her heart despite her weariness. 'Fionn,' she said, unable to hold it back, 'did I ever tell you that you're lovely?'

He smiled, and to her delight, the tips of his ears went pink. 'I don't think so.'

'Well, I'm saying it now.'

'Does that mean you're happy for me to stick around?'

'I guess it does.' She tilted her head to one side.

'What's the "but"?' he asked. 'I know by your face there's a "but".'

She looked away for a minute and then back at him. 'No matter what happens to Evie, I'm not going home to Dublin straightaway.'

'Fair enough.'

'I'm taking time out from the corporate world

for a while. I have some savings to keep me going and – wait for it …'

'I'm waiting …'

She watched his face to see his reaction. 'I'm taking a break to see what kind of painting skills I have,' she said, 'as an artist.'

'Wow.' He smiled. 'That's a biggie.'

'I was always sorry I gave up art after the Junior Cert,' she admitted. 'Down in Heronbrook, I found myself wanting to capture some of the loveliness around me on canvas. I've no idea if I'll be any good or not, but I want to give it a shot. I owe it to Evie and my grandfather.'

'And most of all yourself,' he said, catching her hand across the table. 'That sounds amazing, Amber. I'll be down to check on you, to make sure you're giving it your best shot.'

'I'd like that,' she said.

He had her back at the hospital less than two hours after they'd left, where her parents were sitting in the waiting area, holding hands.

'What happened?' Amber asked, her chest tightening in panic. 'Why aren't you with Evie?'

'Relax,' her mother said, 'they sent me out because they're adjusting some of her fluids. You can see her shortly.'

'I'm going to tell her it's OK to go,' Amber said, a sense of resignation settling over her. 'I don't think she wants to wake up. I know she's full of regrets for what went wrong in her life. She still feels to blame for what happened to little Leah Casey, never mind Lucien, that last weekend in London.'

There had been so much to piece together on Friday evening – the chat with the police and a phone call to Jamie, then Barry on Saturday afternoon – that Amber and her mother had merely skirted around the family history. Now, sitting in the waiting area outside the ICU, her mother shook her head. 'What happened to Dad was nothing but a fluke accident. There's no way Evie was to blame. I know exactly how much he loved her, how much she meant to him. He confided in me himself. He told me he was going to see her in London that weekend, and why, but I respected his confidence and never spoke of it to anyone, especially not my mother. But about Leah Casey … doesn't Evie know the truth?'

'What truth?' Amber said, something in her mum's face sending a shiver down her spine.

'It was one of the reasons why Dad was going to see Evie when he was in London,' her mum said. 'He told me he'd had a big argument with my mother. She was drunk as usual, but this time she taunted him about the cruel trick she'd played on him and Evie. My father was so upset about it – he told me before he left for London that Evie would be equally upset, and that his marriage to my mother was over. I assumed he told Evie the full story before his accident, but some kind of loyalty to Mum – she was reduced to a sad, pathetic drunk and a victim of her own making – kept me silent about everything. I never even thought about it until now. Good grief, Amber, I hope Evie hasn't thought all along that she—'

'What trick?' Amber said.

'Mum was minding Leah when she escaped from her pushchair. She was in the woods spying on Rachel and Barry, too busy watching them to heed the toddler. When she turned around Leah was missing, so she panicked and pushed the empty pushchair into Heronbrook, pretending she was leaving her in Evie's care.'

'And all along, Evie thought *she* was to blame ...' Amber felt the blood draining from her face. 'I have to tell her – I have to tell Evie.'

She had to wait until she was allowed entry into the unit, chafing at the delay, the minutes ticking by slowly. Finally, she was allowed through to where Evie was lying in her cubicle, surrounded by bleeping machines, looking shrunken and pale. Amber sat by the side of the bed and held her hand. She spoke to her, relaying exactly what her mother had said, repeating it over and over, hoping Evie might somehow hear and understand. Time ticked by, the evening came, but there was no change whatsoever in her great-aunt.

Amber sat quietly, dejection sweeping through her. There was nothing for it but to let Evie go.

'OK,' she said, forcing a teasing sound into her voice, 'I give up. You win. You're free to go to Lucien. I won't hold you up any longer.' She continued on a softer note, 'We all love you and we'll miss you, even if you are a crotchety old aunt, but we understand that you have to go. Anyway, it looks like Fionn is going to stick around so I'll be OK.' She held back tears. 'I told him about my plans, Evie. I told him I wanted to stay in Heronbrook for a while – it's so beautiful I want to try and paint it, the colours of the trees, the music of the brook when it spills over the weir, the curve of the old stone bridge, the way the light falls through, how soft it is on rainy days. Not that I might be good enough, I don't think I am, but I want to give it a try.'

She faltered when a nurse came over, examining the readings on one of the machines, scrutinising it carefully. 'What is it?' Amber asked, frozen with fear. 'What's wrong?'

'I think ... there's nothing wrong.' She smiled at Amber. 'Actually, this looks good. I think Evie might be coming back to us. What were you talking about?'

Amber swallowed hard. 'I was telling her about my hopes and plans.'

'Keep talking to her about those plans,' the nurse said, watching a screen and adjusting a dial.

Tears slipped down Amber's face as she looked at Evie's frail figure. 'I want to be an artist,' she said, squeezing her hand and raising her voice a little. 'Remember we spoke about it? I want to go back to Heronbrook and paint everything I can see. The colours of the trees in autumn, the scent of the woods ... the peace ...'

The nurse stayed close by while Amber continued to talk. Her voice was almost hoarse when finally, late that evening, Evie opened her eyes.

Ten Days Later

There was a tree outside Evie's window, the leaves a riot of russet, scarlet, and gold glinting in the beautiful mellow sunshine that typified an evening in early October. A different window, a different tree, a slightly different Jessica walking into the room.

'You're looking a lot better,' Jessica said, coming over to hug her and kiss her cheek, her floral perfume wafting in the air.

'So are you,' Evie said.

Her niece was wearing comfy boots, a pair of dark jeans and a soft pink jumper under a denim jacket. She pulled over a chair and sat down, looking like she had all the time in the world.

'Let's not talk about Tess or Barry or the Caseys,' Evie said. 'Between you, me, and Amber, I think we've exhausted all there is to say. I'd rather just leave the police to get on with the job. Tell me about you and Paul. Are you OK? When Amber was talking to me earlier today, she seemed to think that you'd been got to in some way?'

'I was – there was an issue with the bank,' Jessica said smoothly. 'It could well be related to the Caseys but I've put that in the hands of the police, so we'll see what happens. Either way, Paul and I are fine.

We're off on an overnight break next weekend, Paul has insisted we deserve to take time out.'

'He's right.' Evie smiled. 'How's Jamie? Has he gotten over the shock of you telling him the truth about his father over coffee in a hospital canteen? More drama than *Delphin Terrace*.'

Jessica shook her head and gave a half smile. 'He's OK, still unsettled by everything like us all, but he'll bounce back. He's made contact with Barry, who admitted he "kind of knew about him" – Barry's words – but for the sake of peace with Tess, he kept his head buried in the sand.'

'Peace with his bank balance, more likely,' Evie said. 'Sorry, I'll give him the benefit of the doubt – this time.'

'Jamie said Barry is not going to make any difference to his life,' Jessica told her. 'As far as he's concerned, Lucien was his real father, the man who raised him and loved him as his own. But the whole thing has spurred him into action. He's thinking of going back to college, and keeping on his job in the evenings and at weekends. He wants to open up new possibilities for himself.'

'Good for Jamie,' Evie said. 'It's never too late to find a new path. And when I'm a bit more mobile, do you think it's worth my while trying to see Pippa?'

Her niece considered this before replying. 'I'll suggest it to her and gauge her reaction. It's hard to know what's going on in her head, but sometimes she seems to have moments of lucidity.'

'Thank you. When I thought I was a goner last

week, I regretted not making some sort of peace with her, and now that I know what happened with little Leah, I guess Pippa must have been carrying that hefty burden all along, as well as everything else.'

'If only I'd told you sooner—'

Evie put her hand on her arm. 'Don't, Jessica. Let's have no "if onlys" or "what ifs". It won't change anything. We are where we are. We can only go on from here.'

'Speaking of which,' Jessica said, 'how do you feel about going home tomorrow?'

'I can't wait,' Evie said. 'Amber's all set to collect me at three o'clock.'

'She's at home now going through her winter wardrobe, and from the amount of warm woollies, scarves, gloves, and boots she's packing, it looks like she's in it for the long haul this time.'

'She's planning to stay with me until next spring, at least,' Evie said. 'I think Fionn could be in it for the long haul as well, although Amber has said she's not going to rush into anything.'

'She needs some breathing space. Being with you in Heronbrook seems to suit her – seems to suit both of you.'

'It does,' Evie said. 'She told me she's looking forward to the sabbatical.'

Thinking of her grand-niece, and her plans to follow in her grandfather's artistic footsteps, she felt a warmth in her heart. After Jessica had left, kissing her and hugging her, Evie decided she'd better heed her own words of advice. She was where she was, she couldn't go back in time and change one single thing, but she didn't have to be a bitter old woman in the role of Ma Donnelly, not when she had other, more important, more fulfilling roles in life – sister to Pippa, aunt to Pippa's children, Amber's great-aunt. She might have told Amber that she felt old and cynical and full of withered bitchiness, but life was still fizzing through her veins in all its beauty and messy contradictions, and all its surprises. Once again, it had jumped up and sideswiped her, but in a good way. Which meant, according to Amber, that she was still vital and alive.

Vital. She liked that.

Vital meant being useful, having a purpose. Even now, at her ripe age, she was filled to the brim with purpose, determined to affect some good sea changes. She wanted to encourage Amber with her plans, make sure she knew how wonderful she was and how much she was loved. Her inheritance from the Lawrence family home in Drumcondra had been invested years ago and, thanks to her success, was still largely untouched. No harm in dipping into it a little. She wouldn't see Jessica or Jamie, or even Simon for that matter, stuck, and it was money that would be coming to them in due course.

She had to arrange for Lucien's three paintings to be shipped from London before deciding how best to celebrate his legacy. The agent in London, who'd been tracking them down, had emailed her a few days earlier to say he had secured the final two and was holding them safe. The portrait she had in Heronbrook would stay there, but out on display instead of packed away.

She looked forward to returning to her spirit place, where she could feel Lucien's presence in every nook and cranny. But next year, when things had settled down a bit – if there was any such thing as putting order on this precocious and precious life – she would move back to her apartment in Blackrock. Her driving days were now limited, her mobility slightly compromised after her second fall, and it would be easier for her to meet friends and go to the theatre and cinema and concerts.

She would gift Heronbrook to Amber.

Even though Lucien spoke to her from every corner, and the essence of him was in the sweet breath of air, the leaf buds, the rain-laced trees, and the sunlit brook, he was most of all in her heart, where he would always live. He was with her when she awoke in the light of the morning dawn and in her dreams during the dark, star-filled nights.

But now she could see his light shining through his granddaughter's eyes, beautiful and clear, and it filled her with joy. Because love is not diminished when a life is cut short. Love endures. It blooms in various guises, shapes and forms, and it never ends.

ACKNOWLEDGEMENTS

A huge thank you, as ever, to Sheila Crowley, agent extraordinaire, for inspiration, warm friendship and unstinting commitment, and to the team in Curtis Brown, London, including Sabhbh Curran and Sophia Macaskill.

I am grateful to the super-talented Joanna Smyth for her skilled and insightful editing, patience and guidance, and for the sensitive way she took care of this manuscript. Thanks also to the stellar team at Hachette Books Ireland: Breda, Jim, Ciara D., Ruth, Siobhan, Elaine, Bernard, Ciara C., for all their hard work and commitment behind the scenes.

Thanks to my copy-editor Emma Dunne and proofreader Tess Tattersall for their dedicated work in putting a final polish on the manuscript.

Thank you to Mark Walsh and the team at Plunkett Communications for helping to spread the word about Zoë Miller books.

A special word of appreciation goes to Caroline E. Farrell, author and screenwriter, who responded immediately to my research queries despite the many demands on her time.

A massive thank you to my loyal readers – I wouldn't be in my dream job without your wonderful support; your messages and emails mean so much to me. Thanks also to the unsung heroes of the reading and writing community to whom writers are indebted: book bloggers, reviewers, librarians and booksellers, for passionate support and commitment to spreading the joy of reading.

None of my books could have been written without the steadfast encouragement of my circle of family and friends. But never was that support more needed than when the pandemic hit during the writing of this book and our lives were pulled from under us. The fear and stress of it all hurtled its way into my writing room and onto my desk; I am so grateful for your loving kindnesses, inspiring messages, and the beacons of hope that kept me going through that tough time.

Thank you to my friends in the writing and reading community. At a time when literary festivals and book launches fell by the wayside, social media and online events proved to be a lifeline, keeping us connected. I'm looking forward to seeing many of you, including new virtual friends, at live events in the months to come.

This book is dedicated to my fantastic siblings, Peter, Margaret, David and Kevin, who put up with my early writing attempts when my head was stuck permanently in a book or a scribbler. Love also to the fabulous troup of 'outlaws' – Margaret, Pat, Denise and Hazel, and my extended family including Denis and Mary, Rita and Pat, Angela,

Majella, the two Geraldines – to name but a few of that amazing tribe! Heartfelt thanks to my immediate loved ones: Michelle, Declan, Barbara, Dara, Louise, Colm, and the incredibly precious little ones – Cruz, Tom, Lexi, J.P., Sophia and Éabha. Last but by no means least, much love and thanks to Derek for endless patience and kindness, and for always being there.